Alan Williams was educated at Stowe, Grenoble and Heidelberg Universities, and at King's College, Cambridge. As a foreign correspondent, he covered many stories in the troubled corner of the world where *Holy of Holies* takes place, as well as Eastern Europe, the Soviet Union and the Far East. His previous novels include *Gentleman Traitor*, *The Beria Papers*, *Shah-Mak*, *The Widow's War* and *Dead Secret*. In addition to writing and travel he has a passionate interest in exploring volcanoes and the unusual hobby of building working models of windmills and watermills.

D0716575

By the same author

Alan Williams

Holy of Holies

A PANTHER BOOK

GRANADA

London Toronto Sydney New York

Published in paperback by Granada Publishing Limited in 1982

ISBN 0 586 05096 5

First published in Great Britain by
Granada Publishing 1981
Copyright © Alan Williams 1981

Granada Publishing Limited
Frogmore, St Albans, Herts AL2 2NF
and
36 Golden Square, London W1R 4AH
866 United Nations Plaza, New York, NY 10017, USA
117 York Street, Sydney, NSW 2000, Australia
100 Skyway Avenue, Rexdale, Ontario, M9W 3A6, Canada
61 Beach Road, Auckland, New Zealand

Printed and bound in Great Britain by
Cox & Wyman Ltd, Reading
Set in Baskerville

Granada ®
Granada Publishing ®

For Josephine, who bore the brunt and survived.

Contents

The Touch

1

London. Some time in the imminent present.

It began on that day in November when Charles Rawcliff's wife, Judith, put their telephone number in the local newsagent's window in Battersea, advertising for a baby-sitter. Among the first to call that evening was a man who gave his name as Mason. After Judith had confirmed that he was ringing the right number, she asked to speak to Mrs Mason. The man apologized and explained that *he* was the applicant, and added that he was a bomber-pilot, stationed at RAF Benson, Oxfordshire, and was up in London on a six weeks' training course. He didn't know anyone in town, and thought he might fill the odd evening by getting out of his digs to do some homework, and make a bit of tax-free pocket-money on the side. He gave his full name as Flight-Lieutenant Terence Mason; he was married and had three children of his own.

Judith was amused by the idea: after all, what was wrong with a grown-up man looking after her two-year-old son, even if he was training to drop bombs on people? He had sounded pleasant and sensible, and she agreed to see him at seven the next evening. But first, without consulting her husband, she got the number of RAF Benson and checked with the Duty Officer. Yes, they had a Flight-Lieutenant Mason, but he was away from camp at the moment. Yes, he was in London for a course on Aerial Control. If it was a personal matter, he would have to refer her to Mason's Commanding Officer. She thanked him and hung up.

The candidate arrived punctually at seven. Charles Rawcliff had just arrived back from the office and had poured his first cautious whisky, while Judith was upstairs putting their son, Tom, to bed.

The man in the doorway was stocky, clean-shaven, with

short hair and a healthy complexion. He looked as though he took care of himself. He was wearing a black leather 'bum-freezer' and carried a rolled umbrella. His shoes were cheap and highly polished.

'Good evening. I'm Terry Mason. I talked to Mrs Rawcliff yesterday – about a baby-sitting job.' His manner was awkward, deferential.

'Come in. Charles Rawcliff. Drink?' Flight-Lieutenant Mason followed him down the hall and hooked his umbrella over the back of one of the kitchen chairs.

'I won't, thank you. But tea or coffee would be fine.'

'Sit down, please. My wife said you're with the RAF. What do you fly?'

'Oh, anything they give us – which isn't much these days. Occasionally one gets a crack at a Phantom, even a Harrier – but usually it's just Buccaneers.'

'Dear God, you're not still flying those things? They won't stop the Russians for long!'

'I know, it is rather scandalous. But that's strictly off the record. It's still a free country, except for us blokes in uniform.' Mason grinned, gaining self-confidence. 'We're only allowed to have opinions at election time.'

Rawcliff stood waiting for the kettle to boil. 'I used to fly myself. Civil. Nothing flashy. In fact, distinctly down-market. Mostly package-tours for the Great Unwashed Masses down to the polluted Mediterranean.' He was about to add that he'd been trained himself in the RAF – what seemed a long time ago now – and that he'd become something rather more special than a salaried pilot flying routine missions for NATO. But it would involve too many explanations, many of which were best avoided, especially in front of a total stranger.

Rawcliff poured the young man a mug of Nescafé, and stiffened his own whisky. 'I've gone respectable now,' he added, without irony: 'Got a wine merchants' place across the river. We like to pretend it's Chelsea, but it's really Fulham.'

'Very nice,' Mason said: 'being your own master, with your own business, I mean.'

'Don't you believe it! I'd swap with you, any day of the week. Nice secure job, all found – no worries with VAT and bum creditors and staff who fiddle the books, and trying to unload a case of over-priced Beaujolais on some innocent fool by pretending that it hasn't been pumped through the pipe-line from Algeria. Besides, you can still fly.'

'Can't you? I mean, haven't you still got your licence?'

'Oh yes. I even renew it every year. But it costs money to fly for pleasure.'

They both looked up as Rawcliff's wife came in, carrying Tom. The child's small, semi-continent body was trussed and zipped up in his scarlet jump-suit, ready for bed. At the sight of Rawcliff he let out a shriek of pleasure, followed by a wild babble while his mother had to duck back to avoid his tiny flailing fists, as he struggled to reach out and grab Rawcliff's hair.

He was their only child so far, after they had married late, both for the first time – Judith Rawcliff being nearly ten years younger than her husband. She was a tall, fine-boned girl, dark, with beautiful wrists and ankles, and a clear-skinned, calm-eyed purity about her. A quiet face which seemed to reject her obvious sexuality, to chasten it with a wilful, even stubborn authority. But it was her wrists, and her long slim ankles which Rawcliff remembered noticing first when she'd come into his shop – nearly three years ago now – and asked him for some table wine. She'd wanted something good but cheap; and he'd known at once that he wouldn't be able to fob her off with any rubbish. It was therefore no surprise when he learnt that she was a professional working girl – a fully-fledged executive with one of the big multinational computer corporations.

'Judith, love – meet Flight-Lieutenant Terence Mason' –and he caught her cold glance at his diminishing glass of whisky, before she turned on Mason her wide-eyed smile. 'My wife, Judith, and our son, Tom,' Rawcliff concluded, while Mason repeated that he had three children of his own, and was sure he could handle even a little rascal like this.

Rawcliff had stood back, the proud father. It was an overwhelming, almost unnerving pride – a feeling which, like the whisky in his hand, seemed sometimes to hold a special threat: a reminder, perhaps, that both wife and child were too good for him – that he would never be able to live up to them, and had never deserved them in the first place.

Tom was shouting for a kiss from his father, and Rawcliff had to perform the ritual pantomime of swooping, growling bear-hug, ending with a smacking kiss on his son's wet little lips. *God, how he loved that child.* It seemed almost indecent, in a man of his age – pulling forty, as he preferred to think of himself – which is a good age, providing one was on top of things.

Tom was finally carried off to bed, protesting, clutching his nearly bald, one-eyed teddy; and soon after, Rawcliff and his wife left Flight-Lieutenant Mason alone in charge of the house, with the promise that they'd be back by 11.30, at the latest.

Out in the car Judith said, 'I think he's rather sweet.'

'Probably good enough at his job. And useful if the house caught fire, or somebody tried to break in.'

'I heard you tell him that you've still got your licence.' She took her hand off the gear-shift and squeezed his arm. 'Don't worry about the business, Charles. Something'll turn up.'

Over the next month Flight-Lieutenant Terence Mason baby-sat for them about twice a week. He was the easiest, the most accommodating of men: it didn't matter at what hour they returned, the scene was always the same. Mason would be sitting in the study, working at his figures, with the hi-fi playing soft classical music. He always wiped the records before and after playing them, and washed up the cups he used. He never accepted a drink.

Occasionally he reported that little Tom had woken up, but he had always known exactly how to get the baby off to sleep again. Once he had bought him a rubber turtle which rolled over on its back and wiggled its legs in the bath; but this was his only gesture of intimacy. He had few resources in the way of conversation, which made it all the more surprising when, one evening on which he was not scheduled to 'sit', he called Rawcliff from a pay-phone and asked if he could come round and 'talk something over in private'. He sounded as sober as ever, and very serious.

Rawcliff agreed, with a mixture of misgiving and curiosity. His first thought was that Mason was going to touch him for money. Until now the only awkwardness that he and Judith had experienced with the man was getting him to accept any money at all for his services. He always said, 'Really, it should be me who's paying *you*.'

Before he was due to arrive, Rawcliff said to his wife, 'Give me half an hour alone with him, to find out what he's on about. If it starts getting embarrassing – woman or wife trouble, for instance – I may call you in to draw on your wisdom.'

Mason arrived, as always, on the dot. The only difference was that he was carrying a bag which turned out to contain a bottle of whisky. 'I'm awfully sorry, am I butting in?'

'Not at all Terry – I wouldn't have asked you round if you were.' He led the way into the study. 'What's the meaning of the bottle?'

'I'm afraid it's rather by way of a farewell present.' Mason blushed under his ruddy tan. 'You wouldn't mind, would you, as I'm strictly not on duty tonight, if I joined you in a glass?'

'For Christ's sake, Terry, it's your booze, not mine!' Rawcliff fetched two tumblers and a jug of water from the kitchen. Mason took his drink thin, and sipped it like a liqueur.

Rawcliff had already found that the pilot's presence in the house had a combined disadvantage. The young man not only made him feel his age – he also reminded Rawcliff of what he was missing. For Mason would soon be returning to base, to the pressurized perspex cocoon of a fighter-bomber. Nothing particularly dramatic or hazardous, perhaps – they no longer flew by the book these days, they flew by computers, which was Judith's territory, Rawcliff recalled sourly – but during a few wonderful hours Mason would be up there in the icy blue-black emptiness, streaking along at Mach Two, a tiny disciplined god above the clouds. Free.

Rawcliff had been like that once. Better, he'd been his own man – taken out of uniform and trained almost to breaking point, then let loose as a licensed trouble-shooter, to enjoy all the bogus virility symbols that such a role seemed to demand: a convivial drinker who made free with his loins, while remaining strictly short on emotional commitment. But all that had been in the past – well before Judith and Tom.

He looked across at Mason, sitting tense and alert in front of him, gripping his pale whisky. Flight-Lieutenant Mason was a sensible chap – wary of the demon drink. He also looked trim and fit. And while Rawcliff himself was still a powerful, well-built man, he was made aware that his good looks had sagged, that there were loops under his eyes and a thickening round his waist – all the marks of late-found domesticity and the daunting burden of parenthood.

Mason was moving his glass round between his fingers, clearly nervous. Rawcliff said: 'You told me you had something you wanted to talk about in private. Well, is this private enough?'

'I'm awfully sorry,' Mason began, 'but I shan't be able to come to you after this week. I've been called back to base.'

'We shall be sorry too. But that's not what you came to talk about, surely?'

'No. Charles, I came to ask your advice. I've just had rather a funny experience and I don't know quite what to make of it. You see, we Service chaps lead rather a cloistered life – we don't get around like you London fellows.'

Rawcliff stood up. 'Let me freshen your drink, then you can tell me all about it. Judith'll rustle up something for us to eat. Right – fire away.'

'Well, as I told you, I don't know London, and a few evenings ago I found myself at a bit of a loose end. I went to a pub in Knightsbridge where I'd heard that some of the chaps from base go when they're up in town. I'm not much of a drinking man, but I thought I'd go on the off-chance I might bump into somebody I knew.

'As it happened, I was in for a bit of a surprise. I'd hardly been in there for a few minutes when I caught sight of an all-too familiar face – and one I hadn't expected to see in a hurry. Belonged to a chap called Thurgood. Ex-Flight Lieutenant Oswald Thurgood – with the emphasis on the *Ex*. You know how it is in the Services – everyone conforming, not much room for individuality – so when someone does step out of line, he does it in a big way. Thurgood was one of those. As mad as a hatter. Really bonkers – almost certifiable. For periods he just used to lie on his bunk staring at the ceiling. Sometimes he got these headaches which would keep him off-duty for days at a time. That was usually the signal for him to reappear and do something crazy.

'I hadn't seen him for over eighteen months – since the Christmas before last, to be exact, when he finally went over the top. It was Christmas Eve and most of us family chaps were out of camp, in married quarters. Thurgood wasn't married – still isn't, as far as I know. Anyway, he suddenly grabbed an old Hunter – strictly a training job – and took her up and did a couple of loops over Benson, then buzzed several villages round Wallingford, and finished up clearing the Officers' Mess with about ten feet to spare. He was a damned good pilot. But, as I said, not quite right in the head. His secondary job was radios – bloody mad about them, he was. Built all his own equipment, and used to spend hours picking up places like Albania and Chad.

'Well, after that last escapade, there was a Camp Inquiry, and as a result Thurgood was given the order of the boot. After that he just disappeared – until I bumped into him the other evening. I'd rather expected him to be in jail or an asylum by now. Well, he did look pretty odd in that pub. It was real November weather, if you remember – yet there was Oswald Thurgood, looking like he was dressed for Wimbledon or the Henley Regatta. White ducks, blue blazer, clipped moustache – the works! Very smart and prosperous, too, he looked. It was only his eyes that gave him away – sort of black and staring; I've never seen eyes like them before.

'Well, he remembered me, and we had a couple of beers

together. He was on his own, and told me that he had a hi-fi and audio shop in the West End. Said he was making a packet.' Mason leaned forward and sipped his drink. 'I don't know quite how to explain this, but he'd put on the most extraordinary Oxford accent. You know, plum in the mouth, all that. And very loud. I found it quite embarrassing. I was really glad when he suggested we left the pub and went on to eat.

'He had a big flashy Range-Rover outside, which he said he'd bought through a friend on the fiddle. We went to one of those Chinese places up in Soho. I'm not very keen on Oriental food, but the stuff there was pretty good. Fortunately it was mostly full of Chinese, who didn't seem to notice Thurgood's accent. He ordered wine, and I must admit I got a bit tiddly. I tried to ask him what he'd been doing with himself, but he was very cagey. Then he started asking me a lot of questions – general stuff, about my work at the base and the planes I flew and which I preferred. He also started getting a bit personal – asked me if I was happy in the Service, or wanted to get out and try my hand at something more exciting.

'Suddenly I knew he was fishing. He started mentioning money – saying that a pilot's life is like a boxer's or a racing-driver's. It takes a lot of knocks, and it doesn't go on forever. You have to grab the big opportunity, he said.

'Well, I'd drunk a bit of wine and I rather went along with him. Before I knew what I was doing, I was telling him that I was sick of the camp in Oxfordshire, and the married quarters, and I wanted to get out into the world and see a bit of life before it was too late, and earn some decent money. He managed to get me quite excited. Suddenly he went off to make a telephone call. He was away about ten minutes, and when he came back he had that funny staring look, although he didn't seem at all drunk. And when he started talking again, I realized that he'd dropped the Oxford accent. He asked me what I was doing next evening – yesterday. I told him I didn't know. I was thinking perhaps you might need me, although I didn't let on about my job with you.

'Well, the outcome was that I arranged to meet him again

next evening – same pub, same time. As it was, you didn't need me to baby-sit, and I had nothing else to do. I suppose, to be honest, I was a bit curious. I was sure by now that Thurgood was after something. I was also on my guard – I had to remember, after all, that I was – *and still am* – a serving Officer in Her Majesty's Forces, which hardly makes me a free agent. Still, there's no rule against having a drink with a former colleague, even if the fellow had been cashiered for being cuckoo.

'Thurgood turned up on time, dressed in tweeds this time, and what looked like an Old School tie – though I bet he didn't even get into the local Grammar. Evening classes in radio-electronics would have been more his style.

'Once again, he insisted on buying all the drinks, and dinner afterwards. He'd dropped the Oxford accent completely, thank God, and had become sort of quiet and evasive. He didn't talk a lot, but from what he did say I got the impression that he hadn't been up to much good since he'd been kicked out of the RAF. He'd been in some trouble with the police in Canada, then again when he got back to England – something to do with possessing a firearm – but it wasn't at all clear. There's nothing straightforward or clear about Thurgood, except his craziness. Nothing about him seems to connect up, if you see what I mean?

'All of which should have warned me off him – only I don't mind admitting that I'd had rather a lot to drink. I wasn't drunk, but I'd certainly had more than I'm used to – probably because Thurgood was beginning to make me a bit nervous.

'Anyway, just as we were finishing dinner he went out again and made another telephone call. When he came back, he told me we were both going to a party. He didn't *ask* if I wanted to go – it was more by way of an order. Perhaps it was because of the drinks, and because Thurgood was paying again, but I didn't argue. I thought it best just to go along with him and see what happened.

'Outside we got into his Range-Rover and he drove like a madman out to the City, to a big complex of modern flats, which I think is called the Barbican. All Thurgood would say

19

was that the party was being given by a pilot-friend of his – a civilian who ran his own flying taxi-service.

'Well, as it turned out, the fellow wasn't doing too badly for himself in Civvy Street! I reckoned he must have been making five times what a Wing Commander gets. Thurgood and I finished up in a penthouse flat with suede wallpaper and a lot of modern furniture in chrome and black leather. The taxi-pilot was called Jim Ritchie. Young handsome chap – obviously didn't have a care in the world. Good clothes – you know, fancy open-necked shirt and gold bracelet. Trendy, I suppose you'd call him. And very friendly. First thing he did, as soon as I was in the door, was give me a socking great brandy in a glass half the size of a football.

'Thurgood had said it was going to be a party, but the only other people there were two girls – one of them coloured. Both very pretty and exotically dressed, though Ritchie almost ignored them. I can't even remember being introduced to them. He only spoke to them to ask for more drinks or coffee, or to fetch cigarettes.

'I don't mind telling you, it was a very odd sort of party. At first I thought that I might be in for some sort of orgy – you could never tell with a fellow like Thurgood, although he wouldn't have been the type to take part. He'd have been more the one to organize it. As it was, he just stood by the door watching us, like a sort of manservant, while the taxi-pilot, Ritchie and I sat in the leather armchairs and the two girls wandered about in the background, smoking and listening to a lot of that soul-music on the hi-fi.

'I don't quite know how to explain it, but the whole scene was a bit unreal. What made it more so was that Ritchie was so friendly, so natural – so *ordinary*. I mean, he was so confident and relaxed, and he seemed to take me so much for granted. He and the girls were also being very generous with the brandy. It took me a bit of time to realize that he was pumping me – that I was telling pretty well my whole life-story. The whole *curriculum vitae*, just as though it had come out of my file. Ritchie was particularly interested in the technical details of my flying career – he didn't interrupt much but when he did, it was to ask all the right questions.

'The drink had loosened me up, and I didn't mind boasting that I was an all-round pilot, Class A-1 fitness, and with full flying experience, on all types of aircraft. Then Ritchie started asking me a bit about my private life. He mentioned how boring it must be at base-camp, and what I needed was some fresh air – "the chance to stretch my wings", he said.

'As with Thurgood the night before, I was sure all this was leading up to something, and I was about to ask him straight-out what the hell they both wanted with me, when the outside buzzer went. Ritchie let in a small dark man in a fur-lined overcoat. He had a bloody great diamond ring on one hand and what looked like a solid gold watch that told the time in all the big cities of the world.

'He didn't look English – more the Mediterranean type, Greek or Maltese. Or maybe Jewish.' Then he added hastily, 'Ritchie introduced him as John Newby. He had a slight accent when he spoke – very smooth, very confident. And like Ritchie, obviously doing very well for himself, thank you. He also smelt of perfume.

'The first thing he did was to tell Thurgood to drive the two girls home. As soon as they left he sat down and took out a little black cigar and smiled and said – and I can remember his words exactly – "I think it's a scandal that you RAF boys are paid so miserably, when our whole civilization must ultimately depend upon people like you." I must say, I thought this was pitching it a bit high, and I mumbled something about everyone having to make the best of what they've got in this life, and at this Newby became very excited, and started waving his cigar around and saying, "That's just what I'm getting at, young man! But nothing ventured, nothing gained. Flying should be an exciting business. It can also be a profitable business – as Jim here will tell you!"

'Ritchie just sat and grinned at me. I noticed that he wasn't drinking much, and Newby wasn't drinking at all.

'I said something about it being all very well for freelance pilots in Civvy Street, but in the Services you had to keep to the rules. And Newby said, "Sometimes rules are meant to be broken.'' Then he went on at once to ask me, just as Ritchie had done, about my private life – whether I was married and had children, and so on. I was getting a bit fed up with this line of questioning – and I was also unsure of just how much this chap Newby really knew about me. I supposed that Thurgood must have given some sort of report to Ritchie before we'd met that evening.

'Then Newby asked me about my arrangements for leave. I told him I had three weeks due to me, but that normally I have to give at least two months' notice. Newby pressed me, and I told him that under special circumstances, such as pleading domestic difficulties, I might be able to take all three weeks almost at once.

'He and Ritchie looked satisfied. Then Newby asked me if I had ever flown a Hercules C-130 – one of those heavy four-engined turbo-prop American transports, some of them over twenty years old, and still working. Damn great carthorses that can lift off and land with over twenty tons of pay-load on a three-hundred-yard strip – cruising speed at around three hundred and twenty knots, and a maximum range, with external fuel-tanks, of 4,700 miles.

'Again they both seemed pleased with my answers. Ritchie then fired off a lot of questions, most of them fairly technical. Where had I flown a Hercules? Over what sort of terrain? What sort of weather conditions, and what pay-loads? Did I have experience of landing one on rough ground, with the statutory minimum of 300 yards? Above all, could I handle a Hercules solo?

'I pointed out that a Hercules carries a full crew of four. But Ritchie dismissed this – a full crew included radio and radar operators, and a co-pilot. ''Luxuries,'' he said, which sounded a bit funny, coming from someone in the plush taxi-service racket.

'Anyway, the brandy had made me a bit cocky, and I told them I was sure I could handle a Hercules on my own – after all, what did I have to lose? – and Ritchie went on to ask how I was at low-flying, and I said I could easily manage fifty feet, but would prefer if it was over water or flat country, and he looked at Newby and said something about ''doing their

22

best to manage it,'' and they made a little joke about it. Still very friendly, they were.'

'Yes, I'm sure they were.' It was Rawcliff's first comment since Mason had begun his story, and he regretted it at once. The young pilot, in his eagerness to unburden himself, needed no prompting. At first Rawcliff had listened to him with a mildly patronizing patience – the older, wiser man, following Mason, in his lonely innocence, as he was lured, without subtlety, by the mad-eyed Thurgood to the suede-walled penthouse with its jazzy girls and soul-music and balloons of brandy, and the taxi-pilot, Ritchie, with his drip-dry ladykiller smile, and the oily foreigner, Newby, with his flashing diamond, both paying court to him as the heroic underdog defending the Faith amid the dreary huts and regulated wastes of an RAF camp, *when just look what he was missing*. Forget the rules. Rules were made to be broken.

And slowly, even without realizing it, Rawcliff had been drawn into Mason's place, sharing his frustrations, his feelings of inferiority, with the dawning of an uneasy excitement.

The house around them both was very still. Judith and Little Tom, safe upstairs, were for the moment forgotten. 'Go on,' Rawcliff said quietly. 'How much?'

'What?' Mason blinked dully: it was as though he were reliving that night in the Barbican penthouse all over again.

'How much did they offer you?' Rawcliff repeated.

'They didn't tell me straight out. But Newby did say that the moment I agreed, there would be a down-payment deposited for me in one of those Swiss bank accounts. No tax. Pretty heady stuff for a bloke like me – more the sort of thing you read about in books. I must have looked rather shaken, because Ritchie gave me a refill of brandy; then I managed to ask Newby how much I stood to get at the end of it. He told me it wouldn't be a fortune, but a very comfortable sum, thank you, by English standards.'

Rawcliff interrupted again: 'Did this man Newby say what he did for a living?'

'No. I just assumed he was some sort of business man.'

'Did he strike you as crooked?'

Mason reddened. 'To tell you the truth, things were happening so fast that I didn't really get round to forming an impression. But Ritchie looked fairly straight to me. Seemed a nice sort of bloke – sort of gave the whole business a more solid air. I thought he was the kind of person I could trust.'

Rawcliff nodded. 'That's no doubt why he was there.'

Mason sat forward, gripping his glass as though he were afraid of dropping it, and looked across at Charles Rawcliff with his solemn, innocent eyes, bewildered and beseeching.

'So then what happened?' said Rawcliff.

'Well, everything was left in mid-air. Ritchie finished his drink and stood up, and that was obviously the signal for us to leave. Newby was the first to go, but just as he said goodbye, he told me what he called "a little pre-emptive secret". The advance deposited in the Swiss bank would run into five figures, and the final sum would be five times that. Then he gave me a card.'

Mason reached for his wallet and extracted a white slip. It had the name *John Newby* in embossed script: no address, no profession. But on the back, in pencil, a telephone number with a 499 prefix. Mayfair.

'He told me to go away and sleep on it, and then ring the number, at any time during the morning, when I'd reached my decision.'

'Did he give you a time-limit?'

'Yes. Lunchtime today. I called the number, but it was one of those recorded things – I had to leave a number myself and they'd call me back. I said there wasn't a phone at my place but I'd try to get somewhere where they could reach me.' He licked nervously at his drink, and this time his eyes avoided Rawcliff. 'I'm afraid I left your number, for this evening.'

Rawcliff nodded. 'Any particular time?'

'I said between seven and eight, unless I rang them back.'

'It's gone nine now. Why didn't you tell me this at the beginning?'

'I'm awfully sorry. I seem to have cocked this one up. You see, I thought you might think I was a bit daft, coming in

24

and sitting around waiting for a call from a gang of gun-runners or whatever they are.'

There was a tap at the door and Judith Rawcliff looked in, with a sweet smile at Flight-Lieutenant Mason: 'You'll stay and have something to eat, won't you, Terry?'

Mason had stood up and started to say something, when Rawcliff cut in: 'It's all right, love – we'll have something cold later on.'

She nodded. 'It's curry, so you can heat it up when you want it. And I've left some salad on the side. Good night, Terry.' The door closed.

Mason said, with a slight agonized wince, 'I ought to have said something to your wife about going away.'

'Forget it. You've got other things to worry about.'

Mason sat eyeing the telephone, while Rawcliff poured him another drink. The pilot looked up suddenly: 'What do you think?'

'I wasn't there. But from what you've been saying, it sounds as though they're rushing their fences.'

'How do you mean?'

'Well, let's take it step by step. This fellow Newby's setting up an operation in which he's offering a number of freelance pilots at least fifty thousand pounds – if, as he says, the down-payment runs into five figures and is a fifth of the total. The only sort of operation that would justify that kind of money is something either highly illegal or highly dangerous, and probably both.

'But for some reason they're in a hurry, and any operation conceived in haste is not well blessed. It sounds as though they've got a deadline to meet, and that the whole team had been lined up ready to go, when one of them dropped out at the last minute. Then you run into an old colleague in a pub. You both go out to dinner and he makes a phone call to his boss. Next night you again have dinner with him and the meeting is set up. They have a chance to look you over and ask a few questions. Can you fly a Hercules? Can you land and take off on rough terrain and fly solo – too low for comfort, with a full pay-load? Three pilots so far – which means three planes, with a total pay-load of over sixty tons

– always assuming that there aren't others lined up whom you haven't met. Sixty tons of what, Terry?'

'Actually, I did try to ask them. I forgot to mention it. Newby just told me to relax – that it wasn't drugs, anyway. He promised me that.'

'I'm sure Mr Newby's promises are worth a lot! And we can almost certainly rule out drugs. Christ, sixty tons of the stuff – even grass –' he waved his hand. 'It's too big to think about. Anyway, the professionals would go about it properly – they wouldn't go lugging the stuff around in a fleet of bloody great C-130s. And they wouldn't, with respect to you, go recruiting in a pub and popping the question on the second meeting.

'Guns, as you suggested, are more likely. There's also gold. Even copper. And uranium, of course. Once you reduce it to an ordinary large-scale smuggling operation, it could be any number of things.'

'Do you think it has to be illegal?'

Rawcliff laughed. 'You'd best go and see an international lawyer about that one, Terry. It rather depends on what countries you're flying from and to. As a serving member of Her Majesty's Forces, you'd be in the shit whichever way you turn – but whether you'd be committing an offence here, I don't know. International law is about as clear as a novel by Virginia Woolf. For instance, Britain is one of the few countries which has no law against its subjects enlisting as mercenaries in foreign armies, or even against them being recruited here. And as far as our people doing naughty things abroad is concerned, we leave that to the extradition laws, which are pretty clumsy.

'So, if you ask my opinion, for what it's worth, I'd say that if you go through with this, you run two distinct risks. The first you take as a pilot, and that you can only calculate when you know what the run is, and what sort of country you'll be flying over. The second is if you get caught – and again that depends where it is. You might face a firing-squad, thirty years in jail, or just get your gonads chopped off. Otherwise, as long as you don't mind being cashiered, like your friend Thurgood, you can always disappear with

26

your little Swiss nest-egg and live happily ever after.'

When he finished speaking, he saw that Mason was sweating slightly.

'I'm sorry, Charles, but I'm in a blue funk. That's why I had to come round to see you.'

'You didn't have to leave them my telephone number,' Rawcliff said, without rancour: 'You could have waited for them to ring you in a pub or a restaurant.'

'Yes I know. That was right out of court, I'm afraid. The truth is, I've got the wind up. I didn't tell you, but on that second evening, while Ritchie was calling me a taxi, Newby took me aside and told me to keep my mouth shut. Well, he was a bit more polite than that, but I just didn't like the way he said it. I got a funny feeling that I was committed, and if I said no, they wouldn't let me off the hook so easily.'

'There's not much they can do to you – and you've got the whole Royal Air Force to protect you, for Christ's sake.'

Mason raised his eyes to him, full of that painful innocence. 'That's just the point. Newby's parting words were to say that my superiors wouldn't take too kindly to one of their men considering such an offer. He said it was hardly in my terms of contract, then he gave me a nasty little smile.'

'I see,' said Rawcliff. 'Either accept their terms, or wait for Messrs Newby and Co. to poison your record? Come on, Terry, let's get something to eat, and then you can make that telephone call again.'

'Remember,' Rawcliff said, 'It's only an answering service. That means you do any answering – not them.'

Mason had clamped the phone on the table and dialled steadily. Three ringing tones, a click, and a girl's tinny voice: then Mason banged down the receiver. 'I can't go through with it! I've got my bloody career to consider – wife, three kids – I don't want to finish up like that loony, Thurgood. I don't care if he has got some swank radio shop in the West End. They can keep their bloody money!' For the first time he sounded a little drunk. 'Anyway, they pushed me into it. They made all the running. All I did was to accept an invitation to a party. God, what have I got myself into?'

'You haven't got yourself into anything yet,' Rawcliff said. 'I tell you what you do. You can kip down on the sofa over there. I'll ring that number and tell them to call back here between nine and ten in the morning – I don't go to work until then. If they don't call, forget them.'

'But I'm due back in camp tomorrow!' Mason said miserably.

'Tell them that. Or I'll tell them. Tell them they'll have to go and find someone else. You don't know anything incriminating about them, except Newby's phone number, and the fact that the man's anxious to recruit some pilots to fly Hercules transports, and is offering a hell of a lot of money. You don't know how much, you don't know where they're flying or what they're carrying, or why. Case closed.'

He went upstairs to get some blankets and a pillow. Judith spoke to him, half-asleep, from the bed: 'Everything all right?'

'More or less. Nothing for us to worry about. I'll be up in a moment, love.' And he felt the pang of alarm – he was already thinking deviously, half in Mason's shoes; with the same eagerness, but without the trepidation.

Mason had not moved; he had not even finished his drink. God, Rawcliff thought, I wouldn't like to have him as a co-pilot – heading into an occluded front with the R/T cutting out, heavy icing, oil-pressure dropping on Number Two engine. You would expect all that in a superannuated Hercules, flying solo, half-blind, at maybe tree-top level, for 2,000 miles with an illegal pay-load. Yet this poor sod hadn't even got the nerve to make a phone call to an answering service!

Rawcliff resisted the temptation to have a last drink. It was late, and he saw Mason safely bedded down on the sofa, then went upstairs and undressed in the dark, and slipped into bed beside Judith. She lay with her back to him, the duvet pulled round her naked shoulders, over her slim legs and high-waisted buttocks, and her champagne-glass breasts which had remained undistorted by the birth of little Tom.

He knew how she hated the taste of whisky on his breath; and besides, it was late, and she had to get up early, to get Tom his breakfast, and drive him round to the baby-minder, before she went off to work on her computers. The thought made him guilty, resentful: he was only too aware that she worked rather harder than he did – only because she was interested in her job, and he wasn't – and that she also brought home more money than he did.

His side of the sheet felt cold, starched. Like a hospital bed. For a long time he lay looking at the dark-patterned ceiling. The house was a dilapidated two-up, two-down – barely enough room to bring up one child, and Judith wanted to have at least three. How long could he hold a girl like that? In the old days, it had been high-flying, footloose and fancy-free, at whatever speeds he liked, landing where and when he wanted, using the verbal ejection-seat if the going got rough. It was all a matter of nerves and confidence. His nerves were still pretty good, but his confidence had softened. That bum landing at Gibraltar, with a plane-load of screaming tourists, had only been the last bump on a long slide downwards. He knew it was useless to try and trace back to where it had gone wrong. There were too many starting-points, too many false turnings and blind alleys.

He lay listening to a siren panting somewhere in the night. He was just old enough to remember the sirens in the war – the excitement, as a schoolboy in the country, watching a V1 flying-bomb, or 'Doodlebug', shot down near the Kent coast. By the end of the war he had been able to spot almost every type of aircraft at under 5,000 feet. He was determined to be a pilot, before he left school – one of those minor 'public' schools which most professional men of his class are slightly ashamed to include in the *curriculum vitae*. He didn't try for University. He'd never been much of a learner, although he had a good grasp of technical details, and a natural gift for languages. Instead, he went straight into the RAF, for his National Service.

He had done well, and had signed on. The Royal Air

Force had seemed to offer, at that point, quite as much as a civilian career, with certainly the promise of more excitement. In any case, he had no clear ambitions. At first Service life had suited him. It was during the twilight of the Empire, between the nasty blot of Suez, and a series of skirmishes, from Cyprus and Kenya, to the scuttle of Aden, during all of which the mandarins in Whitehall and the brass in the War House – not to mention the chosen representatives of an indifferent electorate – persisted in their determination that Britain should maintain what they called 'a Presence'.

Rawcliff had become part of that Presence. He had quickly shown himself not only to be an excellent pilot, but to have that one quality that was both distrusted and badly needed in the run-down, postwar British Armed Services. He was an intelligent individualist. He was also rough and tough, and none too amenable to the strictures of petty discipline – which hadn't mattered much, as long as he was thought to be *hard*. He was still in his early twenties when he finished his basic training on the Isle of Man and received his first posting with an Interceptor Squadron, operating out of Norway. But soon after, the long grey arm of the Ministry of Defence had leaned out and plucked him back to England – to a camp outside Cobham, in Surrey. He had been selected to become part of one of those small outfits which thrive in the bathos and phoney *machismo* of Cold War Intelligence work: whose recruits are taught, among other things, all the elegant and inelegant ways of killing one of their fellow human beings.

Rawcliff had graduated into a new career of tension and discomfort, broken up by spasms of acute danger, sometimes death. He had usually operated at night, without lights, from strips in the desert, jungle clearings. He had won the odd 'mention', but no decorations. There were no medals, no glory in that world. If something went wrong, nobody wanted to know. Something did go wrong, but it was slower, more insidious, than a Czech-made bullet or a terrorist's knife. His drinking began to get out of hand. Wild nights in what passed for a 'Mess' – sometimes followed by the theft of

30

a comrade's wife – degenerated into prolonged, solitary benders. He remembered the Australian medic, who used to give him his regular morning jab of Vitamin B-12, saying one day, as he put the needle in, 'You realize, Mr Rawcliff, I'm only painting over rust?'

His nerve had started to go. And his moral fibre, too. LMF, they called it. They found he wasn't so hard, after all – that he had scruples – that he no longer had the stomach to kill. So they'd paid him his derisory stipend and told him to get lost.

He'd been lucky, at first. It had been in the early Sixties, when air-transport was expanding all over the world, and the big airlines were screaming for good pilots. Rawcliff had no difficulty getting himself taken on as a co-pilot for what was then British European Airways. But promotion was by seniority only; the life turgid and stifling; and after he had been passed over a couple of times for Captain, he resigned, and joined one of the smaller charter companies that ran short-haul flights to the cheaper holiday resorts, and where they weren't quite so hot on the occasional absenteeism or on sniffing his breath before take-off. But soon the tedium of scheduled civilian flight – the sad eager air-hostesses, the lonely one-night stands, in foreign towns, with no friends – began to wear him down. Then came the business at Gibraltar, and he found himself once again out on a limb. This time an old SAS colleague had picked him up, and he had spent one hectic, improbable summer punting on the Futures Market, with wretched lack of success. Then a distant aunt had died, and with her modest legacy, he had been able to set up as a wine merchant in Fulham. It had been soon after this that Judith had come into his shop. Three months later they were married – hastily but decently, and at least a month before Tom was conceived.

But now, after nearly three years, he found himself weighted down with worries about tax, mortgage, overdraft – the whole arid litany of stapled paperwork that poisoned a man, drip by drip, like the Chinese water-torture. First you were an unsung hero, then you lost your innocence, then your wings – until a beautiful and intelligent girl came along

31

and pulled you out of the nose-dive. And here he was, once again, with the nose being dragged back down, pulling him into a slow relentless stall. Judith and Tom would have to bail out before the crash. She was too loyal to suggest it herself, even to think about it: but he knew in his heart that Tom was more important to her than he was. And anyway, it was always women and children first, wasn't it?

He was getting maudlin. It was the whisky. Damn the whisky. *And damn Mason*. It was Mason, and his story, which had started him thinking – was keeping him awake, worrying him, tempting him. The wretched fellow had been offered a small fortune on a plate, just to put in some flying time on his leave, and he hadn't even had the guts to say No.

I'm not like Mason, Rawcliff told himself. I'm a man who stands on his own feet, and I've got a beautiful, intelligent, professionally qualified wife to bear witness to it. The savants suggested that women despised failure: but it was not failure, it was weakness they hated. And I'm not weak, Rawcliff told himself. He licked his dry lips and drank some water from the carafe beside the bed; then he got to thinking again about those Hercules.

2

The early morning traffic had started when he finally got to sleep. Judith brought him his tea and the *Telegraph*. 'Your friend seems to have flown,' she said, and handed him a sheet of paper. 'He left this for us.'

It was written in a careful schoolboy hand:

Dear Charles and Judith,
I am afraid I have abused your hospitality. I am returning to camp today, but I promise that if I am recalled to London, I would be more than happy to continue baby-sitting for you.
Yours, with all best wishes,
Terry
P.S. Charles, I have thought things over and have decided to leave well alone. I am sure you will understand.

'What does that last bit mean?' she asked.

'Oh, Mason got a freelance flying offer during leave. That's against RAF rules and he turned it down.'

Rawcliff got out of bed and stretched his big naked body in front of her; and then noticed she was looking at him with her crooked, quizzical smile. 'It's a bit ironic, isn't it?'

'What is, love?'

'That they should have made the offer to him, and not to you. After all, you don't have to get permission.'

'Don't I?' He leant down and kissed her. 'One man you didn't marry is a pilot who is never at home.'

He dressed and joined her down at breakfast. The post brought a final reminder from the Gas Board and a letter from his bank, making the usual terse noises about his account still being out of order and would he arrange funds to be transferred.

Funds, he thought later, as he sipped his third coffee, while shaving. Sell his share of the business, pay off the mortgage, put the house on the market, then what would he be left with? Much tidier to accept a down-payment of five figures in a Swiss bank, do the job, and pick up the other four-fifths: then he could sell up everything, and he and Judith and Tom could buy somewhere in France. A farmhouse in the Auvergne.

Swiss numbered bank accounts had always held a mysterious drama, something almost spiritual, like touching the hem in some mighty cathedral. And all Mason had done was worry about his bloody superior officers. Modern England was fashioned for creatures like Mason. Polite, timid, supine. Rawcliff just hoped that he himself had more balls.

He drove across the river in his old Humber and opened the shop up just after eleven. His assistant, Toby Hyde-Smith, was late. But the early trade was usually slack – a few tearaways from the Earls Court area, buying chilled beer to moisten their hangovers. It gave him time to do the accounts.

Hyde-Smith drifted in, breathless with apology. He had been to 'Chucks' the night before – 'full of those ghastly Arabs, all drinking champagne which they're not allowed to do, are they, under Islam? And you know what one of us did? Put the table-cloth round his head and pretended to be an Ayatollah and gave some wogs at the next table the most wonderful wigging! And the girls!' Hyde-Smith said, a little later: 'The place was positively full of them! And really young girls. I suppose that's how the Arabs like them? Unless, of course, they can get boys or goats.' He gave a nasal giggle: 'Just imagine "Chucks" giving membership to a flock of goats!'

'It must have been frightfully funny,' Rawcliff said. 'Did you know the Excise people have written to us again? They're now threatening us with criminal proceedings.'

Just before lunch time he slipped out to the pub and had a couple of beers. He felt tired and anxious. It was a difficult, indefinable feeling – like when, as a younger man, he had met some girl who had made a special impression on him, and her memory kept nagging at him next day. Sooner or later

34

he knew he would have to call her up. Only this time it was Swiss francs.

As he walked back to the shop, he calculated how long it was since he had last sat at the controls of an aircraft. But that was something they'd have a lot of difficulty checking on. They'd just have to take his word for it.

He had to drive up to Holborn late that afternoon, to take charge of a consignment of Valdepeña, and did not get home till after seven. Judith said, 'Oh, you just missed him. Some man ringing up for Terry.'

'Terry was expecting a call last night. That was one of the reasons he came round here. What did you tell the man?'

'Just that Terry had gone back to camp. He sounded a bit put out – started asking who I was and where I was speaking from, and I'm afraid I got a bit sharp with him. I told him to ring back and talk to you. Then he hung up.'

Rawcliff went through into the kitchen where the table was smeared with the debris of Tom's dinner. He lifted the whisky bottle, when Judith came up behind him. 'Love, isn't it a bit early for that?'

'Just one,' he said staunchly, and poured a glass, neat, almost to the brim. He felt defiant, and defensive. He tried not to avoid looking at her. Her face was pinched and tired, and he knew she was worried, but not just on his account. There was also little Tom.

He could hear the reproach in her voice now: 'Charles, what's going on? It's something to do with Mason, isn't it? He's in some sort of trouble, and now he's involved you?'

'I've got to make a phone call, then I'll tell you all about it.'

He went into the study and dialled the Mayfair number. When the girl's voice asked him to speak, he left Terry Mason's name and his own number, and a message that unless they called back within an hour, he would consider the deal off.

They rang back twenty minutes later. It was a man calling from a pay-phone; his voice was quiet and flat, nothing that Rawcliff could immediately attach to class or nationality. He himself had put a handkerchief partly over the receiver, not knowing if the trick would work or not; but Mason had a particularly featureless voice, like the man at the other end.

'Flight-Lieutenant Mason speaking.'

'We understood that you had left town, Mason?'

'I was delayed. Why didn't you ring last night?'

'There must have been some mistake. We had arranged to contact you tonight.'

Rawcliff thought quickly. Mason was a punctilious fellow whom you didn't expect to make that kind of mistake; but still, on that second evening he admitted he had had a lot to drink, and had been excited and confused.

Rawcliff said into the phone: 'I'm listening.'

'A friend of mine would like to give you lunch tomorrow. One o'clock at the "Escargot" in Greek Street. Do you know it?'

'I'll find it. Who am I to ask for?'

'A Mr Peters. So he can expect you at one?'

'Thank you.' Then with a spurt of adrenalin, Rawcliff added, 'Over and out.'

Back in the kitchen he launched into a carefully prepared, diluted version of Mason's story – some people were looking for a qualified contract-pilot to fly some heavy drilling equipment to the Middle East. He didn't know whether it would come to anything, but he gathered that they were offering good money and he thought he would at least follow it through. His manner was artificially casual, and they both knew that he was a feeble liar; but Judith to emphasize her reaction, said nothing, except one oblique remark about life insurance. He was chronically inept at paperwork and knew that he was poorly insured, should anything happen to him. But he refused to rise to the bait. Just before they went to sleep, she said, 'Do you know how much they're offering for this job?'

'I'll know tomorrow. I'm having lunch with them.'

'Well, it'll be nice to have something to put in the bank. And it'll give you a break, won't it?'

'I suppose so.'

Like hell it would.

He somehow got through the morning, without a drink and without losing his temper with Toby Hyde-Smith. He wondered who they would send. It was unlikely to be the crazy Thurgood – he had been no more than a casual contact. And Ritchie was just one of the hired help. Newby was the most likely, with this man Peters as the next one up in the chain of command.

He considered how they would react. If they were really in a hurry and wanted an extra *bona fide* pilot for the mission, they'd hardly have reason to complain if he stepped in where Mason feared to tread. In fact, they'd have every right to be grateful.

He took a taxi up to Soho, arriving at the restaurant ten minutes after he was due. No point in appearing too keen. 'Is Mr Peters here yet?'

The waiter consulted his book. 'He's expecting you, sir? Table for three, sir, over there,' and he began to lead the way into the dining-room. There was only one man at the table, sitting with his back to them. He did not get up, just nodded, as Rawcliff sat down opposite him against the wall. The waiter said, 'Monsieur would like something to drink?'

Rawcliff saw that the man was having nothing. He said, 'I'll wait for the wine.'

'Very good, Monsieur.'

The man looked at him with a steady grey stare. 'Flight-Lieutenant Mason? Peters.'

'The waiter told me it was a table for three.' Rawcliff glanced at the third place between them.

'He'll be joining us when we've eaten. You know him. Mr Newby.' The wine-waiter arrived, but Peters waved him away, without consulting Rawcliff. 'I was told to expect a much younger man, Mason.'

He had a long, hard, flat face with a sloping forehead, like a cricket bat. His skin was smooth and dry, closely shaven, and his age might have been anything between thirty-five and fifty. Rawcliff was puzzled by his voice: it had the same dull intonation as the voice on the phone, but with an occasional clipped vowel that gave it a curious primness. A colonial voice. South African.

Rawcliff had anticipated the man's remark, and had his answer prepared. He had even made a check-call that morning to the local RAF Recruiting Centre in Wandsworth, and had learnt that he still had more than ten years in hand, as a full-time pilot, before the statutory age limit of fifty-seven. But surprisingly, Peters seemed to let the matter slide. Instead he added, 'How long have you been with the RAF?'

Here Rawcliff had decided to play safe. His true 'Service' background was so murky, its details blurred and often overlapping, that he could afford to be deliberately vague, in the sure knowledge that Peters – and whoever was behind him – would never be able to check his full file, even if such a thing existed.

He pretended to show more interest in the menu, as he said, 'Pushing fifteen years, with the odd break.' He looked up. 'I'm sorry you were hoping for someone younger.' But his smile was not returned.

'Been in the RAF most of your life then, Mason?'

'More or less.'

'I'd put you in your mid-forties. So you enlisted at about thirty? Bit late, wasn't it? What did you do before that?'

Rawcliff paused strategically; the waiter was taking their order. The restaurant was only half-full, the tables well spaced. 'I knocked about a bit. Learnt a few tricks – the odd skulduggery and rough stuff, on Her so-called Majesty's Service, in a few far-flung spots, before we hauled down the flag for the last time.'

'Ever killed anyone, Mason?'

'Sorry, mate. Secrets of the trade.'

Peters' face was as expressionless as the restaurant furniture. 'You mentioned the "odd break", during your RAF service?'

'Oh, the usual stint with the Special Air Service. I'm on the Reserve, of course,' he added, telling the half-lie with casual conviction.

'In what Zones of Operation?'

Rawcliff gave an easy smile: 'Oh come on, Peters, you're not so green as to expect me to answer a question like that?'

'It's something you didn't tell us the other evening.'

'I wasn't asked. I was simply told you wanted a qualified pilot who could handle a Hercules, solo – getting her off the ground and back down again in the minimum space, with a full pay-load, on bad terrain, and flying at low levels.'

There was a pause while the waiter served the first course. 'Have you fixed your leave?' Peters asked.

'You give me the dates and I can arrange it – three weeks compassionate, and more if necessary.'

'Three weeks should be sufficient.' Peters' face was stiff with courteous disdain. 'I thought the RAF were over-stretched?'

Rawcliff ignored him, and poured some water from the carafe. He regretted now that he hadn't asked for that drink. 'Before I make any formal request to my station, I want the answer to three questions. How much money? Where are we flying to and from? And what are we carrying?'

Peters picked a sliver of lettuce from his teeth. 'Ten thousand sterling up front. Another forty thousand when the job's done.'

The two of them ate for a moment in silence. Rawcliff relaxed and smiled. 'No go, Peters.'

Peters just sat facing him.

'It's too much money,' Rawcliff said. 'Five thousand – for a simple contract job – I'd take my leave and jump at it. But fifty thousand? Oh no. You're buying more than a pilot, Peters. You're either buying secrecy or paying danger-money – big danger-money – or both. I've got a secure job and a family to support, and I'm not walking into this like a blind kitten.'

Peters pushed his plate away and touched a napkin to his lips. His eyes did not move from Rawcliff. 'You've obviously had time to think this over, Mason. As a professional serving officer, you must be familiar with receiving your orders on take-off – sealed orders which you only open when you're airborne.'

'Under very special circumstances.'

'These are very special circumstances.'

'The only difference being that I won't be a serving

officer. I'll be doing it for the money. And I shall want to know exactly what the job is.'

There was another pause. The waiter was hovering with two plates of rare steak; a second waiter brought up the vegetables. At the door a small dark man was handing in his coat. Peters glanced across the restaurant, towards the entrance. He looked bored. 'Will you excuse me a moment?'

Rawcliff watched him stroll towards the door. His movements were loose and athletic. Rawcliff noticed that the small dark man had disappeared.

He sat behind his steak and waited. He wondered what they'd do, even in deepest Soho? They'd scarcely put the hard arm on him here. Anyway, what did they have to lose? They wanted to buy a run-of-the-mill pilot for a small fortune, so why shouldn't Rawcliff be their man? With a flash of conceit, he considered himself a cut above Mason. It was just a question of convincing Peters and Newby.

The two of them came back across the restaurant; Peters pulled back the table and the little dark man took his seat beside Rawcliff. He was plump and glossy, with long black eyelashes on a soft round face that looked as though it had been faintly powdered; and he smelt of after-shave. He was one of those people you expect to see at any big international airport, in the bar of the best hotels, the best restaurants, the most fashionable nightclubs; and he would probably specialize in tall flashy girls. Rawcliff would have given a lot to have been able to look at his passport – assuming that he had only one.

The man had taken the wine-list, ignoring Rawcliff altogether. He ordered a cocktail, giving the waiter precise instructions. His voice was relaxed, pleasant, with a faintly cosmopolitan intonation; Rawcliff wondered, like Mason, was it Jewish? Greek? Mongrel Mediterranean?

The man turned to him with a little sigh. 'Who are you?'

'The name is Rawcliff. Charles Rawcliff. I took a call from Mr Peters last night.'

The man smiled. 'As I understand it, Mr Rawcliff, the call was in fact made to someone named Flight-Lieutenant Mason.' He held out his hand, and Rawcliff caught the glint of the diamond ring. 'I'm John Newby. Would you mind explaining how you come to be here?'

'Not at all.' Rawcliff had also anticipated this new scene, and had prepared his lines accordingly. In a way, he felt he had a definite edge over Flight-Lieutenant Mason: for instead of a time-serving greenhorn who could be weaned off the rule-book over a few brandies, Rawcliff was confident that his own career, fragmented though it had been, was much more in line with what this smooth-talking Newby, and his South African sidekick, were pitching for.

He gave them most of it straight – how he had learnt his flying during National Service, giving full particulars of his experience with different aircraft, flying hours, safety record etc., and included only those dates and places where they didn't seem to matter, or couldn't be checked. For the rest, the old Official Secrets Act was implied; and Newby was tactful enough not to press him. Two details which he did leave out were his little trouble with the bottle, and how he had finally flunked the special psychological screening interview which they held at regular intervals back at their place outside Cobham, when he'd one day let slip that he had an unfortunate aversion to killing.

He concluded with a brief, more or less truthful account of his career as a civil airline pilot, until he'd fluffed that one too – though again he wasn't going to volunteer the information unless specifically asked.

Neither of them had interrupted once. Not a muscle in Peters' face had moved; while Newby had sat watching him, almost unblinking, from under his long black eyelashes. When Rawcliff finally stopped speaking, Newby gave a purring laugh and signalled dexterously to the wine waiter. 'You would like a little liqueur, perhaps, Mr Rawcliff? For myself, I sometimes take an iced Grand Marnier. It braces me for the afternoon, without making me too sleepy. Such a bore to be sleepy in the afternoon.' He leant back and patted his well-tailored stomach. 'I must say, I admire your nerve.' He nodded at Peters: 'Ten out of ten for nerve.'

Peters gave Rawcliff a hard glare. Newby nodded his sleek furry head. 'So you no longer fly – professionally? But you

41

still do have a valid pilot's licence, of course?'

'Yes. I fly with a local club outside London.' A lie, but one he'd decided to risk: it made the record sound better. In any case, Newby seemed satisfied.

'Quite so – keeps your hand in.' Newby had glanced at Peters. 'I don't think we should blame Mr Rawcliff too severely for this little muddle. Although I am disappointed in Flight-Lieutenant Mason. I had urged him to be discreet. He seemed a dull young man, but basically sound. Yet I was wrong.' His moist black eyes had moved back to Rawcliff, and his next words held a hidden edge of menace, 'I hope we will not be disappointed in you, Mr Rawcliff?'

Rawcliff was listening to the murmur of lunchtime talk; then Newby added brightly, almost off-hand, 'What do you do now, Mr Rawcliff?'

'I'm in the wine business.'

'I see. And is that profitable? You don't mind my asking, but under the circumstances I feel justified in knowing a little about you?'

'No – to both questions.'

'Quite so.' Newby gave a tactful nod. 'And why did you stop being a pilot?'

'They chucked me out.' To hell with them! he thought. If they were serious – as he suspected they were – they'd have to know sooner or later. Anyway, they were paying for the meal. 'I'd had a few drinks. Nothing unusual. If anyone tells you that civil airline pilots never drink for forty-eight hours before flying, they're talking through their arses. We drink like everyone else – sometimes like fishes, particularly on a long run. It's like driving over the limit – it's all right until you make a mistake and get caught.'

'What were the details?' said Peters. It was the first time he had spoken since Newby's arrival.

'Gib – one of the worst spots in Europe. The regular pilot's nightmare. Runway half out to sea and about 300 yards too short for comfort, with a nasty steep right-angled turn on the approach. It was night, pissing with rain, and I'd laced my coffee with a few brandies. I wasn't in the least drunk – only afterwards my bloody little co-pilot blew the whistle on me. We burst a tyre on touch-down – no fault of mine – and nearly lost a wing. So, after the Inquiry, I had to kiss goodbye to all those hostesses, my pay-cheque and pension rights, and was out on the streets.'

Peters was tapping the table with the edge of his hand. 'You say the runway was three hundred yards too short? Three hundred yards might be *all* you get with a Hercules.'

'So Mason told me.'

'What else did Mason tell you?' said Newby.

'He told me just what you'd told him – which wasn't much. I don't see what the problem is,' Rawcliff added, with energetic self-confidence. 'Surely one pilot's as good as another – for your sort of job?'

'Quite. Providing he is discreet. We are paying for discretion, too, Mr Rawcliff.' He smiled. 'You have a saying, do you not – that discretion is the better part of valour?' He spoke dreamily, as though the words contained some original wisdom which he had only just discovered. 'Discretion and valour – that is what we are paying for.'

Rawcliff said, 'Let's start talking seriously, Mr Newby. Mason's thrown in his hand, and you're probably well shot of him – those RAF boys are trained by the book and they fly by the book. He may have been indiscreet, but at least he put you on to me, and saved you having to waste more time looking for another pilot. I'm qualified, I'm freelance, and the only book I fly by is the plane's handbook.

'Now I'm interested in your proposition – in so far as it goes. Fifty thousand pounds is a nice sum, but it's a lot of bloody use if I wind up dead. I want to know exactly how long the odds are – and I know that for that sort of money they're going to be very long.'

Newby moistened his lips and smiled. He had taken out a crocodile cigarette-case from which he selected a black cheroot with a thin gold band. He offered one to Rawcliff, who declined. 'How sensible,' said Newby, 'I've given up cigarettes myself – they give me asthma. These are not a disagreeable substitute, providing one does not inhale them. You know the Eastern Mediterranean, of course?'

'I've flown to Greece, and Istanbul. But I wouldn't say I

43

knew much more than Ellinikon and Yesilkoy Airports, and the bars of the King George and the Pera Palace.'

Peters' long face was taut with disapproval. Newby nodded. 'You are not, perhaps, familiar with the Middle East?'

'Not so far. Do you originally come from there, by the way?'

Newby's smile stiffened for an instant, but held firm. 'What a curious question. No, I don't, as a matter of fact. I am British.' Two tendrils of smoke curled out of his small nostrils. 'Mr Rawcliff, I think it is perhaps time that we were frank with you.'

'That's fine by me. It's certainly more than you were with Mason.'

Newby took his glass of Grand Marnier and sniffed at it delicately. 'Superb. Your health, Mr Rawcliff.' He was behaving as though Peters were not there. 'Let me first make what may seem an impertinent observation. I deduce that you are not a man who is familiar with the workings of big business?' He tapped off a finger of ash from his cheroot. 'I'm going to surprise you now, Mr Rawcliff. We are in the charity business – international charity.'

'Is charity big business?'

'My dear sir, it certainly is! It is not just a matter of a few old ladies sending in pound notes, or of students and pretty girls rattling collecting tins in the street. Today the business is ruled by committees and sub-committees and commissions, even ministries. It is not only big business, it is *politics*. A pot-bellied child, a living skeleton of a woman' – he made a little circle in the air with his cheroot – 'they have ceased to have any importance in themselves, they are mere statistics. What is important is where they come from. The territorial indicative, you might say' – and he smiled at his obscure little joke. 'What State is responsible for them, or what National Liberation Front is claiming them. It is not so much a matter of which people you help, but of which government or governments are *behind* the people you are helping.' He used his hands while he spoke, tracing elaborate arabesques in the air with his lighted cheroot.

'Are these unhappy starving people oppressed by a nation which is supported by the West? Is that nation in conflict, and if so, on what side? I don't just mean the goodies and the baddies, the Free World versus the rest. Things have now become so complicated. If you smile at the Chinese, you must also smile, behind your hand, at the deposed butchers of Cambodia. If you are a liberal, you may have rejoiced at the revolution in Iran. But do you also rejoice at the renaissance of Islam – a return to the Dark Ages? As I said, it is so complicated – for those who have ideals, that is. Do you have ideals, Mr Rawcliff?'

'None that would worry you.'

'And, of course, you have nothing against mercy missions?'

'Only that the stuff's usually syphoned off into the fat cats' pockets before the starving masses ever get a peek at it. But that's not my problem. I just want the facts – not only my terms of contract, but what that contract exactly entails. How many aircraft? Who are my accomplices? Where are we flying from? And where to?'

Newby blew smoke at the ceiling, then leant forward and crushed out his cheroot. Rawcliff glanced at Peters, whose anger seemed to have temporarily subsided. He was getting worried by Peters – less as a threat, more as an inhibiting presence.

Newby seemed to think the same thing, at the same time. He said, 'Peters, let me have a chat with Mr Rawcliff. I think that I can handle him alone,' he added, with a titter. 'I'll settle the bill.'

Peters stood up, gave a quick nod and walked out.

'Who is that bastard?' Rawcliff said.

'You don't like him? No, I don't entirely blame you. He is excessively security conscious – in the policeman's sense of the word. It has its advantages, but it also becomes socially tiresome. He is not a very cultured man, I'm afraid.'

'Yes, but who is he?'

'He flies planes, like you. He was trained by the South African Air Force. Then he became freelance – what is now fashionably, and pejoratively, known as a mercenary. That is to say, he helped train the Air Forces of several independent African states. He is a professional, without any political axe to grind.'

'So what are his motives? Helping those pot-bellied children and skeleton women?'

'I imagine,' Newby said, with an avuncular sigh, 'that his motives are the same as yours. Money. Money makes the world go round!' And he laid his hand on Rawcliff's sleeve and gave it a squeeze.

'And your motives, Mr Newby? Just money too?'

Newby's laugh purred in his ear: 'Maybe I have a few ideals as well. But you would not be interested in them. You want the facts, the itinerary. Six planes, Mr Rawcliff. Six Hercules transports, purchased, quite legally, from the Americans in West Germany. The planes are not new, of course. Theoretically they are sold off as scrap, when they have completed a certain number of hours. But it is like buying one of your old London taxis. The price may not be high, but you can be sure that the vehicle has been thoroughly serviced and maintained right up to the end.'

'You have a touching faith in London taxis, Mr Newby. If you buy one on the cheap and it breaks down, you take it to a garage. But if you're flying a veteran Hercules over unknown territory and it decides to crack up on you, you're in trouble.'

Newby shrugged. 'Obviously that is a risk. It is one of the risks for which you are being paid.'

'I'm still being paid over the odds. If all six pilots are getting the same as me, I reckon that would cover the cost of the so-called medical supplies many times over – not to mention the cost of the planes, unless you sell them off afterwards.'

This time Newby laughed openly: 'I must say, you are the first man I have ever met who has complained of being overpaid!'

'I'm not complaining. I'm just curious. The itinerary, Mr Newby – the flight-plan?'

The little man put a manicured finger to his lips and shook his head. 'Sealed orders, Mr Rawcliff. I'm sorry, but the matter is politically sensitive, and it will be of no advantage for you to have this information. I am not saying that our mission would meet with the opposition or disapproval of the British Government. It is simply that we cannot risk, at this stage, becoming involved in international controversy. The press, for instance' – and he gave a small theatrical shudder.

The waiter was pouring coffee, while they both sipped their Grand Marnier. 'You can at least tell me where we'll be operating from?' Rawcliff said, when the waiter had gone.

'Not yet. Soon, maybe. When we know a little more about you. It is a mistake, my dear sir, to be too open too early, in matters of big business. In your case, you have rather forced my hand. I must now ask *you* to be frank with *me*. You have not come here, I hope, just to amuse yourself? To satisfy your passing curiosity?'

'Partly that. Partly because I'm greedy. I need the money. I might have a few other motives too, but they wouldn't concern you.'

'In an operation like this,' Newby said softly, 'everything about you must concern me. No large organization employs a man for a high salary without first making quite sure that he is sound.'

Rawcliff finished his liqueur and tasted the coffee. 'I've got a small business that's going bust. And a house that's too small for a family. I'm also a trained pilot, and a good one – at least, that's what they used to say.'

There was a pause between them. Newby had lit a fresh cheroot, but this time sat holding it very still, between the forefingers of both hands. He was leaning slightly forward when he next spoke, 'Mr Rawcliff, permit me to say so, but a man at your station in life, with a business to run and a family to support, does not easily change course in mid-stream, so to speak. You did not come here today, and impersonate Mason, just out of curiosity? Why did you come? Why are you really interested?'

'Because I'm bored. Bored and broke and frustrated. I also want to find myself sitting behind the controls of a plane again. A real plane – not just one of those paper-and-string jobs we use down at the flying club.'

'You can kill yourself just as easily in a small plane. But perhaps the danger does not worry you?'

'That depends on the odds. I've no intention of leaving a widow and a fatherless child. And I don't expect your benevolent organization is likely to pay the second cash instalment if I go down somewhere in a ball of flame, or finish up before some firing-squad of trigger-happy Sambos who can't shoot straight?'

'Now you are being melodramatic. The dangers, I assure you, will be minimal.

'I'm not taking your word for that, Newby.' He paused. 'When do I get the ten thousand pounds?'

Newby lifted his arm and snapped his fingers like a castanette, catching the waiter's eye and calling for the bill. He looked back at Rawcliff with his dark solemn eyes. 'Soon. Just as soon as you make up your mind. But one word of warning. In our line of business we have no lawyers, no tiresome written contracts. Your contract is your word – while ours is a confirmatory telegram to you personally from our agent in Geneva, informing you that the down-payment has been deposited in a numbered account which can only be touched by you.'

'And if something happens to me?'

Newby smiled sadly, 'There is a codicil. In the event of your decease, your next-of-kin will be able to draw the money. You see, we are not monsters. We believe in looking after our employees and in honouring our commitments. All that we ask in return is absolute silence – that you remain absolutely discreet.' He was very fond of that word, 'discreet'. Altogether, a very discreet little man.

He paused to scribble something on the bill and pushed it aside. 'All I need now is your address and – for the codicil – the full particulars of your next-of-kin. Your wife, I presume?'

Rawcliff hesitated. This was getting too close to home for comfort. Newby, acutely sensitive to the atmosphere, laid a hand again on his arm. 'Come, come, Mr Rawcliff, there must be a degree of mutual trust. Your wife need know nothing about the agreement – unless you choose to tell her, of course. Or unless' – he gave a slight shrug – 'you have an accident.'

'I'll give you my business address,' said Rawcliff taking out his pen.

Newby raised his glossy eyebrows. 'You forget that we already have your telephone number?'

Rawcliff felt himself getting angry. Suddenly he wanted to be rid of this oily purring little man with his diamond ring and his cloying perfume. Reluctantly, he wrote down his address in Battersea and stood up.

'Did you come by car, Mr Rawcliff? Then I will get you a cab – private firm. You can never hope to get a black taxi at this hour – they all head for the big hotels.'

He told the waiter to ring a number.

'I prefer to walk,' said Rawcliff.

Newby glanced at the entrance. 'I think you'll find it's raining.' He looked at his watch – the same chunky gold device which Mason had described, with a dial that told the time in Moscow and Cairo and New York and Damascus. Rawcliff wondered if it was just show, or whether it played some small but vital part in the daily running of an international organization.

'And when do I see you again, Mr Newby?'

'I have your number. I will call you very soon. And please, one thing' – he laid his hand again on Rawcliff's arm – 'I do hope you will be more sensible than Flight-Lieutenant Mason. For the moment, I would rather you did *not* discuss this matter with your wife. Not at least until things have been finalized and the money paid into your numbered account.' He gave him a quick sly smile: 'I think that is a good enough reason for keeping a little secret from her, eh? Now, I must go.' He started to push the table forward, just as the waiter came up and told them that Rawcliff's minicab had arrived.

Rawcliff saw the little man into his fur-lined coat and an expensive sealskin hat, and watched him duck out into the rain and get into a blue Lancia which was parked outside on the double yellow line. It had not collected a ticket.

The minicab was already across the street – a Cortina with bubbles of rust along what was left of the chrome. It struck Rawcliff as being distinctly shabby, even for the worst kind of minicab -- unless it was not a very subtle way of demonstrating Rawcliff's present status in the set-up. But there was a chill rain falling, and Rawcliff thought, knew that he could wait half-an-hour for a bus across the river to Battersea, and all afternoon for a taxi.

He crossed the street and said to the driver, 'Mr Rawcliff – for Mr Newby.'

'Hop in.' The man leant back to open the rear door, but Rawcliff got in beside him – a gesture of social guilt, perhaps: a need not to be seen riding on the backs of the lower orders, while people like Newby paid.

The driver was a chubby man with a bad case of psoriasis on his balding head; the only time that Rawcliff had seen a bald man with dandruff. He smoked as he drove, and his teeth and nostrils were dark with nicotine. Rawcliff, with the same uneasy sense of social superiority, was conscious of the weighty silence – like riding with only one other person in a lift. 'Do you often do work for Mr Newby?'

'Newby? Oh yes, him. Now and again. He's loaded. Always the best. I expect he eats in a place like that every day o' the week. You like all that fancy food? Me, I'm not fussy. Can't afford to be.' The rain was coming down heavily now, and he switched on the wipers which made a defective groaning noise. Rawcliff was content to sit back on the cracked vinyl seat and let the man chatter on.

'When I was married, I didn't do too badly. My wife had a lot o' books on French cooking. You like French cooking? Too rich for me. I don't mind a Spanish omelette, mind.' He drove on his brakes, talking between pulls at his cigarette. 'You might not think it, but I've got a seventeen-year-old girl now. I mean, not my own – living with me, like. Passionate, she is. Can't have enough of it. Hates cooking, though. Always wants to go out, pubs, discos – it's exhausting.' He braked, narrowly missing a group of tourists crossing a crowded intersection with Wardour

Street. 'Bloody foreigners, behave as though they own the place!' They had come to a halt, in dense traffic.

'Have you known Newby long?' Rawcliff said.

'A few months. Just the odd job, fetch and carry. He pays well.'

'Any idea what he does?'

'Me? Not a clue. But whatever it is, I wouldn't mind swapping with him.' They crawled up behind a parked van, and the man stopped and switched off the engine. 'Don't mind if I just stop in here for a moment, d'you? Got to have a word with someone.'

Rawcliff watched him hurry into a shop, under a sign: BOOKS - CASSETTES - SOUVENIRS. It had a narrow shop-front with the usual display of magazines. Outside, it was still raining hard. Three young men and a girl with carrier bags came running down the pavement, laughing and trying to push each other off the kerb. A traffic-warden stood in a doorway, bored and wet. Two girls in transparent raincoats and hoods over their hair, looking like a couple of loosely-wrapped sweets, went into a Wimpy bar across the street.

The driver had been gone more than ten minutes now. Rawcliff felt himself getting angry again when instinct prevailed over emotion. The instinct was suspicion – a mental knee-jerk from those distant grinding hours of training back in the Surrey woods near Cobham. If the mini-cab was a plant, elaborately devised by Newby – through prearrangement, perhaps, with Peters – how was Rawcliff to react? An innocent man would probably lose patience and just bugger off, leaving the driver unpaid. While a trusting recruit might be expected to sit tight and wait. But what for?

These people certainly weren't paying for innocence, and they didn't look dumb enough to expect trust. Instead, Rawcliff now acted precisely as he thought they wanted him to do. He was going to see their hand, if only to find out what their play was.

He gave the driver a full fifteen minutes, then slowly got out of the cab. He felt relaxed, sober, flexing his unused muscles, tensing his fingers down the sides of his legs, taking his time, with a quick apparently casual glance both ways along the wet crowded pavement; then went into the shop.

It was harsh with neon and smelt of disinfectant, like a hospital or a mortuary. Empty except for a little dark man who might have been born on the same latitude as Newby, but had clearly not fared as well.

Rawcliff walked down a narrow passage, past shelves marked NAUGHTY KNICKERS / NURSES IN DISTRESS / COLONEL SPANKER'S SPREE / SS UNIFORMS FOR HIRE OR SALE, FULL CEREMONIAL, AS WORN BY INSPECTORATE AT CONCENTRATION CAMPS. At the back was a green door with a Yale lock and a notice saying PRIVATE. The little dark man watched him, saying nothing. Rawcliff pushed the door and it swung open. A familiar flat voice said, 'Afternoon, Rawcliff. We were counting on you to come nosing in. Make yourself comfortable.'

The door snapped shut behind him. It was a small windowless room; there was a bar and shelf of drinks at one end, and about a dozen deal chairs in rows, like pews in a chapel, facing an empty white-washed wall. The only decoration was a Jubilee photograph of the Queen and the Duke of Edinburgh, flanked by furled Union Jacks.

Peters stood beside the closed door, looking calm and relaxed, while the minicab driver leant against the outside of the bar; he smirked at Rawcliff and pulled on his cigarette.

Rawcliff was aware that he had become rather cold. His legs felt heavy, his feet were numb. To steady himself, he tried to think back: had Newby gone out of the restaurant first and had time to instruct the driver, before driving away in the Lancia? But Rawcliff remembered that the two of them had left together. So it could only mean that when Peters had intercepted Newby at the restaurant door and told him that he was dealing with an impostor, a quick phone call had been made – probably by Peters – with a view to teaching Rawcliff a lesson. Newby's sweet talk that followed, and his pleas for mutual trust, were already qualified. These people had their own laws, and once you became involved, you obeyed them.

Rawcliff spoke, with a casual nod at the Royal portrait and the two flags, 'What is this? The headquarters of some kinky far-Right fringe group – black knickers under your SS uniforms, while swearing undying loyalty to the Crown?'

Peters gave a dull yellow smile. 'Got a sense of humour, have you? If you want to know, it's a cinema club. Exclusive, members only.'

Rawcliff attempted to smile back. 'He's got a devious mind, your Mr Newby. Must be fairly sure of himself, too. Suppose I'd decided not to take that cab? Or got bored waiting outside and walked off?'

Peters seemed to be thinking for a moment. 'We might have had to visit you at home. Maybe you would have preferred that? Got a wife, haven't you? And a kid?'

The chill in Rawcliff's limbs changed to a hot surge of blood that raced to his head. Peters, if he knew it, had made a fatal miscalculation. Perhaps he did know it, for he added laconically, 'Have a drink. You look as though you need one.' He nodded to the minicab driver by the bar, 'Give him a drink, Leslie.'

The chubby man lifted the bar hatch. Rawcliff reached for a handkerchief as though to blow his nose. He saw Peters raise his left foot. He was wearing suede chukkha boots with steel caps. Rawcliff dropped both hands, letting the handkerchief float to the floor, and caught Peters' foot as it came up, aimed swiftly and accurately at his groin; side-stepped and jerked the man's ankle hard. He felt the tendon snap like a twig, as he grabbed Peters by the lapels, dragged him down with all his weight and butted him in the middle of his smooth flat face. The rest was easy, like putting the finishing touches to a parcel: a hard chop behind the ear and another at the back of the neck. There was blood on Peters' suit and white shirt; his eyes were half-open, unseeing. He slid down in Rawcliff's arms, onto his knees, and Rawcliff began to lower him on to the floor.

He thought in the same instant, I'm getting careless, forgetful. To have twisted Peters' ankle would have been enough: the rest was just fancy stuff for the spectators. He should have backed away and been ready, as Leslie came out

53

from behind the bar, with surprising speed, and the bottle hit Rawcliff between his left eye and temple. There was a flash of darkness, as his face collided with the lino floor. Then nothing, like a deep dreamless sleep.

He was lying on a large made-up bed. He still wore his shoes, though his jacket had been removed and his tie loosened. He could only focus through one eye and his head slammed with a sharp ache. He started to sit up, through a wave of gagging nausea: carefully felt his arms, ribs and thighs, wriggled his toes. His testicles were intact too.

The bedroom seemed to be in a recess, off a vast open-plan flat. Walls of knotted pine, bare except for an eight-foot span of twin-prop propeller, of polished honey-brown wood. Beside his head, a double-glazed picture window looked out, almost at water-level, across the river to a silhouette of cranes and wharves. From the width of the river, he guessed that he was somewhere below Tower Bridge, probably beyond Greenwich.

He realized that his head was aching to the rhythm of pop music. The room beyond was the size of a tennis court, broken up by rows of thin cast-iron columns; the ceiling a maze of lagged pipes painted white against a chocolate-brown background, like a sprawl of elongated intestines; the floor of coarse scrubbed planking, like a ship's deck. Pure Colour Supplement stuff. There was even a black girl dancing by herself to the music.

He lay back, feeling sick. The bed lurched as someone sat down. He was a thick-set young man with an open sunburnt face, and wore a white cable-knit sweater and heavy silver bracelet.

'You look a bit rough, old sport. Like a spot of brandy?'

Rawcliff raised himself again, slowly. He wished that bloody music would stop! 'Where can I clean up and have a piss?'

The man helped him from the bed, steadied him across the long-haired carpet, to a door with a handle in the form of a gold-plated dolphin. The bathroom beyond was done in chipped green marble pieces, like miniature mosaics; the fittings were all gold-plated, and there was a gold-plated fleur-de-lys on the bidet. The shelves were lined with assorted perfumes and make-up, men's deodorant and cologne, a chunk of soap hanging on a rope, antique telephone by the lavatory, miniaturized TV and radio.

Rawcliff peered at his image in the mirror. A yellowish-green egg had swollen up beside his temple and a puffy blue shadow was closing round his eye. There was no blood. He cooled his face with water, rinsed his mouth out, made his way back into the bedroom. The man in the sweater was waiting for him, smiling. 'Feeling better?'

'On top of the day. Where's the brandy?'

'Coming right up. Jo! One brandy for our stretcher-case!'

Rawcliff sat down on the bed. He had a glimpse of a second girl, white this time, floating up from somewhere across the wide floor of the room beyond.

The man said, 'I'm Ritchie, by the way. Jim Ritchie.'

Rawcliff nodded glumly; he noticed that the man had very good teeth. 'Your pad?'

'Right. Not bad, eh? Picked it up for a snip, before the social mob started moving in. What they call the gentrification of derelict dockland. It's part of an old grain warehouse, actually. Built right over the river.'

'Convenient. If someone steps out of line, they get fished out of the water somewhere below Tilbury? Or perhaps not at all? I thought you had a penthouse in the Barbican?'

Ritchie laughed. 'No, thank God! That's a place we just use occasionally – sort of neutral ground. I can't stand towerblocks – I spend too much time in the air, as it is. When I'm down, I like to stay as close to the ground as possible.'

The second girl had stepped up into the recessed bedroom. She wore jeans and high-heeled sandals, and had a small lightly-freckled face with no make-up. Rawcliff judged her quite pretty, in a neat undemanding way: though it was often the quiet ones, he remembered, who made the most trouble. She had stopped by the bed, holding a kitchen glass and a bottle of good brandy.

'That's a nasty bruise he's got there, Jim.' She hardly

55

glanced at Rawcliff, as she poured a dribble of brandy into the glass and handed it to him. 'Alcohol's not the best thing after concussion,' she added, still to Ritchie, 'I'll get a cold steak to put on his eye.'

'Don't worry, he'll live!' Ritchie leant out and patted Rawcliff's knee. 'Meet Joanna, sport. Jo, to her friends. You've got to take her seriously – she's a nurse. Looks after our every need.' He gave her his white smile. 'You want to watch out for Mr Rawcliff, Jo! He used to be one of those undercover death-and-glory boys. They don't mess about – as our friend Peters can testify!'

For the first time she looked down at Rawcliff. 'If you get any bad headaches over the next twenty-four hours, you should see a doctor,' she said; then nodded to Ritchie, 'See you, Jim!' She had left the bottle of brandy on the floor.

Rawcliff lay and squinted at her narrow haunches moving down the steps and across the bare floor to where the black girl was still dancing with casual energy. He pulled himself up on one arm and swallowed the brandy. 'Which girl is resident? Not both surely?'

'I screw the dark one over there,' said Ritchie. 'Jo's strictly business. So you lay off, see? From now on it's going to be like school – no talking out of turn, no boozing, no fraternizing with the fair sex. Orders of the day – by courtesy of Mr Peters.'

'Where's Peters now?'

'Last sighting was at the Middlesex Casualty Department. The latest I got was a sprained ankle, pulled ligament and a hair-line fracture in the upper vertebrae, in what they call the "hanging bone". Plus two lovely black eyes. You take your chances, don't you, old sport? Peters is rough.'

'He's also stupid. He started to threaten my wife and child.' Rawcliff sat up straighter. 'Let me tell you something, Ritchie. I don't mind you people leaning on me – I can look after myself. But if any of you goes near my family, I'll kill him. That's not a melodramatic threat. I'd willingly go to prison for it.'

Ritchie nodded gravely. 'I'm sorry about that – I really am. I don't know quite how much Newby's told you, but

56

this is a pretty high-powered operation, and sometimes you can't just pick and choose your colleagues. Peters may be a hard bastard, but from what I hear he's damned efficient. You probably rubbed him up the wrong way. You have to be careful with that sort. You *are* coming in with us?' he added, not looking at Rawcliff as he said it.

'Do I still have the option?' '

Ritchie smiled pleasantly. 'No, I don't suppose you have, now I come to think of it.'

Rawcliff drank some more brandy; the floor had stopped swaying and his head had eased. 'What's the exact pecking order in this business?'

'Newby's the boss this end – though I've no idea who's behind it. And Peters is the senior pilot. If he gives an order, we snap to.'

'Who are the others?'

Ritchie paused; got out a packet of cigarettes, offered one and lit his own. 'There's a chap called Thurgood – you've probably heard of him, from your friend, Mason? He's the radio expert. Very odd fish. Then there's an ex-Army bloke called Grant.'

'That makes five – if you include me.'

'I don't know the sixth. Some associate of Peters. Rhodesian mercenary, I understand.'

'Oh God, not another of those?'

'He's abroad, helping to fix things up.'

'Where's that?'

Ritchie paused again and frowned. 'Look, sport, I'm like you – one of the odds and sods. I don't want to speak out of turn. If they need to tell us something, they tell us in their own time. All we do is carry out orders and collect our fifty thou' at the end of it.' He looked up, with his easy smile, man-to-man, 'And there's Jo, of course. Musn't forget her!'

'What's she got to do with it?'

'Did Newby give you any idea what this operation is about?'

'He said something about a mercy-mission, all wrapped up in secrecy to avoid international red tape.'

'Yes. Well, as I said, Jo's a trained nurse. VSO –

Voluntary Service Overseas. She's only over here on leave.'

'You mean she's part of the team? Sits up on the blankets and tents and stretchers like the marzipan queen on top of the cake, just to make it look sweeter?'

'Don't underestimate her, sport. Nurses are a lot tougher than most of us – they have to be, they see too much of the dirty underbelly of life. Anyway, she'll be useful if one of us goes sick or gets bitten by a snake. As well as promoting good relations with the natives.'

'What natives?'

'Ah!' – Ritchie laid a broad finger along the edge of his nose – 'there again you go asking questions I can't answer. I don't know. Honestly. Except it's not Greenland or the Arctic Circle.'

Rawcliff looked at his watch. It was nearly five o'clock. His stomach heaved again. 'I've got to go. Get me a taxi – black cab this time – one whose number I can take if he tries to lure me into another wanker's club to get me kicked in the goolies.'

'Newby's calling round here at seven. He wants to see you.'

'Well he can't. I've got a family to get back to. And they're a bloody sight more important than Newby and the rest of you put together!'

Ritchie sat staring at what was left of his cigarette, then pinched it out in an onyx ashtray by the bed. 'Thank God I'm single.' He looked up and smiled again. 'I'll run you back. Don't worry, I'm not violent!'

As they left, he called good-bye to Jo, who was preparing something in the open-range kitchen. She waved, without looking up. 'Remember what I told you about those headaches, Mr Rawcliff!'

But Rawcliff had other things to remember and worry about. There had been something about the girl that reminded him uneasily of Judith – her calmness and practicality. He wondered how Ritchie had found her. She hardly seemed his type: young Jim Ritchie would prefer his girls dumb and easy, and Jo looked far from being either.

Ritchie had a Jaguar XJ6 which he drove like an aircraft:

calm and skilled, with split-second reactions that dulled any sense of danger. He took the South Bank route, where the traffic was lighter.

'What do you fly?' Rawcliff asked him.

'Beachcraft Duke. Four-seater, twin-engine. Know it?'

'Not personally. Way out of my price range. You do pretty well, I gather?'

'So-so. Not as well as I'd like to. People just haven't the money anymore. When I started, I used to get parties flying down to the South of France – even as far as Italy and Morocco. With optional ferry-tanks, of course. Nowadays you get the occasional bunch of stinking Arabs, or a few millionaires flying back to their tax-havens in the Channel Islands.

'Anyway, I only own forty-nine per cent of the company. The rest belongs to Newby – working out of Lichtenstein. What they politely call "tax avoidance". All nice and legal, too.' He laughed and overtook a juggernaut on the inside; an air-horn blasted at them and made Rawcliff wince. Ritchie's hands were very steady on the wheel.

'Jim, what exactly do you know about Newby?'

'Business man. Wheeler-dealer. Import, export. Likes the good life, good food, expensive girls.'

'Is he a crook?'

Ritchie took the roundabout at the Elephant and Castle at nearly fifty, his tyres steaming off the wet surface. 'Hell, what's a crook these days? If I get three endorsements or done for drunken driving, the computer at Criminal Records stores me away on tape, *et voilà*! – I've got a criminal record – along with your friendly safe-crackers and sex-fiends, and all the rest of the jolly cons!'

'What I mean is, will he be straight with us? Are we going to get paid?'

'Yes, we'll get paid. Newby's got too much at stake to rat on us. Anyway he only has a percentage of the action.'

'He's not the boss?'

Ritchie's face became closed, concentrating on the thickening traffic as they approached Battersea, passing the ugly sprawl of the New Covent Market at Nine Elms, like some freshly erected concrete internment camp. 'Look, sport, don't push me. I told you – I don't know much more than you. And anything you don't know, you'll learn in good time.'

'You're a trusting fellow, aren't you?'

'If you like.'

'And you believe all this cock about a secret mercy-mission?'

Ritchie gave him a grim smile. 'You know, I'm beginning to understand why Peters wanted to work you over this afternoon. I'm not in charge – I don't give a damn. But if you want to make real trouble for yourself, don't think I'm going to throw you a life-belt. I don't want to know. See?'

They drove for some time in silence. Rawcliff had a vivid image of six huge heavy-bellied transport planes shimmering on some sandy strip, while Jo trotted between the six mercenary pilots, serving long drinks and binding up snake-bitten ankles and slapping hunks of cold meat on to bruised faces.

'You can drop me at the corner here,' he said, as they came into Battersea Park Road. 'This car might upset the social harmony of the street.'

Ritchie pulled up and Rawcliff climbed out into the evening drizzle. He was about to close the door, when Ritchie leant across towards him. 'A word of advice, old sport. Play it easy. Newby and Peters mean business. They won't tolerate being messed around again. As for Peters, I'll do my best to square it with him – though it might be a good idea to apologize.'

'What should I do – send him some flowers?'

Ritchie gave his manly chuckle. 'He might appreciate that, you never know! Look after yourself.'

Rawcliff heard the Jaguar's growling whine as he walked under the narrow railway bridge, past the Council estate and down the empty street to his semi-detached. He noticed that there were several slates missing and some of the guttering was gone.

3

At five that same evening, Group Captain Neil Batsford, Station Commander of Benson Aerodrome, Oxon, received a visit from the officer in charge of Camp Security, Provost Branch.

'Small item, sir, may be nothing in it. I logged it just for the record. Bit of chit-chat from Number Four. Waley reported it. He'd been briefing the men for the German posting. One of them's Flight-Lieutenant Mason who's been on that special course in London. Wife, three kids. Waley was expecting him to be rather sore, being uprooted twice in one week. Not at all, the chap seemed as pleased as Punch! Waley got chatting to him, wondering if there were any domestic problems. After all, you know what it's like in Germany, wives don't always take too well to the new environment.'

'Go on,' said Batsford quietly.

'He told Waley a rather odd story, sir. Waley said he checked it with him and took some notes. I've got it all here.'

When he had finished, Batsford sat tapping a pen against his teeth. 'When did we last have this happen, Provost Marshal?'

'Two years ago, I think it was, sir. Those Belgians who got hold of Yates – wanted a chopper-pilot to help them take over a mine in Zaïre. Thank God Mason had the good sense to turn this one up. Though he's still not entirely happy about the incident, sir. That's why he's so keen on the German posting, in spite of the upheaval.'

'You say it was a chance encounter? With Thurgood?'

'Yes, sir. Rum fellow, Thurgood.'

'Quite. Most unsatisfactory character.'

'I wonder if they know about those headaches of his?'

'I don't suppose he's volunteered the information. Are you recommending that I take this further?'

'We might mention it to Special Branch, just for the record, sir. And the Ministry had better know, in case they go sniffing around any of our other bases.'

'Quite. If they strike again, we don't want to find ourselves with egg all over our faces. But if it's a really big op, the Ministry may have a whiff of it already. Six C-130s are pretty difficult things to keep hidden. Waley's report may just help tie up the ends.' He pointed his pen at the Provost Marshal. 'Give me those names again – besides Thurgood's.'

At 7.42 that evening Sergeant Bates, of Military Police, Benson, took a radio call from a Thames Valley Panda Patrol: '*Man identified as Flight-Lieutenant Terence Mason, RAF Benson, victim of hit-and-run driver on A 428 to Warborough. Unconscious, multiple injuries, taken by ambulance to Radcliffe Infirmary, Oxford.*'

Batsford was about to go into the Mess. He said into the phone, 'I want Security up here right away. And put me through to Oxford Central, Senior Officer, priority.' Then he called the Mess and told them to send up sandwiches and a pot of tea.

The Inspector said: 'He was found by a young couple driving a van. The girl stayed with him while the man called us from Warborough. Seems he was conscious at first. Said he was hit from behind by a Range-Rover, T registration, though he didn't get the number or a sight of the driver. The girl was quite sure about that – sharp, very articulate – will make an excellent witness. In the ambulance Mason was already in a coma. He was admitted to the Radcliffe with fractures to the skull and ribs, and possible internal injuries.'

'Is he expected to live?'

'I have no information about that, sir. Two officers are by his bed, in case he regains consciousness.'

'Thank you. And keep this line clear.' Batsford looked at the Inspector, then at the Provost Marshal. 'His wife's been informed, I assume?'

'One of our men drove her to the hospital, sir.'

'Right. I want the local press kept away from her. And I want them kept away from here, too.' He turned to the Inspector. 'I'd appreciate it, under the circumstances, if you'd play this close to the ground. Simple case of hit-and-run, one of our men injured. No mention of his identity, or of the Range-Rover.'

'I'll do my best. But I'm afraid that if he dies, the hospital will release his name.'

'Not if the Special Branch put in the boot, they won't. I'm sorry, Inspector, but there are certain aspects to this case which, in my judgement, should be passed to higher authority. If your men can meanwhile establish all they can about the accident – road conditions, why Mason had stopped – breakdown, puncture – usual drill.'

'It's already been done. Slow puncture in the rim of the rear off-side tyre. Sort of thing you get from vandals, made by any small sharp instrument. Unlikely to have been an accident. No skid marks, but a dangerous bit of road. Blind bend for oncoming traffic.'

Batsford nodded. 'I want to know the moment you hear anything more from the hospital.'

As he spoke, the telephone rang. Batsford snatched it up, nodded and thrust the receiver at the policeman. 'For you – urgent.' He sat back and watched the Inspector holding the receiver with one hand and clumsily jotting down notes with the other. He finally hung up.

'Well that's a break, sir. They've got the Range-Rover.'

4

'Oh you poor fool! I can just about put up with you feeling sorry for yourself, but now you want to be a hero! You talk about this wonderful Swiss bank account, and all you bring back is a bloody great black eye and a sore head.' She was sitting half up in bed, with the light on, while Rawcliff lay facing the wall.

'Do keep your voice down,' he said, 'you'll wake Tom.'

'Yes – Tom! I'm glad you've given him a thought. I suppose it doesn't matter if he's left without a father and I'm a widow?'

'Oh don't be bloody silly.'

'Bloody silly! Who's talking? You said yourself you don't know what the hell it's all about. A mercy-mission, so they told you? Whoever heard of a mercy-mission that was set up with secret phone calls, dangling illegal Swiss numbered accounts in front of your nose, and not telling you what it's all about? Except you've got to fly a plane fifty feet above the ground. That's to avoid radar and missiles – even I know that much! Does that sound like an ordinary mercy-mission to you? Or perhaps you're kidding yourself that you're going into World War Three? God, you ought to be back at prep school.'

'Do turn out the light, love. I want to sleep.'

'You just want to avoid the issue. I'll tell you something, Charles Rawcliff. I can stand being married to a phoney hero. I can just about stand being married to a semi-alcoholic bum who's going broke. What I can't stand is being married to a fool.'

He lay with his eyes closed. She went on: 'I know you think Terry Mason's a dull, wet little man, living his whole life under orders, in his prefabricated married quarters, with a tatty wife and three snotty kids. But I'll tell you something. At this moment he's worth five, ten times what you are! He's

64

got sense. Sense to think the whole thing over and get out while the going's good.

'But not the great Charles Rawcliff. Oh no. Not only does he not have the sense to get out – he doesn't even have the guts. That's the truth of the matter, isn't it?' She was sitting straight up now, glaring down at him. 'You haven't got the guts to face up to anything. You can't face your financial troubles. You're scared of your bank manager, scared of the tax-man, scared of the VAT-man, and now you're running scared of a gang of international crooks who are posing as a charity organization. God, you make me sick!'

His head had begun to ache again. He got up slowly and pulled on a bathrobe. 'I'm going to sleep downstairs.'

'You can sleep on the pavement, as far as I'm concerned. What's the matter with you? We've got a nice house, we've both got jobs, we've got a beautiful child – we've even got two cars. But you're not satisfied. You want to risk your life, and put me and little Tom on the line with you. It isn't fair. It isn't bloody fair!'

He turned wearily. 'It's no good, Judith. Even if I wanted to get out of it, I couldn't. Not unless we're both prepared to go into hiding for a long time.'

'Oh God. So it's as bad as that, is it?'

'It's serious, Judith. They're serious people.' He came towards her and tried to touch her shoulder, but she flinched away.

'Don't you touch me!' she whispered. 'And next time I suppose it won't be just a bump on the head? It'll be me going down to identify you on some mortuary slab. So I'm not married to a fool, I'm also married to a prospective criminal. And perhaps a dead one, at that!'

'You don't know it's criminal.'

'No. I don't even know the world goes round the sun.'

'Turn out the light. We can talk about it in the morning,' he said, climbing back into bed beside her.

'There's nothing more to talk about. If you go, that's the end of it.'

'Right, let's have it,' said Batsford.

65

The Inspector consulted his notes. 'Eight-ten – accident at the roundabout just before Pinkney's Green, near Maidenhead. Ford Escort full of rugger-buggers collided with a beige Range-Rover, registration ELH 283T. Escort has a crushed front wheel and damaged fender. No injuries reported. Two other cars stopped, police were called.

'Before the Patrol arrived, the Range-Rover drove off in the direction of the M4. There was a twenty-minute time-lag before we could get a call out, plus a full description of the driver. No passengers. Man in early thirties, medium build, brown hair combed straight back, David Niven-type moustache. One of the witnesses said he had staring eyes. Another said the Range-Rover had a scratch down the left side, and what looked like mud. The left side hit Mason, sir. Forensic are working on the vehicle now.'

'Where was it found?'

'Harvard Lane, between Chiswick High Road and the M4. He must have driven like lightning, sir, down the motorway. Surprising none of the patrols nabbed him.'

'And he got clean away?'

'I'm afraid so. One of the Met boys spotted the vehicle. That was a bit of luck, at least, in a back-street like that. Parked about two feet from the kerb. Driver must have been in a hurry. Hammersmith are handling it – until the SB muscle in.'

'Thurgood had a moustache,' Batsford said, peering into what was left of his cold tea. 'Though I'd hardly call him the David Niven type. But staring eyes are good. Must be him.'

The phone rang. Batsford listened for a moment and said, 'Thank you.' He put down the receiver. 'Mason's dead. He never regained consciousness.'

5

Simon de Vere Suchard stretched back and crossed his long
legs. The fan-window illuminated his eccentrically
handsome profile. He smiled distantly, fingering the neck of
his cashmere cardigan. 'I am sorry, my dear chap, but
you're going to be rather put out. Just one of those crosses
we have to bear. It's no bite at the cherry on this one. Not
even a nibble, until I say so.'

Addison, of the Special Branch, sat rigidly opposite him,
controlling his irritation: at the same time baffled, amazed
by the number of books, newspapers, loose documents
strewn about the room; by the profuse confusion of the
place; no order, no apparent security – although 'security',
in the most precise and awesome meaning of the word, was
what the whole Department was about.

'You people seem to have decided already that it's a case
of murder,' he said, 'so why not leave it to the local boys?
You've got the evidence. Victim's car's punctured
deliberately, probably by someone who knew his way into
the camp car park. Murder vehicle in the pound. Forensic
checks out, blood matches, plus full description of the
suspect. The Met boys pick him up – Thames Valley handle
the case.'

De Vere Suchard unfolded himself from the button-back
leather chair. 'Drink, my dear chap?' He moved with the
restless agility of a grown-up schoolboy getting the better of
one of his duller masters.

'Gin,' Addison said sourly, 'pink.'

Suchard had crossed the spacious Georgian room and
reached a cluttered antique sidetable, where he stood
rummaging amid a pile of papers, row of bottles and
decanters, unwashed cut-glasses, an ancient electric kettle
and jar of instant coffee. 'Murder indeed,' he repeated,
returning across the room with the drinks; he had poured

himself a thimble of Strega. 'Murder most foul. And crude,' he added, sitting down again. 'Nothing for the future connoisseurs in this one, I fear. Some crumby little RAF pilot had a spot of info that someone else didn't want him to have, and he gets knocked down and killed changing a tyre. Made to look like hit-and-run.' He sipped his drink. 'But as we know, all is not as it appears. This one is as fragile as a Ming vase. Examine, scrutinize, – but *don't touch*.' He gave his flowery smile and recrossed his legs. 'Flight-Lieutenant Mason is dead, and he is going to be buried. In every sense of the word. I have it from the highest authority.'

'You mean, you went up and twisted their arms?'

'My dear Addison, you sleuths have such literal minds. Let us just say, the decision was reached through due process of discussion and evaluation of the case. You'll be pleased to hear that I was able to assure them that I will have your full support. In return, you may call on any facilities you require. It'll be a grand slam, but with all the covers on. A senior Yard man is to be detailed to do the donkey-work, and you'll back him up with anything he needs. No skimping on manpower or expense at your end. But hushed as the grave. *Entendu?*'

He sat back and steepled his fingers together, the tips touching his chin. 'We expect you to have this thing tied up in forty-eight hours. Info, that's all. Facts, details. Names and addresses. Times of meetings. Who goes where, stays where. Forty-eight hours of good hard police slogging. And there'll be no mercy for any stragglers, any slip-ups.'

'Thanks for the tip. And for the drink,' Addison said, putting down his glass. 'There's only one other problem. I've got to ring that Station Commander, Batsford. He's got to come up with some story for Mason's widow. He can hardly say the man died for his country.'

'He may have died for someone's country. The question is whose?'

The Head of Department faced them across the table. He had a long gloomy face, like an intelligent sheep. A couple of pale green files lay closed in front of him. He spoke from memory, while the others took notes.

'Three weeks ago Staff Section got a DAC report from Germany, stating that six C-130 transports had been purchased from the American Air base at Mildhausen, near Frankfurt. All 1962 models, declared obsolete, but in flying order. The purchasers were a Lichtenstein-registered firm called Tallant and Burg A.C. This appears to be a subsidiary of Entreprise Lipp, also registered in Lichtenstein, but with strong French connections. Not' – he paused emphatically – 'so very far removed from official circles. They specialize, as you may know, in high technology, including some of the latest guidance-systems for the French aerospace industry.'

'Rather a long hop from a C-130 transport,' Suchard put in frivolously.

The Head ignored him. 'We know from our French and German friends that the planes were dismantled and shipped by canal into France, where they were taken in two convoys of trucks, to Le Havre and Marseilles. They were billed to be shipped as spares for non-strategic purposes – from Marseilles to Mombassa, and from Le Havre to Port Harcourt. A routine check established that both the Kenyans and Nigerians knew of the shipments – though, after a few inquiries, it appeared that neither government had actually placed an order for the stuff. And Tallant and Burg had offered the spares *gratis*, in exchange for what euphemistically passes for "commercial goodwill".'

'We thought there was something fishy about the deal, and so, to do them credit, did the Kenyans and Nigerians. But the French didn't seem worried. It was more or less their pigeon, so we left it to them. Until the two ships disappeared.' He gave what passed for a smile: 'The one from Le Havre was called the *Delphinia*. 20,000 tons, Greek owner and crew, Liberian registration – all properly registered with Lloyd's along with the spare parts – *and logged through Gibraltar three weeks ago.*' He paused with melancholy emphasis: 'Which would seem to rule out West Africa. As for the second ship, out of Marseilles – same tonnage, same routine. The Suez authorities have no record of either vessel, and Lloyd's have heard nothing. Which leaves us to look round the whole Mediterranean. That, gentlemen, means the Middle East.'

'Or that they're sunk?' said Suchard: 'Scuttled? What was the insurance?'

'The six aircraft were purchased for a total of just over three million dollars, and the two cargoes insured for the same.' He shook his bony head. 'No, not a chance. Lipp are too big for that kind of game. One ship, just possibly, but not both. Anyway, as I said, Lloyds have heard nothing.'

'What about the owners? And the charter company?' asked Suchard.

'The owner is a Greek Cyrpiot called Kyriades who operates out of Larnaca and Athens. Each office manned by a single secretary, both of whom claim to know nothing. And so far not a trace of Kyriades. The charter company is Entreprise Lipp. Which brings me to the central issue. Lipp's main shareholder is a Frenchman called Pol. He's bad news, in about half-a-dozen countries. We've managed to keep him out so far, but he's got some uneasy relationship with our French friends. Which could make things rather tricky.'

'Oh Lord.' Suchard leaned back, rattling coins in his pocket. 'I suppose the moment we start fishing around, some bugger in Brussels or Strasbourg will tell us to lay off?'

'That is precisely why I want you to get to the bottom of this business with the utmost speed, and with absolute secrecy. Now, I would like each of you to give me your assessment of the situation as far as we know it. Suchard, you first.'

Suchard's scrambler rang late that afternoon, connecting him to the Minister's car which was driving down from his constituency in the North.

'I'll make it snappy, Simon. I've got a lot of paperwork and a nasty debate tonight. I just hope you're not going to add to my troubles?'

'God never imposes a duty without giving time to do it.' Suchard grinned into the phone: 'Ruskin, sir.'

'Piss off. Listen, I've got you a man called Muncaster. "Super" at the Yard, excellent track-record, gets on well with the SB. Politically sound, but dull. Doesn't like us or Whitehall, distrusts foreigners, and can't even order a cup of tea in French. Be nice to him, Simon. And make sure that the SB don't walk all over this with their big boots and ruin everything. Muncaster's an obedient workhorse, but he moves quietly, so you don't have to worry about him. He's been fully briefed – at least, with as much as he needs to know. I want a complete report from you every twelve hours, and anything hot served up at once. I don't care if you have to interrupt me in the middle of a speech. It always looks good, anyway. Adds a mysterious dimension to my authority.'

Suchard acknowledged the chuckle the other end, and said: 'Thank you, sir. Good luck with the debate.'

'You bloody hypocrite! Now get on with it.' The line clicked dead, leaving no dialling tone.

The Minister was a slob, but an efficient one. A gritty grammar school boy who played rough but fair – or as fair as anyone in this game. And like most of the players he hated Suchard's guts, but knew a good man when he saw one. Sooner or later someone was going to stab Simon de Vere Suchard in the back, and make an awful mess doing it; but for the moment the man enjoyed the exhilarating certainty that his talents, not to mention his contacts and knowledge, guaranteed him a comfortable immunity from the civilized in-fighting of Whitehall, and of its arcane inner sanctums through which he moved with such immodest ease and confidence.

Detective Superintendent Cyril Muncaster was a small man with a long nose that always looked as though it needed wiping. The man on the Clapham omnibus, Suchard thought. His suit looked at least a couple of sizes too big.

Muncaster had a grubby pocket-book open on his lap, and referred to it like a poor speech-maker reading from notes. 'I decided to use Customs and Excise, VAT division. A young chap and girl. The suspect, Oswald Thurgood, is only an

71

employee – contrary to what he appears to have told Mason. His job is mostly maintenance and repairs. Only he didn't check into work yesterday or today.'

'Of course not.'

'A second man went in under VAT cover – Special Branch, expert in radio and electronics. After a lot of argument the owner opened up his books for the last month. Among the few items which seem to have been transacted legally were six Jap hi-fi sets and eighteen pairs of 18K102 loudspeakers – the most powerful on the market – each with an audio-sensor which adjusts the volume according to outside noise. They were bought, at a discount, from the makers three weeks ago, fully paid for, and air-freighted ten days ago to Athens, apparently to equip a new football stadium. Export licence in order.'

'So?' Suchard touched his mouth as though to suppress a yawn. 'What does that tell us, except that the shop may stoop to a straight deal from time to time?'

'They paid just over twelve thousand pounds for the stuff,' Muncaster continued relentlessly. 'On a banker's draft from Geneva and drawn on the company account of Tallant and Burg.'

Suchard inclined his head. 'Thank you. Go on.'

'During further questioning, the owner informed us that the deal was set up by a Belgian called Rebot – Jean Rebot.' He saw Suchard wince at his atrocious accent. 'The Belgian apparently gave the order and Thurgood selected the goods. Rebot also made a down-payment of one thousand in cash. And it shows on the books. Rather as though, on this one deal, they wanted everything to be absolutely above-board. Later, the stuff was collected in a van by a tall blond man. Didn't give a name, just showed the receipts.'

Suchard's eyes were half-closed with thought. 'And Thurgood?'

'No trouble. We traced him to a service-flat near Gloucester Road tube station. I have the address here. Four men, two cars outside, and one man booked into an adjacent room. And all Port Authorities have been alerted, of course.'

'What have you got on him otherwise?'

72

'He has form. And a medical record. Violent, psychotic. After being tossed out of the RAF, he ran amok in a restaurant in Leicester – got a meat-cleaver from the kitchen and chopped up a few tables, then assaulted a police officer. He was given a two-year suspended sentence, on condition that he underwent regular medical treatment. Didn't finish the course. Hopped over to Canada where he got into trouble carrying a gun. Three months ago he arrived back here. We picked him up a couple of weeks later, on grounds that he'd broken the conditions stipulated by the Leicester Court. His flat was searched and two clips of .38 Magnum ammunition found, but no gun. He was charged, and the magistrate granted bail for five hundred. Case adjourned twice, still pending.'

'Ye Gods.' Suchard had crossed over and freshened his drink. 'And they talk about law and order. Who stood bail?'

'The Belgian gentleman – Rebot.'

Suchard settled back in his chair. 'Yes. I like that.' He sipped his drink. 'And I suppose a high-powered lawyer popped up and tied the magistrate into knots?'

'One of the best, Vincent Colgrave.'

Suchard bared his teeth. 'I see. The Sea-Green Incorruptible himself. Specialist in international law. My God, somebody must have slipped him a packet to have him run round clearing up after a nut like Thurgood! At least it proves they look after their employees – providing they toe the line, of course. What else?'

Muncaster turned his long snout down towards his notes. 'The lab are through with the Range-Rover. Covered in Thurgood's prints. But contrary to what Mason originally stated, Thurgood isn't the owner. We traced it to an outfit in Bayswater, called "Overland Motors". It was hired eight days ago. The girl there remembers it well – mostly because the man paid in cash, new twenties, two weeks in advance. Tall blond man, British driving licence, though the girl thought he had a slight accent. The licence was in the name of Dirk Roger Peters.'

Suchard closed his eyes again and nodded. 'I'm still listening.'

Muncaster had Peters' file with him, prepared over several years by the Special Branch. He had emigrated to South Africa in 1957 and had trained as a pilot, while retaining his British passport. Ten years ago he was caught having illicit intercourse with a Zulu girl – a crime that was compounded by the fact that he had also indulged his tastes by lacerating her. Despite his British nationality, he was sentenced to a flogging and two years' jail. He had then left the White Republic and signed on as an instructor to the new Air Forces of several Black African governments.

He was known to have committed at least two political murders in Africa; and the Dutch police had arrested him a couple of years ago at Schipol Airport, Amsterdam, on suspicion of smuggling arms. West German Intelligence, the BND, had also marked him down as 'surveillance worthy', so far without result. The Italians had no record of him. But the fact that Peters might be too grand for Baader-Meinhof or the Red Brigades gave Muncaster little comfort.

'And we've checked on Ritchie,' he continued. 'He doesn't live in the Barbican, as Mason reported, but has a luxury flat down in Albert Docks. Seems to have plenty of money to splash around. He's a minority share-holder in his company, "Come Fly with Me", which operates out of Lydd. The majority holdings are in Lichtenstein, under the name of Jean Rebot, Belgian nationality.'

Suchard breathed softly and smiled. 'Very neat. Almost too neat for comfort. Any form?'

'I was hoping that you'd be able to help out there, sir. Your people must have taken the file.'

'The file?'

'From CRO. A couple of young chaps came in and helped themselves to it nearly a month ago.' Muncaster's voice was toneless. 'Usual accreditation – had the Met. jumping to attention. Not good for morale, sir, if you'll permit the comment.'

'I see.' Suchard took a quick sip at his drink. He saw only too well: the sort of small, tiresome misunderstanding between the department and the boys in blue which could so easily lead to an embarrassing break-down in relations. But worse, it meant that somebody in the department had nearly a month's start on him, and wasn't letting on. Muncaster would know that too. Suchard didn't like playing blind-man's buff any more than did the regular police.

'So you've got nothing on Ritchie?' he added.

'I did make a few inquiries, sir. Whoever it was even took the trouble to wipe the computer at the Peel Centre, Hendon. That's the sort of thing that makes one curious. But the DS have a separate file. They've had Ritchie in twice for questioning in connection with drug-smuggling from the Continent. Soft stuff, apparently. Customs stripped his plane down a couple of years ago when he did a forced landing near Dungeness. He was clean that time. Of course, without the file, I can't tell you about the other times.'

Suchard stroked his jaw. Muncaster, in his nice polite way, was certainly not sparing him. 'What about the Barbican?'

'The only flat to fit Mason's description – the Penthouse, Coleridge Tower – was taken five weeks ago on a six months' lease by the same Jean Rebot. According to the porter, the lessee was a small, dark, foreign-looking man, expensively dressed, very generous with tips, smelled of perfume.'

'What a lovely witness! I don't suppose you're a gambling man, are you, Cyril? Any odds on our Rebot also being John Newby?'

'No bets.'

'Right. This Newby-Rebot is the bird we want. Only don't forget to stick to the others like clams. Check the Passport Office and Immigration, and have them go through their files until they find him. I don't care how much they squeal about overtime. I want him by tomorrow morning.

'And watch the Barbican – though it's my guess he only uses it occasionally, for meetings. If they've got any suspicions that Mason's talked, they'll keep well away. In fact, they'll probably be preparing to scatter. That's what makes speed imperative.

'Newby sounds as though he prefers the fast life in one of the big hotels. Check them all. Check casinos, private gaming-clubs, all the night-spots – anywhere that a smart, flashy little cosmopolitan picaroon might like to spread his loot. Smart whores, cheap tarts, massage-parlours, S/M, gays, kids, the lot – we don't know his tastes. And drugs. Concentrate on the top people, pushers and the nostril-gentry. Leave no stone, Cyril. Only I don't want the courts choc- ·bloc next week and the press yelling that it's the biggest vice-putsch since the Night of the Long Knives. So don't trip over too many feet, and don't go breaking anybody's arms. But find him.'

6

Ex-Flight-Lieutenant Oswald Thurgood had kept all day to his flat, except for a brief sortie to a nearby pizza-house. He had received no visitors.

Jim Ritchie had been followed to a restaurant in the West End, where he had been accompanied by a coloured girl; he had returned to his flat and had not gone out since.

Muncaster stirred the weak office coffee and turned to the report on John Newby, alias Rebot, or *vice versa*. The Board of Trade had referred inquiries to Kensington and Chelsea Chamber of Commerce. Newby owned two shops, in High Street Kensington and the Kings Road, both specializing in women's underwear – one called 'Knickers Galore', the other 'More Knickers Galore'. Most of his stock was imported from France.

Criminal Records had drawn a blank, both on Newby and Rebot; but the Vice Squad had had their eye on him for some time. At least a couple of smut-shops, with film clubs at the back, both registered in the name of Newby, British subject. But they didn't tell Muncaster anything else, except that they had never heard of Rebot.

Muncaster, of course, knew that Suchard hadn't told him the half of it: but either something was up – something really big – or it would come down and land smack in his lap, like a lead balloon. They weren't merciful, his masters. If he didn't turn out the goods on this one, he might even have to forgo that seaside bungalow on retirement. Somewhere up north instead – a place where you had to wipe the grime off the lettuce-leaves with a dishcloth.

He was going after every scrap, every crumb and titbit. If necessary he'd find out what sort of shoes Newby wore, where he had his clothes made; whether he suffered from nerves, took pills; sexual tastes; did he drink, suffer from constipation, claustrophobia, fear of uniforms?

Find him. Find the little bastard, then go grovelling to Golden Boy Suchard and await his judicious decision on whether to pounce or not. Tie up a murder case, that was Muncaster's job. He had no time for international politics. The FO might get sweaty hands thinking about half-a-dozen British subjects being recruited for tinpot dictators we all have to be nice to, and even give money to, because they happen to be black or brown. Maybe they were even part of the Commonwealth. And by Jimmy, you couldn't have British mercenaries upsetting our Commonwealth brethren – and having them recruited right under our noses, to boot.

Steady Muncaster. Keep your mind on the job. If there's got to be any international rough stuff, leave that to the Hooray Henries in the SAS. Nice and low-key. Remember they've got Colgrave on the payroll. That meant even a psychopathic killer like Thurgood commanded respect.

The telex began to mutter against the wall. Nothing from the four clearing banks; trying Coutts and Hoare, the fringe houses and the internationals, particularly Belgian, Swiss and French. And the new Arab banks. The credit card firms had also drawn a blank. And the Revenue boys still hadn't come through, lazy sods. Though he hardly imagined John Newby to be a model tax-payer.

One of the outside phones was ringing. Sixty-four hotels so far, without result. Why couldn't the British use the registered card system, like they did on the Continent? We were in the Common Market, weren't we, and they regulated the size of our apples and what went into our ice-cream? Why did they have to leave a gaping hole when it came to registering international crooks like Newby? The man could have checked in as Harold Macmillan or Titus Oates, for all they cared.

Nothing from any of the hospitals, and the Harley Street boys weren't giving anything away; nor were the big clinics, private nursing-homes, or the nice little hole-in-the-wall, well-laundered clip-joints where they fed you pills like sweets and charged a hundred pounds a night. So he didn't apparently suffer from corns, trichomonas or withdrawal symptoms.

Of course, the task was made longer and no easier – much time and effort expended, many awkward questions asked and apologies offered – by the fact that there were many Newbys, and quite a few Rebots; though none of them matched the known facts, even on sus.

Check all car rentals. Another blank. And nothing from the Swansea Folly – Vehicle Registration and Driving Licences – either for Newby or Rebot. Or rather, not the right ones.

But the man couldn't just disappear. Or could he? After all, he could have two dozen aliases, for all they knew, and the moment he got just a sniff of suspicion, he'd shuffle passports and redeal.

Muncaster stared through the hard white neon, at the clipboard of the duty-roster, the filing cabinets, rows of telephones, battered typewriters. Six-forty pm. Sandwiches and more coffee. It looked like being a long night.

There was also a call out for Peters. Hotels, rooming-houses, banks, car-rentals. Same routine, same results. A man like that would almost certainly be operating under an alias too: though Petty France confirmed that he had retained his British passport under his own name, and had renewed it for ten years, three years ago. All sea and airports were looking out for him, but so far nothing.

Thurgood was still safely holed up in his Gloucester Road service-flat; and young Jim Ritchie was still apparently dandling his black lady on his knee, in his spacious pad in dockland.

Yet time must be getting tight for them. They'd obviously been worried that Mason would talk, though they couldn't possibly have known how much or to whom. And even if Thurgood had tripped up on that roundabout and had to dump the car in a hurry, they still didn't sound the sort of people who could be panicked that easily. Too much money already invested, too much at stake.

At 1.20 Muncaster put on his coat and went out to the local for a quick pint. When he got back fifteen minutes later, his deputy came up to him and said, 'We've got a line at last, sir. Newby. Seems to fit.'

Muncaster snatched the telex from the officer's hand. *Remus Club, Cheval Place, Knightsbridge.*

'It's a gaming club, sir. High class, very discreet. Mostly Arabs. One of the Special Branch men occasionally gets a whisper, from one of the waiters.'

'Is it clean?'

'As a whistle, sir. Not a chance of a raid. We'd have to break off diplomatic relations with half of OPEC if we did.'

'Forgive my ignorance,' Muncaster said, with muted sarcasm: 'I'm not very well up in these circles. How often does Newby use the place?'

'He drops in most evenings – early. Doesn't usually stay long, but plays high, with cash.'

'Any idea where he hangs out?'

'Not without twisting their arm, sir. But he's booked in this evening – dinner for one, eleven-thirty. They eat late in those places.'

Muncaster had already picked up two telephones. His deputy made the call to Special Branch, Addison direct, while Muncaster used the scrambler to Suchard. He was out of course, no answer. Call Dealey at the Department and leave an urgent message: it didn't matter where the bastard was, get him!

Muncaster began to relax. Once they had Newby, the rest should be simple. As long as they played it long and slow. Everything according to the book. One tiny loophole, and Vincent Colgrave would be through it like a snake.

The phone purred by the bed. Simon de Vere Suchard leant out and answered it. The Minister's voice was thick and rather slow; he'd won last night's debate by a cat's whisker and had obviously been enjoying himself.

'They've found Newby,' Suchard said. 'The SB are staking him out now. We may not have anything positive until after midnight.' He went on to describe his call from Muncaster. Beside him the girl slid closer, curling up her legs and pulling his free hand over her breasts, down across her belly. He began to manipulate her, gently, skilfully.

The Minister's voice was a small bark through the

80

darkened room. 'Good man, that Muncaster. Wouldn't think it to look at him, but he's obviously as smart as two aces back-to-back.'

'He's turned out all right,' Suchard said, through a yawn. The girl trembled and wriggled her head on the pillow.

'Those two boats, Suchard – the *Dolphin*, and whatever the other one's called?'

'The *Delphinia* and the *Ilios*, sir.'

'Any news?'

'Nothing. We've got the Italians and Greeks working on it, for what that's worth, and we've circulated the report to all friendly navies. I'm sticking to my original theory – that they simply painted out the names, paid the crews off and changed masters. They could be sitting anywhere by now. But my original hunch still stands – Tripoli, Libya. Gaddafi's just the lad to offer big money to a handful of bum contract pilots. The question is, what for?' The girl twisted her head and muttered, '*Ah, comme tu parles!*' She drew her legs up further, tucking his agile hand deeper between her thighs.

'If it's Gaddafi,' said the Minister, 'then we're not going to get much bloody change out of the Italians or Greeks. They get most of their oil from the bastard! I still prefer the Lebanon – a PLO job running guns. Heavy stuff. And there's plenty of trouble in Turkey, and Cyprus. Not to mention Iran. That's within range of one o' those planes, isn't it?'

'Oh yes. Even Afghanistan, at a pinch.'

'Shit.'

'You pays your money, you takes your pick, sir.'

'Don't get cheeky with me, Simon. Personally I'm sorely tempted to dump the whole bloody business into the lap of the Americans. After all, they sold the planes in the first place – let them run around picking up the bits. Just as long as we don't get the pilots being recruited over here to fly the things – for whatever dirty reason is behind all this.' He paused.

'So what do we do with Newby, sir?'

There was another pause. 'All right, pull him in. But

absolutely routine. I leave it to you and Muncaster how you do it. As long as you don't crap on my doorstep. And remember, Colgrave will try and get the SB's scalp, so they'll have to have their wits about them.'

'I'll call you as soon as I have any news.' Suchard hung up. The girl shivered against him: '*Ah mon chéri, j'ai joui, j'ai joui!*'

Just before one am the unmarked patrol car at the corner of Montpelier Square reported: 'Subject leaving now. Driving Lancia. No passengers.'

Muncaster nodded. All according to the book. Earlier that evening the Lancia had been traced to an exclusive hire-car firm in Mayfair who had rented it to a blond man giving his name as Dirk Peters. Address, the Penthouse, Coleridge Tower, The Barbican. Payment by cash, in advance.

All Muncaster had to do now was sit and wait for the word from Lucan Place.

7

Rawcliff had begun drinking as soon as he got to the shop that morning, and by lunchtime he was stinking. Toby Hyde-Smith, with commendable presence of mind, put him to rest on the sofa in the upstairs office, and at five o'clock judged him sober enough to go home, by taxi instead of in his car.

His wife was cooking their baby son's supper. She gave him a fixed stare across the kitchen. 'You look awful. A mess.' She turned, tossing fish-fingers into the pan.

'Hair of the dog,' Rawcliff said thickly. 'Touch of the Dutch courage, if you prefer it. You know that Wellington's scum-of-the-earth fought at Waterloo half-drunk?'

'So what's going to be *your* Waterloo?' She spoke without looking at him. 'Or have your new gangster friends let you down? No lovely Swiss francs in the kitty for Mummy and Tom? Is that what's worrying you?'

Rawcliff sat down at the table and raked his hair with his fingers. Tom had biscuit all over his face and was grinning at him. Rawcliff grinned back, like a mask; then stood up unsteadily and went over to the cooker. His wife took a step back: 'Don't come near me! Have a bath and shave and clean yourself up.'

'I was just going to make myself some coffee.'

'There isn't any. Remember, you were supposed to buy some this morning.'

He stood clenching and unclenching his fists, looking at the sizzling pan and the soft white nape of Judith's neck. Tom must have sensed something, because he began to cry.

'There you are, you've upset him,' his wife said. 'And he's hardly seen you for two days. By the way there's a telegram for you. I left it in the hall.'

'Thanks for telling me.' He went over and wiped Tom's face and made his Batman gesture, flapping his arms and swooping down over him, and the child burbled with delight. 'Back in a moment,' he called and went out to the hall.

The telegram had a red border, international. He snapped it open. Dateline Geneva, 11.00 Swiss time. The message was addressed, prosaically, to CHARLES JAMES RAWCLIFF; the rest was largely gibberish. Rawcliff had no mind for figures, and monetary matters were as obscure to him as hieroglyphics carved in ancient stone. There was the figure of 3.75 ¼, which his dull mind just managed to guess was the current rate of the Swiss franc against the pound; then an astronomical figure, well over 37,525.00, in figures and letters, followed by some convoluted telegramese which he slowly deciphered as meaning that the money would be at his disposal on presentation of his person, equipped with a valid passport. The signature was the name of the bank, which was one he had never heard of.

His mouth was dry. He needed a beer, to steady him. He took the telegram back into the kitchen, where Judith was feeding Tom his rice while the fish-fingers cooled. He said nothing, just handed her the flimsy piece of paper. She read it abruptly, frowning. 'Well, you're in it now, aren't you,' was all she said.

He stood by the door, focusing unevenly on her as she coaxed the food into Tom's little mouth. 'Don't you want to celebrate?' he said. 'I can open up the shop and get a bottle of the best. That telegram means ten thousand quid, you realize that?'

'I realize that you've had quite enough already. As for the money, you haven't earned it yet.'

'Oh come on, love – '

'Don't *love* me, Charlie Rawcliff!' she said savagely. 'The great flying-ace, the jet-age superman, all in blue, with his gold braid and peaked cap, and half the air-hostesses in Europe lying with their legs open, just waiting for it!'

'You bitch. Don't bother about supper – I'm going out.' Tom began to cry again, watching them both fearfully.

'What do I do if that man calls back?' Judith shouted after him.

He stopped. 'What man? What call?'

'He phoned just after I got in. He didn't give a name. Said he'd call again at seven.'

'And no message, nothing? What sort of voice?'

'Ordinary, London voice, Cockney. Nobody I know.'

'Probably somebody in the trade.'

'Then why didn't he ring you at the shop?'

'I don't know why he didn't ring me at the shop. Now for Christ's sake stop interrogating me! I'm going to the pub to have a couple of drinks, and I'll be back by seven.'

He went out and slammed the door. His mind boggled with a furious, hopeless indecision. Events were carrying him along, destroying all initiative, probably destroying his marriage. If he couldn't handle his wife, how could he hope to handle Newby and Peters, let alone the people above and behind them? And whoever they were, they certainly wouldn't appreciate it if he went dipping into their ten thousand quid deposit, without having put in even an hour's flying to deserve it.

The pub was a dank shabby place with no carpet and a juke-box and rows of Irish building-workers in knitted pixie-hats and overalls white with cement dust. Its one advantage was that it was near.

He had a couple of pints of draught Guinness, with a whisky chaser, and felt stronger, but still not strong enough to deal with Judith and the delinquent Newby and the horrific temptation of that Swiss bank.

The clock over the bar said 6.50. But it was always ten minutes fast, as the Irish were slow when it came to drinking up time. And as he looked down the row of knobbly, dust-caked proletarian faces, supping their drinks like pigs at a trough, he considered, if the worst came to the worst, that he could always slip one of them a few quid for a bed or a sofa in some decrepit back-room, and talk deformed history and poetry all night. The Irish kept themselves to themselves. Free from Judith, free from guilt, free from importuning telephone calls from international gangsters. Then he saw it.

The man beside him was reading the sports page of the *Evening News*. What caught his eye was a couple of inches on the front page:

POLICE HUNT RAF PILOT'S KILLER

Scotland Yard detectives were called in to hunt for a hit-and-run driver who fatally wounded RAF Flight-Lieutenant Terence Mason, aged 35, of Benson Airbase, Oxon.

The accident occurred on Monday night close to the airbase. Flight-Lieutenant Mason was hit by a vehicle which failed to stop. He died a few hours later in the Radcliffe Infirmary, Oxford. Today Scotland Yard refused to comment on why they had been called in. A spokesman also refused to confirm or deny that foul play is suspected.

Rawcliff had never been directly responsible for anyone's death before. It gave him a horrible corrupt sense of self-importance, and at the same time an awareness of his own fragility. He was trembling, sweating, as he looked at the clock, which now said nearly seven. He left the pub so fast that several heads turned to stare at him; and he ran the two streets home. The *Evening Standard* was tucked into the letter-box. He wrenched it out tearing it and his hands were shaking so badly that he could hardly get the key into the door. Judith was upstairs putting Tom to bed. He started to read the paper as he walked down the hall. It was there on the front page: an agency report, almost the same, word for word. Rawcliff knew little of the journalist's trade, but he could tell when news had been leaked, in drips, still leaving the reader thirsty. He guessed that the police knew a great deal more than they were letting on.

Then he remembered the telegram. There would be a record of it: though not enough to implicate him in an international conspiracy, perhaps – if he decided to pull out now. Which was exactly what Mason had done.

Oh Christ. Judith had been right. She was usually right. She was right about his drinking, about his morbid self-indulgence, about accounts and tax and all the other fiddling obstacles to a smooth and happy life. He didn't need her to be right about this too.

He realized that the telephone was ringing. He snatched it

up and controlled his breathing. The last thing he wanted them to think was that he was nervous.

'Is that 218 1293? Mr Rawcliff? Charles Rawcliff?' A familiar voice, self-assured, cocky. 'I've got a message for you. You're to stand by. Everything's been taken care of. Just make sure you've got your passport. Four o'clock this morning – marching orders. Pack only essentials. I'll pick you up at the corner of your street.'

'Is that Leslie?'

'Never mind, Mr Rawcliff. No rough stuff, I promise. Just your passport and light luggage. And a bit of pocket-money, if you want. You won't need much – it's all found, where you're going. Four am. Okay?'

'How do you know this phone isn't being tapped?'

'I don't. But in this lovely country of ours, it takes time to tap a phone. One of the beauties of democracy and red tape. See you.'

Rawcliff replaced the receiver, then walked slowly upstairs and kissed Tom goodnight. Then he went in and told his wife about Mason and about the call.

8

John Newby stepped out into the damp winter night and stood sniffing the air like a well-groomed spaniel. He had his hands in his overcoat pockets, flapping the sides open and shut, while he waited for the doorman to bring his car round. The Lancia drew up and he pressed a twenty-pound note into the man's gloved palm.

Newby was a fast, selfish driver who took a sensual pleasure in mastering a lethal machine. But at this hour there was little traffic, no pedestrians. He ignored the glare of headlamps in the driving mirror: then saw the flashing blue light as the police car came level with him. He drew up confidently, pushed the switch and his window slid down; then he sat waiting while they strolled deliberately towards him. It was a nuisance, but he knew how to deal with these people.

'Evening, sir. You're in a bit of a hurry, aren't you?'

'I apologize, officer. I may have been going rather fast.'

'For your information, you were touching sixty. You also committed two other moving offences. You shot a pair of lights back there, I'm afraid.'

Newby already had his wallet out and half-open, the inner pockets packed with credit cards and cash. He held it out with a practised gesture, executed with all the guile of one who knows the price of everything.

'Have you been drinking, sir?'

'I beg your pardon, officer?'

A second uniformed man came over with the sealed paper bag. 'I have reason to believe that you may have been drinking,' said the first man. 'Will you just blow into this – a few normal deep breaths.'

'This is outrageous, it is positively indecent!'

'I must caution you, sir. If you refuse, I shall be obliged to arrest you and ask you to accompany me to a police station.'

'I refuse, absolutely. I demand to speak to your superior and to call my lawyer.'

'Very well, sir. I must ask you to leave your car here.'

'Mr John Newby, I am arresting you under Section 8, Paragraph 3 of the Road Traffic Act 1972, for refusing to take the breathalyser test at a police station. Empty your pockets, please.'

'I shall not.'

'Then I shall be obliged to have you searched. Sergeant Hood,' he called, without seeming to raise his voice.

A young man in plain clothes came in and took a long look at Newby. 'Trouble, Sergeant Prentice?'

'Mr Newby here – I've charged him, but he refuses to empty his pockets.'

'Very good. I'll have him stripped.'

'I demand to call my lawyer.' Newby groped, with uncharacteristic clumsiness, inside his coat and brought out a gilt-edged address-book. His soft little hands quivered as he opened it. 'Give me a telephone.'

'I'll have that, for a start.' Hood took the book and stood tapping it against his thigh. He had a hard, sallow face, empty of all innocence and compassion. 'Empty your pockets, Newby.'

'You are no better than the Gestapo!'

'We could be worse,' Hood said, with a joyless grin.

Newby relented. He watched, with stiff dignity, as his possessions slowly began to cover the desk, with Hood intoning each item and the Duty Sergeant methodically writing them down in the charge-book. Newby's wallet had been emptied and the money – mostly in twenties and tens – counted into neat piles. Credit cards, business cards, a number of receipts, club memberships, address-book, three cheque-books; British, Belgian, and international driving-licences, gold watch, diamond ring, and string of worry-beads.

'String of beads,' Hood said. 'Right. Let's sort out this little lot. Total of nine thousand, two hundred and eighty-four pounds. I suppose you can explain how you come to be carrying all this money, Newby?'

'I won it tonight – at a private club. It is most respectable.'

'I'm sure it is. They all are.' He gave a surreptitious nod to the Duty Officer, who removed Newby's address-book, and left the room.

It was very quiet; then an Irish voice shouted from somewhere in the building: 'Brits out! Fuckin' Tans!' 'Shut up, Breakfast,' a voice replied amiably.

'Do they always pay you in cash?' Hood added.

'Invariably.'

'And when you lose? You pay in cash too?'

'Yes, I pay in cash.'

'Don't always trust banks, maybe? You've got at least three different accounts. In different banks. And in different names.'

'My banking arrangements are none of your business. Now, I demand to speak to my lawyer, at once!' Newby's breathing had become tight and heavy. 'And I must be allowed to see a doctor. I suffer from asthma.'

'You can see a doctor and a lawyer, just as soon as we've decided exactly who you are.' Hood looked at him and smiled like a razor. 'Where shall we start? Two of these driving-licences have you down as Newby, the other as Monsieur Rebot' – he pronounced the name passably well – 'and we've also got three names. Quite a choice! Tallant for the American Express and Chase Manhattan. Burg for the Credit Suisse and Diners' Club, as well as an account at Harrods and Fortnum's. Lucky Burg! And a dozen cards for Mr Kyriades of Larnaca and Athens.' He leant forward with both hands on the table. 'Which one are you?'

'I can explain.'

'I think you'd better. You're not leaving here until you do.'

Hood said, 'This is Detective Superintendent Muncaster. We're treating you seriously, Newby – or whatever your name is.' He turned to Muncaster, 'He's not being very cooperative, sir. Four aliases, and this bunch of cards in a Greek name. Says he's an international business man and finds it convenient to have a number of identities.'

Muncaster sat down at the corner of the table. 'Any chance of a cup of coffee, Sergeant?'

'Right away, sir.'

'And you, Newby? Perhaps you'd prefer tea?'

'I demand to call my lawyer. You have absolutely no right to hold me here. I have only committed a minor traffic offence. I know the law of this country! You officials! My God, you will be sorry you ever saw me.'

'You have a British passport, Mr Newby. You also have Belgian nationality, in the name of Jean Rebot. Tallant and Burg are a subsidiary of the French electronics company, Entreprise Lipp.' He spoke gently, watching Newby with a fixed eye.

Newby reached for his handkerchief – the only possession they had returned to him – and dabbed at his upper lip. He had begun to breathe heavily again, in a panting wheeze. 'I have a suite at the Churchill Hotel. I am registered under the name of Tallant for personal reasons. I request to be allowed to return there. I suffer from asthma, and I do not have my tablets with me.'

Hood had returned, with two paper cups, of coffee and tea, in time to hear this last plea of Newby's. He seemed amused; his smile became almost amiable. 'I had an aunt once who had asthma. Psychosomatic, they said it was. Came on when she got nervous. Are you nervous, chum?'

'I refuse to answer any more questions until I have been allowed to make a phone call.'

'Mr Newby,' Muncaster said, 'I don't think you quite appreciate the gravity of your situation.'

'My situation is simply that I am being held here against my will! I was arrested on a charge of having refused to submit to the breathalyser, when I was not even drunk, and now you are treating me like a major criminal!'

'You are being held here, among other things, on suspicion of possessing stolen credit cards and cheque-books. I should add that refusing to cooperate with the police can itself be a serious offence.'

Newby glanced helplessly round at Hood, but found no

comfort in that hard passionless face. Muncaster had leant forward and sat rubbing the end of his long nose.

'All right. Let him make his call, Sergeant. Just the one.'

Newby started to reach inside his jacket, then seemed to hesitate; perhaps he had remembered that they'd taken his address-book. In any case, he didn't ask for it; instead, as though reluctant to call his solicitor direct at this hour, he began to dial a number from memory. The two policemen watched him, closely yet detached – they would rarely watch anyone doing anything in any other way. The line answered almost at once, and Newby said, in a careful voice, 'Peters – it's John. I'm having a little trouble.'

Pause. From somewhere outside, a muffled voice, 'I was only practisin', officer! Honest to God I was!'

Newby said, 'Awkward business, with the police. Yes. Yes. Call him at once and say I need him.' He looked up at Muncaster. 'Which station is this?'

Muncaster told him, and Newby repeated the name into the phone. 'Tell him to get out here quickly. It is most urgent.'

Hood was grinning as he took the receiver from Newby's hands and replaced it in the cradle. 'He's going to love you for getting him out at this hour. What does he know you as, by the way? Newby or Burg or Rebot or Tallant? Or maybe Mr Kyriades, from Larnaca, Cyprus? Whatever it is, he's going to be earning his fee!'

Later that morning Muncaster was back at his desk at the Yard, dog-tired, sipping stale coffee, while his head sang with the ring of telephones, clatter of typewriters and teleprinters, doors banging, boots stamping. Why were today's policemen such a damned noisy lot? He had always believed in doing the job quietly. It was the television that did it, he was certain of it.

They had at least another forty-eight hours in which to hold Newby, who was still at Lucan Place, and still not talking.

Otherwise, all quiet. Thurgood still hadn't stirred. They had traced Peters, through the phone-number which Newby had dialled at the station, to a flat in Bayswater. But either Peters was a late-riser, or he'd taken the hint of Newby's arrest and was lying low. The same went for Ritchie.

Passport Office, Petty France, had come through with some interesting, but somewhat otiose details about Newby. Born Ali Nubi, in Iraq, 1932. Naturalized British, taking name of John Newby, in 1947, father deceased 1949; no details of mother. Passport renewed in Cyprus, 1957, 1962. Present passport valid and correct. No knowledge of dual nationality.

A check with the Cyprus High Commission could tie up nothing definitely with Kyriades of Larnaca, who was apparently a modestly successful figure in the shipping business; otherwise the Cypriots weren't putting themselves out.

The Belgians had also called back, to inform Muncaster that Jean-Baptiste Rebot had been born in Stanleyville, in the former Belgian Congo, in 1932, and that he held a Belgian passport. They weren't prepared to add anything, and Muncaster thought it inappropriate at this stage to start muddying the waters with an EEC ally. But it was all extra ammunition, in case Colgrave started playing for broke.

He was on his tenth cup of coffee and looking forward to a ploughman's lunch and a pint, when Patrol from outside Nelson's Wharf, Albert Dock, called in: girl middle-twenties, small features, brown-to-reddish hair, wearing beige safari trouser-suit, carrying two cases, had arrived at Subject's flat at 10.32 am, left at 11.14, driven in Subject's Jaguar to London Airport. Checked in at 12.45 for Olympic Airways, Flight 296 to Athens, first-class. Name Ms rpt Ms Joanna Sheila Shelby.

Fifteen minutes later the call came from Heathrow. 'Morning, Cyril. Haven't talked to you since we found that plastic eye-ball. How are we?'

'Come on, what have you got?'

'She's twenty-eight and what we vulgarly call out here, "a knockout". Not down on any of our records, but you might know more about that than we do?'

'Well, let's have it.'

'Right, it's all here. She boarded the Athens flight, as you said. Passport has her down as "social worker". Both Customs and Immigration gave her a light quiz, and she said she was working for the VSO in Cyprus, and was going out to Greece for a holiday to stay with some friends near Athens. Only carrying £28 in cash, no travellers' cheques. Nothing fishy about her luggage. Pricey, but not out-of-line.'

Not out-of-line? Nothing fishy! thought Muncaster. A social worker flying to Athens, first-class? There were plenty of pretty girls around, but somebody was obviously picking up a handsome price-tag on this one. Ritchie, perhaps? And Cyprus. Cyprus was cropping up rather too often to be a coincidence.

He registered a quick mental note, as he reached for the scrambler and made his routine call to Suchard. The languid gentleman's voice had taken on a mild sharpness, a reminder to the Superintendent that he was not merely operating in the line of duty – if he stumbled and fell down on this job, there wouldn't be just an inquest. That seaside bungalow was getting no nearer. On the other hand, if he pulled it off – well, he'd get smiles all round, and maybe a commendation. While Suchard, of course, would take all the glory.

'So he still hasn't sung? What are they doing to him down there, for God's sake? Trying to poison him with their tea?'

'His stomach's upset,' Muncaster said, without humour. 'It does tend to interrupt the interrogation.'

'I may have something for you,' Suchard went on. 'Nothing you boys will be able to hang a label on – just what we might call a *canard*. By the way, have you talked to the Board of Trade recently?' he added, with meticulous timing.

Muncaster saw the warning light. He replied carefully, 'All Newby's credentials in that area appear to be in order, sir. We're still waiting for the Revenue boys –'

'I am not interested in the Revenue boys, Muncaster.' Suchard spoke with intense precision. 'You have the record there. Two shops in Kensington and Chelsea, specializing in kinky underwear. Fairly high-class, *and* imported from France. The main supplier is a women's clothing supermarket in Paris, behind the Gare St Lazare. A reputable establishment, according to my sources. Sole proprietor, a Monsieur Charles Auguste Pol.' He paused. 'Are the bells tinkling, Cyril?'

Muncaster said nothing.

'The fat French gangster. The one we don't like. Put it to Newby – gently, just to show we've broken his shell. It might just do the trick.'

'Will do, sir.' Muncaster hung up and sat staring at nothing. I must be getting old, he thought. Suchard had already warned him about Pol: that the man was big time, a real rogue and a menace. The question was, how big was Newby? Big enough to be employed by Pol; but that didn't necessarily mean much. Pol made a habit of employing dispensable people, and if Newby was nothing else, he was eminently dispensable. Any man who walked round London with a flashy diamond ring and his pockets stuffed with cash and incriminating cards of identity must be on a strictly short-term contract, Muncaster decided. It was just his luck that it had taken him this long to realize the connection, while Suchard had pipped him to the post.

Suchard and his mob were one thing. Pol was altogether something else. If the man's file was anything to go by, he brought a whole new dimension to the case.

One of the phones rang. It was Patrol in Gloucester Road, reporting that Thurgood had emerged from his service-flat and crossed the road, to have his solitary midday slice of pizza.

9

When Suchard arrived that day for a late lunch at his club, he was in a light expansive mood. His guest was William Skate, a man whom an earlier generation would have honoured as an Arabist and a scholar – described today as an expert in Middle Eastern affairs. He was the author of a couple of books which had become obscure classics, and was now on the board of several institutions of an eclectic, semi-political nature, as well as a regular contributor to various learned journals. From time to time Suchard picked his brains, in exchange for a bad meal at his club.

They met in the panelled bar, and lunched under the portraits of frozen-eyed Admirals and varnished Field-Marshals. 'I'm afraid the food may be worse than usual. There's some sort of go-slow in the kitchen. It makes the members furious, but I think it's rather funny. We'll make up for it with the wine. As it's fish, we'll have white – they have a very reasonable hock.'

As a companion, William Skate was slow to warm up. He was a thin bone of a man, his flesh wasted away as a youth under the roasting suns of Arabia. He had a high forehead on which grew a tuft of grey hair which he pulled insistently while he talked, like the frayed end of a bell rope.

'So what's new, Willy?'

'Nothing's ever new in my field of work – you ought to know that. We go back to the Middle Ages. Or the Dark Ages.'

Suchard tasted the wine and winced. 'Not up to scratch, I'm afraid, but I suppose it'll have to do. Religion's not in my line, Willy. As you know, I'm an honest-to-God agnostic who believes that if the Almighty really is alive and well, he should be ashamed of himself. But Iran has made us all reach for our reference books.' He smiled indulgently. 'I don't want to batter you about the head, my dear fellow. But I'm an ignorant bastard, and I'm rather pressed. Something's dropped into my lap which might – just might – have a Middle-Eastern flavour. We've got nothing specific.

'Islam seems to be rearing its ugly head – or many heads – right across the spectrum, from the fundamentalists in Iran and the traditionalists in Saudi Arabia, to the wild Left in Iraq and Libya. And religion means oil, and we all know what oil means.

'Then again, it could have something to do with the Yids, but so far we've no direct lead to them. I'm staying away from our Israeli sources, as much as possible. You know what happens if you light a match there – their chaps in the Mossad have it on file in Jerusalem within minutes. Saudi Arabia – absolutely nothing. We've considered the Lebanon, but it hardly seems worth the candle. What I want to know, Willy, is – have you heard anything?'

William Skate tugged at his forelock, as though to release some inner mechanism of the brain. He had the habit of the professional pedant never to answer a question directly, but to lead up to his judgement with a series of expositions, tedious and immaculate in detail. He covered the history and the developing role of the Arab world, concentrating on what he called 'the Holy Crescent of Islam' – a general phrase, he conceded, that excluded the peripheral Muslim areas of Black Africa, the hinterland of the Indian sub-continent, extending into Soviet Russia, and the Muslim areas of the Far East, like those of Indonesia and the Philippines. But what he really wanted to talk about was his speciality – the Middle East, which mostly meant the Arabian Peninsula.

'To understand Islam, it is also necessary to understand that it is, in essence, a very simple religion. In fact, it is simplistic. That is its charm, and also its danger. It is almost entirely uncerebral, and unlike other great religions – Christianity and Buddhism, for instance – it encourages almost no form of contemplation. Islam has no equivalent of monasteries or convents. It does not demand thought – it demands of its followers only belief, total belief.'

'Not belief. Faith,' Suchard said, sipping his thin soup. 'Belief depends on reason, and there is very little that is rational about most religious doctrines.'

'But Islam is a very practical religion,' Skate went on. 'The mosque is not only a place of prayer – it also serves as a town-hall, law court, school, even university. It is also a social centre, in the most literal sense, carrying with it the traditional source of power and influence bestowed on religious leaders since the sixth century. It is that power and influence which are being felt today in what is rather crudely called the "Islamic Revival".

'But there is a paradox here. From its very inception, by the Prophet Mohammed, it has been an all-embracing, pervasive and therefore highly political religion. Far more than is Christianity. And at the same time, as a creed, it is fairly passive, even supine. It also has a very high boiling point. But when that point is reached, it tends to boil over. This happened in the Middle Ages, under Tamburlaine and Saladin, and under the spread of the Ottoman Empire, when Islam carried with it the most advanced civilization of its time. Then, for some mysterious reason, it withered and died – or rather lay doggo. Talk about sleeping dogs. Well, this one isn't just awake – it's getting out of bed.'

'You sound quite Buchanesque, my dear Willy. Next you'll be talking about the Return of the Prophet. Or even the Mahdi – God forbid!' Suchard smiled over his spoon. 'The sword of Saladin replaced by the Kalashnikov rifle.'

Skate continued, as though he had not heard. 'But Islam has another important characteristic which one must remember. The word means to "surrender" – total giving of oneself to the one and only God, Allah. Mohammed, as you probably know, is not worshipped like Christ – he was simply an ordinary merchant from Mecca whom Allah chose to inspire with His Holy Word, which Mohammed inscribed and passed down in what is now the Holy Koran. Unlike the Bible, it is a short work. It contains no real history, no true philosophy except of the most simple and practical kind, and it includes, of course, a kind of rough-and-ready penal code – known as Islamic Law, which in the West is largely synonymous with amputation, flogging, stoning to death. Rather unfair, since when it first appeared, the Koran was a highly enlightened and progressive teaching.'

'So, I dare say, was the Star Chamber,' Suchard said, finishing his soup. 'Except that in the case of Islamic Law, we're talking about the Sixth Century – not the Sixteenth. There were no doubt people who considered trial-by-ordeal, even the sacrifice of the First-Born, as being progressive and enlightened. But this isn't a tutorial, Willy. I want to know about Islam today. Or, more precisely, something that might fit in with the Islamic threat. How do you see that threat?'

'It depends on which side of the mirror you're standing. The Islamic world – which is by no means all Arabic – is polarized between two constants. Oil and religion. For the rulers of all those countries which have the oil, they present an appalling dilemma – one that is only just becoming, apparent. We saw the paradox most vividly acted out in Iran – fabulous wealth, rapid mindless industrialization, the growth of the most vulgar and seductive of Western values, all coming smack up against the rock of Islam, which promised purity, a return to the strict values of the family, the simple life, and a selfless devotion to Allah.'

'Very nicely put, from the dispassionate point of view, Willy. But it doesn't quite answer my question. If Islam's not on our side, is there any way of coaxing him round? Or are we to remain perennial, even perpetual, infidels and outcasts?'

'From the political angle, I don't think you can exaggerate the importance of Islam. What exactly is your problem?'

'The problem is, I don't know. Willy, I look upon you as a sort of seismic counter. As though you register so many points on the Skate-Richter scale, whenever there's an upheaval in the Middle East. Or, more important, whenever there's *about* to be an upheaval. Has the needle been registering anything recently?'

Skate picked a fishbone out of his teeth. 'Put like that, it's moving all the time. Iraq is pulling back from the Soviet abyss. And there you have a complex struggle between the two Islamic sects, the Sunnis and the Shi'ites. While in Afghanistan we have a nice illustration of how Communism, with its soulless atheistic materialism, is just as much an anathema to Islam as is Western society. But, of course, inside that conflict you have all kinds of apparently independent contradictions.

'Iran offers perhaps the best example – a spontaneous, grass-roots revolution, producing an extreme populist regime, complete with revolutionary tribunals, secret trials, summary executions, and such weird offences as "crimes against God". And this regime is not only anti-Marxist, anti-Communist and anti-Russian, but also bitterly anti-Western.

'Then over in Libya we have the eccentric Colonel Gadaffi, who claims to be both Muslim and Marxist, and manages to reconcile the two rather well. His regime is austere, despite its enormous oil revenues; and rather than pursuing the high life, like the Saudis and the Gulf States, Gadaffi spends a lot of money helping any revolutionary cause that takes his fancy, which has included the IRA, the Red Brigades in Italy – even Idi Amin, for no better reason than that the wretched fellow was one of the faithful. What did the FO boys think of that?'

'You know better than to ask me, Willy. Half of them still belong to the old school – Thessiger, Lawrence, even Burton. I often think that some of them were reading Omar Khayyam on nanny's knee, instead of Hans Christian Andersen. The clean desert Arab – honest Johnny Turk. Tough, down-to-earth chaps you can trust. Not like the clever Jew, the smarmy Western Oriental Gentleman outside the pawnbroker's and the bazaar. I do apologize for this fish,' he added, making a delicate incision in a slice of Dover sole. 'They're supposed to fillet it, but it's no good balling them out – we'd have the whole kitchen out on strike. All power to the working class.' He laid down his knife and fork, and pushed his plate away.

'I'm interested, though, when you observe that Islam is just as inimical to the creed of Marx, and Marx's atheistic materialism, as it is to the philosophy and standards of the West. If I'm not right, Willy, aren't one-third of the Soviet Republics Islamic?'

'Not only that,' Skate said, with almost threatening

emphasis. 'It is estimated that by the turn of the century, Islam will claim half the population of the Soviet Union.'

'Allah be blessed,' Suchard said gently. 'And what happens when that can of worms is opened? Perhaps that's the joker in the pack? Otherwise, it looks as though we're betting on Red or Black – the Kremlin's got the missiles and the muscle, the Sheikhs and the Ayatollahs and the mad Colonels have got the oil. Either the Soviet tanks come rolling down Pall Mall, or nothing rolls at all – tanks or cars or anything. Unless somebody can find a middle way.'

'And you want to know if I've heard anything?'

'I can give you a little clue, the faintest whisper. There's some international outfit who bought up half a dozen heavy transport planes and are hiring pilots here in Britain. It stinks, but we don't know what of. There are several options, given the range of the planes, but I've plumped for the Middle East.'

'You could hardly have chosen a wider area, or a more varied one. I was on the point of adding the metaphor about a needle in a haystack' – Skate grinned; he was unused to wine at lunch, and Suchard had ordered a second bottle.

'A fleet of heavy transport planes don't disappear, except perhaps in the Empty Quarter. From what we can gather, they're running on a budget of several million pounds. The backer is a French gangster with close connections with the French hush-hush boys. But the fact that they're recruiting British pilots, suggests somebody wants to bury the French connection. We could nip it all in the bud, but we're curious. The Frenchman's form has one common denominator – he not only has a lot of useful friends in high places who keep him both alive and out of jail, but he also likes to play games. It tickles his fancy to back the small-time players against the big boys. Algerians against the French, North Vietnamese against the Americans.' He paused; chose some cheese. 'We badly want to know what he's up to this time – using British subjects to embarrass us, no doubt, if things go wrong. Or perhaps, even if things go right? The man doesn't play by any accepted rules.'

Skate wrenched at his hair. 'I'm no politician, Simon.

And I'm no strategist. I can give you some idea about the changing political pattern in the Middle East, and I could suggest a few sources that might put up the sort of money you're talking about – unless, of course, it's the French government who are backing this operation?'

'I don't think so. Not overtly, at any rate. They're worried sick about oil but I don't think they're desperate enough to try any rough stuff at this stage.'

'May I ask you something?' Skate scooped out a spoonful of Stilton, to Suchard's polite disapproval. 'Why all the interest in Islam?'

'Just a delicate whiff in the air, Willy. Oil and Islam are the crucial ingredients, as you pointed out. Supposing someone wanted to divide Islam – turn one sect against another, split it down the middle?'

When Skate answered, he had twisted his forelock into a stiff spiral that stuck out vertically, making him look like an ascetic unicorn. 'There is a schism, as I told you, between the traditional Moslems, the Sunnis – and the Shi'ites. But I'd have to belabour you with a lot of high theosophy, and even then, I don't think I could answer your question.' He paused again. 'Haven't you got the slightest clue what these transport planes might be used for?'

'Strictly *entre nous*' – Suchard laid a finger against his lips – 'something that may be important, may not. But we've had a tip that one of the recruited pilots bought up a load of expensive loudspeaker equipment, with six tape-recorders. They were shipped out, quite legally, to Athens, a couple of weeks ago. Enough to equip each plane with six speakers, plus sensor devices to make them carry above any amount of noise. So – what do your grey cells make of that?'

William Skate gave an unexpected smile. 'If you're talking about straws in the wind – well, I've got something that might help. It certainly didn't mean a thing to me at the time. But I've got a Palestinian friend – naturalized, thoroughly vetted, perfectly above-board – who works for the BBC Arab Service. He translates scripts. Doesn't broadcast, so his voice isn't known – which might be relevant. I saw him the other evening and he happened to mention that he'd had a small windfall. A foreign chap – he thought he was French – offered him £250 in cash to make a short recording in Arabic. When I say short, I mean literally about two sentences.

'Of course, he jumped at it, you know what the old Beeb pay, especially in the foreign services! The Frenchman said it was some voice-over for a radio-play.'

'Get on with it, Willy. Can you remember what the sentences were?'

'I can, as a matter of fact. They were rather bizarre. A sort of announcement that the Second Prophet was coming – Ali, the cousin and son-in-law of Mohammed, in the form of the promised Mahdi. He was coming to announce that Allah was displeased with Islam and that he was bringing retribution against Man for his sins. That was about the gist of it – no mention of what the retribution would be.

'The significance of the pronouncement, from a strictly ecclesiastical point of view, is that in Islamic lore, Mohammed cannot return as a prophet, or as the Mahdi. But his cousin, Ali, can.'

Suchard sat fingering his elegant profile. 'More and more like the good Buchan! But it seems a pretty crude way of putting the wind up a few simple-minded Bedouins. Hardly worth an outlay of several million pounds. Still it's worth thinking about. The devil of it is, Willy, there are so many possibilities – so many combinations of terrorism and counter-terrorism. Without a clear lead, it's impossible to move. At the very worst it could be a suicide-strike against Israel – Tel Aviv, Haifa, even Jerusalem. We do know that the pilots are expected to fly very low, which suggests trying to avoid radar or missiles.' He put his hand to his brow. 'And I've got to serve up something concise and lucid for the Minister, by eight this evening. Something simple, which, if necessary, can be turned into a Written Answer.

'So what have we got? Western civilization crumbling in a morass of hedonism, unbridled materialism, social indiscipline, and the rule of special interest groups. No argument there, I think? While on the other side of the coin, an Islamic Revival hardly squares with the Marxist myth of a popular uprising under a vanguard of the Workers' Party. Ergo, the gospels of Marx and Lenin, of Freud, Kate Millett, and the Club of Rome – both the most "radical" and the most "conservative" – all equally hostile to Islam. It's a horrible equation, Willy. If only we could narrow the field down to just one or two targets.'

'I'm sorry, Simon. All I can do is widen the field. Iraq, for instance – an uprising by the Shi'ite minority against the Sunni rulers in Baghdad. Or the Kurds in Iran – though I doubt that they've got that sort of money to throw around. Somebody might be trying to take a crack at the Saudis – trying to ferment a bit of anti-Sunni, anti-Western affluence along the lines of Khomeini. Though they're all long shots, and I don't see many dividends in any of them for this French gangster of yours.

'But it's just occurred to me, you might try another tack. A number of Third World states are trying – God help us – to develop their own A-bomb. Apart from Israel and South Africa, Libya and Pakistan are the favourite contenders. A lot of fancy electrical equipment – ostensibly for domestic use – has been finding its way to those countries, particularly to Pakistan. Not to mention uranium. Most of the EEC countries have embargoed the stuff – but, typically, not the French! Does that mean anything to you?'

10

Muncaster drank another coffee and read the report on Dirk Peters. He was an easy subject to follow, on account of the fact that he evidently had a sprained or broken ankle, walked with crutches, and also wore a neck-brace. He was driven about in a minicab – the firm was checked, without any interesting results – and spent most of the morning moving around, making calls from pay-phones, usually in obscure cafés or pubs. Most of the calls were local. The Special Branch were running a trace on them now. At least two of them were to Jim Ritchie, and one to Thurgood's service-flat. Conclusion – Newby was inside and the rest were getting ready to bolt.

Just after two o'clock Peters made a long-distance call from a public box in Victoria Station – to the growing fury of a queue outside, which included the SB man, all of whom Peters treated with icy indifference. This call was to the President Hotel, Geneva.

Peters then had lunch at a big hotel off Piccadilly, from where he made a second international call. And this time the SB man had used his credentials to get the number from the hotel operator – 010 357 61. Port of Larnaca, Cyprus. Also one of the bases from which Mr Kyriades operated.

Muncaster felt he ought to call Suchard, but the man would almost certainly be out for lunch. While Whitehall lunched, the rest of the world had to wait. But that suited Muncaster. He spent the time tying up a few loose ends before he wrapped the parcel up and handed it to his superiors. The Voluntary Service Overseas confirmed that Miss Joanna Sheila Shelby had recently worked in Cyprus, at a camp near Larnaca, but had been sacked for neglecting her duties. She was no longer working for the organization.

A few minutes later, Athens Airport cabled that Miss

Shelby was booked on the Olympic afternoon flight to Nicosia, Cyprus.

Then, at three-forty Thurgood again surfaced – not to get a pizza this time, but to take the Circle Line from Gloucester Road to Victoria, where he checked in at the British Caledonian office, with a single piece of hand-luggage, and took the train to Gatwick in time to catch the late afternoon flight to Charles de Gaulle Airport, Paris.

Still unable to contact Suchard, Muncaster rang Addison of the Special Branch, who answered angrily, 'You know what my instructions were. Gatwick had to let him go, and from Paris he could be going anywhere.'

Suchard sounded mildly tired, and even more detached than usual, when Muncaster finally got through. The Superintendent told him about Thurgood, and about Peters and the two calls – the second one to the Sun Hall Hotel, Larnaca – and said he was going to try to rouse Interpol and get them to check the guest-list. Muncaster concluded by saying that Ritchie had returned from giving the girl a lift to Heathrow, and hadn't budged since; and that they were still making heavy progress with Newby at Lucan Place.

'I know his type,' Muncaster said. 'He'll play for time, then try to give us a totally false lead. I want him to break of his own accord – get his self-confidence to melt away like a candle, if you see what I mean?'

'Nicely put,' Suchard said wearily. 'I've just spoken to the Minister, Cyril. He's been in for the last hour with the highest of the high. Even the Service Chiefs were there, and I wouldn't be a bit surprised if the wires weren't humming to Washington by now. You've done a good job.'

'Done? I've only just started putting the pieces together.'

'You can forget it, Cyril. Put it all on file, mark it "top secret" and bung it over here. And don't let those SB boys get their hands on it – there's been one leak too many, as it is.'

'What on earth is going on?' Muncaster demanded.

'The Defence lads are half-sold on a theory that the planes are intended for delivering vital material to produce an A-bomb. We think it's probably Pakistan, or maybe Libya.

But keep that tight under your hat. And I don't want your flat-footed sleuths doing anything to scare them off. Above all, do nothing to stop them.'

For several seconds Muncaster stared at the fat girl in the check blouse who brought the coffee round. He sniffed and reached into his box of Kleenex; he was too old a hand to get angry – anger, even disappointment, were not helpful emotions, and they certainly weren't professional.

'So I'm to call them off and shut up shop?' he said quietly.

'And let slip the dogs of war, dear Cyril, straight back to their kennels. Don't worry, old chap, your name is carved in immortality – it'll be worth at least an OBE.'

' "Knickers Galore" is good,' Hood was saying, running the tip of his biro along the cracked seams of wood in the table. 'But "More Knickers Galore" ' – he looked at a second plain clothes man with a pudding-basin hair-cut, sitting with his chair propped back against the wall – 'I don't think "More Knickers Galore" is very original, do you, Punchie?'

Newby had now been at Lucan Place Police Station for nearly fifteen hours, except for his brief excursion to court that morning with Vincent Colgrave. The rest of the time had been spent in the same bleak little room, somewhere in that ugly heartless building, lit by an opaque window high in the wall. They had returned all his belongings, except his credit cards and cheque books, and had supplied him with shaving tackle, and served him a vile breakfast and lunch, assuring him that both came from the canteen where the rest of the officers ate. The English were so genteel in their barbarity!

'It's a pretty silly name,' the second plain clothes man, called 'Punchie', said. 'But then it's a pretty silly business. Silly and dirty. Nasty too – isn't it, Sarge?'

'Oh, it can be. Can be very nasty indeed. Specially when they start getting at the kids. Not just showing the stuff to 'em. Using 'em. Doing things to 'em, and photographing it, even getting it on tape. We've got some tapes, haven't we, Punchie?'

'Yes, Sarge. Brought in last night, after the raid.'

They had both been talking as though Newby were not present. He interrupted in a crumbling voice, 'I'm being held under the Official Secrets Act. So what is all this talk about my shops? It is simple, run-of-the-mill commerce – plain heterosexual up-and-down. Routine stuff, I tell you! I have never employed children! In God's name, I have not!'

'Don't blaspheme,' Hood said, and lit a cigarette. 'Just run-of-the-mill porn, eh? I wonder what they'll say when those tapes are played in court?' He stared lazily at Newby through the smoke. 'We've got you all ways, old son. You'll be lucky to get less than ten years for conspiracy under the Secrets Act. Or five for kiddies' porn. Paedophilia, I think they call it, don't they? Sounds like a skin disease. Nasty, very nasty. Nobody likes that kind of thing – not even the cons.'

Punchie had brought his chair down with a bang. 'Do you follow what the sergeant's saying, little man? He's saying that nobody, absolutely nobody, loves your sort. The public don't like you, we fuzz don't like you – and, my God, the old lags inside won't like you! You'd be surprised how old-fashioned and puritanical our cons can be. Murderers, arsonists, blackmailers, bank-robbers – even terrorists – they're all acceptable members of prison society. But not filth like you. Not people who tamper with children. Christ, Newby, you're going to enjoy that five years!' He turned slowly to Hood.

'I wonder how long they'll take to cotton on to him, Sarge?'

'Usually takes a few weeks, even months. This lad' – with a blind nod at Newby – 'will probably try to get away with it by pretending he's a con-artist or some financial wizard who's been caught with his fingers in the till. Then some nosy old lag – some trustie, probably – will get a peak at the Governor's files. And what does he see? He sees that friend Newby's inside for misusing and molesting minors – little children – for his own perverted sexual pleasure and for the pleasure of others. Tell him what happens then, Punchie.'

The young man with the pudding-basin hair-cut smiled

broadly at Newby. 'I don't suppose, sir, in your circles you get to know much about prison life. All swish hotels with call-girls who come up with the champagne and caviar and go down with the breakfast? That right?'

'Go on, tell him,' Hood said.

'Well it's like this, Mr Newby. The word gets out, you see, and at some strategic time, usually just after exercise all the screws – wardens to you – on your block just happen to find themselves in one place, at one time, nothing secret, just happens like that. And the whole block goes very quiet. The cons who don't want to get involved go to their cells and pretend to be asleep.' Hood glanced at Punchie, both of them ignoring Newby. 'I know all this, from Sharpie, who did the Beaconsfield job. He was in Wandsworth when they played host to the muff-artist who fiddled with those two schoolgirls from the comprehensive.'

'Tell him,' Hood said again.

Punchie told Newby, in laconic and sickening detail. 'They had an inquiry, of sorts, and got two of the blokes on a technical. I think they did some solitary, plus loss of privileges. I tell you, Mr Newby, the fellow was screaming the whole time.'

Newby broke in with a shout, 'I demand to speak to my lawyer.' He tried to stand up, but Hood pushed him down again.

'You've already wasted half the morning with him. Your lawyer's a busy man, Mr Newby. It's no good asking to see him while you're refusing to cooperate.'

Newby felt sick, his head ached with the vicious bombardment of words. 'But I have told you – I have told you everything I know. It is a relief operation, a mercy-mission! Six planes, six pilots – I tell you, what more do you want?'

'Pull the other one,' Punchie said, half-grinning.

'You've told us all right,' Hood said: 'Trouble is, we don't believe you. Just imagine it – sex-fiend runs mercy-mission! If it isn't schoolkids, it's starving women and children. Don't make fools of us, Newby – we don't take kindly to that from your sort.'

They all looked up as a uniformed man came in. He handed Hood a note and stood whispering in his ear. Hood nodded, and gestured to Punchie, who stood up. Hood was frowning. 'You wait here,' he told Newby.

Newby was left alone. Five minutes passed, ten, fifteen. He went to the door, found it locked. It also had a Judas eye in it, which he had not noticed before. He called 'I want to see someone! I want to see someone in authority!' He began to bang on the door. 'I demand my rights!'

A second man in uniform appeared and stood looking him up and down. 'You'll be seen presently. Now you sit down and keep quiet. I don't want any more noise from here.'

Sergeant Hood came back twenty minutes later. 'You're free to go, Mr Newby. A car will drive you to your hotel, if you so wish.'

'What the hell is happening? Is this one of your tricks?'

'There's no question of a trick, Mr Newby.' Hood's face had a numb, stony look. 'Just count yourself lucky – the charges against you have been dropped. You're free to go.'

'But I demand an explanation!'

'You can do that through your solicitor. You have been held on suspicion during investigations. Now that these investigations are complete, it has been decided not to charge you. Do I make myself clear?'

'Get me a taxi.'

'I told you, sir, we have a car.'

'I don't want your bloody car. Get me a taxi.'

'I'm warning you,' the Minister said, patting his thighs and rocking back on his heels. 'If this thing blows up, it'll be your head that'll be on the charger. You'll be served up like John the Baptist. Providing, of course, that I accept your Department's recommendations.'

'*Entendu*,' Suchard said, wrinkling his eyes to make out the Minister's expression, as he stood framed against the tall period window overlooking the parking meters along Queen Anne's Gate.

'Right. Let's look at the map.' The Minister bustled up to the table; he was in his element now – he liked maps, he liked plans, they took him back to his Army days when he'd risen to Captain in a regiment distinguished only by the fact that it had not seen action this century.

'Eritrea? That's where the little sod said it was, didn't he?' The Minister's finger moved busily about on the bridge of the Horn of Africa. He frowned at the browny-grey smudged contours that marked mountains. 'Djibouti – Tigre Wollo – Asmara' – moving up the Red Sea. He paused. 'What is this? Oh for Christ's sake, Turner, it's a bloody Michelin road-map! Is that all you've got?'

'I'm sorry, sir. There's a Bartholomew's.'

'Get it.' He glanced up at Suchard. 'Djibouti – don't like the smell of that. The French still have a lot of influence there. D'you know that Pol was attached to the Elysée Palace under Pompidou? Minister without Portfolio for the African Territories. The Frogs must have been pretty self-confident to have chanced their arm with a fat bastard like him!'

'What happened to Pol?' Suchard asked, sacrificing self-esteem for curiosity.

The Minister gave a little grunt of triumph. 'You mean there's actually something you boys don't know? Watch it, lad, you're slipping.' He grinned cunningly. 'Trouble is, I don't know what happened to him. Nobody does, it seems. But if Pol was playing to form, it was probably some deal that he was involved in – muddy waters, Suchard, muddy waters. And that's what you think we've got here,' he added, as the lissom youth called Turner returned with a Bartholomew's map of the Middle East. The three of them stood over it, while the Minister's thick finger rifled through the pages. 'This is too detailed. What we want is an overall picture. Cyprus to Massawa.'

'Here we are, sir,' Suchard said.

'What's the scale? Let's compare it with the other map. We need a long ruler – tape measure would be better. Haven't you got *anything* in this place, Turner?'

'It's all right, sir,' Suchard said gently, 'I've got all the figures here. Roughly four hundred miles from Larnaca to Cairo, on a more or less direct route. Cairo to Asmara – 1,134 miles.'

The Minister stepped back, patting his hips. 'So. What's the range of a Hercules?'

'Four thousand seven hundred miles, sir. One thousand three hundred and sixty US gallon capacity for two external tanks, to be precise.' Suchard knew what was coming, and knew that the Minister was drawing it out, in order to enjoy the more his discomfort.

'Tell me something, Suchard. Have you got the tiniest – just the tiny-weeniest suspicion that this whole operation *might* be on the level?'

Suchard pursed his lips and managed to look suitably solemn. The Minister was a canny old devil – a hard political pro and a good fighter, one who could make out in the clinches, as Suchard's friends over at the annexe in Grosvenor Square would put it.

'I've considered the possibility, sir, of course. The fact that this man Pol's involved could point us in any number of directions. Assuming that Pol's a front. Or not, as the case may be. May I ask your opinion?'

'My opinion is that it smells. It stinks like a bag of old fish – and I don't want it dumped in my Ministry!' He stood glaring down at the map, playing for time. 'You've got me doing the splits across a very wide chasm – you realize that, don't you? I don't mind messing you people about – that's what you're there for – but I do mind pissing on the Yard's boots, then telling 'em it's raining. That chap Muncaster isn't going to like us one bit. Nor are the SB. They've been building up for a case of probable murder, plus holding a man under the Secrets Act. Not going to like it at all, they're not.'

'It was not on my instructions,' Suchard reminded him quietly.

'Oh damn your eyes! Damn the lot of you! You never instruct, Suchard – you devise, insinuate, kiss the hem and whisper in the majestic ear. You're the smooth cloven-footed archangel of the secret realm. They wouldn't act without you. And even if you keep silent, they can read your silence like a memo.'

Suchard smiled. 'Permit me to say so, sir – but you ought

112

to save that sort of thing for the House. It's a bit short on eloquence these days, don't you think?'

'I'm thinking, Suchard, that either way HMG stands to get her tits in the wringer. On the one hand, we stand to be party to some kind of international conspiracy. But if, by a very remote possibility – and it is the remote possibility that *you* are here to guard against – this milk-run down to Eritrea turns out to be *bona fide*, it's hardly going to look good if we put the kibosh on a genuine humanitarian mission to save starving women and children. Unlikely, I admit. But it has to be considered.'

Suchard bent forward, with his most solicitous smile. 'I can appreciate your anxiety, sir, from the purely political point of view. It could be embarrassing –'

'It could be *very* embarrassing.'

'Quite. Nothing is absolutely foolproof. There's always the zero in this game, whichever way we play it.'

'I'm not interested in your fancy metaphors! Either piss or get off the pot!'

'Thank you, sir. What I would like to say, all things considered, is that at this stage we would do best to sit back a little longer and see what happens next. At least, that's what I think is perhaps expected of us,' he added slyly. The Minister coloured, but said nothing. Suchard went on, 'After all, we don't have much to worry about – yet. So one psychotic hit-man goes free? One small-time international crook may or may not sue for wrongful arrest. And three professional pilots with British passports fly out to Cyprus to earn their loot. So what do you want us to do? We can't even pull them in for currency fiddling, now we've abolished Exchange Control. The only possibility is tax-evasion – and we'd have one hell of a job proving that, with the money locked up in Switzerland. We all know how much cooperation we'd get from the Swiss.'

The Minister nodded impatiently. 'You've forgotten the press. They're already on to Mason's death. And they've got a line on Newby, under the Secrets Act. Give a dog a bone. Christ, then we go and let Newby out.'

'Newby won't talk to the press. He won't talk to anyone –

if he knows what's good for him. If I were Newby now – which God forbid – I'd lie very low and very still.'

The Minister's eyes grew cunning. 'You're so bloody confident, aren't you? You think Pol's got a racket going, and rather than snuff it out – right now, this end, before it causes us any embarrassment, you have to cling on to the finish. Don't worry about me, and fuck the FO – just as long as you lot have your curiosity satisfied.' He took a step forward and thumped the map.

'There are at least three wars going on in this area. The Yemen's bang opposite, across the Red Sea. Then there's the Ogoden, also well within the range of your six Hercules.'

'Minister, would you forgive me if I told you what I think is worrying you?'

'Please do.'

'You're concerned that if my team pull off a coup and thwart some major international criminal operation, you won't be able to claim the credit? A successful operation, or a botched operation – that's news. But an operation to stop an operation is a non-starter. Like saying the Special Branch have foiled a plan to kill the PM. Good show, everybody says, and turns to Page Three.'

'I am not seeking personal publicity or aggrandizement, Suchard. I consider that an impertinent suggestion. And I warn you again, if you lose this little game, you lose everything. I'm not going to help you. I'm not even on the touch-line. You're on your own.'

'So much for Ministerial responsibility.' Suchard began to gather up his notes. 'You'll want to be kept informed, of course?'

'Of course. The sooner the better.' The Minister started towards the door, then paused. 'By the way, there's something I ought to tell you.'

Suchard waited. He had been expecting his superior to slip him a last card; but his elegant features registered no movement, no shade of expression.

The Minister said, 'So happens I got a call this morning from a chap on the Swiss Desk at the FO. It seems that our friend Pol has chums in Geneva who have close contacts with the Committee of the International Red Cross.'

'So you're saying that it *could* be a genuine operation?'

'I'm not saying anything. Just mentioning a fact.'

Suchard nodded sadly. 'Curiouser and curiouser, as young Alice would say. But I suppose even if it were genuine, it wouldn't make much difference? Political sensitivity and all that. Poor little bastards down there!' he added, with uncharacteristic venom. 'That war down there's been going on for nearly twenty years! And now they're not only fighting the Ethiopian government, but also against those bloody Soviet-backed Cubans. God, is there no justice?'

'Very little. The Cubans do the fighting, and the East Germans and Czechs help set up the secret police after "pacification". Don't lecture me, Suchard. Talk to Pol. Pol feels as I do. He's not only a gangster – he's an idealist. It's a horrible combination, I know, but I've had some of the inside reports. Pol does things because he believes in them, only he also likes to skim the cream off while he's doing it.'

'You're convinced I'm wasting my time?'

'I try to judge by the facts. Good afternoon.'

Suchard made a small ironic bow. A cloud of doubt had edged into the scheme of things, which had begun to look rather stimulating, after Muncaster's latest reports – all of which seemed to be homing in on Larnaca, Cyprus.

It *had* to be something else. Pol wouldn't mess around with blankets and penicillin. Maybe just for starters, but not for the main course.

As Suchard walked back across the park, he had to admit to himself that he was a trifle worried. He hadn't liked the way the Minister had talked about Pol. The Frenchman was too much in Suchard's line of business, and if there was one sort of person whom Suchard distrusted, it was a professional rival.

Muncaster was striking camp in his corner of the ops room, folding his files away, to be sent round to St James's, when one of the phones rang. Muncaster was no man to shirk his duty, and he was determined to keep his men on the job until the very last, when the files were handed over.

The call was from Observation Patrol Beta Plus, reporting that Newby had checked into the Churchill Hotel at 4.20, and that half-an-hour ago – 5.17 – the subject, Peters, had entered the hotel and gone up to Newby's suite. He had remained there only ten minutes, then taken a black cab to Euston where he had caught the 5.55 Inter-City to Manchester.

That probably meant Ringway Airport and an early morning flight to the Continent. Peters had been carrying no luggage. But what the hell? It would be no consolation to Muncaster if Suchard slipped up on this one. The Minister and his pack would be baying for blood, and Muncaster wouldn't be spared.

But his policeman's professional instincts remained to the end. A quick call established that Olympic Airways had a flight leaving Charles de Gaulle Airport for Athens forty minutes after Thurgood's British Caledonian flight landed.

It was with a weary sense of resignation that he bound up the last of the files and gave them to the despatch-rider, then stepped out into Broadway, just as it began to rain.

11

Judith had made it easy for her husband. He had not got drunk that evening; there had been no row; he had not overtly lied to her. Yet she seemed, by sinister intuition, to know that he was about to bolt. She went to bed in the study, where Mason had slept that last night; and when he looked in on her, he saw that she had been crying. She was pretending to be asleep. That was the nearest he ever came to throwing in the sponge.

He went on because he was greedy for the money, and because now he was also frightened. Yet this was a double-edged incentive: for it provided him with an atavistic pleasure of anticipation which he had not felt for a long time – since his first flying days, when there had been still enough danger to give salt to the boredom, left up there alone in the clouds hour after hour, with a radio that was like working a boy-scout's crystal set. BEA had never been a patch on them. This would, though. If a BEA pilot refused to fly, he might be suspended, but there'd be no danger of his being murdered.

At 3.30 in the morning he got up and shaved, like a soldier before battle. He had packed only essentials – toilet things, not forgetting his ginseng; change of shirts, socks and underwear, with a tie thrown in, just in case he got invited to the high table at the local Embassy; and a couple of paperbacks – an H.E. Bates war novel, and Waugh's *Black Mischief* – all stowed away in his old pilot's flight-bag, which he had kept as a fond memento. He remembered that they hadn't even left him time to go to the bank; but he had enough cash on him, for bare necessities. He wasn't anticipating any undue expenses, wherever it was they were taking him.

The house was as dark and quiet as a church. The floor creaked outside Tom's bedroom. He hesitated, began to grope for the doorhandle, knowing exactly how the child would look, his little body curled up in his cot, twined round that absurd decrepit teddy, his face resting in perfect, absolute innocence. He also knew that once he had opened that door and looked, he might just as well pack the whole thing in – go back to bed and face the shop in the morning, and every other morning afterwards, until either the Official Receiver moved in, or he got the DT's or had his first cardiac, or whatever happens to old war-weary pilots with nowhere to go.

His whole body had gone rigid, beginning to tremble. He closed his eyes and walked swiftly away from Tom's door, without turning on the light – down the stairs, feeling for each step in the dark, his eyes still closed, fists and teeth clenched tight. This was no time for a last burst of paternal sentiment. He stopped in the kitchen, to switch on the kettle and gulp a finger of whisky. Just one, he thought, slamming the stopper back in. From now on he was going to lay off the stuff.

When he'd made the coffee, he found they were out of milk. Tom must have had the last of the bottle for his supper. The coffee by itself was too hot to drink. He ran the cold tap into it. He was wasting time, already several minutes behind schedule.

No sound from the study. He knew she'd be awake again, lying there on the sofa in the dark, waiting for the snap of the front-door catch, the squeak· of the outside gate. She wouldn't come after him, though. A very determined girl. He liked to think that he wouldn't have married her otherwise. He didn't think of little Tom – didn't dare to. He might still be a hard man but not that hard.

He left the coffee undrunk, remembered to switch off the light; crept down the dark passage and slipped out of the door. Either it was the whisky, or the silence, but for a moment he thought he was going to vomit. He stood clutching the flight-bag, hunching his shoulders against the damp bitter cold.

The street was empty – two rows of low, drab, Victorian bow-fronts under the yellow night-sky that was divided up by the dark fingers of the high-rise tenement blocks near the river. Far too early for the electric milk-float, or for the newspaper boy – bringing fresh news of Mason's murder, perhaps? – or even the old man with the gammy leg across the road, who worked the early shift at the Post Office and usually took five minutes to get his car started.

Still no sound from inside the house. No last-minute click of the door reopening: no glimpse of her pale tired face, no voice calling quietly after him through the darkness, imploring him not to go.

He began to walk up the deserted street, and his steps sounded muffled and heavy, as though he were walking in snow. The air was full of that tangy burning smell that drifted up from the glucose factory on the river-front; and he caught himself wondering, with unnatural calm, if he would ever smell it again?

The car was at the corner, showing only sidelights, its engine idling. The same dilapidated Cortina, with Leslie at the wheel. 'Mornin', squire! No hard feelings, I trust?' The scurf in his thinning hair looked like tiny cornflakes.

Rawcliff got into the back and said nothing. They drove out into Battersea Park Road, past the grey-shuttered shops, catching all the lights on green, with no other traffic in sight. Leslie seemed to take the hint, and they drove in silence, along the South Bank, past Vauxhall Bridge, until they reached Nine Elms, where Leslie turned into New Covent Garden Market; showed a season-ticket at the barrier and drove past a complex of sheds until they reached the Flower Market. 'Here we are, squire. Gate five, over there. Just inside – bay-trees and exotic indoor plants. Ask for the Major.' He winked knowingly, 'There's no charge for the ride – on the house.'

Rawcliff stepped into the chill pre-dawn darkness and walked smartly over to Gate five. The heavy plastic flaps hissed automatically open and he breathed in a nice soggy jungle smell, laced with touches of natural perfume and the scents of exotic flora being marked up for the West End.

The bay-trees, and other diverse evergreen ornaments, were stacked deep and high. A big red-faced man in dungarees was piling fat dwarf palms on to a wooden trolley. Rawcliff stopped him and said, 'I'm looking for the Major.' The man nodded and disappeared somewhere behind the greenery. He returned a moment later and beckoned.

Rawcliff followed him into a little office that smelt of fresh earth. A big man, perhaps a few years older than Rawcliff, sat in a swivel chair in front of a desk. He wore a suit with a chalk stripe and a regimental tie, and had a heavy drinking face – the sort of handsome empty looks that go with the leisured classes who have dallied with the gun and the sword, then sunk back on harder times.

'Sit down, Rawcliff. My name's Grant. Guy Grant. People call me Major – I was in one of the best Highland regiments – but I won't insist on it right now. No ceremony on this one. We're all in this together – sink or swim. Are you a drinking man?' he added, stretching his legs.

'Not right now.'

'Sensible man. This job offers too many temptations. There's one bar round at the back, and two more over the Vegetable Market – both open all night.' He pointed a big finger at Rawcliff, the back of his hand mottled with liver-spots. 'One drink on this job and you're out. And there's no bloody union to protect you. Get my meaning?'

'I've got a fair idea what the set-up is.'

Grant's face took on an expression that was both foxy and brutish. 'So you were the one who busted our CO's ankle? Nearly broke the bastard's neck too, you did. Lucky you didn't kill him. Anything to say for yourself?'

'Self-defence.'

Grant grinned. 'That's what they all say, isn't it? But you want to look out for Mr Peters – he'll try and get even with you when this little caper's over.' He ran a hand through his crisp, greying hair. 'You just another bum pilot hoping to make your fortune?'

'That's about it.'

Grant took a thermos flask off a ledge and poured the cap full of black coffee. He passed it across. 'Got your passport?'

Rawcliff nodded. He sipped the coffee, which was just cool enough to drink. Grant shook himself and stood up. 'That's

120

all the stuff you've got?' He nodded at the flight-bag Rawcliff was carrying. 'Good! I like a man who travels light.'

'Where are we going?'

'Lydd, Kent.'

'Jim Ritchie's outfit? Come Fly with Me? A Beachcraft Duke with seats for four passengers?'

'Good – you're on the ball. But don't make the mistake of asking too many questions. Careless talk costs lives. Let's go.' Grant pulled on a donkey-jacket over his suit and led the way across the crowded, covered hall. 'Want to buy any flowers for your loved ones?' he added, with a nasty laugh, then took Rawcliff by the arm. 'I jest, old bean! But seriously. Take it from me, there are reasons for everything – so keep your eyes front and your mouth shut. If you've ever been in the Services you'll know how it is – you're told just enough, and no more. Bad to know too much.'

They passed through the automatic doors in the grey of the morning. Grant stopped next to a dark-blue Ford transit van with gilt lettering on the side: GUY HAMILTON GRANT, FINEST EXOTIC HOUSEPLANTS. Twenty-four-hour Delivery – Anywhere in the World. There followed a clutch of telephone numbers and a questionable looking coat-of-arms.

'Your outfit, Major?'

'One has to live, old bean. Hop in.'

'What's in the back?' Rawcliff said, when he was in the passenger seat next to Grant.

'*Codiaeum Variegatum* and *Begonia Elatior Hybrid* – at least that's what's entered on the Customs' papers. For simple folk like you and me, read "exotic houseplants which grow wild in Thailand and are cultivated by yours truly near Basingstoke".'

'And bound for?'

Grant had started the engine. 'A little island in the Med: Cyprus. Landing at Paris and Athens to refuel.'

The back of the van was stacked with them – stiff cardboard boxes, about two-foot square and three-foot long, with labels marked FRAGILE – HANDLE WITH CARE, in English, French and Greek.

'Funny sort of stuff to be exporting to Cyprus,' Rawcliff said, pretending to relax as they drew into the one-way system at the end of Vauxhall Bridge. 'Why not send them retsina and olive-oil?'

'It's too early for jokes, Rawcliff. Spare me the wit until we're airborne.' He turned under the sign towards the M20. There was still almost no traffic: just the occasional snorting juggernaut heading for the coast.

'You do this run often, Major?'

'Often enough. Customs people know my face, if that's what you mean. Why don't you put your head down and have a kip? I'll wake you in good time.'

12

At 8.15 that same morning Room Service rolled the trolley down to Suite 12: half a grapefruit, lightly boiled egg, French rolls and butter. As they knocked, the radio-alarm sounded from within: a breezy round-up of sport and traffic news, followed by an advertising jingle. But no answer to the door.

They rolled the trolley back to the lifts and waited until 8.30, when the desk clerk rang up to the suite. Again, no answer.

At 8.45 the floor manager was informed, and he arrived at the suite with a pass-key. Through the door he could hear the rushed words of a newscaster – oil prices up, further price increases on the way, three women executed in Iran. The manager knocked, knocked again, then called out, 'Mr Newby? Mr Newby – your breakfast and your alarm call!'

He waited thirty seconds, then opened the door. The room was tidy, except for an empty glass and a couple of gold-tipped cheroot stumps in an ashtray. He moved cautiously into the bedroom. Curtains undrawn, bed not slept in, although a set of men's clothes was folded over a chair.

The floor manager looked into the bathroom. He did not look long, but went out and summoned the hotel security officer.

Newby's plump white body lay in the bath; the cold water reached just above his black hairy arm-pits. His neck was twisted at an abrupt angle, as though he were trying to reach something under his left knee. The only trace of a struggle was the scum of soap embedded under the finger-nails of one hand, and in the small lump of jasmin-scented Roger Gallet soap floating in a melting mist under the green water.

Detective Superintendent Muncaster did not hear about the murder until just before lunch. He was back on duty at his ordinary desk, dealing with some inquiries involving the disappearance of a Post Office official who had last been seen taking his dog for a walk in the New Forest. The dog was now being cared for by the RSPCA.

Several of Muncaster's colleagues remarked afterwards that they had never seen the old fellow looking so low. He had seemed close to tears.

The Run-Up

1

The Hotel Lord Byron was a three-storey stone building which maintained a courtly charm behind its flaking façade. The vestibule, beyond a faded red-striped awning, had once been a watering-hole for the poorer class of tourist or itinerant scholar visiting the ruins of Kition and the mosque of Hala Sultan. But the Turkish invasion of 1974 had put an end to all that.

The front of the hotel was deserted except for two men at a table behind the awning over the terrace, drinking thimbles of muddy black coffee. One was Rawcliff. He sat rumpled, sore-eyed, barely refreshed by the tepid trickle from the shower in his room, his body still stiff after nearly ten hours' flying, including stopovers, in Ritchie's little Beachcraft Duke.

Since dawn that morning, on the misty airfield at Lydd, the journey had been smooth and uneventful – even suspiciously so. Ritchie was on familiar terms with the Lydd Customs officials, and Grant's eccentric cargo had been cleared with the minimum of formalities, before the two-hour flight to Paris.

But at Le Bourget there had been a delay, during which Ritchie consulted with some plain clothes men, as well as with French Customs, while Rawcliff and Grant were hustled off to eat a scrappy breakfast in the transit lounge. When they took off again, on the long leg down to Athens, Rawcliff saw that there were now only half a dozen boxes in the back, slightly larger than the others, though made of the same cardboard and printed with the same words, in three languages. Neither Grant nor Ritchie volunteered an explanation, and Rawcliff, heeding Grant's advice, decided not to press for one.

They had been cleared in transit through Athens, where they had stopped only to refuel, and had landed in mid-afternoon at the small airport at Nicosia, which, until the recent flare-up between the Turks and Greeks, had been used exclusively by diplomats and members of the UN Peace-Keeping Force. Civilian traffic had used Larnaca, in the south-east of the island; but following the latest troubles, Larnaca's International Airport had been abandoned, and the polyglot Force, mocked and embattled, their morale sapped by obstruction and frustration, had finally hauled down their pale blue flag and departed, in a state of high dudgeon and low farce, leaving the island's two ethnic groups, and their various armed militias, glaring at each other across what was still prettily called the 'Green Line' – a vague barrier that ran through the centre of Nicosia, fencing off the eastern part of the island, and which passed twelve miles north of Larnaca.

When the Beachcraft landed at Nicosia, Customs had again been prompt, almost servile: and Rawcliff guessed that their new cargo was not unexpected. The six boxes had been loaded on to a pick-up truck and driven down to Larnaca by Grant, while Ritchie and Rawcliff had followed in a Suzuki jeep.

Sensing that Ritchie might be more amenable to giving information, Rawcliff had asked half-jokingly what the hell they were doing importing exotic house-plants into Cyprus while engaged on a mercy-mission? And Ritchie had said something about a new-fangled aerial guidance-system – 'Computer stuff – right above my head, I'm afraid' – although Rawcliff suspected that Ritchie knew more than he was letting on. Rawcliff was becoming used to having nothing explained: he would just have to use his wits, to deduce and guess, picking up the odd hint or scrap of information as he went along.

At Larnaca he learnt that the full complement of the outfit appeared to be eight. This included the nurse, Jo; an American called Matt Nugent-Ross, who was apparently some sort of scientist and electronics expert; Mason's original contact, the former RAF pilot, Oswald Thurgood; and the Rhodesian mercenary called Sammy Ryderbeit. It was the latter who was now causing some racket upstairs, being in the throes of what sounded like erotically-tainted *delirium tremens*. Hardly a good portent for a pilot about to embark on a difficult, possibly dangerous mission.

Apart from Peters, who was in overall command, with Grant as Number Two – or so the man had claimed – the others fell into two categories. These seemed to imply social status rather than precise rank. While Peters, Grant, Ritchie, the American and Jo were staying at the town's only first-class hotel, the Sun Hall, the other three – Thurgood, Ryderbeit and Rawcliff – had been booked into this less salubrious establishment, the Lord Byron. The distinction was clearly deliberate, since both these hotels had rooms vacant; while most of the other hotels in town were closed.

Rawcliff's companion at the table in the Lord Byron vestibule was ex-Flight-Lieutenant Oswald Thurgood. A tall, awkward-looking man with a stiff oblong face, clipped moustache and oily hair scraped back from his forehead, he had pale bulging eyes that suggested to Rawcliff a possible thyroid condition. The lower half of the man's face was raw with 'barber's rash'. He glanced down, restlessly round the terrace and through the door to the restaurant at the back where vats of tepid mutton-fat simmered over charcoal grates. The hotel smelt of ripe green peppers and Turkish tobacco and the bitter-sweet scent of ouzo; the air heavy, full of the murmur of flies, the howl of traffic from the street.

'Taki!' Thurgood shouted.

A stocky unshaven man came out, wiping his hands on an apron. His manner was smiling, ingratiating. His two English guests had introduced themselves to him as members of the International Red Cross – a position of obvious importance, which the Cypriot had no cause to question.

But the little man was no fool. Nothing happened in Larnaca without his hearing about it; and he had at once associated his distinguished clients with the two ships which had mysteriously put into Larnaca a week ago, and had been unloaded at night – not at the port, but on a stretch of beach opposite the now derelict International Airfield. Taki had a friend in the Harbour Police who had told him that the cargoes – pieces of giant American transport planes – had been ferried ashore on huge rafts, then pulled up the beach on trailers and stored in the airport's empty hangars.

As he now approached the two men's table, there came a series of thumps from above, followed by a muffled crash. The little man paused, with a pious smile, pretending to ignore the sounds from above. His third foreign guest, Sammy Ryderbeit, also worked for the International Red Cross, and had registered into the hotel with a Luxembourg passport. Having never met anyone before from the Duchy of Luxembourg, Taki had again taken the Rhodesian's credentials for granted. He also liked Monsieur Ryderbeit.

The man had arrived at the hotel before the other two, and he and Taki had spent the first night drinking the Rhodesian's duty-free whisky. And because Taki was a generous host, with a broad mind and sense of humour, he had been prepared to endure Ryderbeit while the man continued to drink all through the following day and the next night. This was the afternoon of the second day and now the hotel was being increasingly shaken by roarings and crashings from the third floor, punctuated by yells for more ouzo. Taki had obliged, not least because he was becoming a little nervous of Monsieur Ryderbeit. At the same time he was worried because the man's behaviour was upsetting his second client, the Englishman, Thurgood. As a good proprietor, Taki wanted all his guests to be happy.

He had stopped in front of their table and bowed, with his fingertips pressed together. 'Please, gentlemen?'

Thurgood said, 'If Mr Ryderbeit won't be quiet, there's going to be trouble. Savvy?'

The little man rolled his eyes upwards, as though in prayer. 'What can I do? He is drunk.'

'I know he's drunk – don't take me for a bloody fool. So stop sending him up your filthy ouzo!' Thurgood had an abrasive voice, and his natural accent was uncertain, slewing somewhere between Bromley and Birmingham. As he spoke, his hand clenched round his coffee cup until his knuckles turned white. Rawcliff also noticed a tiny nerve plucking at the corner of the man's eye. He had decided that he did not like ex-Flight-Lieutenant Thurgood.

Taki shrugged dramatically, with a gesture of infinite despair. 'But please, I send him no drink, he threatens to kill me!'

'A member of the Red Cross threatening to kill you?' Thurgood laughed: a harsh mirthless laugh, like a dog barking. 'You should be ashamed of yourself. Now fuck off. And don't send him up anything more to drink, or you'll have me to reckon with. Okay?'

'Okay, okay.' Taki glanced hopefully at Rawcliff.

'Bring me a beer, please,' Rawcliff said. He waited until Taki was gone, then turned back to Thurgood. 'By the sound of him, it isn't ouzo he needs. It's a girl. Can't Taki find him some local tart, just to keep him quiet?'

'You serious?' Thurgood's bulging eyes had brightened – a momentary gleam of the Cromwellian axe.

'Just an idea – to avoid trouble.'

'You only avoid trouble by maintaining discipline. And strict security. You don't get that by turning the place into a bloody whore-house! This isn't a bean-feast we're on, y'know.' Thurgood ran a finger down his blood-prickly jawline. 'How much have they told you, Rawcliff?'

'Just that we'll be flying solo in C-130s. Carrying relief-supplies, apparently. Can you enlighten me further?'

'I cannot. I do as I'm told – and I should do the same, if I were you.' He paused; and Rawcliff was relieved to see the twitching of his eye had ceased. 'I just know that the planes were crated out in parts. They're being reassembled now by some of the ground-staff – locals who were laid off when the airport was closed. The work should be finished by tomorrow night. Our first job's going to be to check our own aircraft bloody thoroughly. I don't trust these wog mechanics further than I can spit. You got an engineer's certificate, by the way?'

'No. But I know about aeroplanes.'

Thurgood stared at him, his fingers beginning to drum on the table. 'You said you were on civil? Viscounts, eh? Well, you won't find this job quite so cushy!' – then he broke off, staring above Rawcliff's shoulder.

A very tall, thin man with lank hair was standing beside

131

the table. He had appeared cat-like, soundlessly. His smooth, hooked face was the colour of polished ivory. He was dressed in olive-green battle-fatigues and rubber-soled canvas jungle-boots, a red cross was stitched on to one shoulder, and across his left buttoned-down lapel was the embroidered name, in black on yellow: SAMUEL D. RYDERBEIT.

'Afternoon children!'

He stood swaying slightly, and steadied himself against the edge of the table with a slender hand, as smooth as his face.

'That lovely bitch Jo hasn't been prowling round here, wetting her lovely knickers with lust for me? Some hope! That girl's got lock-jaw in the wrong place.' He slipped into the chair between them and leered at Rawcliff.

'So you're the new boy? I'm Sammy. Excuse my manners, but I've been drinking. Pissed as a snake.' He jerked his head round and yelled, 'Taki, you snotty-nosed runt, bring me some coffee!' He turned back, with a smile of evil charm. 'Are you a little confused by me, soldier? A White African Jew flying as one o' the team? Don't worry!' He gave him a painful slap on the shoulder, while Thurgood just glared. For a man who had apparently been on an extended bender Ryderbeit seemed to have recovered remarkably quickly.

'It's not that I'm big-headed,' he went on: 'Just that I never met anyone that's better than me. You want my bumf? I learned my flying down in Rhodesia, in the old days, before they started calling the place Fucking-Zimbabwe and selling out the munts. Married a couple of rich bitches and their daddies supplied me with more or less any plane I wanted.

'I flew up in the Congo during the fun – tree-hopping, picking the munts off with a .44 Magnum. That's another advantage I've got over the rest of you bastards – even over the good Grant. I can shoot. Given the right toy, I can hit a man in the head at a mile. I can shoot a moving snake across a room.' He grinned, as Taki shuffled over with more coffee.

Ryderbeit now turned to Thurgood. 'Not like Oswald

here, eh? Oswald's a special case. He's an old Raffie, kicked out for being a bit of a nutter. Gets these headaches and starts behaving funny. Don't worry, I've seen the record. I'm privileged. Still, Oswald, they say you're very good at twiddling the knobs of a radio. Bit of an Einstein, eh?'

He drank what was left of his ouzo and went on, 'No radio in my day – flying a Piper across the Bush. I used a road-map. Could put that little bird-dog down in the main street of E'ville – Lumumbashi, to you heathen souls. Used to park right outside my favourite bar.

'Trouble with you RAF and civvy types, you fly by the book. Well, as far as Samuel David Ryderbeit is concerned, the book's for the birds. Takes the edge off the game. I tell you, I've never flown drunk – and I've never flown entirely sober either. I like to get up to a certain level, and then pace myself. What would your BEA masters say about that?' he added, to Rawcliff.

Thurgood replied, with malign satisfaction, 'They chucked him out.'

'Yeah?'

'I'd had a couple of drinks and I was unlucky,' Rawcliff said, 'Only I wasn't flying to the Congo – just the Costa del Sol.'

Ryderbeit slapped him again on the shoulder. 'That's the kind o' language I like to hear, soldier! I like you. You've got a good open face, though it looks like it's taken a few knocks in its time. Now look at friend Oswald here. Oswald's got a face like a smoked ham. Getting a laugh out of him's like trying to get a drink down in Saudi!'

Rawcliff saw that the nerve was quivering again beside Thurgood's eye.

'Ryderbeit, I've had my belly-full of you. I can take so much, and no more.'

'Flight-Lieutenant, I am not detaining you,' Ryderbeit said, tilting his chair perilously far back and raising his empty glass. 'You have the freedom of your own room, Oswald. Why not go thither and contemplate thy navel?'

Thurgood stood up, and without even a nod at Rawcliff, strode towards the door, up into the hotel.

'That man's a ratbag,' Ryderbeit said, bringing his chair forward again. 'And a nasty ratbag too. A little birdie whispered to me that he kills people. People who step out of line.' He paused, picking his teeth. 'How did you get into this, soldier?'

'Almost by mistake – or at least, by false pretences.' He told his story to Ryderbeit, who listened thoughtfully. Except for a faint orange glare at the corner of his eyes, the Rhodesian might have been as sober as Rawcliff.

'Playing it a bit wild, weren't you, soldier?'

'Meaning what?' Rawcliff looked at him with feigned innocence.

'Somebody – I can't tell you who – has got a lot at stake in this business. And I don't just mean money, although there's plenty of that too. The people who've been hired are the sort who don't ask questions. The whole business was lined up, ready to go, when the sixth member of the team didn't like the temperature of the water. A Frenchman – oldish chap, Air France captain, retired. Too much of the old book again – seems he started worrying about his pension and whether he'd ever see his grandchildren again.'

'What happened to him?'

'Swimming accident, I believe. He and Oswald Thurgood and Mr Peters went swimming at a little place called St Valérie – on the Somme Estuary. Mud-flats and quicksands. Death through misadventure, all signed and witnessed.'

'But not by you?'

'I was too busy down in Le Havre, helping to load the planes. So the bosses had to look for a new sixth recruit. Third time lucky, it seems?'

Rawcliff nodded. 'The second man got killed a couple of days ago by a hit-and-run driver. Pretty convenient, I'd say.'

'Ah, we live dangerously. Come on, let's get out of this pit and go somewhere we can drink in peace. Peters may come sniffing round, and I'm not feeling sociable.'

The café was little more than a hole in a ruined wall, with a beaded curtain and wooden chairs outside, where rows of old men with white crewcuts sat propped up on sticks, staring at nothing. At the end of the row was a tall, much younger man with dark glasses and a floppy sun-hat, sitting under an ancient image of the Madonna and Child, and a washed-out colour photograph of the late Archbishop Makarios.

Ryderbeit gave him an extravagant salute. 'Hail, magician!' He turned to Rawcliff, 'Meet our scientist and wonder-boy from across the Atlantic, Matt Nugent-Ross.' The American half-stood up, with a slight bow, and shook hands, while Ryderbeit went on, 'Matt, this is the last of the heroes – another bloody Brit called Rawcliff.'

At the sight of Ryderbeit's Red Cross shoulder-flash, a couple of old men nearest them touched their foreheads and moved away, making room for them. Ryderbeit sprawled on his chair, took an aluminium tube from his flap-down breast pocket, tapped out a long cigar, bit the end off and spat the leaf into the dust at his feet.

The proprietor, who might have been Taki's twin brother, took an order for two beers. The American Nugent-Ross was drinking local lemonade. Ryderbeit had lit his cigar, exhaling the smoke luxuriously. His eyes, raw with the exertions of the past thirty-six hours, swivelled between the two of them, settling on Rawcliff. 'Soldier-boy here's rather a classy type of pilot. Used to jetting the plebs down to Majorca. Fasten your seat belts and extinguish cigarettes, this is your Captain speaking – all nice and posh, eh, with bits of scrambled egg on your cap and shoulders, and those lovely hostesses all sighing with expectation.

The proprietor brought them out two glasses of thin beer, half of which was a watery froth. Ryderbeit blew his off and drank thirstily. 'I suppose you still got your licence?'

'You want to see it?' Rawcliff was tired and losing patience with Ryderbeit. Judith had taunted him with almost exactly the same words, about hostesses, only a few days ago.

'A CAA licence? You can wipe your arse on it. A C-130 Hercules needs a lot more careful handling than one of your swish jets. At least, it's going to on this operation! No luxuries on this one, soldier. And our masters have decreed

135

that there's not even time for test-flights. No radar, no proper airstrip. It'll be flying solo, either over unfriendly territory, or so low we won't even be able to bale out. Fortunately, the Hercules is one of the best planes ever built. And ours are veterans, retired.'

Ryderbeit turned to the American, who sat quietly sipping his lemonade. He had tired, finely-cut features, his clothes casual and expensive. Ryderbeit clapped him on the back.

'No such problems for the magician, eh! Matt's the boy who stays on the ground and doesn't take any risks. Not that I reproach you, sir! You're the one that's helped to set the whole thing up this end. Speaks fluent Greek and knows the right contacts, the right palms to cross with the right amount of silver.' He had turned, his hand still on the American's shoulder, leering again at Rawcliff.

'Besides, I don't call him the magician for nothing! Matt here is a cut above us mere mortals who drive planes. He specializes in the toys of the future – computers, robots, automatic guidance-systems –'

'Take it easy, Sammy.' Nugent-Ross had removed his dark glasses and was frowning slightly. 'Not that I have reason to distrust Mr Rawcliff here, but no good pretending we haven't got a security problem.'

'On a routine mercy-mission?' Rawcliff said lightly.

Ryderbeit drew on his cigar. 'Is that your British sense of irony, soldier? Working for the Red Cross is about the nearest I've ever got to dressing up as a nun!'

Only the American laughed. Rawcliff said, 'What exactly *is* the security problem?'

Ryderbeit leant forward, until Rawcliff could smell the sour flavour of aniseed on his breath. 'This is an island. And all islands are small. People can be bribed to keep their mouths shut, but they still talk. It's also close to the Middle East. It's used for what they call a "listening-post" – and by all sorts of people. Not just the Turks and the Greeks. You Brits have still got three airbases here – two small ones just up the road, and a big one at Akotiri, along the coast. Pretty convenient, for the casual over-flight.'

'Then if there's a security problem,' Rawcliff said, 'it

seems bloody stupid to pick Larnaca! Or Cyprus, at all. There must be plenty of disused airbases around this part of the Mediterranean – on the Greek Isles, for instance – or in North Africa?'

Ryderbeit was grinning. 'Sure. Or maybe somebody's not worried? Maybe it's just the odd prying local they want to keep out? Or *in* – in the case of the ground-crews. Or there again, maybe it's just to make Mister Peters feel happy and important?' He downed his beer and called for another.

'All right,' Rawcliff said. 'So perhaps we don't have a security problem, after all?' He glanced at Nugent-Ross, who was peering into his lemonade; he did not look entirely happy. 'And the mercy-mission's obviously a blind. Six free-lance contract-pilots, each hired for fifty thousand quid, tax-free, to fly six clapped-out Hercules. Solo, at low levels, with a cargo of relief supplies – destination unknown. No pilot gets paid that sort of money for a milk-run. Don't worry, I'm as greedy as the next man. But if it *is* a blind, what's that girl doing out here? – Jo, I think she's called?'

Ryderbeit's eyes flickered quickly towards the American, who looked away. 'Ah, our benighted nurse! Better ask Matt all about her – he found her, while she was working out here for some do-gooding organization. Go on, ask him! You're not sensitive, are you, Matt?'

'She's on the level, Mr Rawcliff. She's a sensible kid, competent and well-trained. An experienced nurse is what you'd expect on a relief operation.' He had a soft pleasant voice – East Coast, Rawcliff guessed – almost English – with the leisurely intonation of the rich, or at least of one who has been brought up with all the comforts of the rich. Only his eyes betrayed him – sad weak eyes, with a watery hint of dissipation.

'Funny about that girl,' said Ryderbeit. 'When I first clapped eyes on her I said to myself, Sammy, this one's going to be as easy as picking an apple off a tree. Shake it and the whole fucking lot'll come down! Matt doesn't mind – do you, Matt? Just good friends, as they say.' He blew smoke into the still air. 'I tried my deft hand at her, and nearly got it bitten off. All women are either a mystery or they're trouble.'

Matt Nugent-Ross had finished his lemonade and stood up. 'I'll be getting along. It's been a pleasure to meet you, Mr Rawcliff.'

The other two sat listening to the smack of dominoes and the click of cards from behind the bead-curtain. Ryderbeit nodded towards the American as he strolled away down the dusty street.

'Got a few problems, that boy. The Demon Drink, I'd guess. Educated bastard, good background, come down in the world. What used to be called a "remittance man".'

'What about the others? Peters, for example?'

'A killer. Real professional. You don't mess around with men like friend Peters.'

'And Ritchie? What's so special about him that puts him in the officer-gentleman league staying up at the big hotel?'

'Well, he'a got that nice little plane of his. Touch of class, to impress the locals.'

'That can't be the only reason,' said Rawcliff. 'Five seats, including the pilot – and six, if we crowded it. Easy for landing and take-off, and a decent range. Very handy for a getaway.'

Ryderbeit gave him a crooked stare. 'Rather jumping to conclusions, aren't we, soldier?'

Rawcliff put down what was left of his beer; there was a fly floating in it. 'What about Major Grant?'

'Hell, you've been flying with him all day. You ought to know. I only got it on hearsay.'

'He wasn't letting on much,' said Rawcliff. 'Spent most of his time pulling rank on me. But I gather he was a war hero in Korea. Won the Military Cross holding off a couple of thousand Chinks with one tank, until his guns couldn't fire any more because the bodies were packed up so thick over the turret. And how it was so cold that the anti-freeze went solid in their vehicles, and the troops had to pee in their uniform or their equipment dropped off with frost-bite.'

'Did he say how he learned to fly?'

'Not exactly. Hinted that he was drafted into some hush-hush unit that flew up over the Chinese lines – even flew a few sorties into China itself, so he said. But I got the impression that there were a few gaps in his life that he was keeping to himself. Didn't explain how a gallant Major in the British Army comes to be running a flower-stall at Covent Garden Market.'

'England's greatness,' Ryderbeit said; he took out a fresh cigar.

'That just leaves you,' said Rawcliff. 'You're from Rhodesia?'

'Not any more.' Ryderbeit sat squinting at him through the smoke. 'I got run out of Africa a long time ago. I got run out of a lot of places. Now I'm the wandering Jew – with a nice Luxembourg passport to help me on my way. Not that I don't sympathize with those poor bloody whites in Africa. I haven't much time for blacks or Arabs. In a few years they'll be crawling all over us like lice, calling all the shots. Unless someone stands up and stops them.

'I'll be straight with you, soldier. But this isn't to be shouted from the roof-tops. I've worked a few rackets in my time, like hi-jacking a plane-load of US greens out of South-East Asia. And I always worked for the same man. French bastard called Pol. Fattest man I ever saw – fat and greedy, and cunning with it. I don't like him – don't suppose anyone likes him – but I admire him. Like all high-class gangsters, he has a technique. Distinguishing mark, if you like. I spent a long time on the Veld. I got a nose for these things. And this operation's got Pol's mark stamped all over it.'

'Meaning what?'

'With Charlie Pol it could mean anything. But the man's got a certain sense of humour. Bringing succour to starving women and children, as a front so he can grow even fatter on his various Swiss bank accounts, is just the kind of thing that would amuse him.' He picked a flake of tobacco off his lip. 'But you keep all this to yourself, Rawcliff.'

'And you trust this man Pol?'

Ryderbeit hunched his shoulders. 'As I said, I've played some funny games, but I've always played by the odds. I don't know about you, soldier, but I look after Number One. If it comes to a showdown, I'll settle accounts with Pol personally. And what I'll do to him isn't fit to be heard in decent company – and he knows it.'

They sat for a long time in silence. Rawcliff sipped his second beer and tried to compose in his mind a telegram to Judith. He didn't trust himself with the telephone, even if he could get through without the others knowing. The telephone was a brutish instrument, both too intimate and too impersonal; and a letter would be too slow, as well as too demanding. Anyway, what did he have to tell her? That the Red Cross mission was all in the interests of humanity, and that the rest of the team consisted of a White African Jew who never flew sober; a professional killer; a bum Major; an ex-RAF psychopath; an American drop-out; and a single girl who was alleged to be a nurse. Jim Ritchie was the only one who lent any possible respectability to the gang.

He said at last, 'Look, Sammy. At some stage we're going to have to be told what this is all about.'

'You mean, Pol removing his veils one by one? And stripping off at the last moment? Holy Moses, what a horrible thought! No, soldier. He'll either keep us in the dark, or con us right up to the end. And one thing I am certain of – whatever that end is, it's going to be dangerous and it's going to be bloody. Bloody dangerous and bloody bloody. And I also wouldn't be surprised if it hasn't got something to do with politics – which in Pol's case means dirty politics.' He flicked his dead cigar into the street, stood up and left some money on the table.

'One last thing, soldier. I haven't talked to you and you haven't listened. Okay? Now let's get back to that fleapit and eat some of Taki's filthy food. I don't fancy going up to the Sun Hall – Peters is a flat-arse, he doesn't approve of pilots drinking.'

2

'I think we might start with the salmon soufflé,' Pol said, lifting his broad bib to dab his cheeks and forehead, careful not to disarrange the lick of hair that curled down over one eye, from an otherwise bald egg-shaped head. 'And I suggest a little champagne.'

The early evening was cool, with the french windows of the old house closed against the rolling woodlands of the Upper Rhine, in the crooked gabled town of Illhäusern, a few miles from the German border.

His guest looked unimpressed, despite Pol's claims that this was one of the best restaurants in France, and possibly in the world. He was a spruce, squat man with square-cropped silver hair and thick spectacles, behind which his eyes registered no expression. Pol had noticed, with some contempt, that his suit was of a cheap artificial fibre, with a dog-toothed check *à l'Anglais,* while his shirt looked as though it had been boiled and his shoes had thick rubber soles. A dreary man, but an important one. Charles Pol would just have to make the best of the evening: the food and wine would at least compensate for the conversation.

'Then would you prefer to remain with fish? *Goujonettes de sole et de homard à la nage?* Or perhaps the *noisette de chevreuil St-Hubert?* Both are recommended.'

'It is your choice,' his guest said sullenly. 'I am not experienced in French food.'

The restaurant was not large and all the tables were filled; but from their position by the windows there was no danger of the two men being overheard. Pol had attracted a few curious glances – his wobbling elephantine bulk squeezed into a voluminous suit of slub silk which betrayed patches of sweat under the armpits: his huge face pink and damp, with a little goatee-beard which he fondled as he consulted the menu with benign expectation.

He made the order punctiliously, as though supervising

some delicate technical operation. 'So you are not used to eating in our fine restaurants?' he said cheerfully, when the waiter had gone.

'I am not a gourmet. Food does not interest me. Let us concentrate on more immediate matters. What is the progress situation?'

'Under control. There have been a few minor problems, but they have been resolved.'

'What problems?'

Pol made a vague gesture with his fat pink hand. 'A couple of our recruits were not entirely satisfactory. One of them – a compatriot of mine – had a swimming accident, and another, an Englishman, was killed by a car. I also regret the gentleman whom you know as Monsieur Rebot, the Belgian, died in his bath in London.

'That I know. I read about it in your newspapers. Your methods are very drastic, Monsieur Pol.'

'They are merely methods to fit the situation. I am sure that you, in your position, will appreciate that?' Pol beamed at his guest with a cherry-lipped smile, as the waiter placed before them the salmon soufflé and poured two tulip glasses of very old champagne.

'Have there been any troubles with the police?' his guest asked.

Pol gave a shrug that looked as though it might split the seams of his suit. 'The usual inquiries. But these things take time. More time than we intend to allow them – the authorities, I mean.' There was a long pause, during which he concentrated entirely on his food.

'Is the shopping list complete?' his guest said at last.

'All except for the mining equipment. That is to say, the purchase has been made and cleared, and the ship has already left Marseilles, bound for the island of La Réunion in the Indian Ocean. There is, as you will remember my telling you, some very lucrative open-cast basalt mining there. There are also rumours of uranium deposits – which also might interest you?'

'I'm only interested in the matter at hand. The ship is cleared to pass through Suez?'

'Of course. With a stop at Cyprus.'

'And what are your arrangements with the Cypriot authorities?'

Pol gave him a lewd wink. 'My friend, the Greek Cypriots concentrate on nothing but their hatred for the Turks. What does not concern the Turks, does not concern them. They are blind to the international situation.'

'That is a bold assumption.'

'It is nevertheless a correct one. You know me well enough by reputation – that I never gamble unless the odds are safely on my side.'

'I still need to be satisfied that security is absolute.'

'Nothing is absolute, my friend. Except, perhaps, eternity – and even that has been questioned by Einstein.' He bit into a succulent lump of lobster.

'This is no time to philosophize,' his guest said abruptly. 'What is the bill?'

Pol wiped his mouth and drank some champagne. 'Fifteen million dollars.'

'It is too high. I am authorized to go no further than twelve million.'

'And I am not prepared to argue. I know the situation far better that your people do. But they do know that the project can go no further without me – not at this stage. I have already had heavy expenses myself – an initial outlay of more than three million dollars on the aircraft alone. I will not go into tedious detail, but even the medical supplies from Switzerland have not been cheap. Apart from the fees for the pilots, there are all kinds of sundries – like a brand-new Mercedes Benz for the Larnaca Chief of Police, for instance.'

'So your Cypriot friends are interested in more, after all, than just the Turks?' his guest observed sourly.

Pol sat back with a broad gesture, 'It is a question of goodwill, my friend. One must never forget goodwill. And then there are the ships' fees, paying off the masters and crew, the salaries for the ground-staff at Larnaca Airport – at much-inflated rates.'

'Twelve million, monsieur. That is my limit.'

'Thirteen million. After all, what is a million between friends, when we may be changing the history of the world?'

'You will be making a personal profit of several million dollars.'

'*Eh bien?*' Pol's expression was even jovial, frivolous 'Such a sum is a bagatelle! If I were to have invested the money so far in building hotels on the Côte d'Azur, I could have doubled my profits – trebled them perhaps. And yet your people send you to squabble over a few million!'

'Thirteen million, then. But in return, I hope you will remember our last conversation. If there is any breach of security, any suggestion of cheating or treachery, you will get a bullet in your head. That at least would be cheap.'

Pol giggled and tapped the short sweaty hairs at the back of his neck. 'Ah, my friend, you forget that I have a hard head! But now, let us look forward to the venison.'

3

At 7.30 sharp next morning Guy Grant drove up to the front of the Lord Byron Hotel in an open pick-up truck. He was wearing glasses with mirror lenses and a belted lightweight tropical suit. He allowed Rawcliff to sit in the front with him, while Thurgood and Sammy Ryderbeit rode in the back.

Rawcliff was not in the mood for conversation. He sat back and looked out at the shabby, dusty yellow street, at the low-roofed buildings, the half-derelict shopfronts. None of the garrulous sun-hatted vulgarity of the usual Greek Mediterranean sea-resort – the Turkish Army had put an end to all that, drawn up twelve miles to the north. This was the kind of place where nobody would worry too much, as long as the price was right. Even the police on occasional point-duty looked indolent and in need of a shave.

The town soon gave way to monotonous scrub sprinkled with olive trees and tiny white houses and herds of wretched-looking goats. What had once been the main road out to the International Airport was now shrunk and cracked, bitten into at the edges by weeds and the winter rains. Ahead lay the Salt Flats, already covered by a dull haze.

The sea was on their left, and on their right the Salt Lake came into view, murky-white like curdled milk. They were driving into the neck of a thin peninsula; and Rawcliff saw approaching the high cantilevered wire fence marking the perimeter of the moribund International Airport. In the far distance, along the margin of the lake, lay the hangars and terminal buildings. Then came a gate in the fence, secured by double padlocks. A rusty sign said in Greek and English: PROPERTY OF THE GOVERNMENT OF CYPRUS. ENTRY FORBIDDEN TO ALL UNAUTHORIZED PERSONNEL.

Grant got out and picked up a field-telephone attached to a wire that trailed away into the distance. He said something, then hung up and strolled round to Rawcliff's window, which was closed against the dust. Rawcliff opened his door a little to let in some air. Even outside it was hot and stagnant.

He nodded up at the sign. 'Does "Government Property" include us?'

'For the moment, yes. We're members of the International Red Cross, remember.' Grant had climbed back in and sat waiting, with the engine idling.

'You're not fooled by all this Red Cross stuff, are you, Major?'

Grant turned to him, his heavy face damp with sweat; and Rawcliff saw his own features reflected in the man's mirror-lenses, distorted like two faces seen in a pair of spoons. 'Don't play the dummy with me, Rawcliff. We're being paid to carry out orders, not to question them. "Our's not to reason why", as the poet said.'

Rawcliff nodded. ' "Our's but to do and die." Hardly the happiest quotation.'

Grant said nothing. Across the shimmering Salt Flats ahead they could see a blur of dust approaching. After a moment Rawcliff recognized the Suzuki jeep in which Ritchie had driven him down from Nicosia. It came up fast and stopped with a four-wheeled skid. Peters got out.

Rawcliff hadn't seen him since their encounter in that grubby little cinema at the back of the dirty-bookshop in Soho. The man was now wearing denim overalls, and his left foot bulged out in a white plaster. Round his neck was a flesh-coloured plastic brace which gave him the look of a full-sized Action Man doll, his blank features shielded by dark glasses that hid his still swollen and black eyes from when Rawcliff had butted him on the bridge of the nose.

He hobbled up to the gate, snapped open the two locks with a key, then turned to face Rawcliff – a long stare from behind the dark glasses that might have meant anything. Rawcliff heard Grant chuckle beside him, 'No love lost between you two, eh? Rather you than me, old bean!'

Rawcliff made no comment. They waited until Peters had relocked the gates and backed the jeep round, then began to follow it out across the field, towards one of the hangars, which was at some distance from the terminal buildings. Rawcliff could just make out a Red Cross flag hanging limply from the control-tower, next to a flaccid wind-sock.

Rawcliff now saw what Grant had meant about the difficulties of take-off. Down the centre of the peninsula lay the main runway, like an enormous strip of masking tape stretched across the Salt Flats, its surface already humped and buckled and pot-holed with neglect. To add to which some greedy entrepreneur had removed all the runway lights, all warning beacons, as well as stripping up the miles of electric cable that are the nerves of a modern airport. In their place, half-way down the runway, stood two rows of white-painted oil-drums. Rawcliff judged the distance between them to be barely three hundred yards. With the sea on one side, the lake on the other. And there'd be no help from the control-tower. No radar, not even radio. Those would have been the first to be looted.

Grant nodded ahead. 'The local ground-staff filled in the worst bits, but there's subsidence half-way down. We've got exactly one thousand and eleven feet – which is just over the minimum the Lockheed handbook gives. For landing we bump down and use everything we've got – flaps, air-brakes, reverse screws, and a lot of muscle. If you scrape an engine or a tyre you go into the drink.'

Like Gibraltar, Rawcliff thought: only without a planeload of screaming tourists. At least it would be something to get the adrenalin going.

Ahead there was a stirring like bees in the dark mouth of the hangar, where he could just make out, against the raw sunlight, the huge shapes of fuselages and wings and high triangular tailpieces.

Jim Ritchie came out to meet them. His smile showed through a mask of black grease as he wiped his hands on his overalls. 'Ready for a long day's work?' he shouted, as the two vehicles drew up outside the hangar. 'We've got three of them ready for inspection. But it's slow work. As I warned you, the electricals are going to be our big headache.'

'That's Nugent-Ross's job. And Flight-Lieutenant Thurgood deals with the radios,' said Peters.

Ryderbeit and Thurgood had climbed out to join them – Ryderbeit's fatigues and black hair chalk-white with dust –while Matt Nugent-Ross came strolling out of the hangar towards them.

'Right!' Peters said, to the six of them lined up in front of him. 'You know the drill. Check your aircraft down to the last detail – your lives are going to depend on it. Op schedule is as follows. Fuel and supplies arrive by sea sometime early tomorrow morning. The ground-crews will help with the loading. And I want every man to keep his eyes open. Anyone seen nosing round the field, report to me. And when you're off-duty, you keep your mouths tight shut – these Greeks gossip like bloody women!'

He went on to detail each man to his aircraft, marked 1 to 6 in chalk on the tailpiece; then turned awkwardly on his injured foot. 'Now get to work.'

It was only when Rawcliff was inside the hangar, adjusting his eyes to the blue glare of the arc-lights, that he realized the full size of a Hercules C-130. The six long fat fuselages were drawn up in diagonal rows: almost windowless, except for the control-cabins: matt-grey, all markings painted out, with the swing-down loading-bays open under the massive tailpieces. Each aircraft nearly a hundred feet long, its high-wings appearing to sag under the weight of the four mighty 4,190 hp turbo-prop engines, and the two torpedo-shaped external fuel-tanks. A hulking great, ugly, sensible aircraft – no frills, no nonsense, providing you treated her right.

There were about forty Cypriot ground-crew in airport overalls, crawling over the three aircraft which were still incomplete. The hot oily air was shattered by the roar of fork-lift trucks, by excited shouted orders in Greek, as a wing was levered up into position.

As a professional pilot, Rawcliff was mildly reassured to see that the hangar seemed well-equipped. Besides the fork-lift trucks and heavy welding tools, there was the long-familiar sight of refuelling trucks, generators, pumps and ramps, elevators and hydraulic boosters – as well as a small fleet of Suzuki jeeps, belonging to the airport. All presumably hired from the local authorities for the duration.

He had also noticed, parked outside the hangar near the narrow beach, a number of yellow caterpillar tractors and long trailers with huge soft sand-tyres.

Rawcliff's plane was Number 3, next to Ryderbeit's. Both appeared complete, except for the empty outboard engine-housings. Ryderbeit grinned at him through his dust-caked lips. 'Not quite up to Heathrow! Anything worrying you?'

'Plenty. But that's what I'm being paid for. I'm just puzzled why the aircraft were brought in in bits. Why not fly them down from Germany in the first place? The Red Cross haven't got anything to hide.'

'You're green, soldier. Half a dozen of these big babies attract a lot of attention, what with overflight clearance across Switzerland, Italy, Greece, and most of the Eastern Med. Don't forget, this is a sensitive area – nice and close to the Lebanon and Israel. But most important, you forget the Turks. They've got their front-line just up the road, and the Turk doesn't give a snake's shit for the Red Cross. With six bloody Hercules landing under their noses, they wouldn't think twice. Greek-Cypriot military build-up, and they'd have their Army into the whole Larnaca area almost before we'd switched off the landing-lights! And the Turks don't fart about.'

'What about security? The British still have bases on Cyprus – one just north of here.'

'Raffies. Load of shit. Spend most of their time going to tea-dances and swapping wives.' He raised his arm in a salute, 'You just worry about that aircraft of yours. She's an old lady who's had a long life, and she's probably getting tired.'

Rawcliff turned and climbed the sloping tailvent of his Hercules. Besides the weary, meticulous task of checking and double-checking every control, searching for the tiniest fault, he also wanted to pause, be alone. Have time to think. Time to devise that telegram to Judith. The longer he left it, the more difficult it would be: and he knew that if he left it too late, it would take more than fifty thousand pounds to buy her back.

Yet what could he truthfully tell her, besides describing his unholy mob of colleagues? Tell her, perhaps, that he was preparing to fly a secret mission in a twenty-year-old aircraft that had been stripped down and was now being glued together again by a bunch of Cypriots on a derelict airfield that no sensible pilot would think of using, except in the most dire emergency?

At around noon Peters and Ritchie drove back into Larnaca in one of the Suzuki jeeps. As usual, they offered no explanation. Guy Grant was left in command – a role he clearly relished.

Although Rawcliff was relieved at the absence of Peters – however temporary – he soon found Grant hard to endure. The man seemed less interested in checking his aircraft than in asserting his authority to the full. He had assumed an almost theatrical demeanour of martinet – strutting, snapping, balling out the ground-crew, criticizing wherever possible, even insisting that the other three address him as 'Major' at all times. It was only with a measure of evident self-restraint that he did not insist on their saluting him.

At around 12.30 pm the field-telephone rang. Grant, who had been entrusted with a second set of keys to the gates, drove out to the perimeter wire. He was back a few moments later, followed by another of the jeeps. At the wheel sat a girl, her hair scooped up and fastened under a stiff little white bonnet.

Rawcliff scarcely recognized her, in her starched blue and white nurse's uniform, with narrow blue waist-band, dark stockings, sensible shoes. Grant looked slightly confused, as he escorted her from the jeep into the hangar.

The two of them paused, close to where Rawcliff was working messily under the open cowlings of one of the massive engines. She was prettier than he remembered her – almost demure now, in her uniform, as she stood shielding her eyes against the naked inspection-light.

He climbed down the ladder, wiping his hands on a rag, and heard her laugh ripple above the grinding roar of machinery. 'Mr Rawcliff, isn't it? You're the man with the bump on his head?'

He instinctively touched his oil-smeared face and nodded. Grant said stiffly, 'Mr Rawcliff, this is Miss Shelby. I believe you've met?'

'I gave him a glass of brandy when he wasn't feeling very well.'

Grant was standing rigidly to attention. 'Everything in order, Rawcliff?'

At that moment Matt Nugent-Ross appeared. 'I've got to check the electricals on this one, Major.'

Jo laughed. 'Electricals – that sounds awfully bad!'

Grant was frowning. 'Right, get to work, both of you. We've got a schedule!'

Rawcliff began to turn as Jo said, 'I'd like to have a look inside. It's the first time I've seen one of these monsters.'

Grant hesitated. 'I don't want you getting in the way, Miss Shelby. It's also extremely dirty in there.'

'Don't worry, I've got a spare uniform!'

'It's okay by me, Major,' said Nugent-Ross, 'I'll keep an eye on her. And I've got to start somewhere – might as well be this one.'

Grant watched scowling, as Rawcliff led the way round to the back of the plane where the rear loading-ramp was still lowered. He went first, carrying the inspection-light on its long trailing cable.

The inside was a broad tunnel, smelling of hot metal and plastic and old leather, of hydraulic fluid, lingering kerosene fumes and sweat. Along the floor were two sets of rails, fixed at intervals with free-wheeling rollers, and the walls and ceiling were lagged with plastic-covered padding and hung with a mass of buckled straps and parachute-lines. Everything metal was scuffed and scraped and smeared with an oily grime that had become furry with dust. They picked their way up between the rails to the spacious control-cabin, with anti-glare window-panels on three sides. Above and below the front window were two wide batteries of dials and switches and levers, some of the dials almost indecipherable through the grease, while several panels were missing and bunches of coloured wiring spilled out like entrails.

Nugent-Ross settled down in one of the spacious seats and

reached for the battered flight handbook, issued by the USAF.

Jo stood gaping. 'I must say, it makes my old MGB look rather silly!'

'How does she seem to you?' Rawcliff asked the American.

'Well, she's no virgin, that's for sure. But Uncle Sam looks after his property pretty well. Your biggest danger's a broken connection, either when they were taken apart or reassembled.' He flicked a few switches, peered at the dials. 'Amps reading a bit low – you'll need a charge. Igniters seem okay.'

Jo had stepped over and ran a finger down Rawcliff's brow. 'Poor old bump-head! You were really asking for it, you know – taking on Peters. Still, everybody seems rather delighted!'

'Peters doesn't appear to be very popular?' said Rawcliff.

'He makes my flesh creep. He's so *inhuman*.'

Nugent-Ross turned to her. 'Look, Jo, I don't want to sound mean, but me and Mr Rawcliff have work to do. Why don't you just hop out and get yourself some coffee from one of the ground-crew?'

She turned quickly, and without a word, even a last glance at Rawcliff, walked back between the rails and down the ramp into the hangar.

'Seems a nice enough girl,' Rawcliff said, from the co-pilot's seat. 'What's in this for her?'

'Bread, I guess. And kicks. Mostly bread, plus as many kicks as she can get. Don't ask me. I gave up trying to figure out that kinda girl a long time ago. I guess the only consolation for guys like us is that one day girls like that get old and withered and finally put us out of our misery.'

'You sound bitter.'

'Just practical. I've got a job to do, like the rest of you. As for Jo, she comes along for the ride, and picks up a nice pay-cheque at the end of it.'

Rawcliff looked at him curiously, as the American went on checking the rows of switches of dials and buttons. 'And what's in it for you, Matt?'

'I told you – a job. And some money at the end of it. I'm just part o' the hired help that squares the local brass with the odd bribe, and is supposed to fix fuses and dud magnetoes, and a few other things. You've got a couple of blown fuses here, by the way.' He had taken out a little leather notebook with a tiny gold pen slipped into the spine, and made a quick jotting.

'What other things, Matt? Aerial guidance-systems for instance?'

The American flicked a switch and there was a dull humming noise from under the floor. 'You're mighty curious, friend. You ought to know the law around here. Like the military – the less you know, the better.'

'No harm in asking questions. Not if you don't want to answer them.'

'You been listening too much to that guy, Ryderbeit. What did he tell you about me?'

Rawcliff stared out through the tinted perspex, into the vivid confusion of the hangar. 'Nothing, except about you being some expert in computers and high-technology.'

'That guy talks too much. Maybe he thinks he's got a charmed life – unlike some of us.' He went on working with leisurely concentration while he spoke. 'Did he mention that I'd been to Princeton? And Oxford?' He gave a weak smile, still not looking at Rawcliff. 'I was the model student – the one voted most likely to succeed, and all that crap. Then I got thrown out. Stealing.' He twiddled some more knobs, pulled a lever. 'I got a passion for rare books. Had myself quite a collection, until the Dean of the Faculty dropped by for a drink and recognized some of his old tomes. Faulty connection here – I'll have to get that fixed, for sure!' He scribbled again in his little book.

'I got slung out of Oxford too. Oxford was nice – all those lovely cloisters. Trouble was, I had too much money. Spent most of it living high and fast up in London. Oxford didn't like it. They had a lot of funny old-fashioned ideas about scholastic discipline. So I went home and joined the Marines just in time for the Lebanon landing back in '58. The morning we went ashore I was smashed – woke up in the hospital ship and was rewarded with a Dishonourable Discharge.'

'That's fine,' said Rawcliff: 'You, Thurgood, Grant – all thrown out of the Services.'

'And how do you rate yourself, Mr Rawcliff? Are you another bum – another misfit trying to make a fast buck the dangerous way?'

Rawcliff's narrow Anglo-Saxon instincts closed in: he was not a man to bare his soul to anyone, except perhaps to Judith, and then only with painful remorse. He said slowly, 'If you want to put it that way. Like the rest of us I'm dispensable. I've got nothing to lose, except my wife and two-year-old son. Are you married, Matt?'

'Not any more.' As he spoke, Rawcliff saw the man's face assume a greenish pallor under the glow from the windows. He added, in a hushed voice, 'I'd better go fix those fuses, and that connection. Your lights and flaps are okay. But I'll check your undercarriage – you need just one sloppy mechanic round here and you can kiss us all goodbye.'

He had stood up, controlling his expression with visible effort, and held out a limp hand. 'It's been nice talking to you, friend' – and he started back down the body of the plane. 'If you have any problems, let me know. Technical ones, I mean.'

'Put that fucking cigar out!' Grant roared.

Ryderbeit removed the Havana slowly from his lips, spat delicately between his boots and laughed.

Guy Grant had stripped off his mirror glasses and his eyes held a small mean look. He was holding a clip-board, clasped like a swagger-stick under his arm. 'Right, Flight-Lieutenant.' Thurgood stepped forward, half to attention. His raw bony face was smeared with a congealed layer of dust and oil, like macabre make-up. 'You've checked the radio equipment?'

Thurgood nodded.

'You address me as Major, Fight-Lieutenant! Grant swung round. 'Nugent-Ross!'

'Major?'

'What's your progress?'

'Coming along, Major. Two out o' six. This isn't work you can hurry.'

Grant stood for a moment undecided, his mind working in a vacuum of officious authority. Then he rounded again on Ryderbeit, 'And if you light another match, I'll have your kneecap off!'

Ryderbeit took a languid step forward, then paused. They all looked up as the Suzuki jeep came driving back across the apron and slewed to a halt in front of the hangar. Jo was alone at the wheel. She had driven off only a few minutes earlier for the town. Guy Grant had complained that she was distracting the local labour-force, whose dark faces were now once again turned in sullen curiosity towards her.

She got out of the jeep, leaving the door open, and ran forward, stopping in front of Grant to catch her breath. 'There are some men at the gates.'

'What sort of men?'

'They look like soldiers. Very dirty, in uniform.'

Grant turned again to Nugent-Ross. 'Right, now's your chance to use your Greek. Get into the truck with me. Rawcliff, you look reasonably respectable' – he jabbed his thumb at the Suzuki – 'You go with Jo. If any questions are asked, you're a doctor. Ryderbeit, the rest of you, stay out of sight.'

Ryderbeit stood grinning, still holding his dead cigar.

Rawcliff began to walk over towards the Suzuki, and heard Jo hurrying up behind him. Once outside the hangar the heat hit them like an opened oven, the salt and sand and sea all merged in a shimmering dull glare. Jo climbed into the driving-seat beside him and kicked off her shoes.

'I'll be glad to get out of this uniform and have a swim,' she said, wrinkling her freckled nose.

They heard Grant, in the pick-up truck behind, start up with a roar and come careering round in a swath of dust that swept through Jo's open window, making her cough. 'The bastard! He's just doing it to show off.'

'What's the panic?'

'Peters has given strict orders that if anyone's seen near the wire, they're to be stopped and challenged. Grant's

155

obviously enjoying every minute of it – playing at soldiers again.'

'I suppose he realizes that security can be overdone? All it does is make people more suspicious.'

She had switched on the engine and they started off into the blinding wake of dust thrown up by Grant and Nugent-Ross in the pick-up truck, which was now leading.

'Perhaps they've got a right to be suspicious?' she said.

He looked at her carefully. 'What about you? Are you suspicious, Jo?'

'Should I be?'

'Oh, for Christ's sake, you're on the pay-roll, aren't you? And you're certainly deeper in than I am.'

She shrugged, grinding gears. 'I'm a member of the VSO – Voluntary Services Overseas. One of those nice do-gooders who try to help the underdeveloped countries.' There was a flat edge to her voice, with no perceptible irony, suggesting a deeper side to her character than Rawcliff had so far observed. 'I might ask you the same question,' she added.

'What? Am I suspicious? – or what am I doing here in the first place?'

'Both – although you don't look entirely the type. They pulled you in at the last minute, didn't they?'

'I pulled myself in. I've got a business in London that's going broke, and I want to end my days cultivating my garden, as Voltaire said. As for being suspicious, I suppose that's part of what we're paid for?'

'I suppose so. I'd say it was cheap at the price.' Her voice had become vague now, as she peered ahead through the dust.

'You're Jim Ritchie's girl, aren't you?'

'I'm nobody's girl. I met Matt while I was working out here. He was doing some business with a local shipping agent called Kyriades who has some tie-up with Jim Ritchie's air-taxi firm. So I more or less got drawn in – just came with the package, so to speak.'

'For how much?'

She gave him a crinkled sideways look. 'Enough. Enough to give a girl time to get her bearings.'

156

The faint outline of the perimeter fence was growing out of the fog of dust. Grant and Nugent-Ross, in the pick-up ahead, were slowing up towards the gate. Beyond, Rawcliff could just make out three men behind the wire.

'If there are any awkward questions, just hang back and let Nugent-Ross do the talking,' he said. 'As long as they get a glimpse of your uniform.'

'And as long as that bloody Major doesn't try to be a hero,' she said, drawing up beside the pick-up. Grant was climbing out, adjusting his mirror glasses.

The three men behind the wire wore dark dungarees with shoulder-flaps and belts of Army webbing. Two of them were lounging against the cantilevered posts, the third was squatting down in the dust, chewing the stub of a cigarette. They looked grubby and unshaven and very tough, with an air of mute hostility, showing no interest as Jo walked out and stood beside Matt.

'Who are they and what do they want?' Grant said.

To Rawcliff's untrained ear, Nugent-Ross' Greek sounded very fluent. The two men by the posts said nothing. The third straightened up and kicked his cigarette into the dust. He spoke quickly, abruptly, as though reciting something from memory.

There was a brief exchange, then Matt turned to Grant. 'They claim they're on contract to the airport. They're asking for employment here. Their spokesman claims he's a union official and has the right to see the men's working conditions.'

'Like hell he does. Does he know how much they're being paid?'

'I guess that's why they're here – to get a piece of the action.'

'Ask to see their ID cards.'

This time what sounded like an argument followed: the three men shrugged and talked at once, with their hands in their pockets. Their spokesman broke off and now began eyeing Jo with a snide glint.

Matt turned again to Grant, 'They say they'll show you their papers when you open the gates.'

Grant hesitated, then asked Jo for the spare bunch of keys which he had given her earlier. He undid the two locks and pulled the wire frame open. 'Tell them to get into the back of the truck.' He nodded to Jo and Rawcliff: 'All right, follow us.'

In the Suzuki jeep Jo said, 'There's something funny going on.'

'I don't know. Grant seems very keen to get them inside. I'd lay odds they're carrying guns.'

'Oh Christ.' She bit her lip. 'Are you sure?'

'Not without seeing them. But I don't suppose it's all that unusual out here. Since Independence there's been a lot of hardware floating around in Cyprus, and even more since the Turks invaded.'

The three men were now sitting in the back of the pick-up truck in front; then at the last moment Grant jumped down and came round to Rawcliff's side of the Suzuki. 'We're not going back to the hangar – not immediately. Just keep on my tail – and watch those boys out front.'

They had been going a couple of hundred yards, when Jo said, 'I've got a very handy monkey-wrench in the back. I'll get it out for you when we stop.'

It was nearly a mile to the hangars. But about halfway Grant turned left and began to lead the way out across the cracked, pock-marked apron towards the control tower and the abandoned terminal buildings. He stopped a few yards from the Arrivals entrance. Several panels in the plate-glass front were broken or missing, and the interior had a desolate appearance, chairs piled on tables, the ubiquitous portrait of Archbishop Makarios hanging askew on the wall.

Rawcliff watched Grant and Matt Nugent-Ross jump down from both sides of the pick-up cabin in front, before the three Cypriots in the back of the truck had time even to begin climbing over the tail-board. Jo led Rawcliff round to the rear of the Suzuki. The monkey-wrench lay with the tools and spare tyre. It was heavy and filthy, and she let Rawcliff handle it. He tucked it awkwardly under his jacket, with the screw-jaw pointing downwards.

He heard a crash in front, and saw Grant push one of the

Cypriots back against the closed tail-board of the pick-up. The other two had jumped down beside him and stood watching Grant warily.

'Tell them to stay just where they are,' Grant ordered Nugent-Ross, 'and let's see their papers.'

Rawcliff moved casually up beside the American, who again began speaking in Greek. The one who appeared to be their spokesman muttered something quickly to his two colleagues, then put his hand in to the long pocket of his baggy trousers. It came out, with a swift easy movement, holding a gun.

Heavy calibre: 9mm, Rawcliff thought; probably a Browning picked up during the Eoka days. Pretty useless at anything but close range: but if it hit you, it was lethal. No time to argue, to make fine moral judgements. Rawcliff swung the monkey-wrench out from under his jacket, and with a single flailing motion brought the screw-jaw down on the man's gun-wrist. He heard the bones splinter, and there was a sharp scream as the Browning clattered on to the concrete.

Grant stepped forward and kicked it neatly out of reach. In the same instant, as though the action were unfolding in slow motion, Rawcliff saw the second Cypriot grab for his pocket; and this time he swung the monkey-wrench round like a whip and caught him hard behind his left knee.

The man howled and collapsed backwards half under the tail of the truck. The third man had also got a gun out, and was already backing away. He snapped something in Greek.

Matt Nugent-Ross said calmly, 'Freeze, everyone, or he'll kill the lot of us.'

The man took another couple of steps backwards and spoke again, barely audible above the whimpering groans of his companions. 'He says he'll kill the girl first,' Matt said.

The gun was very steady, held at arm's length with both hands, pointing at Jo's belly. Another heavy calibre, Rawcliff thought: looked like a Walther PPK. Enough to blow a hole the size of a teacup out of a girl's back. Not the sort of gun hoodlums tout about unless they're showing off.

But then these men looked as though they were the sort who carried guns around like ball-point pens.

Grant stood back, thick and sweating, his face the colour of wet stone; and when he spoke, Rawcliff realized that he was terrified. His voice had a coarse, clogged sound, 'What does he want?'

Matt spoke again in Greek and the Cypriot answered, the gun still pointing at Jo's midriff.

'He wants Jo to step over in front of him. The rest of us are to get up into the truck.'

Jo began to walk forward. Rawcliff waited until she was barely three feet from the outstretched barrel of the gun. Matt was still standing tense and helpless, his watery eyes moving quickly from Rawcliff to Grant, then back again.

'Christ, he wouldn't shoot a nurse, would he?'

But even as the American spoke, Rawcliff let out a ferocious yell, to distract the Cypriot's attention: and at the same time made a fast diagonal swerve, since Jo's body was in direct line between himself and the gun. As he moved, he heard somewhere in the far distance a crack and saw the fat gun-barrel jerk away from Jo's belly. In the same instant the Cypriot gave an awkward lurch as though he had been kicked in the side, and something very odd happened to his face. It became blurred, like a smudged photograph, then his eye disappeared in a dark clotted mass, full of pulp and splinters of bone. He went over backwards, his mouth wide-open, and the gun gave a thundering roar, followed by a ringing sound of the bullet bouncing off the concrete apron. Then a harsh dead stillness. Even the whimpering of the other two had stopped.

Jo had turned, the knuckles of one hand pressed into her mouth, staring wildly at Rawcliff. 'What happened?'

She was answered by the sight of a tall, stooping figure racing towards them down the edges of the buildings from the hangar. Through the splintering light they could now make out his lank black hair and hooked profile, and in his hands a long sporting rifle with a telescopic lens. He swerved, zigzagging with astonishing speed, as he came within pistol-range. Rawcliff shouted, 'It's all right, Sammy!'

Ryderbeit slowed and covered the last few yards at a trot. He gestured with the gun towards the two injured men under the truck. 'You want me to spare them any more misery?'

At that moment Guy Grant lurched forward, stumbled round to the front of the truck, and vomited over the front wheel. He stood for a moment, head bent, leaning his sleeve on the burning hot bonnet, his shoulders heaving.

Ryderbeit let out a savage laugh. 'Is that how you won the Military Cross, Major?'

Rawcliff had stepped over and removed the pistol from the pocket of the second Cypriot, who lay with his smashed leg sprawled out beside him, his rancid breath coming in swift gasps. The man with the shattered wrist had crawled into a sitting position, moaning with his eyes closed.

'Give me that gun,' Ryderbeit said, as Grant straightened up and came round the side of the truck. There was a trickle of spew on his chin and down his belted bush-jacket. He turned and stood rigid for a few seconds, his back to them all, staring out across the airfield.

'Go through their pockets,' Ryderbeit said, 'find out who they are.' He was holding the telescopic rifle loosely in one hand.

Rawcliff stepped over again to where the two Cypriots lay under the truck. He still held the monkey-wrench, and was just leaning down over the man with the smashed wrist, about to tear open his tunic and reach for his pockets, when he felt the wrench grabbed out of his hand.

He swung round, but was too late. Grant had brought the weapon down in a vicious swingeing blow, shattering the man's black hairy skull.

Before either Rawcliff or Ryderbeit could fully react, Grant had whirled round and now brought the monkey-wrench down on the second Cypriot's neck, knocking his body back with a thump against the rear tyre of the truck, where he now lay with blood pumping in thick spurts out of his mouth and nostrils, seeping from his ears.

Grant had lifted the monkey-wrench again. Ryderbeit said, 'Hold it right there, Major. This is a .417 Magnum –

elephant gun. You know what that'll do to you.'

Guy Grant stood shivering in the heat, the monkey-wrench still raised above his head, its screw-jaw matted with pulpy blood and hair.

'Drop it like a good boy.' It clanged on to the concrete. 'Now turn round and keep your hands where they are.'

Grant obeyed, with a stiff unsteady motion, like a man drunk. 'I had to do it. Had to.' And he gave a dreadful brutish smile.

Ryderbeit nodded. 'Sure you had to do it, Major. You had to do something.' And he stepped forward. His left leg swung out with a quick scissor-motion like a dancer, and he kicked Guy Grant in the groin. Grant groaned, went down and lay still.

'Let's look at their papers,' Ryderbeit repeated.

'I think I'm going to be sick too,' Jo said, very white against her freckles.

Rawcliff had taken her by the arm and led her round to the front of the truck where he opened the passenger door. 'Better wait inside. Out of the sun,' he added, trying to keep the sarcasm out of his voice.

Ryderbeit was busy ripping open the three men's jackets and rifling their pockets. Two were dead, and the one with the neck wound was clearly dying. Matt Nugent-Ross still hadn't moved. 'What's the matter?' Rawcliff said brutally. 'Never seen anyone killed before?'

'Not quite like this, I haven't.'

Ryderbeit came over with some wallets and folded sheets typewritten in Greek and celluloid identity cards. Nugent-Ross glanced through them, while Guy Grant began to stir on the ground. Ryderbeit looked at Rawcliff. 'Fast work, soldier.'

'You saw it all?'

Ryderbeit tapped the telescopic sights on his rifle. 'As I told you, I've got a nose for trouble. When Granty turned off the track, I got curious. So I grabbed this up and studied the play. And when that joker over there' – he nodded at the dead Cypriot with a bullet through his eye – 'lined up his

162

shooter on Jo I reckoned it was time I dealt myself in. I told you I was handy with a gun, didn't I?'

There was a sudden hush. They all stood listening to the murmur of the sea and the distant mutter of machinery from the hangar. It seemed to Rawcliff that the shots must have been heard as far as Larnaca. Then, with a conversational frivolity induced by shock, he nodded at Ryderbeit's rifle and said irrelevantly, 'That's a pretty unwieldy piece of hardware to tout around, isn't it? How do you get it through airport security checks?'

Ryderbeit replied, with reciprocal nonchalance, 'Comes to pieces – all plastic, conversion of the Armalite. Doesn't show up on the screens. Even has plastic soft-nosed bullets only the casings are metal, and I keep those in my belt.'

Matt Nugent-Ross came over, holding the three gunmen's documents. 'Seems they were some kinda Auxiliary Militia. From what I've heard, they were formed as a splinter group after the National Guard was disbanded in '74.

'I thought the police had been sewn up here?' Ryderbeit said. He turned and shouted, 'Grant, get on your feet!'

Guy Grant crawled onto his hands and knees, levering his heavy body up by holding on to the truck. His eyes were glazed with pain. 'You struck a fellow officer, Ryderbeit,' he said, wincing with every word.

Ryderbeit smiled. 'You're no longer an officer, Grant – not here you're not. You know what the Rule Book says? Lack of Moral Fibre in the face of the enemy. Plus murdering two wounded suspects. That's against the Geneva Convention. And Holy Moses, we're supposed to be representing the Red Cross!'

'They had to be killed. We couldn't hold them here – not with all those other wogs in the compound. Ask Peters. He's in charge of security.'

'To hell with Peters. You're yellow, Grant. Even Jo had a belly-full more guts than you had.' He glanced at Rawcliff, 'Am I right, soldier? Is he yellow?'

'No comment.'

In the distance they saw the white-clad figure of Thurgood

163

coming towards them. Ryderbeit said, 'Right. We're stripping down these bodies and taking them to the end of the beach where we bury them. Keep their clothes to wash off any blood and prevent messing up the truck.'

'What sort of story have you got to explain the shooting?' said Rawcliff.

'I'll think of something. We'll just have to double security round the wire, if anyone starts getting suspicious.'

Thurgood came up, peering curiously at the carnage. 'What the devil's been going on?'

'Don't ask stupid questions,' said Ryderbeit. 'You and Rawcliff get shovels. Jo, you go back into town and alert Peters and Ritchie. Matt, you've got two jobs now – your electrical toys and keeping the labour force quiet. If anyone asks about that shot, tell 'em I'm a White African hunter and I spotted a bird on the shore. Tell 'em I'm going to have it for dinner. Make a joke of it. And make sure it sticks.

'But if any of those boys still looks suspicious, and begins gossiping, make a note of them. It's too late in the day to start being chivalrous,' he added ominously. 'Now let's get to work.'

The three dead men were disposed of, as soon as Jo had driven off into town to fetch Peters.

The bodies were buried swiftly, without ceremony, in a single shallow grave under the Salt Flats at the end of the peninsula. Their clothes and documents were then burned, and the monkey-wrench from the Suzuki washed off and thrown out to sea. Ryderbeit had taken charge of the three hand-guns, while Rawcliff had been given the job of scrubbing the blood and other mess off the concrete apron in front of the deserted terminal.

When Peters returned – alone, without Jo or Ritchie – he listened to their account of the incident in silence. Rawcliff could not know exactly what version the men would already have heard from Jo: but if she had emphasized his own initial heroics, Peters was not passing out any medals. His only comment was to repeat that security should be stepped up round the wire and that there must be special surveillance over the Cypriot ground-crews. Matt Nugent-Ross was to keep his ears open for any loose talk.

Peters then demanded that Ryderbeit hand over the three pistols and his own telescopic rifle. To Rawcliff's surprise the Rhodesian agreed, but with a sly ambiguous grin.

4

The atmosphere inside the hangar had changed. The team had become quiet, wary, oppressed by the salty heat, the perpetual shattering roar of machinery, each guarding his own conscience, of guilt or doubt, satisfaction or relief, at the thought of the three impostors, dead and buried under the blue haze at the end of the peninsula.

Guy Grant had shed all pretence of authority, even self-respect. His manner was now abject, his body still bent with pain, while he worked in a muddled and desperate way, trying to master the baffling complexities of the Hercules' control-panel. Ryderbeit had continuously to go to his assistance, even to help him decipher instructions from the handbook.

At two o'clock they broke for lunch. They ate the same rations as the ground-crew, sitting together at a modest distance from the Cypriots, from where Matt was supposed to eavesdrop on the men's conversation, in case they were having doubts about those two shots. But, since the butchery outside the terminal, the American had become unnaturally calm, preoccupied. He hardly touched his meal, of salami, bread and feta cheese, and only kept up a pretence of listening to the desultory chatter of the local ground-crew.

Later he rejoined Rawcliff at the controls of his Hercules. It was clear that Nugent-Ross drew a certain comfort and reassurance from Rawcliff's presence. The American was essentially a civilized man who found himself confused by the spiritual isolation of the others, shocked by their primitive values – of greed, leavened with varying degrees of violence, as their sole motivating force.

For some time he continued checking the switch-boxes and rows of contact-breakers, while Rawcliff stared through the smoked windows to where Peters was limping about, shouting orders at the ground-crews. Suddenly Nugent-Ross sat back and pulled from under his jacket a miniature thermos flask, leather-bound, with a silver drinking-cap. 'Fancy a dry martini?' He handed it across to Rawcliff, in the seat beside him. 'I think I can guarantee it's the best, and probably the only dry martini you'll get during your stay.'

Rawcliff unscrewed the top, poured it full and tasted it. The American had not been boasting: it had just the correct amount of French, the right chill and sharpness; all it lacked was the olive on a stick.

'Thank you.' He started to pass the thermos back, but Nugent-Ross shook his head:

'Sorry, friend. But I don't partake.'

'Because it's against the rules?'

'The hell with the rules.'

Rawcliff nodded, 'Never drink during the day and never on the job?' He began to screw the cap back on again.

'No, Mr Rawcliff. Never during the day, never on the job, never off the job. *Never, period.* I got my own rules.' He took the little thermos and sat for a moment weighing it in his hand as though it were some object of infinite value; then slipped it back inside his deerskin jacket. He looked at Rawcliff and gave a quick funny laugh.

'It's okay, I'm not crazy. Not quite, anyway. Just that I used to be hooked on the stuff. I carry this little baby around with me, like a kinda talisman.'

'What's the trouble, Matt?'

'Trouble? Nothing. That's the trouble. I don't feel anything. I don't love, I don't hate, I don't even scare any more.'

'What happened?'

It was a few moments before he answered. 'You told me you've got a wife and kid? Must be a darn terrible responsibility coming out here and being at the mercy of people like Grant and Peters and the rest?'

Rawcliff said nothing.

'Did I tell you I was once married myself? It was after I flunked out of Oxford and Princeton, and got my DD from the Marines. My pa fixed me a job out West with a big electronics corporation that was just going into the computer business. Then I met this girl – very special she was. Married her after six months and we had a baby girl. I'd never been too darned keen on children, but my God, I went really crazy about that kid.' His voice was gentle, calm, completely under control.

'Everything seemed pretty good between us. Trouble was, I liked a drink or two – only my wife didn't exactly approve. After the kid was born, she made me give it up. It was okay for about a year, then I began to slip. It was one Saturday morning. I had to go into the office, and afterwards I got together with some of the boys at the local bar. Somehow after the first couple of drinks it didn't seem to matter. When I finally got home I felt just fine. Then I made my second big mistake. I started to justify myself. My God, Rawcliff, there's nothing so disgusting as a drunk trying to justify himself! She didn't try to argue. She just took the kid and said she was going out shopping and that she hoped I'd be sober when she got back.

'That's what did it. I guess I just wanted a fight. I went round the corner and bought a bottle of rye. An hour later she hadn't come back. I went outside and saw the car was still in the garage. She's taken the kid in the stroller. I got in the car and started to drive. I didn't know what I was doing, except that I was vaguely looking for them. Everything I saw was double and I kept on veering over to the left of the road. I took a turn, and must have been going a lot too fast, because I went into a skid and lost control. There was a woman with a child crossing the road and I hit them both.

'I remember feeling the bump as both wheels went over them, and I panicked and pushed the wrong pedal. I finished up in a front garden. The cops were there with sirens and there was an ambulance and damn great crowd, and they pulled me out and I saw the woman and child, and the smashed stroller lying in this great goddamn pool of blood. You can guess the rest?'

For some time the two of them sat and listened to the muffled din of the hangar from through the plastic sound-proofing. Rawcliff had noted that this was the plane's only concession to basic comfort – although it would make little

168

difference when those four mighty engines were at full-throttle.

He was not horrified by what he had just heard, not even embarrassed. He felt merely a pitying disgust – with the man's self-indulgent stoicism, his wretched leather-bound silver talisman full of chilled martini.

He glanced at his watch. With the two hour forward time-zone in London, little Tom would be just about having his tea, before Judith came to collect him: while Judith herself would probably be winding up the last post-prandial conference discussing in-put data and print-outs and interface, and all the other stylized jargon of the computer world.

And he realized, with wry dismay, that his wife had at least one thing in common with Matt Nugent-Ross. Both were computer experts. The difference was that she, and the people she worked with, were professionals. They all had offices and secretaries and stable salaries, and homes to go back to when the day was done. They weren't sitting out on a limb, in a forlorn corner of the Eastern Mediterranean, at the mercy of unknown forces masquerading under the sanctimonious credentials of the International Red Cross. And it was then that the germ of an idea began to nag at the back of his mind. If those six guidance-systems were the computerized lock at the heart of this whole mysterious operation, then Judith might just possibly provide the key which could open it. He was confident that she knew quite as much about computers as this sad, broken ex-lush who didn't give a damn whether he lived or died, and to hell with the mission and the money! Judith would at least be a lot more reliable.

His instincts rejected the idea at once. The very thought of involving her – and, by implication, Tom – made him feel slightly ashamed. But once the germ had been planted, it was not so easily eradicated. It had already begun to mature and multiply.

Presently Nugent-Ross said, 'Well, I guess I'd better get going. That guy Grant's got problems. Forget about the electricals – he can't even tell the difference between the fuel-mixture readings. He doesn't need me – he needs a goddamn flying instructor. Jesus help him when he's alone up there in the blue!'

Rawcliff looked at him solemnly. 'I'm sorry, Matt. I haven't been much help.'

'Sure you have. You listened.' He stood up, stretching his cramped muscles between the two seats. 'Watch yourself. I don't like the idea of Peters having pocketed those three guns.'

'Don't worry. He almost certainly had his own already. And one gun's enough, for a man like Peters.'

The American squeezed his shoulder. 'If you need a friend, you got one. I've an idea they're at a premium round here.'

'Thanks for the drink, Matt.'

'*De nada*!'

It was around mid-afternoon, and Ritchie had been gone for more than two hours. And Peters had driven off once again presumably to inform his masters of the 'termination' of the three Auxiliary Militiamen: for while nominally in command here in the field, Peters was no more than altar-boy in the hierarchy of the organization. When he returned, an hour later, he was alone; he had also shed the plaster from his foot, though his head was still held rigid by the pink halter. If he had any news, he wasn't sharing it. His face was as expressive as a potato.

Rawcliff was up in his Hercules, making a final check of the controls, running through them with the swift precision of a pianist rehearsing to play without music-sheets, until he felt confident enough that he could reach any switch or lever with his eyes closed. Flying a Hercules solo doesn't allow for fumbling, for hesitation or the least error of judgement.

He heard a step behind him and turned, to see Thurgood staring down from over his shoulder. The man's clipped moustache was smudged with oil, making it look as though it had been grown to disguise a hare-lip.

He had come aboard carrying a heavy black case, which he now placed between the seats and opened, to reveal a mass of electrical equipment. He behaved as though Rawcliff were not there. He took out an insulated Philips screw-driver and began to remove some panels under the lower battery of controls.

'Do you mind telling me what you're doing?' Rawcliff asked.

'Fixing the auto-pilot.'

'The auto-pilot's okay. Nugent-Ross checked the circuits and they're all functioning.'

'I don't care what Nugent-Ross said. I'm putting in some extensions.'

'What for?'

Thurgood turned, his eyes swelling open like those of some deep-sea fish. 'Ah yes. Mister Rawcliff. The one who asks too many questions.'

'That's right.' He gave a slow nod, not looking at Thurgood. 'I suppose your extensions wouldn't have anything to do with those boxes of flowers I and Grant brought in yesterday?'

'Fuck off, Rawcliff,' Thurgood said softly. 'You talk like that and you end up under the sand, like those three wog-police this morning.'

Rawcliff nodded again. 'Friendly sort of fellow, aren't you, Flight-Lieutenant?'

The pale eyes stared at him for a moment, then Thurgood turned and reached into the case for a bunch of wires and clips.

Rawcliff was in no mood to start an argument with Thurgood, whose proximity in the cabin gave him a nasty, uneasy feeling, like being with a dog that might turn vicious at any moment.

Without a word he left the man to it, and went down the plane and out into the hangar, to get some of the gritty black coffee which the ground-crew kept bubbling over a kerosene stove. In the absence of Peters he took the opportunity to stretch his legs.

He already knew that the six boxes, which they had flown in from Le Bourget, had been stowed in a locked office at the back of the hangar. But he now made another interesting discovery. At the end of the hangar, beyond the last aircraft, and half-hidden behind two mobile generators, stood a stack of six unpacked cases, each stamped with the name of a well-known Japanese make of hi-fi equipment. And behind them he counted eighteen pairs of huge loudspeakers.

He made a mental calculation, as he strolled casually away: one hi-fi set and three pairs of speakers for each aircraft. Then he observed something that he should have noticed before. The external fuel-tanks under each wing had been fitted with an empty metal bracket through which a locking-screw could be inserted. There were also two pairs of wires running under the wings and into the cabin of each aircraft.

He returned to his own plane, to find Thurgood putting the finishing touches to his work on the auto-pilot. He knew that it would be useless to try and seek an explanation from him, even if Thurgood could give one: although Rawcliff was fairly certain that the man was responsible for the wiring under the wings. It was too menial a task for an expert in high-technology like Matt Nugent-Ross.

Without a word, Thurgood packed his equipment back into the case and lugged it away down the tunnel of the aircraft, out through the loading-bay – leaving Rawcliff to ponder upon two further mysteries.

For a start he decided to assume that Thurgood's work on the auto-pilot was not unconnected with those six secret boxes locked in the back office – each containing, he was damn sure, a computerized guidance-system, to be installed and activated, at some stage, by Matt. Along with a hi-fi set and three pairs of giant loudspeakers – the third pair to be fitted at the rear of the plane, since which Rawcliff had now traced a further pair of wires leading from the control-cabin to another locking-bracket secured above the loading-bay.

At this point his curiosity was tempered with relief. At least you couldn't create much havoc with a hi-fi set and a battery of loudspeakers. A propaganda mission, perhaps? Yet any broadcast, even over the most powerful equipment, would be hopelessly drowned out by the roar of the Hercules' four engines. So why put a fleet of one of the world's largest,

noisiest transport-planes into the air and have them fly
pilotless, merely to broadcast the briefest of messages to
some unknown mass-audience below?

But Rawcliff wasn't here on some fact-finding mission.
What he didn't understand, he was deliberately meant not to
understand. That was part of what he was being paid for,
after all.

5

It was nearly four o'clock when the Beachcraft Duke drifted in over the Salt Lake. Ritchie touched down neatly between the rows of oil-drums and taxied across to the hangar where he tucked the little plane between two of the Hercules. Next to the pair of giants, the Beachcraft looked sleek and fragile, painted in its streamlined white and blue, with '*Come Fly With Me*' rippling down its side, beneath the curtained windows. At least it leant a touch of class to the scene, Rawcliff thought.

At first he had been puzzled by Ritchie's trip. Why hadn't the man flown him and Grant straight down to Larnaca in the first place, instead of landing at Nicosia? But Ryderbeit – a master of indiscretion – had hinted that Ritchie was taking no chances. On all accounts the Beachcraft must remain 'clean'. Its cargo of the six mysterious boxes, which had been surreptitiously exchanged at Le Bourget for Grant's houseplants – probably with the connivance of the French authorities, Rawcliff suspected – would have been 'cleared' well in advance through Nicosia Customs, no doubt after the right palms had been well-greased and crossed with silver. But for some reason Ritchie had wanted to log his flight into Nicosia with all the correct documentation stamped and signed for the record – something that was not possible here at Larnaca. He had also been logged out again, with official clearance to fly to Crete. Only he hadn't arrived; and liaison between the little Mediterranean airports was so notoriously haphazard that it might be weeks before the Beachcraft was registered as missing: and by that time it would be too late.

It was now obvious that Ritchie's little air-taxi had been designated for a vital role in the final act of the operation.

Yet there was a discrepancy here. Four hours was a long time in which to accomplish a bare half-hour drive up to Nicosia, plus the few minutes it took to fly back to Larnaca, even taking into account the laborious sloth and incompetency of Greek bureaucracy.

He seemed relaxed, as jaunty as ever, and even made light of the killing that morning. 'Bit of a bloodbath, old sport – from what Jo told me! According to her, you were quite a hero.'

So Ritchie had called in at the Sun Hall Hotel – presumably before driving up to Nicosia – in order for Jo to have told him about the shooting. And Ritchie's relationship with the girl hardly indicated a couple of hours' malingering round the pool. Like the rest of them, he could ill afford to waste time, and should have been just as answerable to Peters' discipline schedule. So what had young Ritchie been doing all that time, before leaving for Nicosia?

For the moment it would have to remain just one more thing that he was being paid not to understand.

They had broken to eat again at eight pm. The heavy assembly work had finally been completed. The ground-crews had only to finish spraying on the huge red crosses and bogus black serial numbers, using sheets of stencilled plastic, on to the top and undersides of the wings, on the mighty tail-fins and along the fuselages.

Peters had given orders that the minimum of lights were to be shown; but it was a clear night, and although there was no moon the stars were bright enough to read by.

Thurgood was fiddling with a powerful R/T set that looked as though it could rouse Peking; Ritchie had taken off the covers of one of the Beachcraft's engines and was tinkering inside; while Ryderbeit lay stretched out asleep on the concrete outside the hangar.

Only Guy Grant and Jo were absent. Grant had finally succumbed to his damaged groin, complaining of giddiness and vomiting. Peters, without compassion, had told him to take one of the jeeps and to go back to the hotel; while Ryderbeit had taunted him with the image of Jo binding up his swollen balls.

Through the starlit darkness Rawcliff could just make out the faint figure of Matt Nugent-Ross, sitting alone on the beach beyond the runway. Rawcliff, in need of fresh air after the fumes of the hangar, strolled out to join him. The American was throwing pebbles at the slow lapping waves. He did not seem to hear Rawcliff come up behind him; but then, without turning, he spoke, 'Like a drink, friend?' He reached into the pebbles beside him and took out his flask.

Rawcliff sat down beside him and took a sip. Neither of them spoke for a moment.

'Everything okay?' Matt said at last.

'Do you know what all that hi-fi and loudspeaker stuff's about, Matt?'

'Nope. That's Thurgood's line.'

'Okay. So you're way up in high technology. You also got all sentimental this morning about being my friend. I'm going to take you up on that, Matt.' Rawcliff eyed him under the bright vault of the night-sky. 'I want to know about those guidance-systems.'

There was a long pause. The American went on throwing pebbles, watching them skim the crest of the little waves until they disappeared into the darkness.

'I can give you a load o' technical detail,' he said at last. 'Given time, I could even tell you how they work. What I can't tell you is how they're programmed – from where and where to. Nor why.'

'Just tell me what you do know.'

'Well. We can start with the basic principle of the ordinary auto-pilot. You set a two-dimensional course, and if the plane is blown off-course by even a few degrees, the mechanism automatically corrects it. Right. So just imagine that principle magnified a million times, on a three-dimensional pattern. A flight-plan is fed into a computer, but instead of a static number of degrees, you have a constantly fluctuating pattern, sometimes altering every few seconds. A plane can be programmed to fly as low as fifty feet. The distance doesn't matter – just makes the tape longer.

'Now, in whatever direction you fly from Cyprus, you're initially over water, which presents no problem. But sooner or later – unless the target's somewhere on the coast – you hit mountains. And that's where the real beauty of these machines comes in. Every peak and ridge and valley is anticipated – every contour programmed to within a few feet. You're a pilot – you'll know a lot better than me. How many changes of height and direction do you think you'd have to make, flying at fifty feet over mountains?'

'At exactly fifty feet, or even approximately? It couldn't be done. Certainly not in a Hercules.'

'Mortal man couldn't do it, maybe. But these computers send out an impulse which is the equivalent of dialling a hundred long-distance telephone numbers every second. Every contour of the ground, every thousandth of a degree in change of course, is fed to the controls through the auto-pilot. But what's even more beautiful is that if some unexpected hazard crops up – a large ship, another low-flying aircraft, even a ground-to-air missile – the machine instantly picks up the impulse from the plane's radar and changes course accordingly.'

'And in the meantime what's happened to the real pilots? – what you call us mere mortals?'

'I guess you've jumped. You checked your parachute lines yet?'

'Can't these gadgets take off and land?'

'No, that's the one thing those babies can't do – at least, not with any reasonable margin of accuracy.'

From behind them they heard a grunt as one of the fleet of Suzuki jeeps started up, its lights beginning to move fast across the runway towards the gates.

'And what are the odds of one of the machines going wrong?' Rawcliff said.

'On just the one run? Because that's all it's gonna be. Maybe one in a million. Helluva lot more than getting beat holding a running flush to the king.'

'And how much does one of these things cost?'

'Christ. I don't think anybody's ever put a commercial value on them. They're used in the Cruise-Missile, and variations of them have been developed for space satellites. But, so far, only an outfit like the Pentagon can afford them.'

177

'Then who the hell fixed it so that *six* of these bloody machines were slipped aboard Ritchie's air-taxi at Le Bourget? And right under the noses of the French authorities?'

Nugent-Ross sat stroking his jaw. 'You've been listening to Ryderbeit again? He's got a theory that the French are somehow behind all this – though it's obviously not official, and you wouldn't get anyone admitting it. But the French are pretty advanced in modern technology, specially in the line of war-games. And they're not particularly scrupulous about whom they sell to either. Anyway, there's no proof that those airport officials knew just what was in those boxes.'

'Somebody must have known. And from what you say about the cost, somebody with a lot of money. Not to mention influence. You think these things could have found their way on to the open market?'

'Anything can be got on the market, providing the price is right.' The American's hand closed round a fistful of pebbles and he gave Rawcliff a slow smile. 'You're really a lot better off, if you don't push this. Hell, knowing the source of the stuff isn't gonna to pay you any dividends. The prize money'll stay the same – and so will the risks.' He paused and let the pebbles slip one by one through his fingers. 'Don't mind my observing, friend, but you seem a straight enough guy. I might even guess you had scruples. Yet you didn't seem too damned upset when those three boys got themselves butchered this morning.'

'Maybe it's the stiff upper lip. I didn't kill them, remember. I'll go along with the odd bit of grievous bodily harm – in self-defence – but I haven't signed on to kill people. Even if that killing's being done by my own side.' He took another drink from the flask. 'But don't let's fuck about with the health of our souls, Matt. Concentrate on the practical side. For instance, if you were to open one of those machines, how would you go about reading the flight-plan? And most important, the destination?'

'Forget it. For a start, the machines haven't even been loaded yet. And my guess is they won't be, till just before the final mission. But even then, the tape by itself isn't enough. To get a proper reading you'd need a full print-out, and about the only way of getting that would be to track down the original processor that programmed the source-data – in this case, probably a bank of large-scale aerial survey maps, reduced to micro-dots. And you can be darn certain the job wasn't done here in Cyprus. There are probably only a few machines capable of that kinda work in the whole of Western Europe.'

Rawcliff took a last pull at the flask, then handed it back to Nugent-Ross. Then for a wild moment he was on the point of telling him about Judith's work with computers. If what the American had just said was true, she'd certainly be in a far better position – through the resources of her corporation – to trace the material than Nugent-Ross was, stranded out here on a beach in the middle of nowhere.

Together they began to walk up the shingle to the Salt Flats and across the buckled runway. The night air smelt fresh and clean, and at that moment Rawcliff longed for it to swallow him up – longed never to return to that oily stinking hangar, where six giant transports, each bearing the respectable emblem of the International Red Cross, were waiting to be fitted with powerful broadcasting equipment and a guidance-system used in the Cruise-Missile.

It was with weary relief that at ten o'clock he heard Peters decree that they could all return to town and get some sleep. According to Thurgood's radio, the ship was not due now before three in the morning.

Ryderbeit was the only one to stay – officially to keep a watch over the ground-crews – but apparently content to remain sleeping comfortably on the concrete apron under the stars.

6

When he was in Paris, Charles Pol usually stayed at the Lotti, where they kept a permanent suite at his disposal; but on this visit he preferred the relative anonymity of the Hotel Dumini, a small select establishment off the Rue St Honoré, which catered for the better class of American visitor.

On that Monday afternoon, while more than two thousand kilometres away the six Hercules transports were being primed in a desolate corner of Cyprus, Pol entered the wine-red lobby of the hotel, replete from an extended luncheon at Laserre's, to be handed two messages by the liveried porter.

They were two telephone numbers: one in Geneva, one local. Pol sighed and waddled back out to his chauffeur-driven Citroën CX 2400, with its smoked windows and Swiss *Zollamt* plates, which gave it virtual immunity from parking restrictions.

The driver dropped him at a quiet café behind the Place Vendôme where there was a comfortable telephone booth, well-insulated from the other clients. He called Geneva collect and listened intently, the sweat crawling down his great egg-shaped face, while the voice the other end translated Peters' telex message which had been received less than an hour earlier.

Pol made no comment. He was a shrewd gambler and he did not expect the odds always to run in his favour. The demise of the three paramilitary Cypriots would only present minor problems, for he had faith in the absolute venality of Captain Spyromilio of the Larnaca Police – even if it did add marginally to expenses.

He dialled the second number, to an apartment in the Sixteenth Arondissement. It was answered by a woman. He asked for Yves. The man's voice was low and abrupt: he agreed to meet Pol in an hour, at a café on the Champs Elysées.

Pol returned to the hotel where he ordered half a bottle of champagne which he drank in the bath; dried his massive rolls of fat, washing them down with eau de cologne and dusting them off with scented talcum powder; carefully arranged the spiral of hair round the crown of his head and patted down the lick of kiss-curl over his eye; combed out his goatee beard, which had attracted minuscule scraps of his excellent lunch; then changed into a fresh set of clothes, including an outsize slub-silk suit and silk shirt.

He arrived at the café a strategic five minutes late, aware that his appearance always attracted attention. His guest had chosen an inside table, away from the crowd. He was a thin, straight man with a narrow face and short-cropped hair. He had been a parachute Colonel in Algeria and had excellent contacts with *La Police Parallèle*, that twilight adjunct of the French Secret Service, whose existence is officially denied by the French authorities, and whose methods and activities are not inconvenienced by the scrutiny of any Government department.

Pol, with his fetish for intrigue, had soon cultivated in Colonel Yves a useful employee. The man was sipping iced tea when Pol joined him. Pol ordered an enormous cake. The Colonel said, 'You may be having a little trouble – with the Americans.'

'Continue.'

'The man called Nugent-Ross. As you know, he used to work for Westinghouse in Athens. He had dealings with his Embassy there in the early seventies.'

Pol took his time answering. He ordered a *bébé* Scotch with his cake and sat munching thoughtfully. 'You are telling me that he works for the CIA?'

'I am telling you only what I know. You will no doubt draw your own conclusions.'

Pol nodded and scooped up the remains of his cake, leaving his plate as clean as a cat's. He was not troubled by Yves' revelation: his own life was one elaborate web of intrigue in which friendships and loyalties were minor luxuries, to be enjoyed or dispensed with at a whim of the changing wheel of fortune and circumstance. The one essential to Pol was the game. At the end of the day you either won or you lost.

He gave the Colonel his puckish, red-lipped grin. 'I do not take the CIA too seriously. It is a fatted calf, fed on the feeding off thousands of minor agents and informers, some of them professionals, most of them amateurs, many of them charlatans.

'And their information – valuable, useless, or merely planted – is all scrambled up and processed by computers, from whose final data whole teams of keen young men from Langley, Virginia, labour day and night at their infinite reports which are duly studied and evaluated by specialists, committees, Senators, even by the President himself – after which decisions are relayed back to the men in the field, usually of the most ludicrous irrelevance to the problem at hand. And all this takes time. Which means that time, for the moment, is on our side.'

Pol picked some crumbs out of his beard; he always enjoyed a little sermon at the expense of the Americans. He rubbed his hands together. 'No, my dear Yves! We have little to fear from the CIA. Since Vietnam and that *connerie* at Watergate, the organization is an emasculated beast. Besides,' he added, giving his girlish giggle, 'like our late unhappy colleague, Monsieur Rebot, the American's knowledge of the operation is either deceptive or irrelevant. In any event, we must assume that Washington and London know by now about Larnaca. And with your friends with the SDECE and its tentacles into Switzerland, they will no doubt have been able to establish and confirm the existence of the Red Cross mission which is using long-range transport aircraft. And if poor Rebot mentioned to them the putative objective of Eritrea, so much the better. By now they will be scurrying around like blind mice, sniffing the cheese but not being able to find it!'

He sipped his whisky and beamed at the small grey Colonel in front of him. 'You have something else to tell me, I think?'

'There is a man staying at a hotel in Larnaca. Name of Klein. He is a Jew, with dual American-Israeli nationality.'

Pol turned and ordered another cake and a second whisky – a large one this time. 'You don't like Jews, do you?'

The Colonel shrugged. 'They are very intelligent – but it is a morbid intelligence. They are faithful only to their own kind. They are not to be trusted.'

'You are a cynic, *mon cher* Yves. Are you now going to tell me that this man Klein works for both the Americans and the Mossad?'

'The Mossad is to be taken very seriously, Charles.'

'I entirely agree. How strong is your proof?'

'You have a man working for you called Ryderbeit. Another Jew, *n'est-ce pas*? A former employee – from Indo-China?'

'Please don't remind me. I lost a great deal of money over that business.'

'But Ryderbeit didn't?'

'Are you attempting to tell me that Ryderbeit works for the Mossad?' Pol said.

'He used to hold a Rhodesian passport – which was inconvenient, to say the least. He is now a citizen of Luxembourg – thanks to yourself – and has a reputation of being a dangerous mercenary. *Un vrai pro.*'

Pol allowed his belly to swell up over the edge of the table. 'I would not employ him if he were anything else.'

'He is the most serious of your agents in this operation, and the most trusted?'

'He does not know the final objective.'

There was a pause, while the waiter put down Pol's second cake and whisky. Colonel Yves remained content with his half-drunk glass of iced tea.

'You have still given me no evidence, Yves.'

'I have a reliable source in Rome. He has never let me down yet. He tells me that you have a leak in Larnaca.'

Pol raised his scant eyebrows. '*Eh bien*?'

'As you know, Rome is an open city, as far as Intelligence is concerned. Italian security is laughable. The Israelis have a very effective network there, monitoring the whole of the Eastern Mediterranean. They are treating your Larnaca operation as a potential priority.'

Pol sat inspecting his spoon. 'If your contact can identify this Israeli connection, I can promise you a handsome bonus.'

'*Entendu.* But I must warn you, there will be expenses.'

'Yves, you know I have many faults, but meanness is not one of them.'

The Colonel gave a brisk nod and stood up. He felt mildly irritated. Pol's personality was a mass of puzzling contradictions. 'Permit me to say so, Charles, but you seem remarkably complacent about this whole *affaire*?'

'Why not? The gang I am employing in Cyprus – with the exception of Ryderbeit – are bums, riffraff, *de vrais misérables*. The only thing they can do is fly planes. They are not only ignorant of the final objective – they are all totally expendable.

'Now, I think I will finish with a small *glace au chocolat*.'

The Sun Hall was a modest hotel by first-class standards, full of plastic trimmings and potted plants that needed dusting. The whole place had a forlorn fly-blown look.

Rawcliff had driven Matt back from the airfield, and now came in with him, postponing the moment when he had to return to the squalor of the Lord Byron. To hell with protocol, he thought – as long as he didn't bump into Peters.

The lobby was deserted, except for a sleepy clerk; but there were two people at the bar. Jo and Jim Ritchie. Jo was still in her nurse's uniform – presumably to help maintain an 'authentic' image of the mission. But Ritchie had changed into a cream silk shirt under a fawn suede jacket with leather buttons, white linen trousers and moccasins. He might have just put down at Le Touquet, ready for a slap-up dinner and a flutter at the Casino de la Forêt.

Rawcliff guessed that it must have been Ritchie whom he had heard driving away from the airfield, while he was sitting with Matt on the beach. And again he thought that young Ritchie seemed to spend a lot of leisure-time at the hotel.

It was Jo who first spotted Matt and Rawcliff. 'Come and join us! Peters has already turned in, so we can enjoy ourselves.'

Matt made some mumbled excuse and went off towards the lifts; he evidently drew the line at having to stand at the bar, watching other people drink. Rawcliff stayed.

Jo was sucking from a tall glass through a straw. She showed no trace of shock, following the morning's massacre. Ritchie was on whisky, like all good pilots. He ordered Rawcliff a beer.

'You just missed an illustrious guest, old sport. One Captain Spyromilio, Chief of Larnaca Police. All grace and favour, especially with Jo here. Didn't seem to know anything about those three dead hooligans out at the airport. But he's all clued up on the ship that's putting in tonight. *Le Corsaire*, out of Marseilles. He wants to be there, along with one of his Customs friends. Claims it's just a formality – for which they will be duly rewarded with the traditional sweetener, of course.' He sipped his whisky. 'Meanwhile, we've got a little problem – rather nearer home. Major Grant. Up in his room with a bottle of whisky, drunk as a skunk.'

'That's helpful. By the way it looks, we'll be making our first dummy flight sometime tomorrow. Does Peters know?'

'Not yet. If you can get him to cooperate, Jo can give him a jab that'll fix him up. I tried, and got told to take a running fuck at a rolling doughnut.'

Jo smiled over her glass.

'I'll see what I can do.' Rawcliff finished his beer and turned.

'By the way, he's got a gun,' said Ritchie. 'His old Service revolver from Korea. Claims he keeps it as a memento. I didn't wait to find out if it was loaded or not.'

'Thanks for the tip.' Rawcliff paused. 'Incidentally, did you notice anything odd tonight when you drove in from the airport?'

'Like what?'

'Company. Big dark-brown American car. Local plates – just the driver. It picked me and Matt up just outside town and kept with us as far as the turning into Athens Street, on the corner. I didn't try to lose him.'

Ritchie shrugged, 'This is the town centre, after all – and

185

you were following the main road. Maybe he was too.'

'Maybe. Only there wasn't a lot of traffic around, and he was keeping his distance. Thought I'd just mention it.' He began to walk away.

Ritchie called after him, 'Grant's in two-five, second floor.'

'Good luck!' said Jo.

Rawcliff did not answer. On his way to the lifts he passed the switchboard operator, and noticed the telex machine against the wall, at the back. As the lift door opened, a young man hurried up and stepped in beside him. The door closed and Rawcliff pointed inquiringly at the row of buttons. The young man punched the third one, and Rawcliff the second. Neither of them spoke. The stranger had a sallow beaky face and longish, untidy black hair. He didn't look like a tourist, and seemed a little too scruffy to be a visiting businessman.

The lift stopped. Rawcliff nodded to him and got out. Room 25 was at the end of the corridor. He knocked, but there was no answer. He knocked again. 'Major Grant!'

There was a clump and the door clicked from the inside. No word came from the room. Rawcliff waited a few seconds, then tried the handle. It opened and he went in.

The room was surprisingly tidy. Guy Grant sat at a table in the middle of the floor. He was in his shirtsleeves, and there was a tooth-glass in front of him. A bottle of Scotch stood on one side of the table, and a well-oiled revolver lay on the other, its barrel neatly aligned along the edge, pointing away from him. The glass was almost full, but there wasn't much left in the bottle.

He turned and gazed at Rawcliff as though he were a stranger. His corrugated grey hair was damp and ruffled, and there was a puffed glossiness around his eyes, which held a determined glitter.

'Sit down. Have a jar.' His voice was thick and hoarse, but with the careful precision of the practised drinker. 'Who told you I was here?'

'Ritchie. I ran into him in the bar.'

'Sit down.'

Rawcliff remained standing. 'I've come to tell you,

Major, that the cargo's due in sometime tonight. You're expected to be there.'

Grant looked puzzled, like a child who has been given too complicated instructions. 'Cargo?' he repeated; then shook his head and reached for his drink.

Rawcliff stepped forward and dashed the glass out of his hand, shattering it, with a dark stain against the wall. Grant was almost equally quick, moving as though by reflex: he swept up the gun with his right hand and held it, surprisingly steady, pointing at Rawcliff's stomach.

'Y'shouldn'ta done that, old bean. Shouldn't break a man's glass when he's drinking. Damn bad form and all that.'

Rawcliff began to back away, his hands held at a cautious distance from his sides. He guessed the gun was a Webley .38 revolver, British Army issue; but from where he was standing he couldn't see if it was on safety or not. Grant was holding it professionally, with both hands, elbows resting on the table. It was still aimed at Rawcliff's belly.

'Sit down, old bean. On the bed.' Rawcliff obeyed. 'Guess I didn't behave too well this morning?'

'Hardly Queen's Regulations, Major. But then you're not in the regiment now. This is a rough outfit.'

Grant screwed up his mouth and gave a growl of laughter. He had lowered the revolver, but was still holding it in both hands. 'Bloody rough. Bloody rum, too, if you ask me.'

There was a long dismal pause.

'How did you get involved in all this?' Rawcliff said at last, conversationally.

Grant took a gulp of whisky from the bottle. 'Through Peters. Bastard knew an old chum of mine from Korea. They were in the gun-running racket – Morocco, Algeria. Bloody Arabs.'

'And how does Peters fit in?'

'Through that Jew, Ryderbeit. They teamed up down in the Congo, back in the sixties.' He reached again for the bottle, his free hand still holding the Webley, his finger firmly on the trigger.

'Just how much do you know about this operation, Major?'

187

Grant's mottled face grew cunning. 'You think I'm pissed, don't you? You think I'm pissed enough to blow the whole shooting-match?' He was watching Rawcliff with a slack smile. 'Have a drink, for Christsake! Comrades-in-arms, and all that.'

There was a tap at the door. Grant swung the revolver round, as Jo's voice called softly, 'Major? Mr Rawcliff?'

Rawcliff stood up, walked carefully around Grant and eased the door open a few inches. 'It's all right – give me a few more minutes.'

She looked doubtful. 'I'll be in my room. Twenty-one, just down the passage.' She hesitated. 'Is he okay?'

'Everything under control.' He closed the door.

Grant was now sitting with the Webley turned towards himself, squinting down the barrel. 'I guess I fucked up this morning. If I had the guts, I'd finish the bottle, then stick this gun in my mouth and pull the trigger.' His expression became confused. 'Funny thing is, I've never fired the thing.' He grinned again. 'And I'll tell you something else that's funny. Really make you laugh. I'm not a Major. Just a bloody Acting-Captain. It was out in Korea. The Chinks were all over the bloody shop, and we were beating it back to Seoul like a bunch o' rabbits. Yours truly was detailed to take up a rear-guard holding position. Everything bloody chaos – radio on the blink – night, and cold enough to freeze a brass monkey's – when a platoon of those fucking Chinks showed up. I had a Bren and let 'em have it, then finished 'em off with a couple o' Mills bombs. I had a Sergeant who tried to stop me, but I thought he was yelling to frighten the bastards off. You know – they used to come in with bugles and drums, screaming like crazy schoolgirls.' He reached for the bottle.

'There were only three survivors. Chaps from my company.' He chuckled: 'You get the joke?' He took a deep drink, wiping his mouth with the back of his liver-spotted hand. 'Killed my own men, see? God, I almost died laughing – all the way to the glass-house.'

'Go on.'

'I got transferred. Moved down to Malaya where I was

put on an air-training course for reconnaissance. Flying Lysanders – y'know those two-seater World War Two jobs used for tank-spotting in the Western Desert. I finished the six months' course and flew a few dozen missions, then the war packed up.'

'That's not your only flying experience?'

'Oh, I buzzed about in the odd Dak and C46. The real intrepid aviator, that's me!'

'And you think you can handle a Hercules – solo?'

Grant gave a slow nod. 'You're a smug bastard, Rawcliff. You civvy airline boys are all the same – you think it takes a genius to fly an aeroplane.'

'I'm not asking for a recommendation,' said Rawcliff. 'I just don't want you going down in a ball of flame tomorrow morning. You've only got three hundred yards for the take-off, and that whisky's going to be no help at all.' He got up and came across to the table and picked up the almost empty bottle, went into the bathroom and poured what remained into the basin.

When he got back, Grant was again holding the revolver in both hands, staring at the table. Then slowly, without looking at Rawcliff, he turned the gun and stuck it in his mouth. Before Rawcliff could reach him he had clamped his teeth round the barrel and pulled the trigger. There was a sharp snap. Grant gave a choking laugh.

Rawcliff stepped up to him and took the gun out of his hand. He spun the magazine, and saw that all the chambers were empty. 'Listen to me, Guy. Jo's going to give you something to sober you up. And I'm going to get you a pint of coffee. Then we're all going to drive out to the airfield. You can get some sleep there, before the ship puts in.'

'Piss off. You bastards don't need me out there any more. I'm finished.'

'You're not finished, Guy. Just keep thinking about all that money you're going to make.'

Grant gave him a stiff glazed look. 'They'll never pay.'

'Why do you say that?'

'Up the spout – the lot of us. No chance, old bean. We're the children of the damned, working for a bunch of

189

international crooks.' His head sank on to his arms and he began to sob.

Rawcliff had started towards the door, then paused. 'Is that what you really think of the operation?'

Grant peered slowly up at him with moist red eyes; then his face cracked into a ghastly grin. 'Red Cross mission. Succour to the needy. Succour to a lot o' bloody blacks or Arabs. Now fuck off. I wanna sleep.'

Rawcliff put the empty revolver inside his jacket – he wasn't going to take the risk of Grant having ammunition hidden somewhere in the room – then went out quietly, leaving the man gazing at the floor.

Jo's door was unlocked. She was lying on the bed smoking. Against the wall, next to a couple of expensive suitcases, stood her Red Cross medicine-chest. 'And how's the dear Major?'

'Not in good shape. And he's not a Major either – but that story can keep. You'd better go in there and fix him up. Don't worry, he's harmless. I've got his gun. And it wasn't loaded.'

She stood up and looked at her watch. 'I'll have to be quick. I've got a call booked through to London.'

Rawcliff had started towards the door. He now paused. 'It may be none of my business, Jo. But I was given to understand that there was to be no outside communication while we're here.'

She gave him a calculated smile, as she reached down for the medicine-chest. 'Oh come on, Rawcliff! You're not going to grudge a girl one private telephone call? And I'm damned if I'm going to ask for official permission and have that bastard Peters listening in!'

He nodded doubtfully, was about to say something, then decided against it. He was thinking instead of that damn telegram which he knew he must send to Judith, if only to tell her that he was 'having a wonderful time – wish you were here.' He even considered putting through a call himself to London. After all, if Jo dared, why shouldn't he? Hadn't Ryderbeit already hinted that the whole security angle was a bluff, even a double-bluff?

Yet it wasn't the threat of Peters' somehow learning about

190

the call which deterred him. He knew there was nothing he could say to bring Judith any cheer or comfort: he would have to lie, and she would know he was lying.

He went out to fetch the coffee for Grant.

It came bubbling hot, in a conical pewter jug with a pan-handle. Rawcliff rode up with it in the lift and started back along the corridor towards Grant's room. He was just passing Number 21, when he heard the muffled purr of the telephone inside. He paused.

The late night switch-board operator, in an almost empty hotel, would be likely to ring off unless it were answered fairly promptly. Rawcliff tried the door-handle. It opened. The room was empty. He reached the bed and lifted the phone. There was a short silence, then a man's voice said, very clear over the long-distance: 'Joanna? It's Abe. You know the rules about calling here. Is the picnic on?' Rapid and a little nervous, Rawcliff thought: not a young voice, with one of those Americanized accents that no true-born American ever has.

'Joanna? Hello? *Hello*!' A burst of static, then a woman's voice cut in, 'La Cypria, Larnaca? *Parla prego . . .*!'

'Hello! Joanna?'

'Just a minute,' said Rawcliff.

Pause. 'Who's that?'

'I'll get her right away,' Rawcliff said calmly, and rested the receiver on the bedside-table. He could almost see the elderly party sweating at the other end, as he went out to find Jo.

She was in Grant's room, bending over him on the bed, swabbing his arm as he lay back on the counterpane, his face now the bleached colour of washed-up driftwood. In her free hand she was holding an empty hypodermic needle.

'Your call's come through,' Rawcliff said.

She nodded and straightened up. 'See that he lies quiet for ten minutes. That shot should do the trick.' She hurried out, closing the door behind her.

Grant grinned wanly up at Rawcliff. 'So she really is a bloody nurse! Perhaps this is where my luck changes?'

'I wouldn't bet on it.' Rawcliff sat down and stared at his feet.

After a long pause Grant said, 'I don't know what she shot me full of, but I'm feeling like a million dollars. I'm floating, old bean. Even better than whisky! Jesus.'

She was gone exactly eight minutes by Rawcliff's watch. He said nothing as she returned: just watched her pack up the medicine-chest, while Grant lay smiling sublimely at the ceiling.

'The battle may be lost, but not the war! As my old father used to say, "Guy, get in there and win 'em!"' Grant made a feeble effort to raise his head, then fell back on the pillow and yelled, 'I have not hung up my cutlass – but I have rolled up the flag and hoisted the pirate's colours!'

Jo was putting the hypodermic back in the chest. 'He'll be on a pretty good high for a bit, then he'll sleep like a baby,' she said to Rawcliff. 'He'll feel terrible when he wakes, but at least he'll be sober.'

'And in the meantime he's going to wake the whole hotel. Peters included.'

Grant had now begun to recite the Lord's Prayer, in a very loud, clear voice.

Jo shrugged. 'That's his look-out. We've done our bit.'

'I'm sorry, I still feel responsible for him' – Rawcliff had difficulty making himself heard above Grant's incantation – 'and I want Peters kept out of this. Grant's in enough trouble, as it is.'

'So what do you suggest? Take him to the local hospital?' she added, with mild irony.

'Run him back to the airfield. Let him sleep it off out there. He may even be okay when the ship gets in.'

He had already taken Grant under the arms and began to haul him off the bed. Together they steadied him towards the door. He was almost dead-weight, crooning happily, 'My feet aren't even touching the ground – I'm walking on the water – Holy! Holy! Holy! Lord God Almighty! *Per Christum, Dominum Nostrum*!'

They had got him into the corridor and paused, while he sprawled back against the wall, arms flung out, in an indecent effigy of the Crucifixion. 'I told you to sober him up, Jo – not blast him into orbit,' Rawcliff said, catching his breath.

Somehow they lugged him into the lift and out across the now deserted lobby, without meeting anyone – Grant's massive weight sagging and lurching between them like some great puppet whose strings had been tangled.

Rawcliff was surprised at Jo's sinewy strength: very different from his first impression of her, back at Ritchie's riverside flat in London's dockland. He left her propping Grant up against a pillar outside the entrance, and brought the Suzuki round to the steps; and together they managed to bundle their dummy 'major' into the back, where he slumped down, grinning at the roof. Jo then returned inside to fetch the medicine-chest. Rawcliff waited for her, exhausted, leaning on the wheel. He looked up just in time to see the beaky-faced young man from the third floor come down the hotel steps, glance at the jeep, then start away on foot along the sea-front towards the port.

Nothing unusual in that, Rawcliff thought. Except that it was late and, from what he'd seen of Larnaca, there wasn't much to do at night. Maybe the man was just going for a walk? He could hardly follow them on foot.

For the first few streets they drove in silence. Mercifully, Grant seemed to be asleep.

It was very dark, with little traffic. Rawcliff kept to a steady speed, looking constantly in his mirror, but no lights showed behind; nor had there been any sign of a brown American car near the hotel.

'How was your call to London, Jo?'

'All right.'

'Must have been pretty urgent?'

'Why urgent?'

Rawcliff did not answer at once. The houses were thinning out, the road narrowing out towards the airfield. ' *"Our bruised arms hung up like monuments"*,' Grant suddenly began to bellow again from the back-seat, ' *"Grim-visaged war hath smoothed his wrinkled front"* Didn't think I was a literary bod, did you, old bean!'

'Who's Abe, Jo?'

She frowned at him under the dim light from the dash-board. 'Is that any business of yours? It was a personal call.'

'Jewish boyfriend?'

'What do you mean?'

'Abe usually stands for Abraham. Or Absalom, if his parents had a sense of humour. And people called Abraham or Absalom are usually Jews.'

'*By the bowels of the Lord Jesus Christ!*' Guy Grant roared, '*Gird up thy sword, mount thy steed and ride forth to sack the cities of the plain!*'

'Shut up,' said Rawcliff. He slammed on the brakes, locking all four wheels, and they screamed to a halt, throwing Jo forward so that her head barely missed colliding with the windscreen. From behind them came a heavy crash as Grant's body rolled between the seats.

'Are you crazy?' she cried.

Rawcliff switched off the engine and turned to her. 'It wasn't London you were calling. It was Italy. Why did you lie just now?'

'I don't know what you're talking about. You weren't by any chance, helping Grant polish off his whisky, were you?'

'Don't play the dumb dolly with me, Jo. Your friend, Abe, wasn't being exactly discreet – on an open line to a special priority number. He said you knew the rules, so it must have been pretty important. What rules, Jo?'

Her face was now taut with either fury or fear: it was hard to tell in the half-darkness.

Grant was struggling back up between the seats. 'We stopped. Anything happened?'

Jo was sitting bolt upright now, staring out at the empty road which showed white against the jagged black edges of the ruts under the high-beam of the stationary headlamps. 'Do you enjoy eavesdropping on other people's private conversations?'

'I just want to know why you lied to me,' he said patiently; but her next words touched him to the quick.

'What's the matter, Rawcliff? Is it because you don't have anyone yourself to call? No wife? No girlfriend –?'

He hit her hard across the face with the back of his hand. Her head bounced against the side-window. 'You bitch. You know bloody well what I'm talking about! What's the "picnic" all about? The operation? You'd better tell me, Jo. Before I decide to tell Peters.'

'Bastard' – in a small tight voice, as she sat shielding her cheek with her hand, not looking at him. In the silence they could hear Grant's heavy breathing. 'If you must know, he's an old personal friend and the "picnic" refers to the holiday we're planning together when this is all over.'

Rawcliff smiled and shook his head. 'It didn't sound like that to me. He was nervous, rattled – didn't like you calling that number. Besides, he sounds a bit old for you.'

'Yes. He's a very old personal friend,' she repeated softly. 'And since you ask, he's married and doesn't like me calling him at home.' She had straightened up in her seat and her voice was regaining confidence. 'Satisfied?'

'Is he an Israeli, Jo?'

'Go to hell.'

'*Stone, bronze, steel!*' Grant boomed from the back, '*stone, steel, oakleaves, horses heels over the paving. And the flags, the trumpets . . .*'

'Shut up!' Rawcliff started the engine with a roar, slipped into gear, and said, without looking at her: 'Very well, we'll let Peters decide. If you've been talking to an Israeli agent, you're in trouble.'

'*5,800,000 rifles and carbines, 102,000 machine guns, 28,000 trench-mortars,*' Grant intoned from behind. ' "Triumphal March". Eliot, old bean.' He gave his hoarse laugh: 'Rum stuff, eh? But think o' the money it made him!'

Rawcliff let out the clutch and pulled away. A moment later a light flashed into his mirror, and a motorcycle swerved dangerously past them, bouncing over the broken edge of the road. The rider was a civilian, in goggles but without a crash-helmet. Rawcliff let him pull away into the darkness.

'All right,' she said at last. 'Neither of us is that innocent, after all – or we wouldn't be tied up in this business in the first place. I told you this morning that I got involved through Matt, who was working for a local shipping-agent called Kyriades. Or that's what he calls himself here. He's a

195

crook who goes under several aliases. You know him. In London he calls himself Newby.'

Rawcliffe nodded. 'You also told me that this Kyriades-Newby is tied up with Ritchie's air-taxi firm. That may explain how you got involved. But what about Matt?'

A pair of headlamps had crept up behind them. There was an angry hooting. Jo's next words were barely audible, 'Matt's a fool. A sweet weak-minded sucker. While he was working in Athens he got involved with the CIA. Nothing serious, just local background stuff – what they call "situation-colour".'

The car behind was still hooting furiously. Rawcliff cursed and swung over on to the verge, and a Mini Innocenti sped past with a high whine. There was only the driver in it – a man – but he was too low for Rawcliff to see his face.

'And Matt recruited you, I suppose?' he said casually. 'Just for a bit of extra "situation-colour", no doubt?'

'No.' She had begun chewing the knuckles of one hand. 'You don't have to believe this, but it's the truth. Gospel, cross my heart. Through Matt I got to know this man you call Abe.'

'He calls himself Abe. What's his full name?'

They had reached the fork in the road; and Rawcliff could just make out the white skeleton-wire of the perimeter fence ahead, silhouetted by their head-lamps. He guessed that the motor-cyclist and the Mini had taken the right-turn towards the causeway across the Salt Lake, and up into the hills.

After a long pause, she said, 'He's called Abraham Danver. He's an Israeli, but he spends a lot of time in Athens and Rome. He's in the import-export business. Citrus fruit, I think.'

'You *think*?' They had reached the gates, which were locked. Rawcliff turned to her. 'I've got to call Ryderbeit. That'll give you enough time to tell me what else your friend Danver does.'

He had to hang on the end of the field-telephone for several minutes before Ryderbeit answered. He sounded angry that they had arrived back so early.

Rawcliff got back into the jeep. For a moment there was a

dead silence, broken only by Grant's heavy breathing from the back.

'Oh hell. He works for Israeli Intelligence. They've known all about this operation practically from the start.'

'And you just keep them up-to-date?'

'I don't know anything more than you do – more than any of us. Honestly!' She had turned to him, her eyes large and pleading.

'What did you spend eight minutes talking to Danver about this evening?'

She took a deep breath. 'I confirmed to him about the ship coming in tonight. I said that if the planes could be loaded in time, the first flight would probably be early tomorrow. A dummy-run. That's all I know.' She had suddenly slumped in her seat, exhausted.

'Did you tell him about the three dead militiamen this morning?'

'I mentioned it, but he wasn't interested.'

Through the darkness ahead they could see a tiny pair of head-lamps. Ryderbeit had at last roused himself. Jo had stiffened again, turning back to Rawcliff, 'You won't tell Peters, will you? Please! I haven't given anything away that they don't know already.' Her knuckles were again pressed to her lips.

When Rawcliff didn't answer, she took her hand from her mouth and said, 'I can make it up to you.'

'I'm not in the market,' he said brutally. 'Anyway, it would hardly be fair on old Abe, would it?'

Ryderbeit had driven up and was unlocking the gates. He came out and glared at them both, then noticed Grant, curled up in a deep happy slumber.

'I'll explain everything later,' said Rawcliff.

He and Jo were silent as they followed Ryderbeit's jeep out across the empty black field.

7

The whole team, with the exception of Nugent-Ross, were back at the airfield by 2.30 am. The hangar was in darkness, except for a pair of hurricane-lamps, and the glow of the kerosene stove with its constant supply of thick black coffee.

Grant was still unconscious, lying aboard his Hercules where Ryderbeit and Rawcliff had dumped him on the floor of the cargo-bay between the rails of metal rollers. The others, in an unspoken spirit of camaraderie, had been careful not to let on to Peters about Grant's lapse back at the hotel. Nor had Rawcliff told anyone about his exchange with Jo in the jeep earlier that night.

He had still not decided how to react. He knew his duty was to inform Peters. Jo might not have been telling the truth when she said that she hadn't told the Israelis anything they didn't know already. But then the Israelis didn't mess around. If they didn't like the operation, they wouldn't hesitate to wreck it. But not here on Cyprus. Israel had enough on her plate already, without making further enemies – this time among non-Arabs. Besides, the outfit had so far done nothing overtly illegal – if one overlooked the little matter of the dead militiamen, and Jo had said that her contact, Abe, wasn't interested in that. Officially, it was still an International Red Cross operation.

No. The Israelis would bide their time, until the final mission, then intercept the six aircraft somewhere in neutral airspace, then shoot them all out of the sky – after young Jo had tipped them off about when that final mission would be.

There was also the problem of Matt. Did that sad renegade still care enough to betray them? If so, the Americans would probably be more devious. They'd have the influence to stymie the operation here on the ground. Even Pol, and his putative French accomplices, couldn't buy off Washington. And if Washington knew, presumably so

198

would Whitehall. And Rawcliff remembered that five of the six pilots held British passports. Britain might be a puny, pussy-footing, second-rate power; but she still wouldn't look kindly on having five of her subjects involved in some ugly international conspiracy. Unless, of course, the British Government approved?

London, Washington, Jerusalem. Not to mention Paris. Rawcliff was worried, but they weren't the normal worries of a mercenary anxious to earn his money at the end of a hazardous mission, target unknown. He was worried, because in a paradoxical way he was beginning to feel reassured – reassured in the dawning hope that the operation would fail, be thwarted before it even got off the ground.

Jo herself had hardly exchanged a word with him, during the hours while they awaited the others. The two of them had lain under blankets, at a decent distance from each other, and tried to sleep. Ryderbeit, with unexpected tact, ignored them both.

When the rest of the team did arrive, she remained taciturn, withdrawn. She had one brief conversation with Peters, who handed her a sheaf of papers. Otherwise, she spent the time chain-smoking out on the beach.

Rawcliff wondered whether her silence, even hostility, were due merely to injured pride – both professional and personal – or to fear? He also wondered why she was remaining here on the airfield. He joined her outside and asked her.

'Because I'm needed. I have to check the medical supplies from the ship, and the cargoes as they're loaded on to the aircraft. The rest of you couldn't tell the difference between plasma and vodka.'

'Very impressive. A full inventory. Just like a well-run field-hospital.' He watched her light another cigarette, making no effort to help her. 'Just to fool anyone who tries to intercept us during the flight, or at the other end?'

She inhaled, saying nothing. He noticed that the side of her face was very slightly swollen – but not enough to attract attention. Just another little secret between them. He left her alone on the pebbled beach, in her neat nurse's uniform, smoking and staring out at the dark Mediterranean, where at any moment now the lights of the ship would appear.

Back in the hangar the others – except Grant – were sitting idly drinking coffee. The local ground-crew had retired to their tents, to await the ship and help with the unloading.

After the long, hot, hectic day, the stillness and inactivity generated an air of deceptive torpor, charged with an underlying sense of anticipation, of suspended drama. The one trace of animation was the sight of Thurgood, who was doing press-ups, next to his R/T set which gave off a thin continuous whine, tuned to pick up the ship on UHF.

Thurgood was now counting his press-ups, in a high breathless voice: '82, 83, 84 . . .!' Ryderbeit yelled a vivid obscenity at him, but without effect. Thurgood reached a hundred, then sprang up and began jogging out on to the apron, smacking his arms against his hips as he went.

Rawcliff had already noticed that outside the canopy of stars was partially blotted out above the hills behind the airfield, and the close clammy night was now broken with little gusts of wind. The symptoms of an impending sea-storm.

Thurgood was coming back now at a sprint, like an Olympic runner on the last lap of the marathon. He sprang down beside his radio and began to caress the various knobs. The set suddenly let out a garbled chatter. Thurgood gave a whoop of excitement and began calling into the transceiver what sounded like a string of code-names.

The inertia was broken. Peters was giving orders. The ground-crew had appeared from behind the hangar, dividing into groups, each hurrying out to one of the caterpillar tractors, with their inflatable rafts and sand-wheeled trailers, which were drawn up along the edge of the runway.

It was 3.25 in the morning when they saw the dark mass of the ship. She was showing few lights: coming in stern-first, very slowly as she approached shallow water. She dropped anchor about three hundred yards from the shore. A clatter of chains as her rear loading-platform was lowered: lights and movement now in the open cave of the vessel, then a small dinghy with an outboard-motor moved out towards the beach. There was just one man in it.

Peters had limped on ahead to meet him. He was joined by Rawcliff and Ritchie. The man's rubber-soled paratrooper's boots splashed ashore and came crunching up the shingle. He stopped in front of them holding a thick briefcase. '*Qui parle français ici? Je n'ai pas d'anglais.*'

Rawcliff stepped forward. His French was workable, if not brilliant. As he introduced the three of them, the night's silence was shattered by the roar of caterpillar tractors behind them.

The stranger nodded. 'My name is Serge. Which of you gentlemen is in command here?' His French had a marked Midi accent, which somehow managed to make itself heard above the din of machinery.

He was a square, muscular man with short black hair and the quiet self-assurance and natural good manners of a man who does not have to raise his voice or throw his weight around to prove that he is tough.

His whole demeanour was one of complete, unspoken authority; while Peters, immediately jealous of his own rank, was inhibited from asserting it by the language barrier. He was also made to suffer the added humiliation of having to conduct all dialogue with the Frenchman through Rawcliff, whose command of the language had at once invested in him, a subtle superiority over the other two – Ritchie having modestly claimed that his French was confined to 'airport lingo'.

The four of them had begun to walk back up the beach. Ahead, two of the caterpillar tractors were crawling towards them, dragging their trailers which in turn carried the huge inflatable rafts.

'Everything is in order?' Serge asked. He addressed himself directly to Rawcliff, who replied briefly that all the aircraft were now assembled, and, as far as was technically possible, each had been checked out by its pilot. He had just finished translating, for Peters' sake, when they heard the first boom of thunder from behind the hills.

'I desire to meet all the other pilots and to inspect the planes myself. Your first sortie will be tomorrow, as soon as the fuelling and loading are completed. If the weather so permits, of course' – he glanced up at the black sky, as the first drops of rain spat on to the runway. 'Meanwhile, each pilot will be responsible for his own cargo, which must be documented to the smallest item.'

He walked fast, leading the way, and Peters had trouble keeping up with them, hobbling awkwardly behind while Rawcliff again translated. The Frenchman remarked, without slackening his pace: 'Monsieur Peters has had an accident?'

'*Un petit accident d'auto. Rien de sérieux.*'

Peters' temper was not improved by the Frenchman's reply, as relayed by Rawcliff: 'He says that's rather unfortunate. At a certain stage in the operation, we will all be required to do a parachute jump.'

Peters scowled, but made no comment. The rain was coming down hard now. As they neared the hangar, the Frenchman added, 'I am instructed to inform you at once that certain changes have been made to the original schedule. I will give you the details presently.'

'What's he saying?' Peters asked furiously, wincing now with the effort of keeping pace. But Serge continued, without giving Rawcliff time to translate, 'I must also tell you that during yesterday afternoon and tonight our ship's radio picked up unusually heavy traffic in Russian – probably from their embassy either in Damascus or Baghdad – to one of their cruisers lying just north of Cyprus. That is an added reason why the operation must be completed with the utmost speed.'

They had just reached the hangar when they were confronted by a startling sight. Thurgood came running out towards them, this time naked except for a pair of shorts – his tall, thin body a greyish-white, like an animated corpse. He raced past them through the rain, out across the apron and the runway, and down the beach where he flung himself with a great yell into the sea and began splashing around like a demented child.

Serge had paused. 'Monsieur Rawcliff, who is that man?'

'He used to be an officer in the Royal Air Force. He is our radio expert.'

'And he is one of the pilots too?' The Frenchman nodded slowly, without comment.

Jo and Nugent-Ross had come out to meet them, followed by the long ambling figure of Ryderbeit. Serge was punctiliously polite to Jo while leaving the subtle impression that he regarded the presence of a pretty girl as slightly frivolous. But he struck up an instant rapport with Ryderbeit. The Rhodesian spoke a curious mongrel dialect of French Army slang, with a hideous Belgian accent, and the two men were soon locked in spirited reminiscences of shared friends and experiences in the Congo, Biafra, the Yemen. Serge evidently knew Ryderbeit by reputation and notoriety, and regarded him with considerable esteem.

He finally paused, glancing round the hangar. 'Where is the sixth pilot?'

Rawcliff explained, as tactfully as he could, that Grant was still asleep, suffering from a mild bout of exhaustion.

The Frenchman stood looking out through the rain, to where the two rafts were being inflated on the edge of the beach. 'Exhaustion is not a good symptom in a pilot,' he turned back to Rawcliff, 'Tell me, are the others all satisfied with the condition of the aircraft?'

'One can never be satisfied with any aircraft until one has flown it.'

The Frenchman gave a little smile. 'Quite.'

Near them they heard the field-telephone jangle. Peters answered it, then came over to inform them that the local Chief of Police and a senior Customs officer had arrived. He left them, to board one of the jeeps and drive out to the gates.

Thurgood reappeared, his thin naked body gleaming wet, his sodden moustache dripping down his raw chin. He did not pause to be introduced, but raced past them, over to his Hercules, where he leapt on to a pile of crates, sprang up and grabbed the edge of the wing, from which he now began swinging, like some white ape.

'That man is too excited,' Serge observed quietly. 'I trust he will display more self-control when he is in the air.' He paused. 'Have you any particular questions you would like to ask me, Monsieur Rawcliff. Though I do not promise to be able to answer them all.'

'You talked about the original schedule. What was that?'

'It was planned for you to make four flights, carrying full pay-loads of medical equipment and other relief supplies. But it has now been decided to make only one such flight – leaving as soon as the cargoes are aboard.'

'What is the flight-plan, Monsieur Serge?'

'Your instructions will be delivered to each of you immediately before take-off.'

'And the second flight? The final one?'

The Frenchman gave him a calm stare. 'I have not taken you for a fool, Monsieur Rawcliff. Please do not take me for one.'

A few minutes later Peters' jeep returned, followed by an unmarked car bearing two men, one in plain clothes, the other in uniform. Captain Spyromilio was a dark, natty man with well-oiled hair and a bright smile that was spoilt by a black tooth. His companion was stout and morose, in a Customs' uniform that did not look quite clean.

Serge did not go out to meet them. He waited for Peters to lead them both over and introduce them; and again, while maintaining his perfect manners, the Frenchman made it quite clear that far from being daunted by the men's rank, he regarded their presence with contempt. He left Peters to negotiate any *ex gratia* payments.

Outside, through the heavy rain, the first two inflatable rafts had been dragged ashore, each bearing its huge tarpaulin-covered load of cargo from the belly of the ship. These in turn were now being hauled on to the long trailers, with their balloon sand-wheels, ready to be towed up to the hangars by the caterpillar tractors.

The local ground-crew – mindful of Captain Spyromilio's presence – worked with forced enthusiasm: though the two officials showed little interest in the cargo, which arrived in the hangar in separate loads, at about fifteen-minute intervals.

Because of the oil-shortage on Cyprus, all the fuel had been brought by the ship. It was the first of the cargo to be ferried ashore, arriving in two-hundred-gallon drums – fifty drums in each trailer-load. And at the end of two hours Rawcliff calculated that at least 80,000 gallons had reached the hangar – enough for six fully-extended flights by each aircraft. Far more than was needed, even by the requirements of the original plan, which Serge had told Rawcliff was to have consisted of four dummy-runs, with medical supplies. Plus that final, unspecified flight, which was the objective of the whole operation.

But now, according to the Frenchman, there was just to be the one 'mercy-flight'. With that final mission still under wraps. All of which would leave about 60,000 gallons of precious high-octane aviation-fuel stacked in drums at the back of a disused hangar, on a derelict airfield in the south-east of Cyprus.

Serge had closely supervised the unloading, so clearly there was no mistake, and Rawcliff had already decided it would be unwise to question the Frenchman further.

Meanwhile each pilot was responsible for the fuelling of his own aircraft, with the help of a detail from the Cypriot ground-crew and one pumping-engine. Guy Grant had been finally aroused, appearing pale and shaky, out of the tail-vent of his aircraft. Serge, with an immaculate combination of tact and contempt, refrained from introducing himself.

The fuelling was a laborious task, with each drum having to be man-handled into place, its contents syphoned off and pumped through a metal-bound hose, attached to each of the four tanks, like some obscene umbilical cord.

Rawcliff, grubby and exhausted, was beginning to feel the strain, from tension and worry and lack of sleep; while next to him Ryderbeit was working, fast and effortlessly. If the Rhodesian had any qualms, any doubts about the operation ahead, he was keeping them well to himself.

At the next plane in the line was Thurgood, still stripped to his shorts, working with a tireless frenzy, whistling tunelessly, and occasionally breaking into snatches of ghastly song – loud crooning ditties that somehow managed, like an insidious sonar bleep, to carry above the throb of the pumping motors, the clang of fuel-drums being rolled down off the pile on the trailers, the rain ringing on the hangar roof, and the now regular crash of thunder.

Serge presided over the whole operation, strolling unobtrusively between each aircraft, watching but not interfering. However, Rawcliff had noticed that the Frenchman took great care in the selection of those fuel-drums which were to be pumped into the aircraft, and those which were being stockpiled, with the aid of fork-lift trucks, at the rear of the hangar. These were being arranged in two separate loads. Over one hundred drums – enough for at least two full sorties – had been stacked in one corner. But another two hundred were now being unloaded in the corner of the hangar, at the furthest point from the row of aircraft – and free from the indolent eyes of Captain Spyromilio and the Customs officer, who were busy chatting to Jo.

Rawcliff had observed that this second, larger consignment of fuel was handled rather more slowly than the rest, and that Serge had left the aircraft to supervise the work personally. Each one was being lowered off the fork-lifts in a cradle of ropes, where it required four men to roll them into place on the pile.

When the operation was complete, Serge returned to watch the last of the fuelling. Rawcliff chose his moment with care. The Frenchman had stopped to talk to Ritchie, at the last plane in the line, away from the stockpile of fuel-drums. Rawcliff now took a welcome break, and went out to relieve himself behind the hangar. On his way back, drenched and refreshed by the rain, he made a casual detour round the second, larger stack of drums. These appeared identical to the others, except on one – at the bottom end, away from the screw-cap – was some small white stencilling, partially scraped off. It was the remains of what looked like a serial number, and the words PRISES MINIÈRE S.A. VADUZ, LIECHTENSTEIN. Then, in smudged chalk, a scrawl which he was just able to decipher as, *St Pierre, La Réunion*.

Rawcliff returned to his Hercules, his mind made up. Whatever doubts he had had, the lettering on those drums had dispelled them finally. His decision now depended on the weather – on the storm persisting long enough to give him the chance to talk to Matt at the hotel. The American was the only one who had the expertise; and the man's well-bred cynicism seemed to make him both more detached and more approachable. Rawcliff might also be giving him the one chance he had of redeeming his futile existence.

It was growing light, but the new day was bleak and angry, sliced every few seconds by vivid forks of lightning that stabbed down at the dark heaving sea; and the rain showed no signs of letting up.

It was 07.10 hours, on that Tuesday morning, when the *Le Corsaire* finally weighed anchor – the remainder of its cargo now piled under tarpaulins out on the airport apron, waiting to be loaded on to the six Hercules.

Serge had stayed ashore. His only luggage was his briefcase, out of which he now took his personal effects – a compact leather toilet-case, battery-operated shaver, and a plastic, sleeping-bag which folded up into the size of a large envelope. He obviously didn't intend to stay long.

Rawcliff wondered what else he was carrying in that briefcase.

Jo, having finally detached herself from the attentions of Captain Spyromilio and his friend, now stood checking off each item of cargo before it was loaded aboard the various aircraft. A tedious routine job, which she performed meticulously; while the loading itself – under Serge's direction – was executed with military efficiency.

At the end of two hours she had recorded 200 packed tents, 5 tons of blankets, 10 tons of powdered milk, 1,000 yards of bandages, 500 litres of blood plasma, 2,000 litres of saline solution, 60 drums of heating-oil, 500 cheap cooking-stoves, 3 mobile operating theatres, 6 tons of surgical equipment, and 4 tons of medicines, complete with detailed receipts from a reputable Swiss pharmaceutical company, together with all the correct export-licences.

Captain Spyromilio, having reached a satisfactory

arrangement with Peters, and deprived now of Jo's company, had been anxious to leave; but the Customs officer – no doubt in the hope of finding something that could provide him with the excuse to extort further Danegeld from the organization's apparently limitless slush-fund – had continued to nose under the tarpaulins, like an overfed animal rooting for further food.

Among the last items·to come ashore were twelve one-gallon tins of matt-grey paint, six powerful paint-sprayers, a dozen unmarked wooden crates, and a heavy, sealed metal box. All these had been entered on the Bills of Lading as 'miscellaneous'.

The Customs officer poked at one of the crates, and demanded to see inside. Serge obliged, having to break the lid open with a crow-bar. The crate was packed solid with large nuts, bolts and nails. Quite relaxed the Frenchman again used Rawcliff as interpreter, to explain that the contents were intended for ballast. The officer, looking doubtful, gestured with his blue jowls towards the steel box.

This time Serge spoke – still through Rawcliff – directly to Captain Spyromilio, who spoke English with an unhappy Cockney *patios* which he claimed to have learnt as a student at the North London Polytechnic. He listened restlessly, while the Frenchman explained that the steel box contained valuable serum for treating a tropical disease with a name that Rawcliff had never heard before, and which he suspected the Frenchman might have invented. Serge went on to emphasize that the box was hermetically sealed, that the medicine would be ruined once opened, and that hundreds, perhaps thousands of lives would be put instantly at risk.

Captain Spyromilio began to ask Rawcliff why the item was not accompanied by the correct documentation – '*I don't want no bloody cock-up here, I don't, and you can tell 'im that from me!*' – and when Rawcliff had finished translating, as best he could, Serge replied with a short graphic comment on officialdom versus humanity, adding just the hint of a threat concerning what he called '*le petit cadeau*' which had been agreed between the policeman and Peters.

Rawcliff suspected that it was the Frenchman's tone and manner, rather than his second-hand words, which settled the matter. The Captain conceded, with a grin; and Peters was soon escorting the two Cypriots in their car back towards the gates.

8

All six Hercules were fully fuelled and loaded by ten am. The rain had slackened, but the horizon was still dark with ragged cloud, rising into the towering wall of an unmistakable cumulus-nimbus formation, which is the kind of cloud that even the most brazen and experienced pilot does well to avoid.

Thurgood's radio was also picking up reports from weather-stations all round the Eastern Mediterranean, predicting a continued turbulence for the rest of that day. For tomorrow – Wednesday – forecasts remained uncertain. The storm had moved south of Cyprus, and was now stretched in a belt from Malta in the west, to the Lebanon and Israel in the east, and was even reported to be close to the Nile Delta.

Serge waited until eleven, before taking his decision. The first flight was cancelled until further notice. The whole team were to return to their hotels, to remain close to a telephone, stay sober, and to make contact with no one on the outside.

He dismissed them, to their various jeeps, then turned back into the hangar where he unrolled his plastic sleeping-bag.

It was barely a three-minute stroll from the Lord Byron, down to the seafront, and a couple of blocks further to the Sun Hall Hotel. The wet streets were swollen with noon traffic, before the siesta, the pavements a mass of hurrying umbrellas. But Rawcliff still took elementary precautions, in case he were followed.

Along the seafront the palms were bending and writhing in the wind, the waves pounding and sucking at the steep pebbled beach, swamping the upturned fishing-boats. At intervals lay long rows of bleached yellow nets, like the tresses of drowned girls. It seemed a good moment and a good spot to get rid of Grant's Webley. Without ammunition it was useless, except as a possible instrument of bluff; but then he knew well that it is the man who carries a gun who is most likely to be shot. Better leave that sort of thing to men like Ryderbeit and Peters.

He scrambled down to the shore, made certain no one was watching, then flung the revolver far out into the waves.

The desk-clerk at the Sun Hall told him the number of Nugent-Ross' room, on the first floor. This time he took the stairs. He wanted to avoid any close encounters in the lift. He was hoping that the others would be catching up on their sleep; but was particularly on the look-out for Peters. Ritchie probably wouldn't say anything, and Grant was no doubt back in bed. As for Jo, she was in no position to betray him.

He tapped on Matt's door, twice, and was eventually answered in Greek. 'Matt,' he called quietly, 'It's Rawcliff.'

The door opened enough to show the American's ascetic features still creased with sleep. 'Hi.' He stood clutching a barely adequate towel to his waist. 'What time is it?' He glanced down at his watch, realized that he wasn't wearing one and almost lost the towel doing so. He looked again at Rawcliff with a funny smile that was almost a frown. 'Anything new on the flight? I haven't heard anything – nobody called me.' There was something uneasy about his voice, like that of a schoolboy caught cheating.

'Can I come in, Matt? I've got something I want to talk to you about – and I don't have a lot of time.'

The American gave him an unhappy look, then nodded. 'Okay, I guess so.'

He opened the door and Rawcliff walked in. Jo was watching him from the bed. She was lying back with her head on her arm and had made no effort to cover her small breasts. Matt gave a sort of chuckle which sounded more as though he were clearing his throat. 'I guess this is a kinda awkward situation, friend?'

'Not for me.'

'Jo and I are old buddies, as you know.' He was hurriedly pulling on a silk dressing-gown. 'Honey, would you mind if **I talked to Mr Rawcliff in private?**'

She threw back the sheets and stood up shamelessly, kicked on a pair of sandals and pulled on a short housecoat that reached only half-way down her thighs. 'See you, Matt. 'Bye, Mr Rawcliff – have a nice talk!' She brushed past him, and Rawcliff noticed that the side of her freckled face without make-up, was still slightly reddened and swollen. He wondered how she had explained it to Nugent-Ross.

The American locked the door and sat down. 'Kinda anti-climax for you guys, I guess? – having the flight cancelled?'

'It gives me a few hours' grace.'

Matt reached in the pocket of his dressing-gown and lit a cigarette. 'Something on your mind? Okay, I'm listening.'

'Do you know anything about a place called La Réunion?'

'French island in the Indian Ocean – somewhere near Mauritius, I think.'

'And the main port is called St Pierre?'

'Could be – I don't know.'

Rawcliff said, 'La Réunion is highly volcanic, which means sulphur and basalt deposits, which in turn can mean open-cast mining. And open-cast mining means explosives. Do you know anything about explosives, Matt?'

The American sat stroking the light stubble on his chin. 'What are you getting at, friend?'

'What's the most lethal explosive on the market?'

'Depends what market. For open-cast mining – normal rock-blasting – don't they still use plastique? Very stable, flexible, and packs a lot o' punch. You used to be able to buy it over the counter in Switzerland, until the terrorist scare started.'

'What about the really serious stuff? Such as what the military use?'

Matt Nugent-Ross blew smoke at the ceiling. 'You're talking about something like Amatol or Torpex. That way you get a really big bang – if you can get hold of it, that is.'

'How difficult is it to get hold of – in large quantities?'

'How large?'

'Let's say, around sixty tons.'

The American's face remained passive. 'Am I reading you right, friend?'

'Matt, there are a couple of hundred fuel-drums stacked out at that airfield at the back of the hangar. Only they're a bloody sight too heavy to contain fuel. It needed four men to move each of them. And one of them had "La Réunion" written on it, with what looked like the name of a mining company, registered in Lichtenstein. Does that suggest anything to you?'

'Should it?'

Rawcliff sat looking at him for a moment, in silence. 'Matt, don't let's get our wires crossed. You know Sammy Ryderbeit – you've known him longer than me. Ryderbeit's not exactly discreet. Hasn't he ever mentioned to you a big French gangster-friend of his who's been behind a few dirty games that he's been involved in?'

The American had got out another cigarette, but forgot to light it. 'Yeah, Sammy blabs a lot. Specially when he's on the sauce, which is most of the time. What's the tie-up?'

'Just that Lichtenstein is a convenient spot for a big international crook to register a ghost-company with alleged mining interests in a French island in the Indian Ocean. And with enough money and clout to be able to charter a French ship out of Marseilles with a load of high explosive. Which just happens to drop in, en route, unofficially, at a beach opposite an abandoned airfield on Cyprus. I'm not going too fast for you, am I?'

'You're doing fine.' Nugent-Ross struck a match, and watched it burn out, still without lighting his cigarette.

'Sixty tons of HE works out at ten tons per aircraft. Half a pay-load? – what makes up the other half?'

'Okay, tell me.'

'The schedule's been changed – apparently for security reasons. We're now only flying one mission with medical supplies. But there's still enough fuel in that hangar for at least five missions.'

Matt looked gravely down at his unlit cigarette. Rawcliff thought he saw it tremble for a moment. 'Jesus. Six full payloads of HE and high-octane aviation-fuel, in equal parts. That would turn each into one great goddamn napalm bomb, each capable of destroying a vast area – buildings and people. And the lucky ones wouldn't be the survivors.'

'How about throwing in a crateful of nuts and bolts and nails – just for ballast, as our French visitor so deftly put it?'

'Yeah, nice. Then you've got not only a napalm bomb, but an anti-personnel one too. What's somebody trying to do? Break the world-record for genocide since 1945?'

They sat listening to the rain tapping against the windows. 'God, I could do with a drink,' Matt said at last.

Rawcliff sat forward. 'I don't exactly know what you're in this for, Matt. You told me you don't give a damn, one way or the other. But I do. I don't mind earning the odd quid on the side, even if it does mean bending the law. But I've still got a few scruples. As I said I draw the line at killing people.'

Nugent-Ross said nothing. His weak pleasant eyes were staring past Rawcliff, at somewhere a long way away.

'You're lucky, Matt. You're the one who holds the ace. The only one who can activate those guidance-systems. Without you, it's no-go. That's your insurance – which is more than the rest of us have got.'

The American gave him a dull smile. 'Go on – I can take it.'

'All right, so let's take it slowly, step-by-step. We make the one dummy-run when the weather clears. Then we go in for the grand-slam. No blankets and medicines this time – just six Hercules loaded to the gills with HE and aviation fuel. Plus a few nuts and bolts, and a lot of powerful loudspeaker equipment, each wired up to a hi-fi system. Does *that* mean anything to you?'

'I've given up asking questions, friend. I've seen the stuff. I know about as much as you, or as little.' He sounded tired.

'Well, let's forget about the loudspeakers for the moment. I can tell you that at least you guessed right about the parachutes. The Frenchman confirmed it early this morning – that somewhere along the line we all bale out. All except you, that is. And Jo, of course.' He paused, but the American said nothing.

'I suppose someone's checked that we've all had experience. Grant doesn't look as though he's jumped before. Not that it much matters,' he added casually. 'They

214

say you stand *less* chance of breaking your neck on a first jump than during a full training course. So! We're flying a prearranged course, and at a given signal we bale out. And from then on, those nice little gadgets of yours take over? Right?'

'Yeah. They'll need you to get the planes into the air. Those computer-babies can manage just about everything, except a take-off and landing within a reasonable margin of safety. Certainly that strip out here rules them out.'

'So that leaves us all floating down, probably over some bit of lonely desert. And it's here, it's my guess, that Ritchie's little Beachcraft Duke comes into its own. It's going to be parked down there waiting for us. It'll be a bit of a squeeze, but it's just about big enough to guarantee us all a safe getaway. And at the same time none of us – not even you – knows the target, until it's hit. You like it?'

'Except for one small detail,' said Matt. 'Young Ritchie's up there flying one of the Hercules. So who flies the Beachcraft?'

'That Frenchman who's arrived – Serge. Why not? He seems to know a lot about aircraft. And it doesn't take a genius to learn how to fly a plane.'

'I guess not. You've been pretty smart so far, friend. The way you say it, it all fits together – except for those damned loudspeakers.' He paused. 'Let me ask you straight, Rawcliff. Why are you telling me all this?'

'Because even the most perfect operation usually has its Achilles' heel.' He gave him a sour grin, 'You're that heel, Matt. You hold the ace, remember.'

The American gave a sad smile. 'Okay, friend, I'll level with you. Jo told you – and she told me that she'd told you. I used to work for the Company – on a kinda freelance basis. Now I'm lapsed, like a bad Catholic. But you know what they say about Intelligence work? It's like the Church, or the CP. Once you've signed on, it's for the duration. Okay, so you expect me to put it all over on the hot-line to Langley? And what would I tell them, for Chrissakes? Hell, I don't know anything. God's truth I don't! I don't know, and young Jo doesn't know. None of us knows!

215

'But one thing I *can* tell you, friend. Whoever's behind this, is playing it pretty long. And very close to the chest. And my hunch is, it's a mighty big game, and I just hate to think what the stakes are!'

'But you must have some ideas? Another hunch?'

'Yes, I just might. For instance, I just might think like Sammy back there at the café when we first met. That maybe this is one of those games with a fixed pack – and that maybe the house *knows it's fixed*. Or better still, prefers *not* to know. I mean, why do you think they've gone for a bunch o' amateurs and oddballs like us in the first place? Because the professionals have all got records – files a mile high. They'd leave a paper-chase all over the Middle East, if they were let loose. But take a cheap killer like Peters – a chancer like Sammy – a psycho like Thurgood. Or just poor saps like you and me. Some of us may be crooks, some not. But nobody's interested. We don't fit in, we're not programmed, we don't even begin to rate in the big league. So nobody's going to get shit on their fingers when the operation comes off, or doesn't. Either way, one thing's sure – nobody's gonna miss us.'

'Except my poor bloody wife and kid.'

There was a long silence between them.

'God, I could do with that drink,' said Matt. 'Or maybe I'd just better watch you drink? There's still some left.'

Rawcliff ignored the offer. He had drunk too much already, yet he still felt unpleasantly sober. 'Whichever way it falls, I think we're going to be killing people, Matt. They may be people we're not supposed to like, or they may be friends. Israelis, Arabs, Cubans. Even Russians – "advisers", of course. Somewhere down in the so-called Soviet "sphere of influence" – like most of Ethiopia, or South Yemen. All just about within the range of a Hercules, on a one-way ticket. Or Iran. Nobody likes them much – not even the Russkies.'

Nugent-Ross nodded. 'That would be mighty convenient, I guess? Kinda soft on the old conscience. Unless, of course, you're one of those limousine-liberals.'

'It's still killing people, Matt. And killing them in a very nasty way. I'm not going to give you a lot of soft humanistic balls at this stage. I'm telling you straight out that you're the only one who can stop this operation. Screw it up at the source.'

The American leaned his head back and ran his fingertips slowly down his neck. then back up again, his mouth pulling a long, clownish face at the ceiling. 'Okay, preacher, let's have it all! You want me to be the real Good Guy – the one who steps in where others fear to tread and saves thousands of human lives? You want me to take a screw-driver and fuck up those machines just before the final take-off? So you guys jump out and the planes fly on out of control, then crash harmlessly? And who's gonna pick up the price-tag? Because the big boys who are pulling the strings behind this one aren't stupid, for Chrissake! They'll know it's me – or they'll suspect it is. And suspicion's enough for their kind.'

He sat back and lit another cigarette. 'Sorry, friend. You just handed me the wrong script. Heroes are made of sterner stuff. Anyway, what the hell does it matter? Do I have to give you Hamburg and Dresden and all that shit? Not to mention the big bang over Hiroshima. The only difference is, the bastards who flew those missions were just picking up their Government pay-cheques – those that ever got back to draw them. You and I and the rest of us – we'll be creaming it off from some nice respectable Swiss bank, with no questions asked.'

Rawcliff just sat and nodded. 'I think I'll have that drink after all, Matt.' He took a long pull at the flask, then added casually, 'I told you I was married, didn't I?'

'You did mention it.'

'But I didn't tell you what my wife does? She's a clever girl – very much in your line of country.' And he told the American the name of the multinational for which Judith worked.

Now that the moment had come, he felt a kind of frenzied numbness, a resignation to the inevitable. The drink had sapped some of the tension from his body, but the strain was beginning to tell now – the nervous hangover from anxiety

217

and lack of sleep, his muscles already stiffening after the long night's work. Like a good pilot, he must keep his hands firmly on the controls – sit tight, stay calm, wait for the turbulence. Or the crash.

Instead, he found himself again listening to that soothing drawl, as Matt took the bait, 'It's a mighty long shot, friend – with mighty little time to act. But that's one of the biggest corporations in the business. And if your wife's really on the ball –' He let the words hang. Rawcliff gave him no prompting.

Matt had lit another cigarette, taking his time. 'She's ideally placed, of course – London being the biggest computer centre in Europe. All she has to do is make a few initial inquiries. There'd be nothing lost, and it just might pay off. I'm assuming here that the systems were programmed in London. I know the equipment's French. In fact, as Sammy thinks, the French may be behind this whole caper. But London's already been used as the main base for recruiting personnel. It's also not only a computer centre – it has the best mapping services in the world, outside Washington.

'Now it's my guess that they'll have used the most detailed existing aerial survey maps for the source-data – they wouldn't have wanted to draw unnecessary attention to themselves by making their own maps. So I suggest your wife starts with the big London mapping libraries. It shouldn't be too difficult for her to find out if someone's recently used micro-dotted data on the most up-to-date, large-scale aerial surveys, covering several thousand square miles within range of Cyprus. Probably somewhere in the Middle East – including Israel and the area west of the Red Sea and the Arabian Peninsula. Most of it's not been extensively mapped, and most of the maps will be specialized stuff, done for geological surveys looking for oil and minerals, or by satellite reconnaissance, for military purposes. Specialized, but not necessarily classified.

'Or, if she really struck lucky, she might even get a lead on the actual computer that did the original processing. There can't be many of them around – they're not things you pick up at the local hardware store. But her company will have access to them, or at least be able to identify them. And computer people gossip. Programming one of those guidance-systems would have been a big job, and must have attracted attention.

'Once she finds the processor, it should be relatively simple for her to track down the second computer – the one which would have to have been programmed by the first, to feed the data on to tape. Six tapes on cassette, no bigger than cigar-boxes, which at some time, some place, are going to be slotted into those six little machines waiting out at the airport.'

Rawcliff licked his lips. His mouth felt dry and sour with the aftertaste of adrenalin. He could have done with a beer, but didn't want to risk going downstairs again unnecessarily, or drawing attention to himself by calling Room Service. If Peters was doing his job, he'd have certainly bought the complicity of the hotel staff. Which reminded Rawcliff of that beaky-faced young man from the third floor.

He stared back at Nugent-Ross. 'You make it sound too easy.'

'Not easy. But maybe not too difficult, either, with a bit of luck.' He gave a loose shrug, 'It's a lot better idea than risk horsing around with those machines and getting the finger put on us. At least this way we might find out where we stand. The final flight-plan – full details of where you jump, plus the destination and objective of the whole operation.'

Rawcliff nodded. 'It's a better idea, Matt, because it lets you off the hook. Isn't that it?'

The American ignored the taunt. He had lit another cigarette and sat breathing smoke peacefully at the ceiling.

'And what does my wife do when she gets hold of this second computer?'

'If she knows her way around, and has the right contacts, she might get hold of a copy of the print-out. Officially, it would be confidential, but if the job was done under the cover of a commercial firm – as I suspect it would have been – security wouldn't be too rigid. As I said, the computer world's too small – nice and select, like a good club, with a lot of loose talk between the members. If your wife's as good as you think she is, she'll know what to look for, and where to look.'

'And if the new schedule's as tight as Serge suggested it is, she'll have twenty-four hours, from the time I contact her', Rawcliff said. 'Only her company doesn't work a twenty-four-hour day. Or if the weather doesn't clear soon, forty-eight hours, at the most.' He realized he was already trying to stall, find excuses, kill off the whole idea before it got out of hand.

'You can give her at least one hard lead,' said Matt. 'The fact that they're not using the ordinary auto-pilot, but instead, this very latest guidance-system, can only mean one thing. A belly-hugging flight, over difficult and well-defended terrain. Which rules out the sea and empty desert.' He paused. 'Do you know anything about air-defences of the Middle East?'

'Not a lot. Flying BEA, we weren't exactly expecting to be shot at.'

Nugent-Ross nodded without humour, 'Egypt's got the biggest variety of hardware – mostly the old Russian stuff she collected between the '67 and '73 wars. SAM-3's and the later SAM-7, the "Grail". And recently, the US has been equipping her with the "Chaparral". Egypt's worth checking first – an outward flight following the established pattern of the mercy-mission down the Red Sea – to the Ogaden maybe, or to the Horn of Africa – then taking the belly-hugging computerized return flight over the desert. Target – the crowded centre of Cairo. Since the Camp David Agreement, there are plenty of Arab organizations crazy enough to try it. All they need is someone to write out the cheque – someone equally crazy, like Gadaffi.'

'What? Wipe out Cairo? And what good's that going to do anyone?'

Nugent-Ross smiled. 'Good doesn't come into it, friend. You might ask what good did the Olympic Massacre do anyone? Or hijacking aircraft, or shooting up international airports?'

'Okay, Matt. How about Tel Aviv for the target? Or

Jerusalem – preferably when the Knesset's sitting? Only Jo would have warned them first, of course.'

Again the American let the jibe pass. 'Possible. But over their western approaches the Israelis have got the best early-warning system outside the US and the Soviet Union. If these people of ours were trying to hit a target in Israel, they'd more likely send in the flights from the south, over Saudi Arabia. The Saudis have got a pretty good defence-system too, using British ''Bloodhounds'' and the more recent French ''Crotale'' missile – only they've got one helluva lot o' ground to cover, so their air-defences are mostly in the north and east, against attacks from Israel and Iraq – and more recently, against Iran. Not forgetting the Russkies, of course.

'Yeah, we'd do well to consider Saudi Arabia.' Matt spoke as though he were thinking aloud now. 'She may be the traditional seat of Islam, and is also fully committed to the cause against Israel. But she still doesn't have many friends in the Islamic world, outside little Jordan and the Emirates. Camp David has ruled out Egypt, and she's far too reactionary for the leftist Arab states, like Syria, Iraq and Algeria, or a quasi-Marxist religious fanatic, like Gadaffi.

'But then, there's another obvious target – that deranged Messiah in Iran, and his mob-apostles, who regard the Sunni rulers of Saudi Arabia as heretics, damned in the eyes of Allah. And the Saudis are certainly contenders! The Russians don't like her rulers, because they're politically pro-West. While from the West's point of view, Saudi Arabia's an economic pain in the arse. She's got us all over that oil-barrel, and she knows it. Which suggests another possibility. The old Dirty Tricks Department. A freelance operation, under clandestine leadership, financed through a money-laundry in Lichtenstein or Switzerland, with no messy footprints leading back to Washington or Whitehall or Paris, or wherever. Though I doubt the West's got the balls to try it.' He paused, spreading his hands across his naked knees. 'It was just a thought. Otherwise, we'll just have to wait and see what your wife can turn up. Are you agreeable?'

'You mean, is *she* agreeable?' Rawcliff had stood up. 'I can only ask her. But she's going to need some details about these machines of yours.'

'Tell her it's a Tetra-Lipp Retropilot Mark 100/4.'

Rawcliff had found a pad of hotel notepaper by the bed and was scribbling down further technical details, most of which was gibberish to him, but which he confidently believed that Judith would understand. It gave him an odd queasy feeling – this electric bond between her and Matt, which had about it a disconcerting stench of intimacy, as though she were already involved, drawn unwittingly, innocently, into a swamp of conspiracy that was very probably leading to some act of bloody horror.

He looked at his watch. 'The Post Office'll be closed by now. I'm not going to risk calling her from here,' he added in a voice betraying the first twinge of doubt, 'or from my own place – even if I could get through.'

'It opens again at five.' The American sounded too bland. 'Time for the weather to settle – for you to have a better idea of when you'll be flying.'

Or time to change my mind, Rawcliff thought. He had begun to open the door, to make sure the corridor was clear, when Nugent-Ross called after him, 'Just one other thing! Tell her to make sure the track's virgin. I mean, we want to make sure that no one else has been sniffing around before her.'

Rawcliff turned. 'This isn't going to get her into any kind of trouble, is it?'

The American gave him a watery smile. 'What – in a nice civilized city like London? Hell, she'll only be asking a few questions. Part of her job.' He raised a limp hand. 'So long, friend. Good luck.'

Rawcliff again took the stairs, and again met no one. The clerk was snoozing behind his desk; the man didn't even notice him leave.

He waited up in his room in the Lord Byron until 4.50, before slipping out, unseen. The street was still full of wind – short tepid blasts that churned up the dust and slammed

222

windows and shutters, and set the nerves on edge. A subtle feverish wind, like the mistral or the sirocco, which can unhinge even the most balanced mind.

It was after the siesta, and crowds hurried and jostled down the pavements, as he headed east on to Kitieus Street, past the Swedish Consulate, grey and shuttered, and remembered wondering afterwards, what the hell did the Swedes need a. Consulate for in a Godforsaken place like this? Presumably a relic of the old UN Force. And a lot of bloody use *they'd* be to him now.

It was at the turning down to the Post Office that he knew he was being followed. It was a visceral instinct, like that of a nervous animal. Nothing more than the tap of ghost footsteps, and when he looked back, just the hurrying crowds – black cropped hair and shawled heads bent against the wind. An empty cigarette-packet came bouncing and spinning down the gutter towards him.

He arrived outside the Post Office at a few minutes past five. The big iron gates had been folded back and the first crush had already passed through, ready to grapple with the mindless obstructions of the local bureaucracy. Rawcliff was busy looking for the counter which dealt with international telephone calls, and for a moment his guard dropped. Another couple of seconds and he would have walked smack into Jim Ritchie.

Perhaps it was the neurotic effect of the wind, after the long waiting, with too many of Taki's thick Greek coffees, but he now reacted with that same fearful instinct, stepping swiftly sideways behind a marble pillar. He knew at once that it was absurd, that he was getting jumpy, losing his grip, for Ritchie was the one member of the team – with the possible exception of Ryderbeit – whom he didn't have active cause to distrust.

Ritchie had just come out of one of the phone-booths reserved for local calls. He had paused and stood studying a slip of paper; then he crumpled it up, seemed about to toss it into a spitoon, changed his mind and stuck it in his trouser pocket.

Rawcliff was reminded of that sheet of hotel note-paper

from the Sun Hall, with his scribbled instructions to Judith from Matt Nugent-Ross. He had spent nearly half an hour lying on his bed, memorizing them – a string of computer jargon and meaningless digits – until he had felt confident enough to flush them down the lavatory.

Ritchie had walked past without seeing him, and had now disappeared into the street. At the same instant Rawcliff knew, with irrational certainty, that someone was watching him.

He edged his way round the pillar, his eyes smarting from the dust and wind. Huddled queues, patient faces peering through the grilles. He waited twenty seconds, then pushed his way back towards the entrance. Through the moving gaps in the dense rackety traffic, he saw Ritchie opening the front passenger-door of a car parked directly across the street, under a 'no-waiting' sign. It was a big chocolate-brown American sedan. Rawcliff glimpsed the beaky profile of the driver, with his untidy black hair, as Ritchie climbed in beside him.

But instead of the car starting, a second car now appeared, and pulled up directly behind the first. It was a Mini: and although Rawcliff could not see, he knew that it would be an Italian-built Innocenti. A tall man in an open-necked shirt got out. He did not look like a Cypriot, nor did Rawcliff think he was English: a long scooped-out face, high forehead and rimless spectacles. Rawcliff watched him through the traffic, as he came round the Mini, paused by the sedan, and opened the rear door.

Rawcliff had started down the steps of the Post Office. He could see Ritchie turned in his seat, talking to the man in the back. Then the driver joined in. A few more words were exchanged. Ritchie nodded, reached over the seat and shook hands with the tall man. It was an oddly formal, un-English gesture for Ritchie. He said something to the driver, then got out and began walking rapidly away down the street towards the seafront. The tall man had climbed out again and gone back to the Mini.

Rawcliff did not stay to see the two cars drive away, but returned to the cool vault of the Post Office hall. He was still in no real hurry – the two-hour time difference meant that his call would reach Judith at her office around 3.30 pm, which, with luck, should catch her nicely between lunch and her regular Tuesday afternoon sales conference, which Rawcliff knew to his annoyance often went on late. But first he had to endure the maddening anxiety of waiting a quarter of an hour in a queue, before he could place his call, through the international operator; while another ten minutes passed until a woman's shrill voice called out his London number, with the 499 Mayfair prefix barely intelligible above the babble of the crowded hall.

He still had that uncomfortable feeling of being watched, though his sense of disquiet was now concentrated on what he was going to tell his wife, as he pulled the padded door shut, sealing himself off in the hot airless cell of the telephone-booth.

He lifted the receiver and stood listening to the familiar English girl repeating mechanically the name of the multinational for which Judith worked. He gave her the extension number. No tell-tale clicks. It was a public switchboard, for Christ's sake. The line was very clear, as he now heard that exasperating languid voice of his wife's secretary. He explained who he was, and she told him to hang on. He could feel the receiver already growing clammy under his hand.

'Hello, Charles?' She sounded very close, in that dark quiet place, and at the same time stiff and remote, a tone he recognized all too well from when he rang her up after a row the night before, waking with a headache, to find that she'd already left for the office.

He kept the preamble down to a minimum. Told her not to worry, and that he was doing his job in Cyprus, that it would soon be over, and that he was all right – above all, *he was all right*. He didn't give her time to press him. He asked her to get ready to take notes; then he rested back against the wall of the cabin and began to recite, slowly, like some idiot incantation, the instructions that Matt had given him.

This time she was too confused, or perhaps still too angry, in her quiet, over-controlled way, to ask for a full

225

explanation. She let him go on, telling her to cover the whole area of the Middle East and north-west Africa, concentrating on the full area round the Red Sea – Egypt, Saudi Arabia, the southern approaches to Israel.

Even before he had finished, he was feeling foolish, aware of the melodramatic absurdity of the whole thing. It was not only preposterous, impossible, it was bloody daft – a deliberate diversion by that American to keep him happy, or at least keep him busy.

Somehow he managed to maintain the pretence, stressing the urgency of her task, and of the maximum time-limit of forty-eight hours in which to accomplish it. There was a dead silence. It was very hot in the booth and he was prickling with sweat. He heard her cool voice, 'It's no good my asking what all this is about?'

'No, love. But it's very important – that's all I can tell you.'

Her next words had the sudden chill edge of hysteria, 'Oh God, Charles, I hope you know what you're doing! *Please* – for the sake of me and Tom –!' But he cut in quickly, closing his eyes with dread, promising to call her again, without fail, at eight o'clock tomorrow evening – Wednesday, her time. He calculated, perhaps recklessly, that the relief-flight must be back well before then.

He hung up with a sense of weary anguish. He had forgotten about Ritchie and the ubiquitous beaky-faced young man from the Sun Hall, and the tall stranger and the familiar two cars. He didn't even worry any more about being followed, as he stepped back into the noisy hall and paid the woman at the desk, from a grubby wad of Cypriot notes which he had changed, at a humiliating rate, with Taki. The call to London had taken a sizeable bite out of his remaining cash resources.

Outside, the wind had not let up and the sky was crowded with scudding grey clouds – the shreds of the cumulus-nimbus, still rising dark above the sea. Dusk was closing in and he returned to the Lord Byron, feeling deeply depressed. The hotel had a clogged, grimy smell that made him feel dirty. Taki was presiding behind the empty bar. No sign of

Ryderbeit or Thurgood. A radio played very loud *bazouki* music. Taki beamed at him and gave a broad gesture, 'You drink, my friend?'

Rawcliff stopped long enough for a beer. The Cypriot added, 'Today weather no good for aeroplanes! Perhaps tomorrow good – yes?'

'Yes.' Rawcliff considered going up to find Ryderbeit on the chance that he might be sober and awake. But what did he have to tell him? That he'd just put in motion a ridiculous plan to try and scupper the operation? Ryderbeit wouldn't like that. He wouldn't like it at all. He might be a shatterpate adventurer, but he was also a professional. He had been paid to do a job, and he would do it, and make sure that he got paid at the end of it. Judith would be wasting her time, as far as Sammy Ryderbeit was concerned.

Rawcliff finished his beer and went up to his cheerless room. No lifts in this hotel. No sound from the other rooms. He imagined Thurgood's gruesome white body stretched out somewhere near, his manic energy spent, recharging himself for the next bout. God knew what Ryderbeit was up to.

He stood naked in the narrow shower cubicle, watching the water drain away in a rusty pool round his feet. There was a cockroach on the wall, like an enormous blood-blister. He reached out to squash it with his thumb, and heard the door of his room click behind him. He had left it unlocked. He turned and saw Jo staring unashamedly at him. He nodded to her, as though he were expecting her. She was wearing a nondescript headscarf and plain cotton skirt – which was no doubt why he had failed to pick her out of the crowd in the Post Office, or in the street outside, although he had known all along that there'd been someone. A professional. At least he could give her credit for that.

She came in and sat down on the bed. 'Tit-for-tat, Mr Rawcliff. I call Rome, you call London. Only you spoke for longer than I did.'

He bent down and picked up his pants, noticing with mild relief that they were clean. 'It was my wife. Any objections?'

'Why should I? I don't know about Peters, though.'

He pulled on his pants. 'What do you want, Jo?'

'I want to get a few things straight. What did you come up to talk about with Matt today? Don't worry, I'm not upset about being caught *in flagrante delicto*! As I said, Matt and I are old friends. I just want to know what you're cooking up with him?'

He nodded. 'So that you can pass it all on to Mossad?' He stood in front of her, his hands hanging loosely at his sides. 'Why have you been following me, Jo?'

She looked up at him, her face calm, determined. 'I think it's time you started answering some of *my* questions for a change. You still haven't told me what you spent all your time talking about with Matt?'

'I should ask him yourself – during your next bit of pillow-talk.'

She had taken off her scarf and sat shaking out her hair. 'Oh come on! – that's a bit cheap, isn't it?'

He took a step forward until his knees were almost touching her skirt. 'I slapped you around last night, Jo, because I was angry, and because I wanted you to talk. Well, you're going to do some more talking.'

She dropped her lower lip and gave a small laugh, both furtive and cunning. 'And if I don't feel like talking?'

'You didn't come up here just to hold hands. You're a big girl now.' He stood, still almost touching her, flexing the fingers of each hand. This wasn't quite what they'd prepared him for, all those years ago in Darkest Surrey, where – despite the propaganda of popular fiction – girls were still not accepted as part of the British undercover curriculum. The camp at Cobham, after all, had only been a step down-market from White's Club and the Travellers.

Jo sat looking up at him with sly anticipation. She didn't move, didn't speak: and Rawcliff, enervated by exhaustion and the jarring strain of his call to Judith, knew suddenly just how it would be, even before it happened – that there was nothing he could do to prevent it, even if he had wanted to, and that it was irrelevant anyway. Afterwards he had a remote image, in the dying light from the window, of her narrow haunches cleaved into hemispheres of brilliant white against the pale tan of her legs and shoulders, skin dry-cool in the muggy stillness as he closed with her in a skilful passionless ritual, its timing perfectly synchronized, undistracted by sentiment, even affection. He felt no shame, no guilt. Since involving Judith in the operation, he was now beyond such exemplary emotions. When it was over, all he felt was a dead utter tiredness.

He must have slept for only a few minutes. He watched Jo slip gracefully off the bed and move towards the shower cubicle; and he lay and stared out of the window, at the flat roof-tops with their fringe of washing-lines and TV aerials framed against the raw twilight. He heard the water stop, and saw her come back in and start quickly, methodically, hitching up her panties, smoothing her dress, reaching for her watch on the bedside table.

'If you were at the Post Office this evening, you must have seen Jim Ritchie?' His voice had a thick disembodied sound, as though it came from somewhere outside him, from across the room.

She had put on her shoes and now sat stiffly on the edge of the bed. She might have been a secretary waiting for dictation. 'What did you say about Ritchie?'

He could not read between the dim lines of her profile and realized that he had not even kissed her.

'He was in the Post Office making a local call. Left just as I arrived – got into a big American car outside – the one I told you about last night – that followed me and Matt in from the airfield. Driven by a young man who's staying at the Sun Hall, third floor. Come on, Jo, you're a pro – you're supposed to find out about these things. Who is he? And who was the tall man in rimless glasses who drove up in the Mini?'

She ran her fingers along the edge of the frayed counterpane. 'You expect an awful lot from me. And don't give much in return.' But there was a cynical tone to the words and he did not respond. 'Oh all right, what the hell! The young fellow you saw in the car is called Klein. He's got dual American-Israeli nationality.'

'How do you know?'

'You forget that I have contacts with the Israelis. I told

you last night.'

'And Klein's another of their agents?'

She shook her head. 'It's not as simple as that.'

'My God, I hope not!'

'Klein's what's known in the trade as an "information-broker". What you'd call a "double" – or perhaps a "treble", in Klein's case – which is not unusual in this part of the world. He peddles to the Americans and to the Mossad, and occasionally even to the Russians, when they ask for it. He's tolerated because he's useful all round. It's one of the ways Washington – and Moscow – keep tabs on what the Israelis and Arabs are up to. For instance, if one side wants to fly a kite – say, a new initiative involving the PLO, or some other sensitive issue – they'd use Klein as middle-man. He's trusted enough for the other side to believe him. But if they don't like what he tells them – or there's a press leak and a big international row – nobody is officially to blame. The ministers and diplomats concerned can honestly claim no knowledge of the business – they'd never dirty their hands dealing with a little shit like Klein. That's left to the small-fry – the stringers.'

'Like you? And young Jim Ritchie, so it seems?'

Rawcliff had put on his trousers and took a clean shirt out of his suitcase which lay on the floor still half-unpacked. 'And what about the tall man from the Mini?'

'I don't know who he is. I've never seen him before.'

'Why not ask your friend Ritchie?'

'No. I'm sorry, but it's not in the rules of the game. And unless you know the rules, you just can't hope to understand.'

'I'm doing my best.' He didn't like being patronized by pretty girls who came uninvited into his room while he was taking a shower and provoked him with their neat little naked bums, then lectured him with a lot of big-talk from the inside-track of the Intelligence racket. Jo was either too ingenious, or too bloody crafty. Both ways, he didn't like it.

He stood buttoning up his sleeveless shirt, letting it hang loose over his trousers. 'So you say it's all a game? Which is what I've always believed about the so-called spy-world.

Neither side has any secrets left any more – none worth guarding, anyway. Most of the technical stuff has usually been published somewhere, if you know where to look. And the really big info, like troop build-ups and rocket-silos, is all monitored by satellite. But the Intelligence people have to do something to justify themselves, so they play around with young amateurs like you and Ritchie, buying and selling the odd tit-bit of hush-hush information, thus making everyone feel important and satisfied. Only people on the outside, like me, don't feel so satisfied. For a start, who's Ritchie working for?'

'For us, I should think. I mean, the British. Strictly short-term contract – to buy himself insurance, or ''good-will'', as our authorities prefer to call it. Which in Ritchie's case probably means a guarantee of immunity next time there's a tip-off that he's running over a load of hash in that little plane of his.' She smiled: 'Don't look so surprised! It happens all the time. You don't have to be a big-shot in the art world any more, working for both the Kremlin and the Palace, to get the preferential treatment. Whitehall's much more democratic these days.' She tried to smile again, but was inhibited by the look in Rawcliff's eyes.

'Listen, Jo. This isn't a game, and these aren't titbits you're buying and selling through Klein. This is a big, serious, nasty operation, and there may be many thousands of lives at stake – mine included. While at least two members of the operation – leaving out Matt for the moment – are busy blowing it to the Israelis, the British, the Americans – even the Russians, if what you say about Klein is true.'

She had again begun sucking the knuckles of her hand, which he took to be a sign of nervousness.

'You can't just let it hang out like this, Jo. What's Ritchie told Klein?' She said nothing. 'What have *you* told Klein? You're going to tell me. And you may get more than just a spanking before you do.'

She had taken her hand from her mouth, and said quietly, 'I haven't had anything to do with Klein. I deal direct through my contact in Rome.'

'But you must know what Ritchie's told him? You're a

231

friend of his, for Christ's sake! You're at home in his London pad – and you're both in the same racket.'

'You don't understand. It's one of the first rules that we don't swap info between ourselves.'

'What about Matt? Haven't you talked to him?' He realized it was the first time that he'd thought seriously about Matt, since Jo had arrived, but he certainly wasn't going to start having a sense of remorse on his account. After all, the American had been a willing accomplice in involving Judith, and Rawcliff felt a sudden irrational hatred of the man.

'Leave Matt out of this,' Jo said.

'Like hell I will! Matt's got his own line to the CIA, if he chooses to use it.'

'Matt's neutral. I'm sure he is.'

'No one's neutral – not in this operation. But even if Matt isn't officially on the US payroll, that still leaves you and Ritchie. Now, since you won't level with me about Ritchie, I'll just have to assume for the moment that you and he know about as much, or as little, about the operation as each other. Ritchie may be working for the British, but he's also feeding his stuff through Klein. And if Klein is what you say he is, that means that Washington and Whitehall – even Moscow, God help us! – must all know what you've told the Israelis. But you said last night that all you'd done was keep your friend in Rome up-to-date on the operation?'

'That's right. Honest to God.'

Rawcliff clamped his jaw shut, controlling his temper. He took a deep breath, then said slowly, 'And you've no idea if the Israelis know what the operation is all about?'

'No. They'd never tell me anyway. They just say "thanks, and keep up the good work".'

'If they *do* know,' said Rawcliff, 'why don't they do something about it? They've got enough friends in Washington to be able to lean on the Cypriots, however much the local big-boys have been paid to keep their noses out of it. Unless, of course, they don't *want* to know?'

This time she did smile. 'Clever Mr Rawcliff! And if Jerusalem doesn't know, or doesn't want to know, you can be sure nobody else does.'

'All of which seems to suggest an unofficial operation that has everyone's tacit blessing?'

'It rather does, doesn't it?' She stood up. 'Perhaps it's as simple as that. Or as unsimple.'

'Why have you told me all this, Jo? It's not because you're really that frightened of me, is it? What I'd do to you is nothing to what Peters would think up, if he ever found out.'

'I trust you. You're an innocent outsider, but you're also one of the team – and I've got a pretty good idea that you don't like the way things are going any more than I do. But my hands are tied. I just do what Jerusalem tells me. You can do as you please – although I'm certain that the last person you'd confide in is Peters. He's just waiting to get even with you – to hang you up by your balls, and take his time doing it. And don't think you can buy any favours from him, by blowing me and Ritchie, or even Matt. Peters isn't that type. It would be enough for him that you'd even been talking to any of us.'

She had picked up her headscarf from the bed and turned towards the door. 'I suppose I just have to take your word that you were ringing your wife this evening?'

'The Post Office'll have a docket of the number. I was ringing her at work – if you're thinking of checking.'

'I will, don't worry.'

He stood for a long time staring down at the unmade bed. She had left the room so softly that he had not even heard the door close behind her.

9

From Judith Rawcliff's point of view, her husband's telephone call, coming in the middle of that Tuesday afternoon, could not have been more inconvenient or less helpful. She had a stack of world sugar forecasts to finish by tomorrow evening; and he had interrupted her with an urgent demand that managed to be both vague and complex – a task which at best was going to keep her on the telephone for several hours. Nor had his call done the least to reassure her: indeed, far from resolving the riddle of his disappearance, it had merely deepened the mystery. He had hung up before she had been able to ask him where he was in Cyprus, let alone what he was doing there.

He had just said that it was very important: and while he had still given no direct hint that it was anything illegal, even criminal, she decided to do as much groundwork as she could without involving any of her colleagues or superiors in the company. At this stage she did not even enlist the help of her secretary.

She began by making a full list of the main London mapping libraries. Beside the British Library, at the British Museum, and the Royal Geographical Society, the only official Government source available to the public was the Directorate of Overseas Surveys, attached to the Ministry of Overseas Development, whose offices were out in Surbiton. Typically, they closed at 4.30, and the information was disclosed by appointment only. She risked using the company's name to get through to a senior official in the cartographical department, who told her that the only parts of the Middle East to have been recently surveyed was the Yemen Arab Republic – otherwise, non-Communist North Yemen – and large chunks of Sinai, which had been covered by a joint Israeli-Egyptian·oil prospecting team, working together in the 'new spirit of Camp David'.

She made a provisional arrangement to drive out tomorrow during her lunch-break. Her husband had not mentioned the Yemen, telling her to concentrate on Egypt and the north of Saudi Arabia; but he had also specified the area around the Red Sea, which included both North Yemen and the South, Marxist, Soviet-infiltrated Peoples' Democratic Republic of the Yemen.

She drew a blank at the British Library and at the Royal Geographical Society, although she was able to discover that a firm called 'Hunting Surveys' had made a geodetic survey of Saudi Arabia back in 1970; but they had no report of anyone recently inquiring about the information, or of using any data for computer work.

That left her with the Copyright libraries, all outside London – in Edinburgh, Oxford and Cambridge, and at Aberystwyth. But it was already getting late. And she cursed her delinquent husband and those sugar quotas. She couldn't stay on late at the office, because of collecting Tom from the baby-minder; while her boss, a hyper-active American called Cy Reynolds had demanded those 'futures' forecasts by six o'clock tomorrow. But, knowing him, he'd then probably forget to use them for another week or ten days. At least she knew her way around Cy; and in spite of everything, her husband had to come first. In the end, he always did.

He had told her that she had, at the very outside, forty-eight hours, but that he would call her again at home tomorrow at eight in the evening.

She now had two deadlines to meet. It was almost five o'clock, and she had made no progress in either direction. She unlocked a drawer of her desk and took out a packet of cigarettes. It was her first for three weeks; but self-denial had its limits. The cigarette made her feel bolder, and slightly sinful. She now decided to try her computer contacts direct.

There was a man at the University of London Computer Centre, called Matlock, who owed her a couple of favours. She caught him just as he was leaving. He had never heard of a Tetra-Lipp Retropilot, but guessed that it might be something to do with missiles, and said he didn't think she'd get much joy out of the Ministry of Defence, even if the thing wasn't still strictly classified.

Although Judith had no idea what her husband was playing at, she was shrewd enough to guess that – if only for his wretched sake – she must steer well clear of the military establishment in Whitehall. Even Surbiton might be getting too close.

She read out to Matlock the full details which her husband had given her. He replied that it sounded like a very big specialized job, and that he himself knew of only two computers in the country capable of processing such data at source. One was an ICL 1902 belonging to the Directorate of Military Surveys, which sounded a great deal too official – both for her, and for this job. The other took her back to the old DOS out in Surbiton.

Matlock was apologizing for not being more helpful, when he remembered something, and told her to hang on. She was already on her third cigarette when he came back.

It was a long shot, he said, but he happened to have heard from a colleague that over four months ago – around June, he thought it was – one of the Centre's own computers, a PDP 11/35, had been used for a huge run, transferring already processed source-data on to tape. He couldn't say offhand who had commissioned the job, but he'd heard that the data itself originated from a small private mapping firm that specialized in geodetic surveys, mostly for the big oil companies. He agreed that this might tie in with the Middle East. The name of the firm was AREX Surveys, with offices off the Charing Cross Road.

She thanked him, and he promised that if he heard anything more he'd let her know. When she hung up it was just gone 5.15. She called AREX Surveys, but there was no answer. That would have to wait until tomorrow. And by then, the deadline would be eighteen hours closer.

Tomorrow, Wednesday, looked like being a long day.

Rawcliff on that Wednesday morning, woke, dazzled by a spear of sunlight from between the shutters. Outside, the weather was bright and calm, the sky a clear blue. The beginning of a perfect Mediterranean winter's day.

Downstairs he found Ryderbeit and Thurgood engrossed in a game of 'spoof'. From their expressions, it was evident that Ryderbeit was winning handsomely. He was leering and cackling at his opponent; while Thurgood's long pale face was flushed with blotches, and his bulging eyes had a cloudy look. He kept shifting on his chair, his fingers drumming on the table and the nerve tugging at his left eye. Occasionally he would break off the game to scratch himself vigorously on both arms, and at his shoulders and chest; then would pinch his moustache and say, with bogus hilarity, and in an accent that was a cross between Bertie Wooster and those pre-war BBC commentators – a preposterous drawl, abruptly clipped at the end, 'Damn well played, Sammy! By Jove, you had me there!'

Rawcliff remembered that back in London Terry Mason had told him, only last week, of how Thurgood sometimes got these 'turns', when he was in the habit of assuming a parady of what Mason had called an 'Oxford accent' – hinting that they usually portended some drastic and unpredictable behaviour on Thurgood's part.

The man totally ignored Rawcliff, as he sat down beside them. Ryderbeit offered him a glass of neat ouzo, but Rawcliff declined. 'We may have to fly soon, Sammy.'

The Rhodesian jabbed a sharp fingernail into Rawcliff's ribs. 'Don't nanny me, soldier. I know how to drink and I know how to fly. I also know how to play spoof. The Flight-Lieutenant here now owes me precisely two thousand, eight hundred and fifty pounds. And he's bloody well going to pay me, too!'

'You're a thumping fine fellow!' Thurgood said, wincing and scratching his shoulders and arms.

Rawcliff ordered a double Turkish coffee and yoghourt.

Thurgood had lost another five hundred pounds to Ryderbeit when the phone jangled behind the bar. Taki came out. 'Mr Sammy, sir, telephone!'

While Ryderbeit went to the back of the room, Thurgood began his scratching routine again. Rawcliff asked him what the trouble was.

'Bites, old man. Damn well bitten all over, I am.' He undid his shirt and pulled it wide open. Rawcliff stared aghast. The whole of the man's torso was covered in a livid network of pustules, strangely reminiscent of a map of the London Underground system, each station represented by a dark swelling, capped with a yellow head, and linked by red weals.

'Christ. Those aren't bites,' Rawcliff said, as Ryderbeit came strolling back.

'Right children! That was Peters. We're off the ground and flying.'

'Just take a look at Thurgood's chest,' said Rawcliff.

Thurgood was holding his shirt proudly open. 'Itches like the billyoh!'

Ryderbeit peered down at him. 'Holy Moses, you better get that seen to, Flight-Lieutenant. And make sure you keep well away from me. It's either scurvy or the bubonic plague!'

'I say, do you really think so, old man?'

'Get Jo to look at it. I'm sure she'll find it highly attractive.' Ryderbeit lit a cigar and led the way out to the Suzuki. 'He sits in the back,' he said, jerking his thumb toward Thurgood, 'and don't breathe over us. Keep your windows open and your poxy germs to yourself!'

Thurgood sustained his asinine jabber all the way to the airfield. It had ceased to be comic, and now took on the sinister guise of the true psychotic: he was like an automaton that has been programmed to utter a string of irrelevant phrases, each delivered without the least facial expression, 'Dashed fine to be getting the old kites flying, eh? I'm looking forward to this shufti!' – scratching all the time as he talked.

Occasionally Ryderbeit would tell him to button his lip, but it was as though the man had not heard. Nor did he seem to pay the least attention to Ryderbeit's comments to Rawcliff, 'The bastard's blown a fuse. Holy Moses, I'm glad I'm not going to be up in that plane with him!'

'He looks and sounds sick to me,' said Rawcliff. 'What's that rash he's got?'

'God knows, but it's something pretty horrible. Just our luck to have one of us go sick, on the morning before take-off. Grant was bad enough – now we've got this! A bloody rabid hyena in the back. If there was a moon, he'd be fucking barking at it!' In his keenness and excitement, Ryderbeit displayed an almost childish innocence. His only concern about the operation was that it should proceed without mishap. He believed in doing a dishonest job honestly – unlike half the other members of the team.

By eight am they were all assembled out at the hangar, with the exception of Matt Nugent-Ross; he would not be needed until the final flight, when he was to load the guidance-systems, and activate them at some stage during the mission.

Jo was there, in her nurse's uniform, with her Red Cross case. She greeted Rawcliff with a casual nod, while chatting to Ritchie. Rawcliff had to admire her nerve, but then it would have been part of her training. Ritchie gave him his boyish grin and asked if he'd slept all right 'in that flea-pit of yours', to which Rawcliff made some dim joke about cockroaches. He found that he was looking at Ritchie in rather a different light now: no longer as the playboy taxi-pilot hopping over to Deauville for the weekend, but as a cheap informer on a one-night-stand with Whitehall, as well as dealing through a professional street-walker like Klein, whose clients included Langley, Virginia, and Dzerzhinski Square, Moscow.

They were joined by Guy Grant, still sallow, with mushroom-pouches under his eyes; but he had turned himself out in a smart biscuit-coloured suit, and his crisp grey hair was carefully combed and varnished back. He looked at Rawcliff and Jo with a pinched smile, 'It was damned white of you both to look after me the other night. I behaved abominably. Sorry I didn't apologize before, but what with all the loading and everything –' He had drawn Rawcliff aside. 'That Frenchman hasn't said anything about me, has he?'

'I haven't seen him since the other night.' Rawcliff had noticed that Serge was busy listening to the weather reports on Thurgood's radio.

Grant nodded. 'I must say, old bean, I'm as nervous as a kitten!'

'You'll be all right when the time comes,' Rawcliff said, without conviction. 'The waiting's always the worst time.'

Jo came up to them and said, 'I've been asked to look at Thurgood's chest. Sammy thinks he's got foot-and-mouth.' She giggled, just as Thurgood strutted over to them and once more, with evident pride, ripped open his shirt for her to see.

She stood examining him with professional dispassion. 'How long have you had this?' she said at last.

He gazed at her with his cloudy eyes, the pupils shrunk to black pin-heads, and answered as though in a trance, 'Must've come up during the night. Didn't notice till this morning, when it began to itch.' He had spoken in his normal voice, as though the ventriloquist's doll had been returned to its shelf.

Ryderbeit shouted at her, 'I should keep your paws well off him, Jo, my darling – he's probably picked that up from some scabby whore. Oswald, you're an evil poxy sod.'

Thurgood stared at her blankly. Jo said, 'I don't think it's anything to worry about. Most likely a parasite you picked up from the water, or from something you've eaten.'

'Bloody bilharzia,' Ryderbeit said.

'If you come with me,' Jo said, 'I'll give you something to stop the itching.' Thurgood followed her meekly away to where she had left her Red Cross kit.

Peters now approached, still wearing dark glasses and his pink plastic collar. 'Right, that's enough talking. Get into line.' He stepped aside, as Serge arrived. The Frenchman was carrying six plain buff envelopes, which he distributed among the rest of the pilots; then he addressed them, again through Rawcliff, 'These contain your flight-plan. You will have ten minutes to study it before take-off. Remember, you are flying a normal mission, fully accredited to the International Committee of the Red Cross. You will maintain normal radio-communication – but you will not, on any account, contact me. If, at any point, ground-control orders you to alter course, or even to land, you will obey without question.' He paused, while Rawcliff translated. Peters listened with a slight scowl.

Serge went on, 'Each envelope also contains your Red Cross identification papers, a certificate of your plane's airworthiness, insurance documents and a full inventory of your cargo. There are also certificates of vaccination against smallpox, typhoid and cholera. You will remember to sign all these before take-off.

'Now – each of you has a valid passport and your pilot's licence? You will see from the flight-plan that you will be maintaining a height of four thousand metres, so as not to interfere with normal civilian air-traffic. You may be requested to alter height and direction round Cairo. You will also remain vigilant to the presence of unscheduled military aircraft.

'You will be flying in close diamond-formation, one hundred metres between each aircraft. Monsieur Peters here will lead the formation' – his calm eye ran across the faces in front of him – 'with Monsieur Grant flying to port, alongside Monsieur Ryderbeit. Monsieur Rawcliff will assume port in the second row, with Monsieur Ritchie to starboard. Monsieur Thurgood will take up the rear.'

Thurgood had come sprinting over, fresh from the attentions of Jo, and stood stiffly to attention, his clipped moustache twitching slightly.

'Your special clothing is over behind the planes.' Serge paused. 'Are there any questions?'

The words sounded almost facetious to Rawcliff. Yes, there were plenty of questions: and as always, not the faintest bloody chance of their being answered. The Frenchman concluded: 'So if that is all, *au revoir et merde!*' – which Rawcliff translated, rather lamely, as 'Goodbye and good luck!' At least the man hadn't said *Adieu*.

They broke away at a trot, like eager schoolboys – all except for Peters who limped morosely behind, still jealous of the Frenchman's authority, and harbouring his deep, festering hatred for Rawcliff.

The special clothing consisted of fur-lined flying boots, standard issue, leather gloves, lunch-packs, and leather jackets lined with lamb's wool, each with a red cross on a white background stitched to the back – seven apiece. Jo took hers and, without discussion, boarded Ritchie's Hercules. It seemed to Rawcliff a gratuitous act of provocation on her part – unless it were her way of showing that she didn't belong to him, and owed him nothing. Ritchie, after all, was her old spookmate, and perhaps sharing the same flight-deck meant as much to her as sharing the same bed? Rawcliff just hoped she'd be safe up there with him – that, considering the amount of time that Ritchie had spent away from the field, he'd done his homework on the plane.

Once inside his own plane he felt the old familiar surge of excitement, as he switched on and checked each dial, which he had wiped clean of grease: checked flaps, air-pressure, oil and fuel-mixtures, hydraulics, undercarriage, brakes. All humming smoothly. He turned on the R/T, cleared the static and listened to the jabber of voices. Ryderbeit was saying to Grant, 'Keep it cool and steady, old soldier. You just follow me, keeping your wings level with mine. Just do what I do, and you won't go wrong.'

Rawcliff slit open his envelope. The flight-plan curved out south-westwards across the Mediterranean, then settled down south-south-west to the Nile Delta: and from there due south between Cairo and Suez, bearing south-west over the Galala Plateau to join the gulf of Suez, and down now on an almost fixed south-by-south-east course following the length of the Red Sea, keeping well out of Saudi Arabian and Sudanese airspace.

Peters' leading Hercules was already warming up all four engines, and Serge had crept under the wings, ready to kick away the chocks. Rawcliff started his Number One outward port-engine, waited for it to fire, with a shudder and blast of black oily fumes, and heard, with the thrill increasing, the deep growling roar as he fed it more throttle. He started Number Two engine and felt the whole aircraft vibrating and tugging forward against the chocks. He glanced quickly at the other documents from the envelope.

The vaccination certificates had all been issued in Geneva during the last week. They looked uncannily genuine. He also noticed, with a quick sinking feeling, that the Red Cross documents were filled in with his full name, together with his home address, place and date of birth.

He let all four Lockheed engines start in turn, slowly warming, feeding each just enough mixture so as not to overheat the weary old machinery – remembering that they might have sat idle for months, even years, on a damp airfield in Germany – soothing and caressing the four colossal turbo-props, while he looked through the rest of the flight-plan.

Nearly five hours' flying, with only Egyptian airspace to cross – and that had been fully cleared. The rest was down the centre of the Red Sea – far down to an area just north of Massawa, on the Eritrean coast, where they were to veer due west. The drop-zone, a tiny place called Oudgan, lay a hundred miles, or twenty minutes' flying time, from the sea. No airstrip there. Any airfields in Eritrea had either been recaptured by Ethiopian Government forces, or ripped up by Soviet-built missiles. The Hercules were simply to go in low, at minimum speeds, then put their noses up and let the cargoes drop out of the rear loading-bays.

No heroics at the end of this trip – except, perhaps, the stray MiG or a bright-eyed boy watching his latest SAM-scanner. But it was a long chance. The odds were no worse than against a pile-up on take-off or a crash-landing, or against not even being paid at the end of it. Otherwise, with a freefall over the drop-zone, the mobile operating-theatres and most of the surgical equipment would be smashed, useless. But what the hell? They were only intended as expensive props, in case the mission were intercepted en route.

Anyway, there'd still be the tents and bandages, and perhaps a few drums of heating-oil, and tins of powdered milk – enough to survive the drop and salve Rawcliff's mercenary conscience.

Rawcliff watched Peters' aircraft begin the short run up to the first row of white oil-drums, then lumber slowly round, its high wide wings sagging above the hot concrete. Peters stayed several minutes at the holding-position, still warming his engines, while the air was now filled with the shattering roar of all twenty-four mighty turbo-props.

Peters now began his final run. The Hercules appeared to move very slowly, on its broad eight-wheeled undercarriage, and in the last split-second seemed to judder almost to a halt, before its nose-wheel lifted off the ground, with perhaps thirty feet to spare before the second row of drums.

Grant was the next to go. He took his time manoeuvring up to the end of the short strip, and an agonizingly long time turning the plane. Ryderbeit talked to him all the time, like a father coaxing his child on its first swimming lesson. Grant finally held steady and began the run-up to the take-off. He had all flaps hard down, and suddenly jerked them up and the plane rose with its black-painted blunt snout pointing into the sky. Ryderbeit was shouting over the R/T, 'Level her out! Get her nose down – less throttle, more flap! Holy Moses!'

Grant at last levelled out and fell into formation behind Peters. Rawcliff found that his hands were sweating, tingling with the vibration of the 'stick'.

Ryderbeit and Ritchie each made an almost perfect take-off. Now, through the tinted perspex shield, Rawcliff saw Serge duck under his port-wing, to kick away the chocks. Rawcliff's mouth was dry with adrenalin, with the long pent-up exhilaration, as he felt the huge machine roll forward towards the strip.

She was heavy – heavy as hell. All aircraft handle differently, and a pilot must know how to adjust to each one, and this is often more a matter of touch, of pure instinct –

something he can't be taught, and can never even learn after however many thousands hours' flying. It makes the distinction between a good pilot and a brilliant one.

Rawcliff had always put himself somewhere in the middle, though now grown rusty at the edges. He was also handling a strange aircraft for the first time. He had swung round in front of the first row of oil-drums. The second row looked terrifyingly close, through the shimmering heat filtered by the perspex.

Besides his excitement and anxiety, he now experienced professional pride, wondered what his old BEA colleagues would have to say about it. Every commercial airline pilot has his least favourite airports – usually a too-steep approach between mountains, like Bogotá or Hong Kong; or short runways built out to sea, like Corfu, and that bloody one at Gibraltar where he'd come unstuck. There were also runways that were too wide or too narrow to gauge safe visible height and distance on take-off and touch-down; together with poor air-control and scanty back-up facilities in case of an accident. This do-it-yourself strip at Larnaca incorporated all these faults, with a vengeance.

He made a last check of temperature and revs, adjusted the mixture to the engines, saw the small figure of Serge far below give him the thumbs-up sign, and began to move forward.

For perhaps three seconds the row of white oil-drums ahead seemed to remain static, a watery indeterminate barrier – the limit between safety and a horrible death. Then they were racing towards him, and he was easing back the throttle, no flaps now, more mixture, finer pitch – and still the heavy drumming vibration through the floor. Come on you old bitch! Get up – get your snout up! Get that front wheel off the ground! Less than three hundred feet to go. Oh Christ. More throttle. The sudden lift, the vibration ceased, the white drums disappearing below.

He heard the clonk of the undercarriage folding into the belly of the aircraft and felt the extra surge of speed. And as he veered south, closing into tight formation behind

Ryderbeit, with Thurgood now rising at his rear, he heard Peters' prim voice over the R/T, instructing them to climb to 12,500 feet.

The sea levelled out, grey-green and marbled with shallows, reaching away now into the deep blue calm of the horizon. Behind them the huddle of the airfield was growing tiny next to the pale Salt Lake; and in the smoky distance he could just see the smudge of Larnaca.

Dry Run

1

On that Wednesday morning, Judith Rawcliff arrived early at the office-block behind Park Lane, in time to make her call to AREX Surveys, and to catch her boss, Cy Reynolds, before he became locked in the ritual round of conferences and meetings. For she realized now that random telephone calls, except to insiders like Matlock, would be unlikely to elicit any useful information, certainly of a confidential nature. To achieve any results would require bringing the full weight of her company's name to bear. Discretion had to be measured against the time-limit: and time was running out.

If her husband were mixed up in some dirty business, she would just have to hope that Cy would never hear about it; and if he did, all he could do was fire her, which he wouldn't.

She got through to AREX Surveys, and was put on to a man called Sampson, who was in charge of aerial cartography. She had assumed her most authoritative voice, with an edge of beguiling solicitude. After identifying herself and the company – careful to use her maiden name – she said, 'We understand, Mr Sampson, that last summer – I think in June – you were asked to supply survey data for a large computerized job covering an area of the Middle East?'

When the man made no comment, she launched into her practised monologue about not wanting to breach any confidentiality, and that anything Mr Sampson said would be strictly off-the-record, etc, but that it would be saving a lot of time and expense if he could supply her – again in the most absolute confidence, of course – with the name of the client who had originally commissioned the material.

There was a pause. The voice the other end was soft, cagey, 'Who did you say you were again?'

She repeated her credentials, patiently.

Another pause; then, 'All business we do for private firms

is of a private nature, unless our client instructs us otherwise. I am sorry, I cannot help you.' He hung up.

Five minutes later she was up in the handsome office on the top floor, watching Cy Reynolds pacing the carpet in front of the double-glazed windows which insulated him from the roar of Piccadilly.

'A Tetra-Lipp Retropilot Mark 100/4?' He stopped short and slowly removed his spectacles. 'That's in the semi-classified area, honey. Getting pretty close to the Pentagon – only the Tetra-Lipp's a French design. This company business?'

'No. It's personal, Cy. A very old friend of mine, a journalist, is working on a story involving one of these things. He's asked if I can get him a lead from the computer end – something that would indicate either the source material or the final print-out. It's somewhere in the Middle East,' she added.

Cy Reynolds had paused, engrossed in the 'Newton's Cradle' on the corner of his vast leather-topped desk. He looked at his watch. 'Look, honey, I gotta run – I got a meeting. But try Laraby, fourth floor – he deals with all aerial survey work. Only make sure that whatever this newspaper friend of yours writes, he keeps the company's name out of it!'

Don Laraby was a greying man with a smooth face and gold-rimmed glasses; he looked like a college-boy grown prematurely old, surrounded by a mass of gadgetry: machines whirred and chattered and clicked, telephones tinkled, lights winked. He wore armbands round his shirt-sleeves and suspenders on his socks.

She repeated to him what she had just told Reynolds, but giving a more detailed and technical version of what her husband had told her yesterday afternoon from somewhere in Cyprus.

Laraby listened, frowning, fidgeting, making little notes with a gold pencil. 'The Tetra-Lipp?' – he shook his head – 'that's a damn tricky one, Mrs Rawcliff. Hey, wait a minute!' – he sat up, his eyes searching the ceiling as though for some magic inspiration – 'yeah, I think I might know who can help.' He snapped his fingers twice. 'People called Metternich, Dettweiler – they're a small Swiss outfit in Conduit Street. Their head office's in Geneva and they deal with a lot of this kinda stuff.'

'And they might know about the source material? Or perhaps put me on to the machine that processed it?'

Laraby's jaw muscles were working as though trying to dislodge some piece of food. 'It's possible – if they're willing to talk.' He shifted some papers on his desk, shifted them back, leaned forward and pressed his thumbs against the edge of the desk. 'You're looking for something pretty special – a machine that's been programmed over years to handle a data-bank of A-S maps. What's the OZ, by the way?'

'I'm sorry?'

'Operational Zone. The area you want. For the AFP – Aerial Flight Pattern.'

She hesitated only a moment. 'The Middle East. Round the Red Sea: Egypt, Saudi Arabia, Israel. Possibly the Yemen.'

He gave a hooting noise, as though he were about to sneeze, 'That's a damn wide area! You're talking about millions of square miles – hundreds of thousands of grid references.' He sat up and snapped his fingers again. 'Wait a minute, I got it – Skate, William Skate, Institute of Contemporary Middle East Affairs.'

He flicked the switch on the desk. 'Sally, get me Skate at the ICMEA.' He sat back and smiled enthusiastically. 'Skate's what they call an "Arab watcher". One of their best, so I hear. If there's anything we want to know about the Middle East, he's your man.' He grabbed up the phone, muttered something, then began talking very fast and quietly, the receiver tucked against his shoulder, his hands weaving patterns, as though he were conducting a piece of frenetic music.

A long pause followed, while he sat crouched forward listening, occasionally nodding and staring owlishly at Judith across the desk. He had mentioned the company's name and had twice emphasized that it was a confidential matter – just a favour between buddies, so to speak.

He finally hung up, exhausted. 'Yeah, I was right. Metternich, Dettweiler – they're your people. Skate didn't sound too happy about it all, so I think you'd better keep his name out of this. But he did say he'd heard that this Swiss outfit commissioned a big run some months ago, covering the Red Sea down to the Horn of Africa. He couldn't be more precise than that.'

She had stood up. 'You've been very helpful, Mr Laraby.'

He raised both hands. 'Any time. Only one thing, Mrs Rawcliff – I got the impression from friend Skate that this business may be a little dodgy. I'd appreciate it if you kept my name out of it, too.'

She left him smiling nervously after her.

Back in her office, her secretary mentioned to her that the switchboard had called, to check on the extension for a Miss Jenkinson – Judith's maiden name.

Of course, she should have warned them both first! The caller had not said who he was, but her secretary admitted that she had told him that there must have been a mistake and that this was a Mrs Rawcliff's extension.

Judith felt the first rush of panic. With some impatience she told her secretary to take a coffee-break. Her hands were shaking as she looked up Metternich, Dettweiler, of Conduit Street, and rang them on an outside line. Twice she got a wrong number. Finally she spoke to a prissy emasculated voice, with a slight accent. He did not give his name, merely said he was the firm's chief London representative.

Judith began her *spiel* all over again, but this time with her confidence blunted by weariness and anxiety. 'Yes, of course, yes, I quite understand your position – quite appreciate' – she was groping guiltily for her sixth cigarette – 'appreciate the need for confidentiality in this matter, but as I said, since our company also happens to be interested in commissioning a similar survey of the Red Sea area, I thought that it might be in all parties' interests if we could reach some agreement with your clients?'

She swallowed a lungful of smoke. The voice said, 'What is your extension, please, Miss Jenkinson?'

She felt another twinge of panic, as she repeated the number into the phone. It was one of more than a thousand such extensions and, besides, she had a whole massive multinational to protect her – not to mention Cy's own erratic but influential friendship.

The man said he would call her back. He did so, twenty minutes later, speaking now with a certain cloying intimacy, 'Yes, Miss Jenkinson, I find that you are quite right – Messrs Metternich, Dettweiler were commissioned to do survey-run of the area you mentioned. As it so happens, one of the partners, Mr Dettweiler himself, is in London at the moment. He suggests that you might talk to him personally, in order to explain your company's requirements in more detail. He is lunching at the Carlton Tower Hotel today, but he can meet you for fifteen minutes in the bar downstairs. At 12.45. Will that be convenient?'

'Fine. Many thanks.'

'Not at all, Miss Jenkinson.'

It was only 11.30. Judith was in no mood to get on with Cy's sugar forecasts, and it was only ten minutes' brisk walk to the hotel. She'd use the time to ring *Computers Weekly* and try and get a further line on AREX Surveys, and on Metternich, Dettweiler in particular, as well as anyone else who might have run off an extensive job, probably using a PDP 11/35 machine.

She found him at once, half concealed behind a pillar in the bar overlooking the Rib Room. A pencil-thin man with a sallow grainy complexion, his black hair combed across the scalp to hide his baldness.

He seemed to recognize her instantly, from behind his copy of that day's *Neue Zürcher Zeitung*. He folded the paper under his chair and began to rise, 'Miss Jenkinson? I am enchanted!' – his hand was hard and bony – 'please, will you sit down. I am Klaus Dettweiler. So, what will you drink?'

She had come to the hotel already braced by a Scotch. 'I'll have a Manhattan, thank you.' She took out a cigarette and

253

the man snapped at it with a black lighter edged with gold, 'Permit me, please!'

He sat back. 'I regret that I do not have much time, Miss Jenkinson. First, allow me to ask who informed you about my firm?'

'Oh, you're very well known, Mr Dettweiler! I understand that you specialize in this kind of thing. Aerial-surveys, and so on,' she added rather wildly; and noticed that his eyes were cold and oily and had never once left her face.

'We specialize in a great many things.' His English was very correct, with only a trace of that ugly *Schwitzditsch*. 'But you mentioned a specific job, which we had commissioned in June? A survey of the Red Sea area, is that not so?'

'That's right.'

He gave her a bloodless smile. 'It has been explained to you, I think, that all work we do for clients is in confidence?'

She smiled with him, as the waiter put down her cocktail. The Swiss was drinking mineral water. 'I appreciate that, Mr Dettweiler.' She began to tap out her cigarette with rather too much energy. 'My company would, of course, respect that confidence.' She shifted slightly to avoid his cold black gaze. 'We are not in the least concerned with your client's identity. But we would be interested in acquiring a copy of the print-out.'

'Miss Jenkinson, if I understood correctly, a client of yours is anxious to obtain mineral rights in the area concerned?'

She nodded vigorously. 'But unfortunately, owing to some unexpected last-minute competition, my client finds himself very short of time. I'm sure you'll agree that it would be unnecessary and wasteful, in both time and resources, if we were to duplicate the work which you've already done?'

'Yes, I would agree. Assuming, of course, that there is no conflict of interests between our clients? Permit me!' he added, leaning over and lighting another cigarette for her. 'You see that we already have a small problem here.'

She drew on her cigarette, and took a long sip of her cocktail. Her lips felt dry, her throat harsh from so much smoking. 'I don't think I would be breaking any confidences, Mr Dettweiler, if I told you that our client has mining interests out in Australia.' She was improvising now, calculating that whoever was behind her husband's escapade in Cyprus was unlikely to fall into this category. She'd been surprisingly lucky so far, and just hoped that her luck would hold out.

Dettweiler said, 'Thank you, Miss Jenkinson.' His sallow Swiss face was giving nothing away. He licked at his glass of flat water. 'The Red Sea covers a large area. Can you be more specific?'

She reached for her glass and saw that it was almost empty. 'I wonder if I might have another one of these?' She needed time to think.

'Of course!' Dettweiler had the eye of the waiter almost at once. Judith finished her drink and handed the man her glass.

She decided to play a little dumb. 'I'm afraid I haven't been fully briefed on the exact details. But I understand that our client may be interested in Egypt or part of Saudi Arabia. Or possibly areas further south.' She smiled brightly: 'I'm sorry I can't be more specific than that, but you know how it is with these large corporations like mine. They love to keep secrets!'

'Quite.' Dettweiler did not smile, and his eyes still did not leave hers. 'By when do you require this information?'

'As soon as possible. Within twenty-four hours?'

He gave her a long stare. 'Miss Jenkinson, if I may say so, you seem a little nervous?'

She laughed again. 'I'm just overwhelmed at your kindness in agreeing to see me so soon.'

'Yes, you are fortunate to find me in London. But as for my helping you' – he broke off abruptly and stared across the bar. Much as she would have liked to, she refrained from following his glance.

'Miss Jenkinson, if you will excuse me a moment, I must make a telephone call.'

She made her second drink last, and smoked two more cigarettes. He was away nearly ten minutes: at this rate Mr

Dettweiler was going to be late for his lunch engagement.

He came back rubbing his hands. 'Miss Jenkinson, I have arranged an appointment for you to meet a colleague of mine at four o'clock this afternoon at the Cumberland Hotel, Marble Arch. His name is Sims – he will know how to recognize you.' He gave a short bow. 'I have been enchanted, Mademoiselle. Please stay – I have ordered you another drink.'

'Oh, just one last thing, Mr Dettweiler.'

'Please?'

'Has anyone else approached you for this material? I'm referring to our client's competitors.'

'No, Miss Jenkinson. Be assured, you are the only one.' He gave another little bow, and she watched his narrow shoulders disappear behind the lunchtime crush along the bar.

He was not, as she expected, lunching in the Rib Room. Perhaps a private party in one of the hotel suites? A man like Dettweiler would have his secrets too.

She didn't wait for her third Manhattan. As she left, she noticed that the Swiss had forgotten his newspaper.

Charles Pol took the call from London, just as he was preparing to leave Geneva's President Hotel for an excellent meal at La Taverne du Postillon, across the French border, at St. Julien-en-Genevois.

He listened with his usual good-humoured patience. 'You are sure the name was Rawcliff?' he said at last. 'And she used a different name to you? I see.' He took a silk bandanna from his breast pocket and mopped his face. 'Well, I see no serious problem – providing she is shown the correct results of your work. You follow what I mean?' Pause. 'And she must on no account be suspicious. Provide the usual problems, and charge a good price. Then your agent can perhaps come to his own arrangements with the lady. But I don't want any stupid bungles. If there are, the consequences could be grave.' He listened, nodding a couple of times: *'Bien, bien. Entendu!* I shall expect your call before eight this evening. And invoice me for the usual expenses.'

He went out into the fresh cool air by the lake. He had found the call more irritating than disturbing: it was too late in the day, and the operation too advanced, to have to deal with these awkward little last-minute obstacles. Still, Pol was an eminently sanguine man and he knew that the success of any campaign depended on its commander being able to countenance the least difficulties, however unexpected. It was the unexpected which had destroyed so many great men.

In any case, he was determined that the incident should not spoil his appetite.

'We've had a sniff, sir. Wife of one of the pilots. Name of Rawcliff. Husband's on file – former SAS – but we don't think that's relevant, as far as this case is concerned.' Simon de Vere Suchard held the scrambler-telephone in one hand, and with the other shook a couple of artificial sweeteners into his cup of black instant coffee.

'That's right, sir, and Willie Skate's confirmed it. Yes, sir, seems she works with computers, knows the form.'

At the other end, the Head of Department was short, to the point. Suchard frowned and stretched himself on the sofa. 'Isn't that rather gilding the lily, sir? It isn't as though we had any real *control* over the press – unless we try using the new Act, which could mean everybody getting mauled, the Department included. In my considered opinion, sir; the issue is too sensitive to risk feeding Fleet Street in at this stage, even as a favour. And Number Ten aren't going to thank us for having it dumped in their lap, either!'

He lay listening for several moments; swallowed a yawn and said, 'Very well, sir. I'll see that it's put in hand, right away. We've got a full description of the woman – there shouldn't be any problems.'

He hung up, reached over and snapped a cassette into a tape-recorder. The room filled with a soothing chorus of trumpets, oboes, bassoon – Bach's Orchestral Suite No. 3 in D minor. Then Suchard lifted the scrambler-phone and called Addison, of Special Branch, with instructions to contact the car-pool and order a priority surveillance.

2

Forty minutes after take-off, flying in a slightly lopsided formation, with Guy Grant drooping to starboard, the six Hercules transports were approaching the Nile Delta: a lush green fan veined with glittering snakes of water reaching back into the blurred horizon over the industrial towns north of Cairo.

The sun was almost at its full height, but up in the oily gloom of his control-cabin, behind the anti-glare windows, Rawcliff was aware of the intense cold. At over 12,000 feet, even in these latitudes, it would be only 6° Centigrade. Cruising at around 300 knots, unpressurized, with the back-vent of the fuselage hanging open, he had fastened his leather jacket, and was wearing his boots and gloves, while his legs were frozen numb. It was perhaps a sign of his lapsed experience that he had neglected to bring warmer clothes of his own. As Ryderbeit had said, there were to be no frills on this one, no luxuries. It was becoming increasingly clear that they'd be earning every little Swiss centime of their money.

The first exhilarating thrill on take-off was long dissipated, and Rawcliff had now settled into the *ennui* of the pilot flying a steady course through apparently perfect conditions. Unlike the driver of a car he was not constantly working, though part of his mind had to remain ever alert, watching the battery of flickering dials, warning lights, correcting the tiniest deviation on the radio-compass against the meticulous flight-plan that Serge had given them. Meanwhile his physical senses were lulled by the pounding roar of the engines, each with its own peculiar pitch and rhythm, an incessant subliminal whine that changed imperceptibly every few seconds, nagging at his subconscious with the constant threat of a choked feed-pipe, short circuit, a fractured tension-wire controlling the pitch of the props.

Even the regular weather reports, which continued to give

conditions as good, were not always reliable. The flight's relatively low altitude ruled out the various 'jet-streams' to be found in the tropopause – that no-man's-land between the edge of the Earth's atmosphere and space. And at anywhere under 20,000 feet they were unlikely to run into that other nightmare weather-freak, CAT – Clear Air Turbulence – which plagues the high-flying jet-pilots, and can strike out of a clear sky, without warning. But these lower altitudes did not exclude troughs of localized turbulence and rising draughts of hot air which can tear rivets out of even the strongest aircraft within a few seconds.

There was also the danger of the 'Haboub' – the local wind over Egypt, which is sister to the mistral and the sirocco, and can make low flying, especially landing, extremely hazardous. Over desert areas its progress is usually marked by sandstorms; but across the cultivated and populous Nile Delta, it hides unseen.

Cairo was ahead now, to their right, and the radio was picking up, above the static, the harsh Arab voices from Cairo West. Rawcliff tuned in on their wavelength and presently heard someone intoning their call sign, in that international English that is the *lingua franca* the world over of hotel-clerks, high-powered salesmen and air-controllers: 'Mission Humanity, state your position and flight path.' Peters' South African accent came over very clear – hardly a tactful introduction to the African continent where all South African over-flights are rigidly banned. A minor detail. Rawcliff reminded himself that it was too soon to start getting windy.

Below him, the city sprawled away under a brown haze, pierced by the white pencil of the tower at Gezira. Here they made a slight change of course to the east. The Pyramids lay ahead now, very small, like toy bricks lying on their side half-buried in the sand. The Nile, crawling between its belt of blotched green, fell away behind them to the west. Ahead, the monotonous glow of the desert reached to the rim of the horizon.

Fifteen minutes later he saw the blurred neck of the Gulf of Suez, with the Sinai Peninsula coming up on their left, as they followed in close formation the south-south-east course down towards the Red Sea, which even in winter, is one of the hottest places on earth.

Rawcliff removed his gloved hands from the controls and again slapped his frozen thighs. Hardly any turbulence so far: no trace of the 'Haboub,' no sudden deviations to avoid the swift unexpected path of low-flying military aircraft.

Another half-hour, and they were past Sharm el Sheikh. Below, the Red Sea extended interminably, like the desert, its metal-blue surface broken occasionally by the tiny white wake of a ship or tanker. Despite the thin, icy, inebriating air, he now felt that dangerous drooping of the eyelids. He started jerking his head up every few seconds, massaging the muscles in his neck and shoulders. For he was beginning to realize, as he headed on through the clear empty blue, that his greatest hazard was no longer the weather, or a mechanical fault or failed radio, but lay in himself: in the sheer boredom that was now compounded with an overwhelming urge to sleep.

He considered switching on to the auto-pilot and taking a short nap; but then there would be nothing to wake him – nothing except a sudden emergency, by which time it would probably be too late to react.

He started wondering about the others. About what Ritchie and Jo would be discussing, if they could make themselves heard above the engines. Or did the 'rules of the game' – as Jo had put it – exclude their both talking shop?

He wondered how Thurgood was making out, at the rear of the formation; his inflamed body racked with itches under his leather jacket or perhaps just flying high on whatever magic potion Jo had given him?

In the Hercules directly ahead he could just make out, in the open loading-bay under the tail-piece, the lean silhouette of Ryderbeit. He must have put the plane temporarily on to auto-pilot, and now stood holding one of the parachute-lines, urinating out of the back. Rawcliff noticed that he was wearing neither flying-jacket nor gloves. Ryderbeit was truly a man for all seasons.

At 13.15 they were three hours out from Larnaca, and cruising now fifty miles off the Saudi Arabian coast, twenty miles north-west of Jeddah. Then things started to go wrong – nothing very serious at first, for an experienced pilot, on what should have been an ordinary flight. But this was not an ordinary flight; and at least one of them, Guy Grant, was clearly not an experienced pilot.

Grant's plane, flying ahead and to the right of Rawcliff, in the second line of the formation, had again begun to tilt to starboard. His nose was also going down, and Ritchie – flying directly behind him – came over on the R/T, correcting his course and warning him that he was losing height.

Grant, out of stubborn pride perhaps, did not reply; and after several long seconds managed to climb back into line. Five minutes later the same thing happened again, only it was more serious this time: his starboard wing dropped as though he were preparing to break away into a dive. The plane held steady for a moment, then again began to lose height. Peters cut in on the R/T, speaking with an angry urgency, 'Grant, do you hear me? What's your problem?'

Another pause followed, until Rawcliff wondered whether Grant's radio had failed. Then the man's voice came over, tight and abrupt, 'Right flap jammed down – getting a lot of drag – can't get the bloody thing up!'

Rawcliff could imagine him, his heavy face sweating in spite of the cold, his shaky liver-spotted hands wrenching at the controls. First rule, never force them, like squeezing the trigger of a rifle – never pull. Easy does it.

Grant was obviously rattled. 'Can't move the fucking thing – jammed down. Those bloody wogs back at base – skimped on the job, the bastards!'

'It can't have jammed down unless you were using it,' Ritchie said reasonably. 'You were okay until just now. What happened?'

Another pause, then Grant came back, sullen now, but with fear beginning to sound in his voice, 'Hand must have slipped. So many bloody controls for just one man. These things were built for a crew of bloody four!'

'Try again,' Ritchie urged: 'Slowly this time. If nothing happens, slow your Number Four engine.'

Grant was no longer losing height, but he was wobbling badly. Then they saw the next problem – two of them, to be exact, flying towards them, but higher, at around 15,000 feet and ten miles away, and closing fast. A pair of fighter-bombers. Five miles ahead they broke apart and came streaking down at the formation, one on each side – Saudi Arabian Air Force F-5's, like two plump drooping bats, their wings heavy with air-to-air missiles.

Rawcliff was watching for the tipped wing signal – once for follow, twice to land. The planes passed close to Mach 2, leaving their long thin trails of exhaust, then veered off on either side, climbing on to their backs and heading away east toward the coast.

He spoke into his transceiver, 'What was that all about?'

Ryderbeit's voice came back, 'Just nosey. We're well outside their airspace. The Saudis just like to keep a beady eye on us bloody pagans passing by. But it all helps to establish our pattern.'

Ten minutes off Jeddah, at 13.30 hours, they saw the jets returning. Slower now, closing in like pincers around the formation, and this time they got the tipped wing signal, clearly visible on either side. The R/T picked up the Arab voices, in broken words of English: 'Instruct Hercules us accompany!'

Peters came back with, 'Wilco', as the two F-5's looped around and set a course due east, flying at their minimum speed with a curious waddling movement, their noses in the air, like ducks walking on their tails. Occasionally, as though to exercise themselves, they would sweep round and fly several miles behind the Hercules formation, then come chasing back up at around 450 knots, their squat bat-wings clearing the wide span of the transports by only a few feet.

It must have been obvious to them that Grant was slightly lame, but they made no allowance for him. His aircraft seemed to shudder and wince every time one of them passed him. He began to talk continually over the R/T, 'Bastards!

What do they think they're trying to do – force me into the fucking sea?'

'Steady as she goes,' said Ryderbeit. 'They're calling us into Jeddah. Probably a spot-check. No sweat, Granty – they'll have that flap of yours fixed in no time!'

'Bloody wogs. Just because they think they've got us by the balls with all their bloody oil. Well, I'm not putting up with it, I tell you. Not from bloody wogs, I'm not!'

'Careful,' said Ryderbeit, 'They might hear you. They're sensitive in these parts.'

There were mountains ahead now: high naked ridges, one upon the other, rolling back bluish-brown through the haze. Then a pool of jagged white – tiny sky-scrapers growing like a fungus down to the shore. They could see the tankers lined up in the port, and now the wide modern streets jammed with gleaming ant-like traffic.

The airport, just outside, looked as though it were entertaining some massive rally: thousands of white-clad figures bunched along the edge of the runways, overflowing between the airport buildings where there seemed to be an unusually large number of aircraft on the ground.

The two F-5's closed in again in front, wiggling their wings, and Peters gave the order to follow them down. Rawcliff's hands moved over the controls, watching the altimeter drop: 1,200 – 1,000 – 900 – 700 – 500 ... The fighters were leading them down towards a runway in a far corner of the field, away from the crowds and the rows of parked aircraft.

Rawcliff could feel the heat now, blasting through the rear of the plane, smelling like hot iron, as though an oven had been opened. He had no time to tear off his jacket. The sweat began to itch down his face, settling in the fold of his eyelids, and he could see the heat bubbling up off the glaring concrete below.

Peters went down first – a short landing, turning off abruptly to the right, in accordance with the instructions which were now coming from the control-tower. Grant followed. His starboard wing was still perilously low, although he seemed now to have got both main flaps down, without difficulty. His right tyres, like two punch-balls, hit the ground and bounced several times. The port wheels came down and the aircraft began to slew drunkenly to the left.

He had a good seven hundred yards in which to make the landing – more than twice that needed by a Hercules – and he seemed to be using all of them. At the last minute, while both main and nose-wheels were still just skimming the ground, he reversed the four screws. He had all flaps down now, and the whole plane shivered and seemed for a moment to rear up, its enormous wings heaving with the strain. Grant tore part of a fence down, before coming finally to rest on the sandy verge at the end of the runway.

'That Granty,' Ryderbeit intoned, 'is one of the worst farts of a landing I've ever seen.' As he spoke, he gave an exhibition performance of his own, touching down and pulling up effortlessly, in the minimum of three hundred yards.

Rawcliff followed. He was less worried by the problems of landing than by the sight of two white police Land-Rovers that were now driving along the perimeter to meet them.

Ritchie had landed and was just taxi-ing up to join the others, where ground-control had ordered them to park in line, facing the mountains. There only remained Thurgood's plane. He was coming in smoothly, his wheels just about to touch down, when he suddenly gave the engines full throttle and roared upwards, his main under-carriage barely missing Guy Grant, who had somehow managed to turn his aircraft back on to the runway, manoeuvring slowly into line with the others.

Rawcliff watched, with a kind of horrified entertainment, as the crowds scattered like geese, shrieking and wailing even above the noise of Thurgood's engines. He noticed that many of them were veiled women with children.

Thurgood now headed towards the control-tower, and this time he passed so close that it looked as though his wing-tip would slice the roof off. He wheeled round and came back again, brushing up another crowd, which included scores of terrified ground-staff.

The two police Land-Rovers had swerved to a halt: but not before Thurgood had seen them. He had just finished his second run and was steadying the Hercules, still at fine-pitch and full-throttle; and now came bearing down on the two vehicles, like some monstrous grey albatross.

The Land-Rovers' doors were open and eight policemen flinched and threw themselves flat, as the aircraft's undercarriage roared over them, missing them by less than a foot, its huge wheels revolving idly on their own momentum.

Thurgood executed another immaculate turn, straightened out, and made a smooth unhurried landing, taxi-ing up alongside the other five aircraft.

The eight policemen were on their feet and running towards him, each carrying a long cane.

3

She sat among the cups and saucers and the chattering coachloads of trippers from Oxford Street. She was drinking coffee and had lost count of how many cigarettes she had smoked.

He stopped opposite her table: a large young man, shiny and well-scrubbed, with a high complexion that looked as though he had never shaved in his life. In his big pale hand he held an incongruous bowler hat.

'Sims,' he said. 'Miss Jenkinson? May I?' He sat down, placing the bowler on the table between them. 'You've already ordered? I'll have tea. Coffee makes me nervous.' He had a squeaky, sing-song voice that was out of tune. He looked at Judith and smiled: a genteel smile, yet sly and suggestive. She noticed that he was overweight and that his head seemed too small for his body.

'You know what this is all about?' she asked, to break the silence between them.

'Oh yes. Yes indeed I do.' He smiled again and sat waiting for his tea.

'What line of business are you in, Mr Sims?'

'Oh this and that. Public relations, mostly.' His tea arrived and he poured it with the care of an experienced woman.

'So you represent the firm of Metternich, Dettweiler?' She spoke with increasing impatience.

'In a manner of speaking.' He sat blowing on his tea. 'You want to purchase a certain item, I understand?'

She nodded. 'I assume you've been told the details? A certain aerial survey print-out which you were commissioned to have computerized in June.'

'And the area surveyed?'

'Mr Dettweiler and I have already discussed that.'

Sims looks at her blankly. 'I'm instructed to make an

266

outright sale. Ten thousand pounds. COD.'

She stared past him, above the women's hats, at the appalling decor – all plastic 'leather' with bronzed gilt, in the style of up-dated twenties. She had known all along that this was the most likely 'rub', and that there was no way round it. Even if she sold the house – and even if her husband agreed – there'd hardly be enough left over after paying the mortgage. Of course, he'd talked about that money in Switzerland, but he had to go there first to touch it, and from what he'd said, by then it might be too late. Sims didn't look the type who would take a promissory note on a secret Swiss bank account, even if he could be trusted, which she doubted.

From her call to *Computers Weekly*, she'd learnt enough about Metternich, Dettweiler not to expect an easy deal: their interest in computers was only peripheral to their main activities, as middle-men for the French aviation industry, particularly on the military side – which, in less polite parlance, meant that they were arms-brokers. That explained their demand for a straight cash-deal across the table, with no messing about.

She suddenly felt very tired. She'd smoked too much, drunk too much at lunch, and now this odious flushed young man was trying to screw her for money which she couldn't possibly raise.

'You're putting me in a very difficult position, Mr Sims.' She lit another cigarette, 'As I thought I'd already explained, and as Mr Dettweiler appeared to understand, my clients cannot contract to purchase this material unseen. As it is, there are likely to be only a few areas of the survey which will be of interest to them – in connection with winning an urgent mining contract, you understand?'

Sims tasted his tea, and added a spoonful of sugar. 'Which areas would those be exactly?' he asked, in his high, precise voice.

She hesitated: wondered just how much he knew, how much he would guess, how readily Metternich, Dettweiler would pass the information back to whoever was controlling her husband's destiny, and blow whatever fragile 'cover' he had constructed for himself. The full danger of what she was doing had only just dawned on her: and if she hadn't been acting on Charles' urgent instructions, she would have fled from that tea-room, and from her oafish pink companion, then and there.

Sims was sipping his tea with exasperating slowness. 'Of course, Miss Jenkinson, we might possibly be able to come to an arrangement.'

'Go on.'

'I always find that there are ways, and ways, of doing business.'

'Come to the point, please.'

'I was about to say,' he said, fingering the rim of his bowler hat, 'that if your clients are only interested in certain specific items of information' – he paused, with sinister emphasis – *specific* items, then perhaps I might be able to help you on – how shall we put it? – a strictly personal basis.' He drank the rest of his tea and leaned forward; he smelt of soap. 'My terms would be quite reasonable, under the circumstances.'

'Do you have access to the full print-out?'

He licked his lips and smiled: a horrid obsequious smile that was at the same time triumphant. 'Miss Jenkinson, may I be frank with you?'

'Please do.'

'Just let's say, I happen to know that this isn't an aerial mining-survey. It's more in way of a flight-plan.'

'How do you know?'

'My employees specialize in aeronautics, not mining. So you will not think me impertinent if I make a guess? Your clients are interested in knowing the beginning and end of this flight-plan?'

'The end will be enough. The destination.'

'The destination. Quite.' He was turning the edges of his bowler hat round in both hands now. 'I think that could be arranged without too much trouble. For two hundred pounds? Cash, of course. By this evening.'

'Very well.' It would mean drawing all the petty cash from Charles' shop; and if that wasn't enough, she could probably

268

cash a cheque at a restaurant. 'Where do I meet you?'

'You know South Kensington? There's a bookshop on the side going up to the Exhibition Road. It's called Oppenheim's – it's open till seven on Wednesday evenings. I'll meet you there at ten-to.'

She stood up. 'Thank you, Mr Sims, for the coffee.'

Judith Rawcliff had always been an observant girl, with a quick eye for detail, and an even quicker one for spotting the unusual or unexpected. She had first seen the blue Volvo outside the Hilton when she had left at lunchtime to walk to the Carlton Tower Hotel. There was just one man, who looked like a chauffeur waiting for someone.

She had seen it again afterwards, when she had hailed a taxi in Sloane Street. It had kept behind them, at a leisurely distance, until she had reached the pub in Mount Street where she often had lunch, then it had disappeared. Nothing very surprising so far, perhaps: Mayfair is a tight community, like a well-heeled village, where businessmen sometimes have their chauffeurs drive around during their employers' extended luncheons in order to bypass the parking restrictions.

But now here it was again, waiting at the lights on the Edgware Road, as she drove out of the side street where she had left her car during her visit to the Cumberland Hotel. The same man was at the wheel, as far as she could see. She kept behind him, drawing into the outside lane; and as the next set of lights went green, she executed a neat illegal U-turn. She raced back into the perilous scrum round Marble Arch, and was sworn at foully by a taxi-driver and two boys in a van, as she swept round into the Bayswater Road. She had an insight now into the magnetic attraction that poor Charles felt for this kind of thing. No wonder he was prepared to do it for fifty thousand pounds!

She turned up right at Lancaster Gate, round the hotel and crossed back over Bayswater Road into the park. Passing the Serpentine her mirror showed clear behind. Then she ran into a sluggish line of traffic leading up to Prince's Gate.

At her next glance in the mirror she saw the Volvo four cars behind.

This time she felt a slow dumb terror. What was she going to do? More important, what was the man in the car behind going to do? If she went to the police, what would she tell them? She had no definite proof, beyond her own certainty. Then she thought of the awful Sims and her appointment with him at 6.50. She guessed that once the man in the car saw them meet for the second time – she was now convinced that he must have seen them together at the Cumberland Hotel – he would know that she was in possession of incriminating material.

She had just entered the top end of Exhibition Road, when she had a crash – or, to be more exact, she bumped into a taxi in front of her. The driver was a young Cockney, obviously fresh to the job; he was no match for Judith's coolly concealed frenzy. Both had pulled over to the side, and she had managed to get her little car into a space against the kerb. The traffic moved round them, and among it was the blue Volvo.

The taxi driver stood inspecting his scarred paintwork, complaining that he had to pay the first fifty pounds himself, plus loss of earnings while the damage was repaired. It was the tired ritual argument, during which the police did not appear. Meanwhile, the blue Volvo had gone.

Judith had a sudden change of heart. She offered to pay him fifty pounds, spot cash, if he drove her to Charles's wine-merchants' shop.

He relented and agreed.

There was no sign of the Volvo all the way to Fulham. Toby Hyde-Smith broke off in the middle of trying to sell a couple of Iranian students some over-priced Beaujolais. He hailed her with a superfluous gesture: 'Madame! While the boss is away, the mice will play. What can I do for you, Mrs Rawcliff?'

He had only £89 cash in the till. She took it all and told him he'd have to shut up shop: he was going to have to give her a lift – urgent business, on her husband's behalf.

It was just gone 5.30. She decided on Chelsea Rare Books,

at the corner of the Kings Road and Beaufort Street, where her husband had a long-standing account.

Hyde-Smith got rid of the Persians, and together they made it through the evening rush-hour, with just three minutes to spare before the shop closed at six. The proprietor, who dealt mostly in cheques, had only £47 in cash. Judith had £23 of her own. Toby Hyde-Smith, with enormous relish, advanced her the remaining fifty, boasting with bogus nonchalance that he had 'cleaned up' at the Clermont last night.

With no difficulty she persuaded him to run her back to South Kensington, where she spent the extra £9 on groceries and household goods in the supermarket under the station arcade. A woman walking with shopping bags never attracts attention, she persuaded herself; but she was still keeping a keen lookout for the blue Volvo. The thought had occurred to her that whoever her pursuer was might have changed cars, or that there might even be several, operating in relays: but she was now too tired to care anymore.

She reached the bookshop several minutes early. It had SALE pasted across the windows and most of the stuff was at half-price: big colour volumes on the history of steam-engines and tanks in World War Two and Soviet air-power in pictures. She found a book on animals for Tom, and began to fret that she was going to be late for the baby-minder. Nor was she going to have much time to get Tom to bed, before her husband telephoned again, at eight o'clock.

'Miss Jenkinson.' He loomed beside her, his vivid pink face staring down at her. He had not bothered to remove his bowler. 'You have the money?'

'Yes. Yes, I have.' He'd caught her off balance and she fumbled for a moment with her bag. The cash was in a confusion of five and ten pound notes, with a few singles thrown in; she had not thought of arranging them in their correct denominations. 'It's all here – two hundred, as we agreed.' At the same time she felt every browsing eye turned to watch them.

He took the bundle of money, without even attempting to check the amount. A man bumped into them both, carrying a book on vintage cars. 'I should count it if I were you,' she said defiantly.

He stuffed the notes inside his jacket. 'It looks all right to me.'

'And the information?'

He took a plain vellum envelope from his side pocket.

She tore it open. On a sheet of bank-paper, folded double, were typed the words: Sa'al, Kaur El Audhilla, People's Democratic Republic of Yemen.

He tipped his bowler. 'I hope that is satisfactory? I went to some trouble to get it.'

'I'm sure you did. Thank you, Mr Sims.'

She paid for Tom's animal book and left, just as they were closing the shop. Five minutes later she reached her car, where she had left it up Exhibition Road, and drove back to Battersea, collecting Tom from the baby minder on the way.

She had already decided what she would do. During their first months of marriage she and Charles had mixed with the motley and not always desirable social residue of his bachelor days. One of the more spectacular reprobates, for whom she had always retained a sneaking affection, was one Frank Smollett, a Fleet Street lag of indefatigable resource and experience who had survived employment by almost all the national newspapers. He had the manners of a hog and the nose of a ferret; and there were few tremors on the official grapevine that Smollett somehow, somewhere, didn't hear about. But he was redeemed by one surprising virtue – he was discreet, when he had to be. 'Protecting his sources', was how he put it. This time Judith intended to use *him* as a source.

The names which she had bought for £200 from Sims meant nothing to her: but then she'd been more or less expecting that. Computers, with their arid world of print-outs and feedbacks and interfaces, were her domain. International affairs, and their unseen tentacles, belonged to Frank Smollett and his kind.

Otherwise, all she could do was sit and wait for that damn husband of hers to ring at eight o'clock. It had gone 7.30 now. He'd better not be late.

She remembered the Volvo that afternoon, and shivered. She ought to turn the central heating up. It was cold and very lonely in the house, with only Tom upstairs.

Suchard had had a trying day. Not that the work had been arduous: on the contrary, there had been an embarrassing lack of it, except to keep tabs, through Addison, on the Special Branch's surveillance of Mrs Charles Rawcliff. The rest had been left to the private machinations of the Head of Department.

All day Suchard had been aware of secret meetings, usually with only two or three senior personnel present. What was known in the Department as the 'Magic Circle'. Officials and their confidential secretaries had hurried between the inner sanctums – those preferred few who were in the know maintaining a prudent privacy, while those excluded, to disguise their ignorance, aped an air of furtive conspiracy.

Suchard was among the latter. In times like these he was discreetly but cruelly reminded of his true place – among the odds and sods, the other ranks. They had allowed him to cover up two murders, bugger the Yard about, let the whole ugly business hatch under their very noses – his in particular – before they had brought down the shutters and put on the muzzle, padlock and all.

Suchard knew that it was useless to protest. Already, over the past twenty-four hours, he had watched the regular cables arriving on his desk – particularly from Western Europe and the Middle East – becoming noticeably fewer, and scrappier and more ambiguous in content, until he felt sure they were being doctored before reaching him. Codes had also been changed, without explanation; and files removed or marked for the eyes of Head of Department and the Cabinet Office only. But at least he did not have to endure his ignorance in solitude. Plenty of others seemed to be in the same leaky boat. By afternoon, of that long wintry Wednesday, he had begun receiving pained calls from his opposite numbers in the Foreign Office, complaining that their own cables were going astray, and even accusing him of being responsible. Meanwhile, the annexe in Grosvenor Square appeared to have shut up shop since noon; and the French were being even more sulky and bloody-minded than usual. Brussels, of course, knew nothing and probably didn't even care.

But what worried Suchard most was that he had lost all contact with the Minister. Even his most urgent calls were now being stalled by some unknown secretary: leaving him, as the lights came on, to ponder the Minister's warning, over the map of Eritrea: that if the whole thing blew up, and the archangels got egg all over their faces, it would be Suchard's fastidious head that would roll. And all because he had carried on regardless, in the line of blind unquestioning duty.

His one real task that day had been performed on the personal instructions of the Head. It was one in which Suchard was the acknowledged master: that of the official leak. Though in this case, no more than a dribble. Lunch at one of his favourite restaurants in Charlotte Street, where he entertained a tame Fleet Street editor, with a whisper over the cheese. Nothing confirmed, mind – probably no more than a loose tongue wagging out of the War House. If anyone brought it up at Prime Minister's Question Time, it would be denied. Just a whiff of rumour, and the official 'denial' would be regurgitated on to several million British breakfast tables – but not before the damage had been done.

Suchard was now convinced that something very big and unusual was going on, or they wouldn't go to the lengths of planting such an explosive cover-story. It was to satisfy certain people in the field, so they said. And it was implied that at the last moment the front-line troops might baulk at their orders, unless they were given reasons. Though God knows, it was a high price to pay – threatening to inflame an international crisis over a remote desert country 'of which we know nothing'.

Suchard could already see the sub-editors sharpening their pencils: SOVIET NUCLEAR THREAT TO RED SEA... RUMOURED PLUTONIUM PLANT IN DESERT HIDEAWAY...

RECKLESS MOVE...COME OFF IT, IVAN! WHAT IS BRITAIN GOING TO DO ABOUT IT? Pluto, the evil guru, the lamplighter of perverted science. Hints of contaminated waste; the stench of another, greater Three Mile Island; the earth's atmosphere poisoned for a thousand years.

All grist to the mill. A divided tribal state, Marxist dictatorship, Soviet infiltration, political assassinations – one recently in London, within spitting distance of Hyde Park – violent, unstable, 'not one of us.' And it was further reported that they were using East German scientists. The ideal bogeymen in the English psyche. It would take more than a Government statement to make this one lie down in a hurry!

But by early evening – well before the first editions went to press – the rumours had already started. Suchard himself heard a wild whisper that it was all a plot by the French, a final broadside to sink Britain with the EEC. Even the soundest minds seemed to be growing soft in the fever of speculation. Willy Skate, for instance – who could usually be counted on to know most things – had quite lost his scholarly detachment and assured Suchard, solemnly over the open phone, that it was all something being got up by the Zionists. America reneging in the Middle East, a new Palestinian threat in the wake of Afghanistan and Iran, with a massive back-up from the Soviet Union.

And now this shock-horror rubbish about Yemen. Somebody was playing pretty fast and loose with all of them, and Suchard did not like it one bit. He wrote, in his flowery hand: *Acquiesce: to agree tacitly: not object: to accept.* To pass by on the other side, hear no evil, speak no evil...God help us! Or perhaps it should be *Insha allah – Allah akbar!* God be willing, for God is great!

Suchard was not a sentimentalist, and he had never been impeded by ideals, which he saw as a vain luxury. He preferred to think of himself as an intellectual pragmatist, an enlightened cynic, if only because 'intellectual' and 'cynic' were held to be *pejoratif* by the Anglo-Saxon races, among whom Suchard did not count himself one. His job was dirty and demanding, and above all flexible. Unlike the sewage-worker and the dustman, he had to be able to know, by a wink and a nod, which pile of faeces was to be removed, which left to fester in the national interest.

At six o'clock he locked up his papers and went home. Tonight he was going to get quietly, deeply drunk.

4

The room was small and bare, chilly with air-conditioning. Through the double-glazed windows rows of civil aircraft, belonging to most of the Arab national airlines, were drawn up like slim silver fish seen through water.

'You mad bastard,' Ryderbeit said, sinking his hooked face on to his arms. 'You know what you've just done, don't you? These crowds out there are pilgrims going to the *Hadj* – the pilgrimage to Mecca. Buzzing them is like crapping on the steps of Buckingham Palace on Coronation Day.'

His raw yellow eyes moved gloomily towards the desk on which their passports were laid in a neat row, next to their vaccination certificates, Red Cross papers, licences, and each aircraft's documents, together with the inventory of its cargo.

Peters, his blond head still supported by its pink halter, said, 'Thurgood, you're likely to be in serious trouble. Don't expect any help from us, or from the British authorities here. The Arabs have a strict code of law, and sacrilege against their holy pilgrimage to Mecca may well be a capital offence. That could mean the chop, Thurgood – literally.' And he sliced the edge of his hand down against his thigh.

Thurgood sat expressionless, his face flushed mauve with the aftermath of excitement, one leg stuck stiffly out in front of him. The policemen had not spared him with their canes, beating him thoroughly about the fleshy parts of his body; and one had struck him a hard nasty blow behind the knee so that he now had difficulty walking.

'Holy Moses!' Ryderbeit sighed wearily. He counted the team off on his fingers: 'Two semi-cripples. And one who behaves as though he's not even out o' flying-school. That only leaves us with our beautiful credentials.' He had got up and stood flipping through the pile of passports on the desk. 'Grantie describes himself as a bloody *florist!* Very convincing. And Rawcliff's a *wine merchant* – which should go down well here! Mr Dirk Peters is a businessman. Christ. Come to think of it, I'm one too, though it sounds rather better in French – *homme d'affaires*. And Oswald's supposed to be some kind of engineer. About the only honest one of you is Ritchie – described as straight *pilot*. And I was forgetting Jo. *Registered nurse*. Without the fucking veil.'

He sat down again and leered at Thurgood. 'I don't fancy your chances, Oswald-boy. Not one bit, I don't!'

Thurgood had begun scratching again. He seemed far more distressed by his superficial skin complaint than by the treatment he had just received at the hands of the airport police.

'I've heard stories about this *Hadj* to Mecca,' Ryderbeit went on. 'They get up to five million pilgrims passing through here – some of them have saved up all their lives and travel like cattle, and they crawl out of the holds of ships like a walking laboratory, full of every germ known to mankind. The Saudi authorities are very strict about sickness. God knows what they're going to make of that skin of yours, Oswald!'

Thurgood touched his moustache. 'At least I've given them something to think about.' His pale eyes stared at the wall. 'I hope I did, anyway.'

'You're going to hope you were dead,' Ryderbeit said, 'when this lot have finished with you!'

Rawcliff broke in, 'There's something funny about all this, Sammy. The Saudis couldn't have known about Thurgood's skin trouble – or that he's a nut-case, for that matter. And it's highly irregular for civil aircraft to be intercepted and arrested outside a country's airspace.'

'What are you suggesting, Rawcliff?' Peters sat watching him with angry curiosity.

'I think they were tipped off. So somebody can establish that the cargoes are *bona fide*.'

Ryderbeit turned to Thurgood, 'What were your instructions, Oswald? Did someone tell you to fuck up just before you came in to land? Pay you a bonus to get us all locked up?'

Rawcliff shook his head. 'No, Sammy.' He looked despairingly at the mute, passive figure of Thurgood, his mania once again expended, his body left bruised and itching. 'I don't think Thurgood's little act was written into the script. Though God knows where it leaves the rest of us. I should think it rather depends on whether Islamic Law recognizes collective guilt.'

The seven of them sat in moody silence. Occasionally, from outside, came a slow wailing and chanting, sad and dissonant, and full of alien menace, as the crowds of pilgrims fell to the ground in abject prayer. Thurgood's acrobatics must have seemed to them, in their primitive piety, like some divine intervention.

The door was unlocked and a tall man came in, wearing a white robe fastened around his head with a black and gold band. He had a stern grey face like smoked leather, a black beard, and deep black eyes. He bowed and sat down behind the desk. At first he made no mention of Thurgood's performance. He ran through each of their documents, in a careful deep-throated English which he had obviously learned in England. He wore sandals and a gold watch. He was immensely courteous. 'Which of you gentlemen, please, is the leader of your group?'

Peters stood up. White mercenary Infidel confronting the black-bearded emissary of Islam.

'You represent these gentlemen?' the robed man asked. He made no reference to Jo.

Peters nodded.

The Arab's questions were not hostile. He wanted to know how long they had worked for the Red Cross: whether they had any special interest in the conflict in Eritrea, and had they ever flown a mission like this before?

He seemed satisfied and bade Peters be seated again; then placed his long hands on the desk and fixed each of them with his black stare. Only when it came to Jo did his eyes pass on, as though she did not exist.

'It would appear, from your passports, that you are British citizens, with the exception of Monsieur Ryderbeit. I shall therefore instruct a representative of the British

Embassy here in Jeddah to visit you in due time. Unfortunately, Monsieur Ryderbeit, Luxembourg is not represented in our city. However, in such a case as yours, the French Embassy will attend to your interests.'

'In what such case?' Ryderbeit said.

The Arab looked at him – at this tall, lean, athletic Jew from Southern Africa whose almost virgin passport described him as a 'man of affairs' from the plump little Duchy of Luxembourg. The Arab's face was calm: a face of authority, of virtue, of a terrible certainty. He knew his duty and nothing would deflect him from it.

'I refer, Monsieur Ryderbeit, to such a case as a party of foreigners entering my country under circumstances which might provide grounds for suspicion.'

'We did not ask to enter your country,' Rawcliff put in. 'We were brought here under armed escort, from well outside the limits of your airspace.'

Peters said, 'By making an aerial arrest and forcing us to land, you are obstructing the work of the International Red Cross.'

The Arab looked at him, unmoved. 'You will be permitted to submit any complaints you may have to the representative of the British Embassy. Now I speak of the conduct of Mr Thurgood here.'

He pronounced the name with impressive accuracy; then added, 'You appear to be distressed, Mr Thurgood?'

Thurgood had again begun to twitch and shift in his chair. Their interrogator looked puzzled. Jo piped up, 'Mr Thurgood is suffering from an allergy.'

The Arab ignored her. Thurgood was now scratching and plucking at his armpits like a monkey picking fleas. 'Remove your shirt, please,' the Arab ordered.

Thurgood obeyed with alacrity. In spite of Jo's earlier ministrations, his condition had deteriorated: to his own efforts of scratching and slapping were now added the livid weals from the policemen's canes, so that his pale torso this time resembled one of those wartime aerial maps of the Ruhr after a particularly savage raid; splotches of brown and red and purple, while little nests of fresh pink tumours were already sprouting up, each with a ripe yellow head.

The Arab stood up. 'The man has a sickness.' He gathered up his robes and turned towards the desk.

'It is an allergy,' Jo repeated, 'It isn't serious.'

The Arab did not look at her. 'He will be examined by a doctor. The rest of you will remain in detention while investigations are made.' He collected up the passports off the desk. 'Your identities will be fully checked and each of your aircraft will be subjected to a search. The case of your colleague, Mr Thurgood, will be considered separately.'

He started towards the door, somehow managing to conceal the passports and documents within the folds of his robes. 'I shall now make the necessary representations to the British and French Embassies. It is necessary that everything is done correctly, according to the law of my country.' He bowed and left the room, and the armed policemen outside locked it after him.

'Oh Christ.' Guy Grant sank his head into his hands. Despite the air-conditioning he was damp with sweat. 'SNAFU – situation normal, all fucked up. God, I could do with a quick one.'

'You're in the wrong bloody country,' Ryderbeit said, leering maliciously. 'Unless you want a hundred whacks on the bum. Still, you're a public school man, Granty – I expect you could take it.'

'Oh God,' Grant murmured.

5

Charles Pol did not like the town of Vevey. He did not like Switzerland, and he did not like the Swiss; although he continued to take full advantage of their multifarious banking arrangements.

He had only agreed to meet here, because his guest had insisted on it: an obscure café overlooking Lac Leman. The place did not even serve alcohol, and Pol was having to make do with a mug of chocolate. His guest, he noted with contempt, had ordered warm milk.

The squat silver-haired man sat opposite him, hands folded in his lap like a pair of napkins. 'I have just heard a bulletin on "*Europe Radio Un*." It reported that a plutonium plant is being established in the People's Democratic Republic of Yemen.'

'*Eh bien?*'

'You are the source of the item, Monsieur Pol.' The man's eyes were like oysters behind their thick lenses. 'You should have consulted me first. This is a serious development, which could have grave consequences. You should have consulted me first.'

'I thought it was agreed that you wished to be involved as little as possible? That I was to provide a subterfuge – a little *canard*, by way of a distraction.' Pol took a slurp of chocolate to hide his impish grin.

The man spoke with icy pedantry, 'This little *canard* of yours, Monsieur Pol, could precipitate an international crisis.'

This time Pol disguised a smile at his guest's discomfort. 'We cannot play for high stakes, my friend, without taking high risks. And the greater the risk, the greater the deception. We are already agreed that all the powers involved *must* be deceived. That they even *want* to be deceived.'

'You are a cynic, Monsieur Pol.'

'I come from a nation of cynics. I am also a realist. We both are.' He gave a grand shrug. 'As for your crisis, let the politicians and the international bureaucrats worry about that. It is what they are paid for. Your job is to fund the operation, and to ensure the necessary political back-up. My task concerns tactics, which include subterfuge. Already there are many people sniffing about – many mice at the cheese, you might say. *Alors*, I have provided this small diversion – so that they get the wrong piece of cheese! Also, it may be something to feed the pilots before the final mission. And we must not forget the pilots. They may be scoundrels, but in the heat of battle one should never underestimate the infantry. They need motives too – or at least, something to satisfy their curiosity. Even sweeten their consciences, perhaps?' This time he giggled openly at his guest's evident malaise.

The man sipped his warm milk, holding the glass with both hands. 'I still say, you should have devised something less drastic. This story of yours is a provocation which will seriously embarrass many people. You had other, less sensitive choices. Iran is in the hands of the Devil. Iran would certainly have offered a more correct diversion. Or there is Pakistan, with its imminent nuclear capability.'

'*Mon ami, les jeux sont faits. Rien ne va plus.*'

'This is not a game, Monsieur Pol.'

'Not a game, perhaps. But a gamble. Maybe one of the biggest gambles the world has ever taken.'

'I have provided the stake money,' the man said sulkily.

'Thirteen million dollars? A mere *bagatelle*, considering what we stand to win after the final *coup*.' Pol patted his fat little hands together. 'We came here to discuss the new schedule, which impinges upon my delicate relations with the International Red Cross, which in turn has already made full preparations for all five flights.'

His guest stared into what was left of his milk, which was now covered with a wrinkled skin. He spoke slowly. 'The change of schedule is already a matter of policy. Such policies cannot be questioned.'

Pol wiped some chocolate-foam off his upper lip. 'It is also a matter of the calendar, *n'est-ce-pas?*' When his guest did not reply, the Frenchman continued, 'You surely do not expect me to believe that such a change of plan simply involves security? We both know where we stand on that score.'

Pol's guest had carefully scraped the scum off his milk with a blunt forefinger. 'It is a matter of policy,' he repeated. His face remained quiet, closed. Secretly he hated Pol. The Frenchman treated him like some superior messenger-boy: showed a contemptuous lack of respect for one who was used to power, to cause his fellow beings, often men in high authority, to cringe and whiten in fear for their careers, their whole livelihood. But Pol was unimpressed, unmoved; efficient no doubt, but a rich, individual hedonist, someone alien and untouchable. A horribly imposing creature, and a dangerous one.

The man continued, in his pedantic French, 'You do not intend to question this decision, do you?'

Pol's shoulders heaved with laughter. 'Come, you know me – at least, you know my reputation! You think a little more blood on my hands worries me at my age? But I must admit, when I first heard that the schedule had been changed, I did suspect a certain reluctance on the part of your people to go through with the plan.'

'There is no reluctance. Once my superiors have reached a decision, that is final.'

Pol swallowed his chocolate and ordered another. Besides the waitress, they were now the only people in the café. 'Very well. Give me the necessary details.'

Twenty minutes and three hot chocolates later, Pol sat back and gave his most voluptuous grin. 'But you must not be so sensitive, my friend! The world will be disabused of my little invention within twenty-four hours. By tomorrow they will have forgotten the radio broadcast. They will be using today's newspaper to wipe their arses with!'

His guest winced with disapproval. 'I think that concludes the meeting, Monsieur Pol.' He stood up and shook hands formally.

'This new schedule,' Pol added, as the man was turning,

'it will mean not only the difference of five days, but the difference between a modest killing and a gigantic massacre.'

'So?'

Pol giggled, 'You and I, we are in the same game, we have no secrets. Tell me – what do you estimate the total score at the end of the day?'

'Score?'

'*Le grand match*, on Friday. How many dead, injured, maimed for life? I'm only asking for a provisional estimate, of course.'

The man paused, raised one hand and showed two fingers, then a third. Pol nodded, and watched him walk out of the café on his squeaky rubber-soled shoes. An undistinguished, even down-at-heel figure here in Switzerland, Pol thought: he might have been a minor civil servant or banking official. A dull grey man working towards retirement and a safe pension.

But as the Frenchman sat staring at the cloudy remains in his guest's glass of milk, he wondered what those two or three fingers had meant. Had each finger indicated a thousand, a hundred thousand, a million, perhaps?

Pol was not a man who liked to ask too many questions: and in this case he decided that he did not want to know the answers.

6

By 7.45 Judith Rawcliff was calm enough to fix herself some scrambled eggs and a second drink. Tom had gone to sleep without fuss, so at least that was one worry out of the way – for the moment.

She had no idea how reliable communications were with Cyprus, so she must use the phone as little as possible. But she was anxious to ring Smollett's office and speak to him in person, or get a message to him, before he vanished on some wayward mission. She also wanted to talk to an old friend – a girl she had been at school with, who now lived up in Richmond, wonderfully married to a man who was with Lloyd's, and had a huge house which she and Judith jokingly referred to as the 'Rawcliff bolthole'.

She would have arranged to go up there tonight, with Tom, had it not been for Charles' telephone call, which was due in just a few minutes now. Of course, if she'd had time after first spotting that bloody Volvo, she might have been able to have his call from Cyprus re-routed up to Richmond. Lovely safe Richmond. Why couldn't *her* husband find himself a nice sensible job? She didn't want anything fancy, like a tennis-court or indoor swimming pool. Just something that wouldn't mean her being followed by strange cars and making secret assignations in second-hand bookshops with horrid young men in bowler hats, and have threatening letters pushed through the door, and now having to sit waiting for that damn phone to ring.

8.10. 10.10 Cyprus time. She stiffened her drink; she'd only been able to eat half the meal. She wanted to talk to someone – Smollett. Anyone. Though Smollett was the most important. Just a couple of words with the News Room, telling him to ring her back. But she dared not occupy the line, even for a minute.

She would have gone next door, leaving her own door

open so that she could hear the ringing; but her immediate neighbour was away; and the people who lived on the other side, and opposite, were not on the telephone. It was that kind of area.

She was also frightened. For Tom, more than for herself. She realized it after she had double-locked the front-door and was making sure that the back one was bolted, and that all the windows were secured – something she never did, unless they were all going on holiday. She now had most of the lights on and the radio playing loudly – a merciful symphony concert.

By 8.30 he had still not rung. She called the international operator and tried to make inquiries, but it was futile: she was only monopolizing the line. She also considered the possibility of the phone being tapped – the sight of that Volvo had alerted her to all manner of suspicions – but decided that it was one of her lesser worries.

At 9.30, in desperation, she called Smollett's newspaper. After an agonizing wait, she was told that he was out, and no one seemed to have any idea when he'd be back. She left her message, emphasizing that it was urgent; then willed herself to do the washing-up, before the next cigarette.

She tried to imagine what her husband would be doing. What did one do in one's free evenings on a secret mission to Cyprus? He surely wouldn't be in some jolly taverna, swilling the local wine and swaying to the strains of 'Zorba'? Had he crashed? Was he dead, horribly mangled, lying without help in some lonely corner of the desert?

The telephone rang. She tripped over the cord in her haste to grab it. 'Charles?'

'Judith, me old love!' It was Smollett.

'I can't talk for long, Frank. But this is important. I want to know if you can help me?' Damn, she'd left her bag in the other room. 'Hang on a second.' She came running back a moment later and read out the names from the sheet of paper which Sims had given her.

'South Yemen? Hardly Rudolph Valentino country! Didn't know you were interested in that kind of thing?' He sounded reasonably sober.

'Do the other names mean anything to you?' She looked at her watch. Nearly ten o'clock. Come on, you drunken hack, get on with it!

'Read it to me again.'

She controlled her voice. '*Sa'al,* – she spelt it – '*Kaur el Audhilla.*'

A maddening pause. 'Rings a teeny bell. Yes, South Yemen – I think we're running something on it this evening. I'd better call you back.' She started to hang up. 'No chance of telling me what this is all about?' he added.

'Sorry, Frank.' She slumped down into a chair and finished her whisky.

Later she went upstairs to Tom's bedroom, to check that he was well-covered, and on the way down again she thought her legs were going to give way.

At 10.30 she again rang the international operator. Had her call from Cyprus come through while she'd been talking to Fleet Street? The operator said they usually cut in with long-distance, if the line was engaged for more than a few minutes.

Smollett rang back just after eleven o'clock. He sounded a little tight now. 'What are you playing at behind our backs, Judith old darling? We don't like outside competition!'

'What have you got?'

'Strong rumours of a Soviet plutonium plant being built at this place you mentioned – Sa'al, in the deserted interior of South Yemen. Big flap. Talk of the second Cuba crisis. It's against all the Treaties.'

'Thanks, Frank.' He started to add something, but she hung up, and only just made it to the sink before she was sick.

So her beloved Charles, the father of her son, had thrown up everything and gone off to bomb the Russians. People like him never grew up. They were also born too late. He'd have had a lovely time in the war and been killed having it.

Her limbs felt heavy and her throat harsh with bile. She'd just have to start getting used to being a widow.

7

Rawcliff was alone in a very small room with a high window, well air-conditioned, furnished with a table, chair, and a bench with a single blanket and no pillow.

The man who came in was short and stocky, dressed in khaki, with what looked like a dish-cloth round his head. He had a short black beard, and the rest of his face, which was of the texture of stale bread, had not been shaved for several days.

He questioned Rawcliff at length, about his professional background as a pilot, how he had been employed, how long he had known the other crew-members, what his connections were with the International Red Cross.

Rawcliff answered with careful innocence. Wherever possible he answered honestly, or nearly honestly: he was an ex-airline pilot and had been recruited on a short-term contract which he was undertaking for humanitarian reasons. Apart from his employer in London – a Mr Newby – he had never met any of the mission's organizers, nor had he met any of his present colleagues until a few days ago.

The Arab watched him intently while he spoke. He took no notes and listened without interrupting; then finally got up, as though bored, and left without a word.

The view from the window was of a hot white wall that gradually turned to the colour of a blood-orange, sliced with deep blue shadows as Rawcliff's watch crept on. The door was unlocked and a smiling little man draped in white brought him dinner – a plate of *mezze*, a hunk of hamburger like a burnt cowpat, an envelope of pitta filled with houmus, and a Swiss-wrapped cheese – all on a plastic tray with a plastic bottle of mineral water.

The representative from HM's Consulate in Jeddah arrived at the airport just after ten pm that Wednesday evening. His name was Hicks, a sandy-haired man with sun-parched cheeks and a whisky-nose. He had a shy, awkward manner that might have been mistaken for shiftiness, and which he tried to conceal by fiddling with a small black pipe.

'Apart from everything else, your colleague's got some funny skin complaint. I've had our own medic called in, and he says it's a simple infection that can be treated with antibiotics. But the local chaps won't buy it. They're windy as hell – particularly at this time of the year. With the *Hadj*, the place is riddled with every kind of disease. I don't honestly blame them for being strict.

'But then again, this chap of yours – Thurgood – apparently did some dangerous low-flying over the pilgrims. He's put up a black mark there, I can tell you. I wouldn't be in his shoes for anything. Not on your life, I wouldn't!'

'What does that mean?' Rawcliff said idly. Thurgood's imminent fate concerned him only insofar as it delayed their departure: for Rawcliff was far more anxious about being able to make his phone-call that evening to Judith, to catch her at eight, London time. He now had barely an hour left.

'He might get off with a public flogging,' Hicks was saying, 'plus a stiff fine. Or he could spend ten years in jail – and that's something I wouldn't wish on any white man. Twenty men to a cell, and only one window, in this stinking heat, with just a hole in the ground for sanitation.'

'On what charge?'

'Sacrilege. These Saudis are funny chaps.' He gave Rawcliff a doleful smile. 'They're a law unto themselves. They call it the Koranic Law, but they rather make it fit the occasion. You know how it is – they're all so damned Westernized, with half the ruling families putting in part-time at the Hilton and the London Clinic – while basically they're all still living in their tents in the oasis.' He sucked noisily at his pipe. 'No, your chap Thurgood's really put the lid on it – for the rest of you, that is.'

'What are you getting at?'

Hicks began tamping down his pipe. 'The authorities here are suspicious. Don't like the smell of your outfit.' He paused to light a match. 'You might as well come clean, old chap – anything I should know that isn't quite according to the book? I'm only here to help,' he added hastily.

'Our papers are all in order. And they must have searched all the aircraft by now. What the hell do they suspect?'

Hicks had another match going, glancing at Rawcliff through the jumping flame. 'You're dealing with the desert Arab, remember. Tricky chap, as I said. No good quoting Judges' Rules at him, or applying for Habeas Corpus.' He stared at the diminishing patch of sunlight on the wall outside. 'God, this is a bloody awful place. Before this I was in Rio. That was okay, except for the kidnappings. You could spread your wings there.' He turned slowly back towards Rawcliff. 'Are you still telling me that this is just a Red Cross mission down to Eritrea?'

'Whose side are you on, Mr Hicks? You've seen our papers – you've talked to the others. Go and look at the cargoes.'

'Yes, I've talked to the others.' Hicks smiled shyly through a puff of dense smoke. 'Funny bunch. That chap Ritchie's all right. But Grant – says he's an old Army bloke. Something a bit fishy there, I thought. And I didn't much care for your boss, Peters. His passport's a bit dodgy. It's genuine all right, but our people have a way of marking these things – something the Saudis won't have spotted.'

'Is that some kind of hint?'

Hicks stared out of the window, like a bank manager considering a difficult loan. 'Just that our Immigration chaps like to keep tabs on people they don't like. Seems they don't like Mr Peters much. Nothing to pull him in on, of course – no grounds for taking away his passport.' He paused again, knocking his pipe against the side of the table. 'I said this was an awful place, didn't I? Well, I must say, chaps like you make a difference. Most of our lot out here are oil engineers or fellows in shipping – not to mention the secretaries. They all keep to their compounds, with their own supermarkets, tennis clubs, swimming-pools, even their own bits of beach where they can wear bikinis. The girls are the worst,' he added quickly. 'They come out because of the high salaries, all hoping it's going to be like *Kismet*, with a hundred Ronald

Colmans thrown in – and all they get is the boy next-door, hemmed in by a wire fence, and cocktail parties that are rather like drinks in the dorm.

'Only last week I had to deal with the case of a girl who was sacked after three years' service with one of the oil companies. And you know what for? She was found alone in the same room with her boss! I protested, but nothing doing. She had to pack her bags and go.' He looked up, tugging again at his pipe. 'To people who've just arrived here I always say the same thing – tread carefully, because you're treading on broken glass.'

'I've already told you,' Rawcliff said patiently, 'We didn't choose to come here – we were escorted in by two of their fighters. I can't speak for that nutter, Thurgood, but the rest of us were going about our lawful business.'

Hicks nodded energetically. He had got out another match, but did not light it this time. 'I understand that Customs have found an impressive amount of medical supplies. They're searching those planes pretty thoroughly, I can tell you.'

'I should think some of the stuff – plasma, for instance – will have to be refrigerated, if we're going to be held much longer.'

'That is the least of your problems.' Hicks took his time playing with his pipe and contemplating the bleak decor. 'I've never been much of a betting man,' he added, 'But I can say that I know my way around this country better than most of our chaps. I have a couple of good friends in the Saudi Government. Two brothers. Government's all very much a family concern out here. I mentioned it to Mr Peters, since he claims to be in charge. I was able to persuade him it was your only possible way out – unless you wish to spend weeks, even months, sitting around in Jeddah while they decide what to do with Thurgood. Justice here is either very swift, or very, very slow.'

Rawcliff waited, infuriated by Hicks' manner, which was becoming increasingly leisurely and oblique.

'The normal fine, I estimate, would be around 60,000 Riyals. That's just over £10,000. Fortunately, Jeddah is a first-class banking centre, with excellent communications. Mr Peters has agreed to cable the appropriate authorities in Geneva and to request that the money is deposited at once with the Central Bank here.'

'And if that satisfies the Saudis, will it satisfy you, Hicks?'

The man sat clicking the stem of his pipe against his upper teeth. 'Hardly for me to judge. I'm just a mediator – my job's to get you chaps out of trouble. But I still can't say I'm too happy about the whole business. We'd heard nothing about your flight. It certainly wasn't cleared through the normal channels. And this is a sensitive area – you must realize that? Embarrassing, when a flight of former US aircraft with Red Cross insignia come flying down the Red Sea unannounced.'

Rawcliff's impatience was turning to mild anger. Hicks knew a lot more than he was letting on; and he was trying to find out just how much Rawcliff knew, or suspected. Rawcliff let his anger break: 'Well check with Geneva, for Christ's sake! Check with Cyprus. And Egypt had us cleared. As for the Saudis, it's got nothing to do with them. As you know, we were well outside their airspace.'

'Yes, you were.' Hicks looked up, with his tired smile. 'Very well, Mr Rawcliff, I'll try to do my best. Thurgood's skin trouble doesn't help, but I think in the end the Saudis can be persuaded that the best way to deal with it is to throw the man out. Now, if there is anything else you wish –'

'There is. I promised to ring my wife in London at eight, London time. She'll be as worried as hell if I don't get through.'

'That may be a little tricky. Officially you're being held incommunicado, except with our own people. I'm afraid that when the Saudis get suspicious, they tend to get suspicious of everyone.'

'Perhaps you could make the call for me?'

'I'm afraid that might be even more difficult. I'd require higher authority from our own people – and the First Secretary's on leave, and the Head of Chancery's in Riyadh.' The excuse sounded palpably false, and Hicks seemed to know it.

'What about your bloody Ambassador, then? Doesn't he take any decisions at all?'

'Matter of protocol, I'm afraid. Very strict, we are here.'

I bet you are! Rawcliff thought. You wouldn't get His Excellency dirtying his hands with a lot of seedy hush-hush men in MI6. Much better that HM Ambassador knows nothing about it – especially if Hicks' superiors were anxious that the flight should get on its way, all passports and papers examined, cargoes checked – the whole operation signed and sealed, with no snags, except for a psychopath called Thurgood who was going to cost someone £10,000.

'You see, it's also a matter of priorities,' Hicks was explaining: 'Either we raise the fine and spring you, or I try to get a call through to your wife, while you stay locked up. We just don't have time for everything, I'm afraid. But I promise I'll see what I can do.' He gave a timid smile and let himself out.

This time the door was left unlocked, although Rawcliff was aware of the two policemen standing outside.

At 5.15 am, Thursday morning, Rawcliff was woken by a police officer, already in dark glasses, with a wicked-looking cane under his arm. The man led him down the air-conditioned corridor, into a larger room with Arabic inscriptions on the walls. Through the windows, under the pink dawn, the crowds of waiting pilgrims were still gathered along the edges of the runways like rows of white flamingoes. All through the night Rawcliff's heavy, overdue sleep had been punctuated by the regular roar of aircraft bringing in more pilgrims, then taking off again, empty.

The other six were brought in at almost the same time - Jo in the charge of a black-veiled lady wearing severe spectacles. Thurgood looked distant, inert, no longer twitching or scratching, apparently impervious to any sense of guilt or fear over what had happened.

'This has cost you £10,000, Flight-Lieutenant,' Peters said, looking sallow in the early light. 'I was up half the night fixing it, so we could fly out.'

Thurgood did not even appear to have heard.

'So Swiss banks work through the night, do they, Peters?'
Ryderbeit leered and tapped out a cigar. 'Or maybe you just
knew the right big boy to telex, who only had to whisper in
the Saudis' ear, and hey-presto! we're sprung?'

Peters sat angry and silent. Ryderbeit lit his cigar and
leant across to Grant, blowing smoke in his face. 'Don't
worry, old soldier, we'll soon be out o' here, then you'll be
able to have a nice big drinky! Or maybe you'd prefer we
were made to stay, and have the aircraft impounded, so that
someone else has to fly you out?'

Grant pressed his hands together and said nothing.
Rawcliff did not like the look of him: he was flushed, sweaty,
and his hands were shaking. He looked hardly in a fit state to
drive a car, let alone take over once again, single-handed,
the controls of a Hercules.

A policeman threw open the door and the first black-
bearded Arab, in the white robes, came in. He bowed
graciously to each of them, with the pointed exception of Jo,
and placed their pile of passports and papers on a table,
arranging them in an apparently casual but elegant, fan-
shaped pattern. Then he turned to the six men and bowed
again.

'I am pleased to be able to report that our examination of
your aircraft and their cargoes has been completed and
has been officially "okayed".' The colloquialism jarred
comically with his imposing demeanour. 'The incident concerning Mr Thurgood' – he paused, and his eyes stared
past them at the black wall – 'has been satisfactorily
terminated, with the proviso that he does not again enter the
territory of our Kingdom.'

No mention, Rawcliff noticed, of any fat overnight
transaction from Switzerland into the Central Bank of Saudi
Arabia. After all, the man looked the type who would guard
his dignity above all else.

The Arab concluded by telling them that their aircraft
were ready and cleared for take-off. 'A fighter-bomber of the
Saudi Arabian Air Force will escort you out of our airspace.'
He bowed yet again, lower this time, with the murmur,
'*Allah akbar*!'

As they walked into the dry warm air, Ryderbeit slapped Guy Grant painfully between the shoulders. 'You could do with Allah riding as co-pilot, couldn't you, Granty? As a flier, you're as much use as a one-legged man at an arse-kicking contest!'

During their enforced stop-over, on that Wednesday night, one detail had been overlooked: to have a mechanic check Grant's flaps. But they were all in too much of a hurry to get clear of Jeddah for anyone to start worrying about that now.

Their F-5 escort was already taxi-ing into position. They waited while two PIA charter-flights landed, packed with pilgrims; then, at 06.02 hours, the control-tower gave them clearance to take off.

They left in the same formation – Peters rising into the lingering exhaust from the F-5's after-burner. Grant followed, taking most of the runway to get off the ground, while the others watched keenly over their controls. His plane shuddered a little as he gave it full throttle; the wheels slowly lifted, then bounced twice before he finally left the ground, again climbing too steeply; and again Ryderbeit was coaxing him, cutting in above the jabber of Arabic from the control-tower, urging him not to give her too much throttle and keep her nose down; then joined him a moment later, after a swift taut take-off, flying almost wing-to-wing with Grant, making a wide circle against the mountains and the desert beyond, still climbing into the path of the F-5.

Rawcliff was also relieved to see Thurgood fall into position at the rear of the formation, having executed an exemplary take-off.

The sea was now like beaten copper, the sun a huge melting orange, and for a few minutes the air in the cabin, despite the oily metallic smell and ear-pounding roar, had a sweet freshness that was both exhilarating and relaxing.

Their escort led them due west towards the rocky Nubian Desert on the far shore of the Red Sea: then it tipped its wings in salute and veered off back towards Jeddah, while Peters dutifully resumed their south-south-westerly course according to the flight-plan, down the 400-odd remaining miles to the northern borders of Eritrea.

It once again became bitterly cold, as they reached their agreed height of 12,500 feet: and again, looking sideways at the plane to starboard, Rawcliff wondered what kind of anodyne report Ritchie and Jo would be concocting for their disparate Intelligence agencies, and whether this interlude at Jeddah had in any way upset their plans, or whether it had merely reinforced their purpose?

They began their descent seventy minutes later – a steep drop for the final fifty miles of low flying which had to take into account the possibility of the odd Ethiopian MiG. Rawcliff had heard that they used Soviet and East German pilots, and wondered if these would have the nerve to shoot on Red Cross planes? It seemed more likely that they would try to force them south, over Government-held territory, and make them land at Addis Ababa.

But before any such contingency arose, Grant began to have trouble again. This time it seemed to be with both flaps, his plane dropping in steady jolts – about fifty feet at a time, like a lift going down. And he was losing power rapidly. Ryderbeit went down to join him – several hundred feet now below the others, – 2,800 feet showing on the altimetre, as they all continued their descent to 200 feet, as prescribed on the flight-plan.

Ryderbeit's voice over the R/T was growing more impatient, and Grant's replies more muddled. Peters did not help by breaking in and telling the man to 'pull himself together!' Grant's voice was peevish and panic-stricken in turn: the aircraft was too heavy, the controls weren't responding, he needed a co-pilot – it was crazy to try and fly one of these juggernauts with just one man! He couldn't keep the nose up, couldn't keep control of the descent, his revs were going, flaps all crazy, stuck down, couldn't get them to budge! He wanted to make for land.

'You keep over the sea, Granty!' Ryderbeit called.

'I can't swim,' Grant replied desperately.

'Nor can a Hercules. But you can stay afloat long enough to get your life-raft out!'

'If you go into the sea,' said Peters, 'you're on your own.'

'I'm making for fucking land!' yelled Grant. 'I'm making for a beach! There must be a sandy beach down there somewhere. Desert country – must be sand.' His voice had a horrible cracked sound over the intercom.

He had now dropped well below 500 feet, and seemed barely in control of the plane. Its downward flight had become erratic, its high tail drifting, yawing dangerously; then his outer port engine completely lost power, its lifeless propeller setting up a drag that pulled the aircraft down even faster.

'Cut your outboard Number Four engine!' Ryderbeit yelled. 'Full throttle on your two inners, and pull your flaps up! Haven't you got any muscles left? And use your rudder to correct that bloody yaw!'

This time there came no answer. Grant's limping, lurching Hercules was sliding and sinking away from the main formation – westwards towards the jagged rim of the coast. The sky now was like burning steel, the sun behind them throwing their fat rippling black shadows on to the burnished waters below. Peters called, 'Ryderbeit, head him off!'

Ryderbeit dipped and swooped down over Grant, falling in just in front of him, then throttling back so hard that their great wings were almost touching. 'I need help,' Ryderbeit called. 'Ritchie, get down here – let's see just how good you are!'

Ritchie's voice came back smooth and deadpan, 'Sorry, old sport, aerobatics in this baby isn't in my contract.'

Rawcliff strained forward, watching through the side-windows in stupefied fascination. He didn't know whether to be sorry for Grant, or enraged by him. At the same time he kept anxiously staring ahead into the glare, scarcely dimmed by the tinted glass, for a glimpse of those tell-tale dots that would mean Soviet fighters coming up from Ethiopia to intercept them.

Grant was just holding enough height to reach the Eritrean coast at a spot mid-way between the towns of Mersa Teklay and Gulbub – seventy miles due north of Asmara, and only a few minutes' flying time now from the drop-zone.

'Ritchie, you're a bastard!' Ryderbeit had brought his starboard wing up underneath Grant's port, with its inert outer engine; with extraordinary power and skill he somehow managed, for several seconds, to steady Grant's downward course.

'Ryderbeit, get away from me!' Grant's voice was almost a scream, muted only by the flat intonation of the R/T.

But Ryderbeit – perhaps out of some obscure gallantry or a mere natural show of heroics – persisted in his almost impossible feat. He continued to carry Grant's plane at a steady height of 500 feet. 'Thurgood! Come on down, you crazy bastard! Let's see what the bloody RAF taught you!'

But there was no answering call from Thurgood. At that moment, Rawcliff, in a kind of numbed trance, as though reacting like a man drunk, all inhibitions dispelled, lowered the flaps and pushed the nose down. He felt the soft thump of air and heard the scream of the screws churning downwards, the cargo creaking under its straps behind him.

His gloved hands were pressed stiff against the controls, bringing the plane down in a howling dive, tensing himself just as he got almost level with Grant's starboard wing: then he used all his force, throttle full-back, all flaps up, dragging with the whole weight of his body against the 'stick'.

He could feel the sweat all over his body, and could hear Peters' voice somewhere through the singing in his ears, 'Get back into line, Rawcliff! That's an order!' then Ryderbeit's cackle, 'Holy Moses, it's BEA to the rescue!'

At that moment both Rawcliff's port engines lost all power. He now felt himself being dragged violently down, in the wake of Grant. He got one engine started again, saw the other one coughing black smoke; while Ryderbeit, hidden by the vast bulk of Grant's plane, was still issuing calm instructions, only to be interrupted by Grant's voice, in a rushed furious whisper, 'Get off me, Ryderbeit! And you, Rawcliff! What the fuck are you both trying to do? Tip me into the fucking sea!'

Rawcliff's second port engine had ignited at last, and he steadied the wing under Grant's, feeling the perilous weight of that mighty stricken aircraft, as both he and Ryderbeit struggled to give Grant more time – time to regain control of himself, to fight to get his flaps up.

Ryderbeit was talking to him again, but Grant was now more interested in a strip of grey beach less than 500 feet below, on his right, and coming up fast. It looked smooth and clear, and Grant was either fool enough, or desperate enough, to think that he could judge terrain, even from that height.

Peters' voice cut in, 'Ryderbeit – Rawcliff – regain altitude. That's an order! At once!'

Something in his cold, prim voice may have jolted Grant more than Ryderbeit's patient persuasion: for at the last moment, as the tail of his great Hercules began to rise again, with his speed still holding at less than 150 knots, he appeared to make one final, frantic effort to lift his nose.

Rawcliff felt the lurch, as his wing was almost torn off. Grant was flying for himself,and for no one else. Rawcliff heard a familiar obscenity from Ryderbeit, and saw the Rhodesian's aircraft drop skilfully below Grant's, out of range. Grant had now totally lost control.

Everything that happened in the air, Rawcliff reflected, is either very long, gradual – a leaking fuel-tank, freezing up of the wings – or it happens very fast, often so fast that you have no chance to react or make a judgement. In this case, Grant had already made the judgement for them. He had refused their help, and was once again set on his own downward course to disaster.

He must already have seen how hopeless the beach was. He still had his R/T open and said, 'Oh fuck'. It was sloping rock-gnarled ropes of dead lava running steeply down into the sea, each one forming a broad hump that would be like trying to land on a vast sheet of corrugated iron.

His nose-wheel snapped off and sprang upwards, tearing a gash in the aircraft's belly. Some of the cargo began to sag out, like some horrid mechanical hernia: and Rawcliff had difficulty concentrating on his own controls, as he watched, with the same numb fascination. The black nose of Grant's Hercules crumpled, its mighty wings flopping down with exhaustion, three of the engines wrenched from their housings, while the great tail began to rise – very slowly, it seemed, like some grey monument to the Red Cross being erected in this massive wilderness.

A slow swelling cauliflower of flame now began rippling up the body of the Hercules, whose skin shrivelled and peeled away, showing the white-hot bones of the fuselage, while all around rivers of burning fuel spilled out, spitting and crawling between the ropes of dead lava.

Rawcliff felt the thud of hot air, as he banked steeply, struggling round rapidly to regain height. There were two dull explosions as Grant's external tanks went up, and now an oily black smoke was coiling round the buckled wings, rising from the bubbling flames in a single column, straight and steady into the still air – a beacon that would be visible for fifty, perhaps a hundred miles. And all as a result of four half-empty tanks, plus a payload of harmless medical supplies.

He tried not to think of what Grant's last moments would have been. The man would probably have been crushed under the weight of the controls, strapped helplessly in as the tanks exploded. His arms and legs would have lifted up, with the tension of his roasting muscles, his sweaty face charred white to his grinning teeth; while the rest of his body shrank, except for his belly which would have swollen up and burst, its residue boiled out of existence by the intense heat.

Rawcliff drew back into formation, leaving space where Grant had been flying. He had never seen a man die in a crash before. In that moment all the flavour and excitement of flying was gone.

Peters was ordering Ryderbeit back into line. The Rhodesian seemed reluctant to leave Grant's resting place – almost as though, on some crazy impulse, he wished to go down and somehow drag his remains free from what was left of the burning Hercules.

'Prepare to dump cargo and return,' Peters ordered.

Ryderbeit's voice came back, 'We're two minutes from the drop-zone!'

'And risk a few MiGs up our arses?' Peters snapped back, with uncharacteristic coarseness.

Rawcliff joined in, 'These people in Eritrea are starving. The stuff we're carrying is life-blood to them!'

Peters had already banked his plane round in a wide south-westerly circle, beginning to head out towards the Dhalak Islands. His only response to Rawcliff was to read out the new flight-course. 'When you're steady, go on to auto-pilot and cut loose the cargo-bindings. Then prepare to climb.'

Rawcliff yelled into his transceiver, 'But this is bloody insane! We've come all this way, then we dump the stuff in the piss – like bloody murder in reverse! There are women and children down there, for Christ sake!'

'He's right, hero,' Ryderbeit came in. 'We farted back there – or rather, Granty did. First rule when you fart, get out of the area!'

The smoke had now risen several thousand feet, its stem thick and black above the still boiling orange roots, at its full height beginning to drift and spread out like a Roman pine. It would signal every Ethiopian look-out in the whole war-zone: but with any luck, and with their inexperience and confused communications, they would think it was the result of one of their own air-strikes.

Bitterly, cursing Peters and the miserable Grant, Rawcliff switched on to auto-pilot, then went back and snapped off the belts. He could hear the canvas-covered cargo already shifting on its rollers. He stood gripping the parachute-lines, waiting for Peters to give the order. The formation had now closed into a blunt 'U', with Ryderbeit pulling up to port of Peters.

Peters gave the order to spread out, each aircraft at 500 metres from the one in front; then he gave the signal to climb.

Rawcliff strained back hard and felt the weight lift from him with a sense of physical release; the shrill scream of the rollers, even above the engines, as the cargo went bumping and trundling down the steep floor; then the sudden uplift, jerking forward as the whole plane put on at least 40 knots' airspeed, and for a moment he had difficulty controlling her, holding down the flaps so that she didn't roll over and go into a downward spin.

302

He watched the cargoes spew obscenely out of the rear end of Peters' and Ryderbeit's aircraft, then the tiny splashes of haphazard foam as the loads of milk and medicines and tents and stretchers and surgical equipment scattered and smashed into the rocky shallows of the Red Sea. Whoever was financing this little caper must have a fine sense of how to balance his accounts.

Peters gave the order to head back to Cyprus.

With their increased speed, they came in sight of Larnaca just before noon. The return flight had been mercifully without incident: and as Serge talked them down, Rawcliff's main worry was once again his frustrated phone-call to Judith. She must be frantic with worry by now.

As soon as he had switched off the engines and climbed out, he was aware of a sense of urgency. The Beachcraft Duke had been brought out of the hangar; and besides Serge, Matt Nugent-Ross was there to meet them, together with the full complement of the local ground-crew.

Serge now gathered them round in the hangar, and demanded a full debriefing – concentrating on the incident at Jeddah and the death of Guy Grant – again using Rawcliff as interpreter. He listened impassively, interrupting only to elucidate some small point. He was an experienced commander, not given to venting his feelings. He would know the right time at which to apportion blame. Peters made a meal out of Thurgood's performance, and was clearly disappointed by the Frenchman's apparent lack of response.

Serge then ordered them to check their watches and to return to their hotels for some rest. The five of them – excluding Jo – were to be back at the airfield at 20.00 hours. Final take-off 01.00 hours, weather permitting – which left five clear hours for the refuelling and loading of the five deadly cargoes.

Before they left the field, Rawcliff noticed that some of the ground-staff had begun bringing out the loudspeaker equipment from the end of the hangar. He also guessed that at least five of those precious boxes, in the locked office at the back, would be produced in due course.

He already saw, as he drove away, that Matt Nugent-Ross was remaining with Serge on the airfield. The American's expression was detached, enigmatic; he gave no gesture, not the least intimation of sharing a secret with Rawcliff, let alone an incubating conspiracy; and Rawcliff, having nothing to report, made no overtures of his own.

He rode back into town with Ryderbeit. The Rhodesian, with his hooked nose sniffing the wind, said, 'Tonight's the big one, soldier! I'm going to have a few stiff drinks first. You've got to keep your wits about you, one step ahead – or you finish up like Granty.'

'Matt's got his computers out.'

'Yeah. That confirms that the poor bloody Eritreans can kiss goodbye to our next few loads of goodies. From now on we drop the mask and start earning our money!' He sat with a long cigar jammed between his white teeth, his single yellow eye squinting down the dusty road ahead.

Several times Rawcliff checked behind them for a glimpse of an Innocenti Mini, or a brown sedan driven by a young man called Klein who was staying at the Sun Hall Hotel.

'What's the matter?' Ryderbeit said. 'You got a worm up your arse?'

Rawcliff again wanted to tell him – about Ritchie and Jo and the meeting outside the Post Office, even about the cynical, dispirited Matt Nugent-Ross, and about his own call to Judith – but while Ryderbeit still appeared, in his loose, independent way, to be perhaps the straightest, even the most honourable, of them all, Rawcliff's capacity for trust was now badly corroded. He trusted no one except his wife, and she was more than two thousand miles away.

8

Rawcliff had had nearly forty-eight hours, since his call to Judith on Tuesday afternoon, in which to make his plan. It had a pathetic simplicity: he would take a taxi to the capital, Nicosia, and if anyone followed him, he would at least know where he stood.

He waited until Ryderbeit was busy with his third ouzo, before slipping out to the cab-rank at the corner of Athens Street. The shops were already closing for the afternoon. He felt uncomfortably conspicuous.

The drivers were all dozing, curled up in front of their stifling, ramshackle Mercedes diesels. He had to haggle for the price, which would include waiting-time and the return journey, but he was too tired to extract a decent bargain. The taxi was sweating hot, full of flies, the seats of humped cracked leather with broken springs; and his driver treated the road with the dumb abandon of someone playing Russian roulette with the rest of the traffic, which at this hour consisted mostly of very old trucks and donkey-carts, goats and sheep.

Rawcliff sprawled out and closed his eyes; it would be a comic irony if he were to be wiped out now, in a squalid car accident on a lonely road in Cyprus.

He woke up instead outside the Nicosia Hilton. The hotel was quiet in the hush of the afternoon, the interior cool and discreet, full of the mewing of musak and officiously polite liveried personnel; while a few locals – heavy black-chested men and their overfed spouses – lolled around the swimming pool. There appeared to be no other foreigners, and for the moment, no suspicious faces.

The girl at the desk got his call through to London almost immediately – just before one o'clock English time, so that he should catch Judith before she went to lunch – exactly sixteen hours later than he had promised her.

He stood in the sound-proofed alcove and once again endured listening to the artificial Mayfair voice of his wife's secretary telling him that Judith was in conference. And once again he told her who he was, and that he was calling from abroad and that it was urgent; and she replied, with patronizing satisfaction, that Mrs Rawcliff was in conference with Mr Reynolds, and that Mr Reynolds must never be disturbed. Rawcliff said something to her which she probably hadn't heard outside the bus-queue home or in the local disco – certainly not on a long-distance business call to a reputable multi-national – and for an instant he thought he heard the quick hiss of her indrawn breath.

She told him to wait. He half turned, glancing out of the alcove, down the passage to the corner of the lobby beyond. Business was not brisk at this outpost of the Hilton empire. A porter appeared, carrying what looked like a small bulky vanity-case of soft white leather with gold fittings. He was followed, several paces behind, by an immensely fat man with a little beard, in a flapping oyster-white suit and an old-fashioned Panama hat. He waddled along until he reached a group of empty chairs, then dropped into one and began fanning his great balding head with his hat, while the porter put down the case beside him and pocketed a bundle of local currency, with a reverent bow.

Judith's voice cut in, clear and breathless: 'Charles! Charles, *is that you?*'

As before he wanted to be brief – as brief as decently possible – but for all his wife's normal self-control, he realized that she was nearly hysterical with anxiety and relief. He spent a couple of valuable minutes explaining about Jeddah.

He tried feebly to reason with her, appease her, to point out that he was now so deep in, he couldn't draw back; but the words were no comfort to her. They served only to exasperate her, to drive her back now into a confusion of impotent rage and misery. She told him that he was totally selfish, that he was a foolish greedy man and that he had no thought for those he left behind. She dismissed herself, but held up his infant son Tom as a hostage to his better judgement. He began to regret that he had ever called her: her words were both wounding and fearsome – far worse than the most deadly confrontation with either Peters or Serge.

They had been talking for some minutes now, and in a moment she would start making ultimatums – giving him the alternatives of either coming home or of losing her and his son. He tried to distract her. 'Did you find out anything? About that computer survey? The route? The destination? Hello, love! – are you still there?'

His term of endearment only exacerbated her further. Her tone was now one of passionless fury, deadened by the anonymity of the telephone. 'I did what you asked. I spent the whole day doing it.'

'What did you find out?' His hand was shaking, growing moist again round the receiver, although it was cool in the little alcove. The fat man down the passage was drinking a half-bottle of champagne.

Her voice was now brisk, matter-of-fact, drained of all emotion. 'All right, Charles, if you want to be an international hero now's your chance. I got your destination – and I was able to check it with that old hack-friend of yours, Smollett. It's all over today's papers – I'm surprised you haven't seen it.'

'We don't get any English papers in Larnaca,' he replied lamely.

'Larnaca?' she repeated. Pause. Out in the lobby the fat man sat watching a waiter top up his glass of champagne.

'It's a new Soviet nuclear base in South Yemen,' she went on: 'And you're obviously supposed to go in and bomb the shit out of it. Oh, for God's sake, Charles! Forget about the money, we don't need it! We can manage without it! – get the next plane – come back!'

'Judith – take a hold of yourself. Where is it – exactly?'

She told him to get out pen and paper, then spelled the target out to him: 'Sa'al, Kaur el Audhilla, Peoples' Democratic Republic of Yemen. It's either a missile site or a plutonium processing plant – which is why there's such an almighty flap on.' Her voice broke, 'No wonder they're paying you so much – it's blood money, Charles! They're using you! Don't you realize it, you poor bloody fool! They're sending you in as a suicide-squad! For God's sake get out – !'

Rawcliff was too distracted to hear the soft step behind him. A hand closed round the wrist that was holding the receiver; and at the same time something hard pressed into his kidney. Peters' voice said quietly, 'Replace the receiver, Mr Rawcliff.'

He heard Judith say, 'Charles, are you there? *Charles*!'

His arm had gone limp. He did nothing to prevent Peters replacing the phone for him. In his free hand he was still holding the piece of paper on which he had scrawled his wife's message. Peters took it and nodded.

'Mr Rawcliff, put both your hands in your pockets and turn round slowly. I have in my hand a small-calibre Magnum automatic. You will now walk a little in front of me – this way.'

They moved down the marble passage, past the telephonist clerk who smiled and told him that the charge would be 630 Cypriot pounds for eleven minutes to London, which included the one hundred per cent hotel charge. Rawcliff saw the opportunity to play for time, if for nothing else. He would have to change more English money, if he were going to pay for the telephone.

Peters said to the girl, in his prim, steel voice, 'The gentleman will pay later.' And without pausing, he guided Rawcliff on towards the lobby where the fat man sat sipping his champagne. Rawcliff knew that if he were a true hero, this would be the moment to act: Peters was still slightly dragging his left foot and his neck was still braced in its hideous pink collar. If Rawcliff chose both spots with care, and moved quickly enough, Peters would spend more than just a few hours being patched up in the local hospital.

But would the man use the gun first? It was pressed hard, unflinchingly, into Rawcliff's back, close to his spine. A .22 he guessed: a nasty little weapon, impossible to miss at point-blank range, with no kick and very little noise. Above the musak and the sleepy hum of the hotel, it might even go unnoticed – except, perhaps, by the fat man. The hotel management wouldn't be very happy, but the police were surely well used to people being gunned down in cold blood in the middle of Nicosia? They'd worry about him being a foreigner, of course, but those worries would come later, and they wouldn't help Rawcliff, or his wife and son.

The moment passed. The fat man was smiling up at him. Peters murmured something and handed down Rawcliff's note. The fat man unfolded it and made a little clucking noise. 'Sit down, Monsieur. You speak French? *Bien*! Then we can behave in a civilized manner.' He made a quick gesture to Peters, who slipped the gun almost unseen into his side pocket.

'Your arrival is timely,' the Frenchman continued. 'Monsieur Peters here does not speak French, and my English is abominable. You will have some champagne?' He had already signalled for the waiter.

'I'll have brandy,' Rawcliff said, sinking down opposite him. Peters remained standing. The fat man gave the order for a large cognac, the best the hotel had.

He beamed at Rawcliff, 'I regret that I cannot introduce myself, Monsieur. I would find it inconvenient at this stage – for reasons which you will no doubt appreciate? As for Monsieur Peters here, he is merely doing his duty. Security is such a vital element – I'm sure we all agree?'

Rawcliff nodded, and even managed to share a desperate grin with the fat man. He had no doubt at all that this was Ryderbeit's master and mentor, Monsieur Pol. There was about the man's size, his whole revolting demeanour, a hint of the freak: but it was a freakishness that had to be taken seriously. There was also something about him that was permanent, ageless; one of those men whom it was impossible to imagine having been a child, or even young. Something immutable, menacing. Even his ease and good humour carried with it the threat of false reassurance.

Pol also had an aroma – more than just a whiff of sweat and expensive scent. It was, quite simply, Rawcliff decided, the smell of power – of a man inseparable from all the forces

309

that power both requires and generates. Riches, influence, greed and gluttony, a relaxed ruthlessness – wilful, cunning, and merciless, when necessity dictated; and necessity would be no more than what Pol happened to want at any given time.

The one thing that Rawcliff could not determine was whether his knowledge of Pol's identity gave him some obscure advantage over the man, or made him an even greater hostage to fortune.

Pol looked down at his enormous marsupial lap, where he was holding the scrawled message which Rawcliff had taken down on the telephone. The fat man giggled. 'I must congratulate you, monsieur! – your sources of intelligence are remarkable!' He drank some champagne and licked his soft red lips. 'You are Monsieur Rawcliff, *n'est-ce-pas*?' And he raised his hand, like a freshly-peeled shrimp, the finger nails pink, trim and shiny, 'Ah, you see there are no secrets from me and my organization! You are the last one to have been recruited – *hein*? The civil airline pilot, I believe? Such a pity the way they treated you! These big national organizations, they have no sense of humour, no pity – no *largesse*! However –' he stroked his beard and gave another giggle – 'You have been very naughty, *mon ami* – *tres méchant*! This' – he tapped the piece of paper – 'is a very dangerous piece of information. You realize that?'

Rawcliff said nothing. The fat man sighed. He looked at Peters. 'Telephone – pay and check details, plees!' His English had a sing-song Cockney ring. Peters frowned, then turned and moved away again towards the passage. He was obviously unhappy at leaving Rawcliff alone with his employer.

Pol deduced Rawcliff's thoughts and cooed happily, 'That man Peters is a good employee. But a bad man. He has no emotions, no compassion – above all, no imagination. He would have made a good policeman. And I despise policemen.' He nodded as the waiter put down Rawcliff's balloon glass of cognac, and lifted his own glass of champagne.

'I hope we understand each other, Monsieur Rawcliff? You are naturally suspicious of our little operation. I do not

310

blame you – I am a very suspicious man myself. I would not hold the position I have had I been otherwise. Your health!'

Peters returned and handed the Frenchman a second slip of paper. 'A London number, Monsieur Rawcliff?' The fat man nodded. 'But not, I perceive, that of your home address?' Then added, with a chilling little smile, 'So I must understand that it belongs to the organization for which your wife has the good fortune to work?'

Rawcliff noticed Peters' hand move casually down to his side pocket. 'Just try me, Peters. I'll kill this fat bastard first! I'll kill you both. You just leave my wife out of this!'

Pol gave his mischievous grin. 'But, my dear friend, I would gladly do so! It is you, however, who appear to have been so unwise as to involve the good lady. So it is not my responsibility – it is entirely yours.' He raised his glass and drank.

Rawcliff emptied his cognac in a gulp.

'You are a poker player?' Pol asked. 'Then you will appreciate that while the game is one of supreme skill, there is also that element of luck involved – which includes bad luck. It was bad luck for you to have chosen the Nicosia Hilton at the precise moment at which I arrived, on my very brief visit.' He leant down and tapped the bulky white case beside his chair. 'My cards, Monsieur Rawcliff – I have them in here. Hidden, ready for the final hand. But for the moment I must concede a small victory to you. The ultimate objective of the operation, for which you have been hired, has been deliberately kept secret, for security reasons. It was my intention to reveal the true nature of the target only at the last moment, before final take-off. You will, of course, appreciate the desire for secrecy? Some greedy, or even stupid member of the team' – he used the sporting word *l'équipe* – 'might have been tempted to sell the information to an unscrupulous dealer.'

He sat back, his fat pink fingers holding the stem of his glass. 'The RDPY, I think your wife told you? What is agreeably known, *mon ami*, as *La République Démocratique Populaire du Yemen*.' He grinned hugely, 'Your wife must be an admirable woman! I should enjoy making her acquaintance. A woman who can work so fast, with such aptitude, is indeed rare, in my experience.'

'You just dare touch her,' said Rawcliff.

Pol shook with laughter. 'My friend, I am too old for that kind of sport! A man of my age and appearance is left to enjoy those few pleasures that remain until the grave – good food, good wine, and from time to time, perhaps, a little excitement.'

'Like blowing up the latest Soviet plutonium plant in the Middle East?'

'Ah, you and Madame Rawcliff are indeed very astute! Again I must congratulate you both.'

'So it seems that we both hold the same hand?'

'Not necessarily. The final hand has yet to be dealt' – he winked sublimely – 'and *I* shall be dealing it.' He gestured again towards the leather case beside him. 'This contains, among other things, your flight-plan. As you see, I entrusted it to no one, let alone the international mails. Instead, I risked bringing it here myself and entrusting it personally to Monsieur Peters, who will duly pass it on to my lieutenant, Monsieur Serge. As I told you, you will only receive your final orders just before take-off.' He shrugged, 'A standard precaution – one practised by all Air Forces and secret missions in time of war.

'Now, I am not a vindictive man – not, at least, on account of such a minor pecadillo as yours. In fact, I find it rather amusing, rather *sportif*. However, this is a serious business. It has already been reported to me that one of your number has been lost, together with his aircraft. That leaves only five of you – and one of those, I understand, is afflicted by bizarre tendencies. Some nervous complaint, yet?'

Rawcliff stared at him, still saying nothing. Pol sipped the last of his champagne. 'But while discipline must be maintained, time is too short, and the stakes too high, for me to indulge in the petty luxury of retribution. I had to pay a relatively large sum to the Saudi Arabian Government to procure your release from prison last night. Your compatriot, Monsieur Thurgood' – he pronounced it 'Troged' – 'will have the sum deducted from his final payment. His behaviour was childish and irresponsible. But in your case I shall be more generous. I admire a man with enterprise, even if it should slightly inconvenience me. You will remain my guest at this hotel, Monsieur Rawcliff, until you are required to complete your role in the operation.

'Meanwhile, you look as though you need some sleep, *mon cher*! And a good meal will do you no harm. You may order what you wish – though I advise against alcohol. Any personal effects you need, you may purchase here through the hotel staff. In due time, a car will collect you and drive you back to the airfield at Larnaca. Your mission will then follow its normal course. At its successful completion, the balance of the agreed sum will be paid into your Swiss bank. I think that is reasonable?'

Rawcliff knew there was a catch: there had to be. 'Thank you. But what's the price?'

'Only the minor inconvenience of having Monsieur Peters here to keep you company. I understand that you are not the best of friends?' – he broke into his giggle – 'but I am sure Monsieur Peters will be very discreet and will leave you alone. I would enjoy having a late lunch with you, but I must return on the next plane. As I have said, time is short, and it moves fast.' He began to heave himself to his feet; the effort brought the sweat glistening to his forehead and round the edges of his goatee beard.

'*Au revoir, Monsieur Rawcliff.* There is always the chance that we will have the pleasure of meeting again. And just one thing – look after Madame Rawcliff. As I said, she is obviously an admirable woman. It would be unjust if she had to suffer on account of some foolish indiscretion on your part.'

Rawcliff's fists tightened at his sides, and he saw Peters reach quickly for his left-hand pocket. He stood up and shook the fat man by his podgy pink hand. He wondered what the Frenchman would say if he were to be told about Ritchie and Jo – that the ears of Washington and Moscow and Jerusalem, and no doubt London, were already tuned in to every move of the operation? That might just perhaps be Rawcliff's winning card.

Peters nudged him by the arm and led him away to the reception desk.

9

'Hey, Judith, are you feeling okay?' Cy Reynolds had taken off his spectacles and was peering curiously at Mrs Rawcliff.

She had come back to the table and sat down, without a word. She now began to shake.

'Honey, you look ill,' Reynolds said. The others round the table were obviously embarrassed; she was the only woman among them, and while they accepted her as a professional equal, feminine emotion was ill-favoured in the boardroom.

She managed to get a cigarette alight and said, 'I'm sorry, Cy. It was long-distance, from the Middle East..I was cut off half-way through. I couldn't get back.'

'Anything important?' Cy Reynolds' voice had become a fraction harder.

'A personal matter, Cy. They tried to get through last night, but all the lines were engaged.'

Reynolds had put his spectacles back on and turned again to his notes. He frowned. 'Now, what have we got? Some idiot here has written, "Extended Binary Code for Decimal Interchange Characters". I've said always use the abbreviation, EBCDC.'

'Excuse me, Cy,' someone said. 'Last week you put in a memo to all staff to avoid abbreviations, so as not to cause unnecessary confusion.'

Reynolds seemed not to have heard. 'Judith, you've thrown my thoughts. For Chrissake, try to take your personal calls out of the conference-room!'

She flared up. First her bloody husband had buggered off, then he'd sent her on a wild chase after a computer 'write-out', and she'd had to raise £200 to pay off some morbid horror in a bowler hat to sell her some info. about a Soviet plutonium plant that was all over the day's papers. She'd got herself chased by some spooky 'chauffeur' in a blue Volvo, then spent an agitated and sleepless night, only to be able to bawl her husband out next morning, and be cut off in mid-sentence. Now she had her flat-footed American employer creasing up his forehead and complaining like a child that she had interrupted his flow of magnetic thought.

'I think you'd better get on without me,' she said, standing up. She turned and walked out of the room.

Back in her office she was informed of what she already knew: that there was no way of tracing an STD international call, even through the agencies of Interpol. But she had at least something to go on. He had said that he was in Larnaca. A quick check with the Tourist Information Office of the Cyprus High Commission told her that there were only four hotels in Larnaca open in winter.

Again she considered the possibility of the line being tapped. To be absolutely safe, she should put through her calls to Cyprus from the Hilton, round the corner. But the precaution seemed a luxury, and a waste of vital time. But also, secretly, she was unwilling to pander to her husband, in something that might amount to criminal activity. Judith Rawcliff had a certain rectitude where the law was concerned, and it was in an ambivalent mood of wifely concern tempered with bloody-mindedness that she made her first call to Larnaca, to the Sun Hall Hotel, which she had been told was the largest in the town, and therefore the most likely.

After a delay, she was told there was no one registered there in the name of Rawcliff. Then she remembered that he'd said something about operating under the suspect cover of an international relief organization. Yes, the clerk at the Sun Hall informed her, there were five members of a Red Cross team staying at the hotel. After another delay, she was put through to one of them.

'Yes?' a man's voice said carefully.

'My name's Judith Rawcliff. I want to speak to my husband.'

'I'm not sure I can help you. Who are you again?'

'Don't be a bloody moron! Who do I sound like? – his bank manager?'

'I'm not a moron,' Ritchie said with feeling. 'But your husband is not registered at this hotel.'

'Then where is he? Please – I beg of you! It's a matter of life and death.'

'All right. But don't call back here – I take no responsibility. He's at a place called the Lord Byron Hotel.' And the line clicked dead.

The man's last words had hardly reassured her. The Red Cross must be running a very tight little ship down in Larnaca.

She got the number of the Lord Byron from international inquiries, but it was only on the fifth attempt that she managed to get a ringing tone. The line was very bad. Finally a monosyllabic Greek came on the line. 'Mis-tair Rawcleeff?' it repeated twice, stupidly. 'Okay, I call 'eem!' She could hear confused noises in the background, like the sounds of a party.

A strange voice came on the line, sharp, yet laconic, 'Yeah, who is it?'

'I'm Mrs Rawcliff. I want to speak to my husband, urgently.'

'Holy Moses! Where the hell are you?'

'I'm calling from London. Please, is my husband there?'

'How the hell did you get on to this place?'

'He called me, but we were cut off. Please, this is desperately important.'

'Hang on, I'll get him.'

She waited at her desk, limp and trembling. The line cracked and whined; at any moment, she feared, it would go dead again. She had fumbled another cigarette into her mouth and was drawing on it, when the man came back on the line: 'He's not here, lady.'

'Where is he?'

'How the hell should I know? I'm not his nanny. He's pissed off. Hey, Taki, you bastard – fill me up again!'

'Will you give him a message?' she cried in panic.

There was a pause. 'What was that?'

316

'Please,' she said slowly. 'Give him a message. Say I rang. It's private, family business. Ask him to ring me back as soon as he gets in. I'm at the office.'

'All right, I'll tell him.' He hung up.

She sat at her desk staring for several long minutes at the column of figures. CAP Sugar quotas for the past six months; marching down the page like soldier-ants. She was wondering how much more of this she could take. If he now knew the mission's target, and they had just been cut off, why didn't he ring back? It was now nearly an hour since she had talked to him, and even while her own line had been engaged, the switch-board would have registered any incoming calls. The girl confirmed that there had been none.

The light on her intercom winked and Cy's voice came on. 'Forgive my harsh words, darling! Let's interface over lunch and think laterally – solve your problem. Club sandwich at the Hard Rock. Collect you in ten minutes.'

'Sorry, Cy. I've got to wait by the phone. It's Charles – he's going to ring me back.'

'If there's anything I can do, honey?'

'I'll let you know.'

10

Rawcliff's first, overwhelming temptation, on entering the antiseptic luxury of the Hilton bedroom, was to flop down into a deep dreamless sleep. Even Pol's malign jollity could not jar him out of his bone-aching weariness. He knew now that he was in serious, perhaps mortal, peril – that he was already marked down as a potential traitor to the operation, and that his only remaining hope of salvation lay in the fact that the fat man and his accomplices could not at this stage afford to lose another pilot.

But as soon as the operation was over – even supposing that they survived – the moment of truth would come. But Rawcliff was no coward. His weaknesses were more those of self-indulgence and sloth, rather than lack of moral fibre. But nor was he naturally given to heroics. He knew one thing for sure. He needed an ally. Of all the bunch, Ryderbeit was the only possibility. The Rhodesian was a loner, a seasoned adventurer, a wild man, and a killer. He might well take chances, even reckless ones, but he would surely draw the line when the odds seemed hopeless. Rawcliff felt that as long as the Rhodesian was in on the deal, the hand was not entirely lost.

But there was another reason why he needed Ryderbeit. The Rhodesian evidently enjoyed some 'special relationship' with Pol; and while Pol might be amused to indulge Rawcliff, on a temporary basis, the whim might pass. Like Robespierre, Pol was a man who would wake up in the morning with a whim, and by afternoon it would be law.

The Frenchman had left Rawcliff with a wish that they might perhaps meet again. But he had also left him with a warning. A warning about Judith.

Rawcliff, in his greed to know the final objective of the operation, had involved her, imperilled her. And the thought of her and Tom, alone in that little house in Battersea, made him feel slightly ill.

He must somehow warn her.

The solution was obvious – it lay right there by the bed. Whatever the power and influence of that fat French gangster, Rawcliff doubted that they extended so far as to corrupt the international sanctity of the Hilton organization – though the man had not done so badly, he remembered, with the Red Cross.

Rawcliff reached the bed and lifted the telephone. A girl's voice came on immediately and he asked for a call to be put through at once to London. She chimed at him, in her cheerful trans-Atlantic accent, 'Thank you, sir – I'll call you right back!' He put down the receiver and heard a faint click behind him. The communicating door into the next room had opened and Peters stood looking at him. He had the little .22 in his hand, pointing low.

'You're a stupid man, Rawcliff. You answer that phone when it rings and I'll shoot off both your big toes. You'll still be able to fly, after Jo's patched you up, but you won't walk again.'

Rawcliff stretched himself out on the bed. 'You're a charming fellow, Peters. How have you managed to live so long?'

'I'm careful.'

The phone purred beside the bed. Peters reached it in a couple of strides. 'Cancel that call to London,' he said, and replaced the receiver. His cold brutal face smiled down at Rawcliff. 'It's all right, your end hadn't answered.' He stepped neatly out of Rawcliff's range. 'So there's no chance of your little wife tracing you here – if you haven't told her already. And if you have, too bad. For her, as well as for you.'

Rawcliff closed his eyes. When he opened them again he saw Peters sitting by the window. 'Like a bloody night-nurse,' he muttered.

Peters did not move or reply. A moment later Rawcliff was asleep.

He was woken at 6.30 by the floor-waiter, bringing fresh-cut English sandwiches and a pot of black coffee. Peters had still not moved. They ate quickly, in total silence.

At 7.15 exactly they left the hotel together, Peters again just a step behind him, with his right hand in his side pocket, pressed against Rawcliff's side. In his free hand he carried the small white leather vanity-case.

A smart new BMW, with a Cypriot driver, was waiting for them outside. Peters opened the rear door and climbed in beside Rawcliff, the little gun now pressed hard against his ribs. The driver obviously knew their destination and drove off without a word.

The silence endured throughout the drive, down across the rocky yellow hills towards Larnaca and the sea. The chauffeur drove fast and skilfully. He took a short cut round the scruffy outskirts of the town and joined the road out to the airfield. On the last stretch they came up in the dusty wake of one of the Suzukis. They stopped together in front of the gate, which was opened for them by Serge. The driver dropped them on the near side of the runway; and, without exchanging a word, turned the car around and drove away.

Peters handed the white leather bag to Serge, who took it with an air of grave ceremony. Rawcliff wondered if the Frenchman already knew about the interlude in Nicosia; but if he did, he gave no sign of it.

It was a fine evening and the weather reports from all coastal stations predicted perfect flying conditions for the next twelve hours. The loading and fuelling routines followed the same arduous pattern as two nights ago, except that this time they had to manhandle, with the help of the fork-lift trucks, the segregated drums which had been earmarked for mining operations in the Indian Ocean. These had to be rolled up into the hold of each aircraft and lashed down separately; and when the floor was covered, they were followed by a second layer of the identical but much lighter surplus fuel-drums – five layers in all, two of high-explosives, three of JP fuel – while the fork-lifts finally served each Hercules with one of the crates packed with half a ton of loose nuts and bolts and nails, which were now sprinkled and shovelled down every crevice between the murderous drums, and the floor and walls of the aircraft. Each a monstrous club sandwich of death.

Rawcliff worked and watched with a sense of suspended morality, as though all his values, his standards and beliefs, had been short-circuited. If, at this late lethal stage, he did pause to wonder, even to question the validity of the task ahead, it was only to ask himself why such a massive demolition job should have to include five half-plane-loads of precious high-octane aviation fuel, as well as a heavy seasoning of cheap sharp metal that would rip white-hot through the skin of each aircraft, travelling at the speed of a bullet, slicing through roasting flesh and charred limbs; while it would be the power of the high explosive – only half the cargo – which would heave up and crack open whole bunkers and underground silos of ferro-concrete.

Matt Nugent-Ross had told him that each plane would become one giant napalm-cum-anti-personnel bomb. If so, half their mission must be to kill and maim, as well as to destroy. A Soviet nuclear installation would mean foreign technicians – Russians, as well as a few ubiquitous Czechs and East Germans; and they might even have tossed in a brigade of Cubans to guard the perimeter. All of whom might be considered fair game, in the sub-morality of the Cold War. But that would no doubt still leave an array of wretched locals – primitive, innocent tribesmen, press-ganged away from their tents and flocks of sheep, or just left watching helplessly from the touch-line, waiting to be blasted and spattered across the rocky desert of what it pleased some people to call the Peoples' Democratic Republic of Yemen.

The mystery was compounded towards midnight, by the sight of Serge coming out of the office at the back of the hangar, carrying the small steel box which was supposed to contain hermetically-sealed serum. He broke it open, in full view of the five pilots, and Rawcliff saw, neatly packed inside a cushion of polystyrene, what looked like six shell-casings, or the magnified tips of ballpoint pens.

Matt Nugent-Ross had appeared beside Rawcliff. Until now, the American had continued to work silently, and largely unseen, fitting the complex electrical circuits of the guidance-systems into the auto-pilot of each Hercules. But the sight of the open steel box seemed to have animated him, either prompting his curiosity or his conscience. He nodded down at the six steel points. 'Barometric detonators. Beautiful! Set to go off when the aircraft sink to a certain altitude.' He spoke with the detached respect that a professional reserves for a true work of craftmanship.

Rawcliff turned, frowning. So far the American had not even paused to inquire about how his phone call had gone. 'Detonators?' he repeated, nodding up at the row of Hercules, and at the same time remembering the flaming pyre of Grant's aircraft as it blew up on that lava beach in the Sudan. 'To set off that lot?'

'Sure – if you want maximum spread. *Zap*! *Wham*!' Matt turned his slim hands palms upward and smiled. 'That way somebody'll be getting up into the Hiroshima stakes.'

He did not give Rawcliff time to comment, but slipped effortlessly away into the shadow of one of the planes. And Rawcliff knew that he should share his knowledge of the target. Expensive, inanimate technology – most of it – probably buried underground. No need for such elaborate devices as barometric fuses, or crude non-essentials like nuts and bolts. Even the blazing heat of the fifty-odd tons of fuel would hardly be sufficient to make much impact on deeply-concealed bunkers.

Rawcliff knew there was something badly wrong here. Something wrong with Judith's information, perhaps? Yet while she was now involved in whatever messy, murderous mission lay ahead – and it wasn't just a few nuclear reactors hidden out in the desert, he was sure of *that* – he also remembered that Matt still might have an open line to the Americans. All Rawcliff had to do now was condemn Judith, if only by his association with Matt, as a CIA informer.

Oh God. He rested on a crate, watching dully as Serge began to hand out five of the detonators, to be loaded aboard the fleet of aircraft, each lodged under the co-pilot's seat. They all had timing devices which were explained to the pilots: a circular screw-dial, with a fixed setting, which was only to be turned on when Peters gave the final order. Rawcliff could see little scope here for the odd bit of calculated mischief. The fuses looked very solid, and there appeared to be no way of damaging them, without it being obvious to Peters, or anyone else inspecting them.

In the last hour, after midnight, another mystery was again aroused, and again left unsolved. Thurgood, with the help of some of the Cypriot ground-crew, began supervising the installation of the loudspeakers – three to each plane, as Rawcliff had observed: two under the wings and one over the open rear loading-bay.

Five of the hi-fi sets were also unpacked and installed in each cabin, next to the compact guidance-systems, which they indeed innocently resembled, except that the computers were attached to a mass of wiring and telescoping tripods which joined together like the arms of some gleaming stainless-steel octopus, each tentacle attached to a control on the co-pilot's side.

In that last hour the tension slackened, and was replaced by the firm professional self-control which all pilots learn to exhibit before any kind of dangerous flight. They were all keyed up, wide awake with too much black coffee and a surplus of adrenalin; but as usual, Ryderbeit was the most relaxed.

As Rawcliff was making a perfunctory, last-minute inspection of his nose-wheel mechanism, he glanced round to see the Rhodesian leering evilly down at him. 'Hello, soldier! Pity you fucked off this afternoon. Your wife called you at the hotel – at least, she said she was your wife. Nice voice she's got. You can tell a lot from a voice.'

Rawcliff felt a chill, and grabbed him by his loose combat jacket. 'What did she say? Tell me!'

Ryderbeit prised Rawcliff's hands away; his breath had the rancid aniseed smell of ouzo. 'Anxious, eh? You bloody well ought to be. How did she know where to find you?'

'I rang her today – from Nicosia.' He suddenly spoke calmly, his mind made up. On the pretext of checking the parachute lines, he led Ryderbeit up into the rear of the plane. There, in the oily darkness, wedged against the drums of HE and fuel, and keeping a keen eye open for Peters or Serge, he finally confided in Ryderbeit. He began by telling him about the afternoon's events.

The Rhodesian leant his long body back against a drum of Amatol and wagged his head. 'So you got bought a drink by old Charlie Pol, eh? Quite a privilege. See, I was right about that old French bastard, all along. I could smell him on this one from the start. But your meeting with him could mean trouble for you, soldier. Maybe trouble for us all. Pol's so crooked he can't even shit straight!'

'What did my wife say when she called?'

'What wives usually say when their hubbies have gone AWOL. She said she wanted you to ring her back – urgently. Well, I guess she'll just have to sweat it out until this bloody business is over.'

'Listen, Sammy. I need your help. You're the only one here I can trust – if that word isn't too loaded for you? Peters is after my blood. Thurgood's crazy. Matt's hopeless, and Grant's dead.' He deliberately drew the line at including Ritchie and Jo.

The omission was not lost on Ryderbeit. 'You're a discreet bastard, aren't you? Or maybe you didn't think I knew?'

'What?'

Ryderbeit's teeth gleamed in the dark. 'About young Jim Ritchie and little Jo – playing footsie with the big boys?'

'Okay, Sammy. Exactly how much do you know?'

'Too fucking little, soldier. But just enough to make me angry. I don't expect that French bastard, Pol, to trust anyone. But nor do I like being left out on a limb, while people like Ritchie and Jo are running to Nanny.'

'Several nannies, it seems. Ritchie reports to London. And Jo has a line to the Jews. Holy Moses, unless every spook in Europe is asleep, this operation must by now be as public as the Olympic fucking Games!'

'How did *you* find out? Through Jo?'

'Jo's pretty transparent. Which is maybe why they're using her. Anyway, in one way and another, I managed to talk her into telling me rather more than she should have.'

'That's not difficult,' Rawcliff replied, with a sense of wounded chivalry. 'Does Pol know?' he added.

'He'd be losing his touch if he didn't! Don't be dull, soldier. Jo, Ritchie – and Matt. Don't worry, I know all about the Magician! The CIA have got their hooks into him, and those boys don't let go.' He leant forward and spat thoughtfully into the dark. 'Having the three of them lining us all up under the unofficial spotlight is part of the game. You and I – we're about the only honest bastards around. Unless you count Peters and Serge.'

'Talking about Peters – did you manage to get your rifle back?'

'Still confiscated – like a naughty boy.' Ryderbeit laughed. 'Unlike you, Peters doesn't seem to trust me. I'd be bloody insulted if he did!'

'And you haven't any other guns?'

'Hand-guns, you mean? Don't believe in 'em – except as frighteners.'

'Peters, at my latest count, now has four. Those three heavy jobs he took off the dead militiamen, and that .22 he showed me today.'

'Peters is the kind of man who needs a gun. He doesn't have friends, and he makes enemies like Errol Flynn laid girls! – God rest his soul!' He straightened up. 'Stick around, soldier – it may come all right in the end. It's just possible that old Pol has taken a liking to you, in which case you're quids in, like me! Pol believes in looking after his own.' He started back towards the rear loading-platform.

'And you still don't know what this is really all about?' Rawcliff called softly after him. 'What all this loudspeaker stuff's for, for instance?'

'I wouldn't tell you if I did. Unlike little Jo, I've got a mouth as tight as a snake's arse-hole!'

'What's happened to Jo, by the way?' Rawcliff asked, with a kind of desperation, as he watched Ryderbeit's silhouette move further away.

'She took the evening plane from Nicosia to Athens – with Charlie Pol. You must have missed her.'

'What does she do it for, Sammy?'

'How should I know? She's a bit of a screwy kid – half Red Sea Pedestrian, like me – on her mother's side. Got a soft spot for the Promised Land.'

'Christ. To think that my wife was doing it just for love! And you're still going to go through with this, without a gun, Sammy?'

'Soldier, there are ways of killing a man without having to use a gun.'

11

That Thursday afternoon, Suchard drove back in his handsome obsolete sports-car, from lunch at his club, to the house overlooking St. James's Square. There was a message on the scrambler answering-service, telling him to ring the Minister, urgently. The Minister was in the House and would ring back. But before he did, the Head of Department called.

'That Yemen story. Call your original contact and kill it. I want it stone-cold by tonight. You can blame it all on our Washington friends – misread satellite reconnaissance photographs. It's a new weather-station being set up for the benefit of Soviet naval operations in the Indian Ocean. The Minister will give you the quotes. Nothing too sanguine – we don't like the Russian Navy, remember, especially when they're cruising round our old hunting-grounds off East Africa. But no question of huffing and puffing and blowing the house down.'

'Might I suggest, sir, that we sweeten it a bit by saying that Moscow has offered facilities for the use of Western merchant ships? A sort of crumb from the Feast of Détente?'

'I shouldn't go overboard, Suchard. We're not tucked up in bed with the Russians yet. Just kill everything nuclear. The Soviet embassy will be issuing a strong denial, in their usual subtle way, and the Minister has agreed to eat humble pie and confirm it. It's what's called politics, across the road.'

Suchard replaced the scrambler and dialled a number in Fleet Street, wondering just how many people would want to read about a new Russian weather-station covering the Indian Ocean.

On that same Thursday afternoon, at about the time that Suchard was ringing Fleet Street and Peters was threatening to shoot off Rawcliff's big toe in the Nicosia Hilton, Judith Rawcliff's secretary came into her Mayfair office, to tell her that there was an outside call for her.

She seized the telephone as though it were a weapon. It was a local call. She recognized the voice of Geoff Matlock, her contact at the University of London Computer Centre, to whom she had spoken two days ago.

'Hello. Mrs Rawcliff? Matlock here – hope I'm not disturbing you. But you were asking about that aerial flight-pattern, somewhere in the Middle East? Well, it's rather a coincidence really. I was chatting to a couple of our blokes this morning, and to cut a long story short, it seems I may be able to give you just what you need – or near enough. Just happens that one of our machines – a Techtran 8421 – was used for the job, transferring on to a Hewlett Packard Floppy Disc. The input data came to us privately. I can't check off-hand who it was invoiced to, so I can't give you the source, I'm afraid. But as luck would have it – your luck' – he chuckled – 'our machine developed a few glitches during the job. We made a couple of botched run-offs and somebody stuffed the dumped print-outs in my in-tray! I don't know if they're complete, but there's a damned great pile of the stuff – well over a thousand sheets, I'd say. Somebody with a sense of humour, no doubt.'

'When was this?'

'About three months ago.' He laughed, 'It must have been just before I went on holiday – I don't usually let things pile up like that, you know.'

'And you've no idea who commissioned it? It wasn't a firm called Metternich, Dettweiler?'

'As I said, 'fraid I don't know. Chap who dealt with it's up in Birmingham at the moment. If you can wait till Monday –'

'Doesn't matter. Geoff, can you send the whole lot round by special messenger? It'll be paid for this end.'

There was a moment's hesitation. 'Ye-es. I s'pose so. I should point out, Judith, that it was a confidential job. But since you're in the business –'

'I'd be very grateful. But if you *could* do it as soon as possible? This afternoon?'

'All right – anything to please the fair sex. I'll get one of our own men to do it. More reliable. But remember, if there are any repercussions, I don't know what you're talking about.'

She hung up wearily. Her energy was only sustained by nervous momentum – anything to distract her from the tedious agony of waiting for that call from Cyprus. At least, provided Matlock were right, the dumped print-outs would either confirm or deny the information she had bought from Sims: and if that wretched creature had swindled her out of two hundred quid, that was going to be the least of her worries. She still had the problem of contacting her husband. The voice at the Lord Byron Hotel, Nicosia, had not been reassuring. She wondered whether she ought not to dump little Tom with the baby-minder for a couple of nights and fly direct to Cyprus, using the company's credit facilities, and if necessary drag her husband physically back home?

She had already arranged to stay for the next few nights at her friend's house up in Richmond. As tomorrow was Friday, at least she would have the weekend for herself and Tom, without having to put on a brave executive face.

She would decide what to do about her husband only after he phoned back – if he ever did.

Her intercom lit up and Reynolds' voice whined out at her. 'Judith, remember, I want that sugar data by six.'

'I'll have it for you, Cy,' she lied, knowing that he would probably have forgotten about it by then. Tomorrow he'd be back on his old hobby horse – forecasting a Soviet oil famine.

Forty minutes later her secretary appeared, laden with three large Jiffy bags, each as fat as a telephone directory. Judith told her to put them on the floor, and that she was not to be disturbed for the next hour, unless it was for an international call.

The stacks of print-out were, as Matlock had told her, dumped, or rejects. And there were, as he had also said, well over a thousand sheets, many of them torn or crumpled, several splashed and stained with coffee rings. Although clearly numbered, they were in no kind of order; and soon she had them strewn across the carpet around her desk, engaged in what looked like some gigantic game of patience.

Each perforated sheet was covered in sets of figures, arranged in columns of five, occasionally interspersed with letters: about ten figures across each column, and at least two hundred deep. What she was most interested in were the final pages – the destination of the flight-plan. But here she had an obvious problem. Without sorting every page into its exact sequence, she had no idea whether the print-out was complete. She could see why the run had been dumped. On several sheets the columns of figures veered and zig-zagged, sometimes in an illegible mess.

After nearly an hour she had sorted the last hundred pages into sequence. Only eight were missing – two from the final batch. Unless there had been more sheets, which had been mislaid or destroyed, she could feel fairly confident that she had enough to satisfy her curiosity, as well as her earlier investment of £200.

The task had at least one other advantage: it had distracted her from worrying about her husband's call. She piled up the two batches of sheets and called Don Laraby's secretary. Yes, he was in his office. She did not bother to make an appointment. She left a message with her own secretary, telling her to put through any international calls to Laraby's office; then rode up to the fourth floor. The American looked as though he had not stirred since yesterday, seated in the midst of the cosmic chaos of advanced technology, struggling in his hushed breathless voice with several telephones at once. About the only sign of order in the place were his sock-suspenders. At this hour even his drip-dry buttoned-down shirt was looking rumpled.

She settled herself down in the comfortable swivel-chair opposite him, careful to show him enough leg but not too much, and dropped the two stacks of print-outs down on to the mayhem of his desk. He jerked up with a start, almost dropping one of the telephones, broke off two conversations and adjusted his eye-glasses.

'Mrs Rawcliff! Please, sit down,' he added superfluously. 'What can I do for you?'

'Have you any way of reading that?' She nodded at the two piles.

He peered at the top sheets and wrinkled his nose. 'Jesus, what is this – ''Purple Code''?'

'It's part of that AFP I told you about yesterday. Programmed by a Techtran 8421 for a Tetra-Lipp guided system. A retropilot Mark 100/4.'

His smooth boyish face lit up with slow understanding. 'So – those Swiss people, Metternich, Dettweiler, were helpful, were they?'

'Very helpful. This stuff should give the take-off and destination. I think I know the destination – I just want to check.'

Laraby spent a long minute shuffling the pages, fidgeting and frowning and crossing and uncrossing his legs, then peered hard at one sheet while a telephone rang unanswered at his elbow. 'You just wanted a straight map reference, huh? He paused; the telephone went on ringing. Judith glanced nervously at it, wondering if it was that call from Cyprus.

Laraby leant out to answer it, just as it stopped ringing. He sat blinking at her from behind his glasses. 'Seems the first two sets of figures on each column are simple latitude, longitude,' he said at last. 'Straightforward enough. Starts with Latitude 26 64813N, for North. And Longitude 38 – 82681 East.' He looked up. 'We don't need a reader for this stuff – we need a magnifying glass and a good map.' He pressed a button. 'Miss Hale, have them send up a world atlas from the library – right away!' He turned to the last page of the second sheaf.

'That's the most important,' she prompted him.

'Yeah, yeah, this is it: 21 265 – Christ, whoever gave you this stuff looks as though they've been having breakfast off it! What a mess. Dumped, eh?' He paused. 'Here we are – 21 26598 North. These are pretty damned exact readings! Must have been taken off a specially commissioned ordnance survey.'

She had been quickly jotting down the figures on her pad. '21 26598 North,' she repeated. 'That's latitude again, I suppose?'

331

'Should be. Unless someone's been playing funnies on this one. The Tetra-Lipp's still pretty secret. But you can get just a little too secret at this kind o' game – no good programming a computer if at the end of it even God can't understand it.'

'What's the final longitude reading?'

'You're gonna ruin my eyesight, you know that?'

'The longitude,' she repeated patiently.

Laraby screwed his glasses hard back on to the bridge of his nose. 'Longitude 39 49882 East. You got that?' He beamed at her. 'I should be charging Cy overtime for this.' And when she didn't smile back, added, 'Is that what you were looking for?'

'It should be somewhere in South Yemen – the last reading, I mean.'

Laraby shook his head knowingly: 'Oh no! The Yemen's down around Latitude 14. You're way up on 21.' He smiled again. 'Just so happens you've come to the right man. I used to do aerial surveys for an oil company in the Middle East.'

'You never told me that.'

'You didn't ask me. I spent whole days reading these damn references. While other guys were dreaming about girls, Don Laraby was dreaming about latitude and longitude!'

She felt the dawning of a terrible excitement. Laraby's phone was ringing again. 'Then if it isn't in South Yemen, where is it?'

A pretty girl with a helmet hair-cut came up to the desk, gave Judith a quick once-over, and handed Laraby the heavy world atlas.

'Thanks, Cynthia. Somewhere in Saudi Arabia – round about the middle, I'd say. Latitude 21 would put it somewhere close to the west coast. The Red Sea.' He was clumsily turning the pages of the index. 'Jeddah, maybe?'

She sat very still; and there was a low ringing in her ears that had nothing to do with the machinery in the room.

The American kept up his easy, exasperating banter. 'Hell, I ought to know the references for Jeddah like I know

332

my own National Insurance number. I lived in the damn place for nearly a year.' He had found the right page in the index and was poring over the tiny columns of place references. 'Jeddah – damn! See Jiddah.'

Judith's pen was quivering in her hand.

'Yeah, here we are. Jeddah. Latitude 21 30 North. Longitude 39 10 East.' He paused. 'Now what have we got on your stuff?' He began shuffling about on his desk for the final sheet of the print-out. 'Latitude 21 26598 North.' He peered up at her again.

'21 26598 North,' she repeated; and her voice sounded as though it came from someone else. 'That's not right, is it?'

The room seemed to have grown quiet, like a crowded church.

'Longitude 39 49882 East – according to your stuff.' Laraby's voice was dead-pan, but with a hint of apology. 'That puts it about fifty miles off, to the east. Unless it's been programmed wrong, and that's why it was dumped?'

'What's the correct reading, Mr Laraby?'

After some more fumbling he found the page for the Arabian Peninsula. When he looked at her, he saw that she was very pale. He said, 'Mrs Rawcliff, can you give me any idea what this is all about?'

'I'm afraid I can't. I'm doing it for a friend, as a favour.' She spoke in a dull, choked voice, as she stared at the final sheet of the print-out in his hand. 'Come on – where is it?'

Target

1

By 00.30 hours, Friday morning, Cyprus time, the five Hercules transports stood fully loaded and refuelled, the guidance-systems, detonators, hi-fi and loudspeaker equipment set in place. It only remained for the computers to be activated and the hi-fi sets fitted with their cassettes.

Each pilot had chosen one of the four parachutes that came with his plane. Rawcliff had never jumped before, let alone over wild, unknown terrain. There was also the possibility that the packs had been tampered with, or that he'd just be unlucky, and go down in a 'Roman candle'; or the chance that he might overfly the drop-zone and be left to fry, without food or water, on some rocky wasteland or in blistering desert; or maybe the Beachcraft Duke was just a blind, and there would be no drop-zone – perhaps Matt had been 'doubling' all along and had already activated the guidance-systems, and it had been intended from the start that the pilots should go down with their exploding planes? The detonators might already have been primed, without any of them knowing. No guarantees, no promises. Nothing certain, except their greed for the balance of that £40,000 in a Swiss vault.

It was a warm, clear night, and they rested, refreshed by tepid water from jerry-cans and by the bitter black coffee. Smoking was rigorously forbidden; and there was little conversation. Now that the final hand was about to be dealt, there seemed to be nothing to talk about. It was certainly no time to start expressing doubts.

Shortly before one am at least one puzzle was solved. Serge, carrying a mapcase and goggles, boarded the Beachcraft Duke. If Jim Ritchie had any qualms about his pretty air-taxi being flown by a total stranger – a foreign mercenary with no visible credentials or licence to show – he was keeping his feelings to himself.

Rawcliff had long despaired of any forthright explanations, even for the simplest action or incident. Throughout this mission, even when you were not airborne, you were left to operate by instinct, deduction and suspicion. Just after Serge boarded the Beachcraft, he was joined by Matt, who climbed into the seat beside Serge, carrying the white leather case which Peters had collected from Pol in Nicosia. Rawcliff guessed that it contained the computerized tapes for the guidance-systems and the cassettes for the hi-fi sets.

Whoever was behind all this was leaving nothing to chance or to trust. No risk that one of the pilots might decide to turn off and land with his deadly load at some friendly airport, ready to turn them all in for a reward. Without the computerized tapes there would never be any proof of the final target – except Judith's word over the phone, and a scrawled message which Peters would certainly have destroyed. And whatever mysterious evidence was held in those cassettes, to be relayed over the massive loudspeakers, could easily be wiped off by either Matt or Serge, if anything went seriously wrong.

The strip of runway was now lit by half-a-dozen hurricane-lamps down either side. It was all right for Serge in the little Beachcraft, Rawcliff thought. Even at night, in an aircraft like that, a competent pilot can take off and land in a field or an empty street. But for a Hercules, in the dark, they were going to have to calculate to the nearest foot.

They had all done this short take-off once now – even poor Grant – but it had been achieved in daylight, with perfect visibility. And Rawcliff knew that even with the most experienced pilots, there were always the times when the nerves began to jump, the sweat started up and the stomach grew heavy. He was worried that he had drunk too much black coffee; his bowels were feeling loose.

While the Beachcraft Duke stood warming up its engines, Rawcliff asked Ritchie, as casually as possible, if he knew where the plane was going. Ritchie sounded almost off-hand. 'They've got permission to do some aerial reconnaissance for a French geological institute – somewhere over the empty

338

part of the Nafud Desert in the north of Saudi. And they've been cleared for Egyptian and Saudi air-space clearance – no problems.'

The Beachcraft took off at 01.15 hours, on that last Friday. For a few minutes they watched its lights and heard its engines pulsing out over the sea: then it was gone, leaving behind a heavy silence. It also seemed to leave a vacuum – an absence of true authority, in the person of Serge – as well as the departure of Rawcliff's specious accomplice, Matt Nugent-Ross.

Peters was now back in full command, and determined to make the most of it. Only one set of items remained to be loaded on to the Hercules, through the side-doors, where they would be easily accessible: five drums of grey paint, five sprayers, and five light extendable ladders.

Peters now handed each pilot his buff envelope; but before dismissing them to their aircraft, he stood rigidly to attention and made a short speech. It was an incongruous, even comic performance. To Rawcliff's ear it was obvious that it had been translated, almost certainly from French, and that Peters was reciting it, in his prim 'colonial' voice, which rendered some of the more lyrical phrases into passionless platitudes.

He began by saying that he was about to announce the full significance of their mission, which would be of historic proportions. He paused dead-pan, his eyes avoiding Rawcliff's, as he went on: 'And while I am unable to divulge the precise nature of our ultimate target – for reasons of our own security, as well as that of others – I promise that each of you will be striking a major blow for the defence of Western civilization, for freedom and democracy, against the increasing threat of alien and barbarian forces.

'Unfortunately, for reasons of international security, your identities must never be known, although by the end of the day you will be the unsung heroes of the Free World. You are about to undertake a mission of a magnitude which the supine governments of the West are too craven even to contemplate. But I assure you that next to the enormity of this mission, the risks you run will be minimal.'

Peters concluded his homily with more practical details. In approximately eight hours they would have returned, having made a rendezvous with the Beachcraft at their primary destination, as marked on their sealed flight-plans. The mission would then be officially concluded, their contracts terminated. At the same time, each of their bank accounts in Geneva would be credited with the balance of forty thousand pounds sterling, at the prevailing rate.

Peters glanced maliciously at Thurgood. 'With the exception of the Flight-Lieutenant here, who will be receiving thirty thousand.'

At the mention of his name, Thurgood straightened up with pride, shoulders back, heels together, his eye twitching ominously.

At 01.30 Peters ordered them into their planes. Ten minutes to study the flight-plan. Take-off 01.40.

Rawcliff settled into his seat, checked ignition, contact, undercarriage, flaps and hydraulics, R/T and radio-compass; then he broke open the buff envelope.

The flight-plan followed the previous path across the Nile Delta, down as far as Latitude 28, where the Gulfs of Suez and Aqaba joined the Red Sea.

Fifteen miles south of Sharm el Sheikh they would turn due east and cross the Saudi coast, flying at 200 metres. altitude, up over the Harrat ar Raha mountains. It would be first light and they would be relying on their Red Cross markings for 'protective colouring'; the rest would depend on their flying skills, and on luck.

There was only a marginal danger from ground-to-air missiles; but this time, if they were intercepted by fighter-planes, they were to scatter at once, still keeping to the minimum altitude, using their radios to pretend they were lost.

Their destination was the south-west corner of the Nafud Desert. Here they would rendezvous with Matt and Serge in the Beachcraft. They would spray out the Red Crosses and other markings, and take off again, heading due south, altitude 100 feet: switch on the guidance-systems, as Matt would explain to them, set the detonators, then bail out as

340

quickly as possible and make their way back to the Beachcraft.

They took off in column formation this time: Peters leading, Ryderbeit and Rawcliff behind, Thurgood and Ritchie taking up the rear.

Weather reports as far as the Red Sea continued to give flying conditions as good.

The sky warmed and flared a bright mauve, turning to burning gold over the craggy southern point of the Sinai Peninsula.

In the black hours before dawn Rawcliff's legs had again been numbed by the cold. If it hadn't been for those hopeless attempts to call poor Judith, he might have stopped long enough to buy himself a pair of extra trousers. He had noticed that nowhere along the line had anyone been offered, or asked for, a blanket. He imagined Ryderbeit making some crack about having a stewardess along too; and Rawcliff wondered what had happened to Jo. Had she flown from Athens on to Rome, to meet old Abe, of the Israeli Secret Service? or was she heading for some rich play-pen, waiting to snuggle down with the hapless Nugent-Ross and enjoy their combined bounty of £100,000? Or perhaps she would just return to Ritchie's fashionable London dock side pad?

But what the hell did Rawcliff care what happened to her? Something else worried him far more. If young Klein really did trade happily between Langley, Virginia, and Dzerzhinski Square, Moscow, and if the Russians therefore knew about the mission, they'd have that nuclear site in the Yemen bristling with SAMs, the skies swarming with MiGs, so that by the end of the day there would be just five huge glorious bangs over the desert, with probably no one any the wiser. At no point had there been any mention of the full payment of money being contingent on the mission's success.

Rawcliff shivered, hunching himself over the controls. It wasn't the kind of mission where you had a contract with witnesses and lawyers. You just bumped into somebody in a pub, and were introduced to a little man called Newby, and you took his word for it. Right down the line. You trusted, you believed. People will believe anything for money.

At this point Rawcliff had only one job in hand: to fly his Hercules according to the flight-plan, avoiding radar and interceptors, and somehow get her down and up again, off unknown and probably unfriendly country, then manage a low parachute jump without breaking his neck. He refused to worry about whether Matt or Jo or Ritchie, or all three, had already betrayed them. It was Peters' business to worry about security. So leave it to Peters. Rawcliff had been hired to drive a plane – no more, no less.

Keep your mind on the job, eyes on the horizon. Don't think about Judith, that you may already have dropped her in the shit. Or about little Tom. Just think that the high pounding roar of the four great turboprops on either side is earning you around £1,000 a minute.

Peters' voice came over the R/T, 'Begin descent to 800 feet. Formation spread out to 200 metres distance – prepare to scatter if ordered.'

They went down steeply, and even above the noise of the engines Rawcliff could hear his dreadful cargo groaning against it bindings. He began to chew hard, his ears popping painfully. The sun was now hard in his eyes, as he watched keenly for those telltale specks coming up at them over the horizon. But nothing except the clear, deep azure of dawn: the coast of the Kingdom of Saudi Arabia passing below them at 1,500 feet: naked ribs of mountain unfolding back over the yellow rim of the earth.

The plane began to bounce and sway and shudder with the first draughts of early-morning heat. Their flight-pattern now zigzagged, well south of the little town of Tabuk on the road on up into Jordan.

Great patches of sandy wasteland opened up, climbing into the wall of purplish volcanic mountains, pitted and scarred like a lunar plateau, its razor-sharp ridges racing towards them, often barely a hundred feet below.

Rawcliff's eyes were becoming strained, his muscles stiff and aching as he worked incessantly at the controls, dipping, rising, changing every fraction of a degree as marked on the flight-pattern, following the luminous electronic compass and the agile movements of Ryderbeit's high tail-fin ahead.

Their destination was some 240 miles inside the country. They were some ninety miles from the spot, passing close to the oasis-town of Tayma, when Ryderbeit spotted the plane coming out of the sky from the south.

It was flying well above them, closing in at about 600 knots, and seemed to be alone.

Rawcliff's radio picked up a stream of Arabic, as the fighter flew down low over them, then arched up on to its back and shrieked up towards the horizon. It looked like one of the older marks of Mystère, and he noticed that it was not armed with missiles. Just taking a look at them: but as soon as they got the message down in Jeddah, they'd be likely to have half the Saudi Air Force up looking for them. They had no friends in Jeddah, Rawcliff remembered – thanks to that loony Thurgood.

Peters called over the R/T, 'Formation scatter – at will.'

Ryderbeit's voice cut in, 'The rest of you bugger off in all directions. I'll take the bastard. Leave him to me!'

While Ryderbeit spoke, his Hercules rocked nervously and banked downwards, his port-wing narrowly missing a sharp peak. The Mystère had come out of its climbing turn and seemed to be hesitating, as though its pilot could not decide which plane to chase. Ryderbeit's was the nearest and the lowest. The Mystère dived down, its stubby blue shadow rippling over the rocks below, and Rawcliff felt the thump of its hot exhaust as it swept overhead, swooping down now towards Ryderbeit.

It executed a neat pass over the Rhodesian's lumbering Hercules, which again wobbled ominously, and for a moment Rawcliff, as he pulled away in a wide turn, wondered if by any chance Ryderbeit had lost control or lost his nerve. The Arab pilot must have been thinking the same thing. His voice came over the R/T for the first time in English, calling Ryderbeit's number. He had a young, cocky, trans-Atlantic voice, a cowboy enjoying the kicks – although he seemed to forget that he was flying on an old horse. 'C 130, BZ 462, follow me – just do as I say!'

'Fuck you and your mother and all your sisters,' Ryderbeit said calmly, and pushed the Hercules' nose hard down. He was almost clear of the mountains now, beyond their gleaming pool of sand, its horizon already lost in the haze.

For a moment it looked as though the Arab had jerked his plane to a standstill. He didn't reply to Ryderbeit's taunt, but rolled up on to his back and went down again, in another ferocious pass, this time looking as though his belly might scrape down the roof of the Hercules fuselage. Ryderbeit was down to 50 feet, and the Mystère had to pull up quickly.

Rawcliff was watching from a distance of around three-quarters of a mile and a height of about 500 feet. Ryderbeit was still wobbling and swaying, as though trying desperately to pick a spot to land. Then suddenly he wheeled his mighty plane round, straight into the dazzle of the sun; waited a couple of seconds until the Mystère had levelled out again behind him, closing fast, then wrenched back the throttles, pulling up straight into the jet's path. The Mystère reared up like some terrified animal, until it appeared to be riding on its tail; then went into a sudden shuddering spasm and began to sink forward into the slackening slip-stream.

Rawcliff realized that he was witnessing one of the nightmares of all modern jet-pilots. Ryderbeit's apparently ungainly performance had lured the Arab into the classic trap to which single-engine jet-fighters are the most vulnerable. The Mystère had cut its air-speed so abruptly that it had gone into what is known as a 'wing-stall' – as though the whole aircraft had been seized with mid-air cramp, its jet firing impotently against the static air-flow.

A couple of seconds later it went into a 'super-stall', and began spiralling gently, helplessly downwards, like a dead butterfly.

Rawcliff was able to catch a glimpse of the pilot behind his goggles and the ugly snout of his oxygen-mask, as he struggled, too busy even to send out a Mayday signal. He did not even try to eject. Perhaps his fierce Islamic pride, savaged by Ryderbeit's obscenity, refused to allow his assailant that small satisfaction.

He hit the desert with a thump that was audible above Rawcliff's engines, and was followed by Ryderbeit's triumphant cackle over the R/T.

Peters broke in, 'Formation reassemble – proceed destination, 100 feet, 310 knots, total radio silence. And keep your eyes on the sky. There may be others.'

They were flying now above a bone-white wasteland, strewn with boulders and broken up by banks of wrinkled sand, like some petrified sea on which the occasional bleached skeleton-palms of a dead oasis swooped towards them under the rippling, racing shadows of the five huge planes.

Rawcliff's eyes were still narrowed into the rising sun, muscles tensed at the controls, ready at any moment to throttle back at the sight of some towering rock, some sheer precipice thrown up by the accident of Nature. The compass-reading, against the detailed flight-path, showed that they were getting very close.

The sky was still as empty as the desert – a vast dome of burning glass, under which the five fat grey transports, hurtling along at nearly 300 miles an hour, belly-hugging the sand, would have shown up with the clarity of insects moving across a sheet of clear paper.

It was just a question of whether that lone Mystère pilot had signalled back to Jeddah, before he spun down to his death.

Peters called, 'LZ at two to three minutes. Slow to 180 knots – decreasing. . .'

Rawcliff could hear the slight drop of the engines, the soft push as the nose tried to go down. 'Undercarriages!' Peters called. The dry whine and clonk, the nasty drag as Rawcliff kept his arms braced, nose up, trying to plough up through the stagnant air and regain that few feet of altitude.

'LZ dead ahead!'

Through the shields of perspex Rawcliff could just make out the blue-and-white fleck ahead: a slender bird resting on its fragile legs. Then, as they came down, two planes abreast, he saw Ritchie's motto 'Come Fly with Me', looking faintly frivolous in the arid vastness of the Arabian sands.

The small dark figures of Serge and Matt Nugent-Ross could be seen resting in the meagre shadow of one wing. Serge came out, signalling with a white flag.

The zone had evidently been chosen with some care: a flat tract of desert that seemed to have been cleared for about 500 yards of all stones and boulders, lying between a steep cliff of rock on one side and a shelving sea of soft sand on the other. It was as safely hidden as anywhere in the desert can be, in the harsh light of day.

Peters and Ryderbeit landed first, almost simultaneously, on either side of the Beachcraft. As soon as their main wheels touched down, the dust exploded behind them in two rolling mushroom-clouds that almost instantly blotted out the little plane, and soon obliterated the margin of the makeshift landing-strip.

Rawcliff throttled back fast and did a high howling turn, out over the sloping sand-sea. This was no time to make mistakes, he thought, as he brought the Hercules round, back through the dense dust, and could see Peters' and Ryderbeit's planes drawn up at the end of the airstrip.

Both Ritchie and Thurgood were good enough pilots not to have questioned what he was doing. He levelled the plane, with the windshield now smudged a cloudy-yellow. He chose the side of the Beachcraft that ended with a wall of rock, guessing that it would be firmer than the side closer to the sand-sea. Not that it would make a blind bit of difference, he thought, if either Ritchie or Thurgood made a too soft landing and stuck – nose down, tail rising, with the image of Grant's final seconds coming vividly into focus. On this run it was all or nothing. There would be no survivors.

He felt his wheels bump down, grinding, slewing slightly: watching frantically his long starboard-wing and measuring the distance from the bare rock-face. Then he felt a jarring thud as the wheels gouged out four deep channels in the sandy surface. The four engines screamed at the hot dry air, as he reversed the props, slammed on the airbrakes, the wings shivering, as he bounded and lurched to a stop. He switched off, and heard his ears ringing, felt his body drenched with sweat; got the cabin-door open and lowered himself down into the blinding light.

His nose-wheel was very slightly buckled and half-bedded in the loose sand. He watched, a little dazed, as Ritchie and Thurgood came in through a fresh cloud of dust, taxi-ing noisily up to the end of the strip next to the other three planes.

Although it was still not eight o'clock, the heat was scorching, airless, seeming to burn one's throat and lungs with a rasping mixture of sand and dust and kerosene fumes.

All the engines had been turned off, and the silence was gigantic, terrifying. Just the scuff of the pilots' boots as they came, already panting, blinking through the sweat, towards the Beachcraft. Matt Nugent-Ross was carrying the white leather case from inside the little plane.

Peters gave orders. They each had ten minutes, no more, to spray out all the Red Cross markings on the five aircraft. Then they were to fasten parachutes and prepare for immediate take-off. At altitude 200 feet – absolutely no lower – they were to prime the detonators, before jumping. Any pilot who overdropped the DZ, or who was injured and unable to make it back to the Beachcraft, would be on his own.

Rawcliff realized that Peters was not necessarily excluding himself from these conditions. And, since he still had his bad ankle, there was no denying that the man was brave. He had probably lived too near the margin of death for it to matter much now. The same would go for Ryderbeit. Thurgood looked as inscrutable, blank-eyed, as ever. He would have made a fine kamikaze pilot, Rawcliff decided.

Jim Ritchie looked calm and serious. Young Ritchie had more to worry about than getting his plane back off the ground and making a smooth parachute landing. Rawcliff wondered at what moment he had planned for the Americans or the Israelis, or even the Russians, to arrive like the flying-cavalry and remove those lethal detonators?

Five miles above, the tiny silver speck of an airliner crawled across the sky, trailing a thin white wake of exhaust. Probably an early flight from Athens or Cairo, Bombay or Karachi. They would be serving breakfast now: smiling hostesses bringing the fresh piping-hot coffee up to the pilots sitting comfortably in their pressurized air-conditioned cocoon of instruments, everything legal and correct, according to the book.

Spraying out the Red Crosses was a more horrible task than Rawcliff had anticipated. It also struck him as unnecessarily dangerous. The skin of the aircraft was rapidly becoming too hot to touch; and the fierce spray of paint bubbled and wrinkled ominously as he swept the nozzle back and forth, desperately trying to erase those last emblems of international respectability.

It took longer than Peters had predicted; long enough for a squadron of Saudi Arabian F-5s to be making a broad sweep of the Nafud Desert, in a search for their colleague in the drowned Mystère. But Rawcliff remembered that searching the desert is like searching the ocean: there would be no more left of the little fighter-plane than a few scraps of blackened flotsam.

His face was sprayed with a thin mask of grey, his eyes burning with paint fumes and sweat, his head pounding with the heat. When he got back inside the plane, nothing had changed, except that Matt had now armed the neat metal box that contained the computerized guidance-system. The hi-fi set behind the navigator's seat had also been loaded with a cassette.

Rawcliff strapped on his parachute, made sure that the line was secure, and breathed a meaningless prayer that the nose-wheel would not come loose. God, what he'd have given now for a chilled beer!

The sound of Peters' and Ryderbeit's engines shattered the awful silence, like eight powerful explosions. They took off in the same order, at two-minute intervals. The dust was again crouching over the whole airstrip, as thick as fog. Rawcliff calmed himself, reminded himself of that first meeting with Newby and how he had claimed that they were offering too much money. Maybe there were certain things that didn't have a price. Like getting a Hercules off the ground in the equivalent of a static sand-storm – visibility perhaps ten feet, no helpful voice from the control-tower, a gammy front-wheel and a runway as smooth as a wrestler's grip.

He steadied her, gave full throttle, felt the nose-wheel break off with a nasty scraping, wrenching sound, as the floor of the cabin slid along the rocky sand. Then suddenly the nose bounced up, the engines took control, and a few seconds later he was above the dust-cloud, turning steeply again out over the sand-sea which disappeared into an invisible horizon; and now he was concentrating on the altimetre: 160 – 170 – 190 – 200... He leaned down and turned the screw-head dial of the detonator; flicked the little white switch on the guidance-system; pulled back, to maximum throttle, waiting for the strip of churned up landing-zone to come sliding round towards him at just under 500 feet; then released the controls, feeling the guidance-system take over, while he made his way down between the rails and the creaking steel drums to the open rear vent, and smelt the hot blast of the slip-stream; saw the landing-zone passing almost directly below now; then jumped.

2

On that same Friday morning, Don Laraby received his visitor promptly at 9.30 am, London time, in a small side-office, as quiet as a cell after the confusion of the big room next door.

Had it not been for the man's card, and a couple of phrases of introduction, Laraby might not have been inclined to take him seriously. An old-style Britisher straight out of Central Casting: three-piece chalk-stripe suit, pepper-and-salt moustache, tie of obvious distinction, though one whose origin eluded Laraby. No subtlety here, he thought. Laraby had had a few dealings with the Intelligence racket during his stint in the Middle East, and he'd never found subtlety yet. He guessed this breed to be almost extinct, except in a few London clubs, far-flung embassies, and among those Englishmen who worked as Stateside representatives for Rolls-Royce and malt whisky distillers. All that was missing was the rolled umbrella.

Laraby wasn't worried, or even puzzled; just slightly irritated that his visitor declined a chair. The American disliked formality. He said, 'Yeah, she got a stack of print-outs and brought them up to me. Fairly straightforward. Flight-path for somewhere in the Middle East, due south. She was expecting it to lead to the Yemen.' He grinned sadly, 'I guess that Soviet nuclear base you've all been getting so steamed up about?' He lifted both hands in a mock gesture of surrender, but without effect. He might have guessed that the Englishman would not be amused.

Laraby fidgeted with a pen-holder. 'Hell, I was just doing the lady a favour. Helped her check out some of the grid-references, using an ordinary atlas.' He smiled innocently. 'What's all the sweat?'

'But you did check the final reference?'

'Sure. The last reference that showed, that is. The stuff

was dumped – a real mess – lotta sheets missing. I got no guarantee it was the *final* reference.'

'What was Mrs Rawcliff's reaction when you told her?'

Laraby's manner became wary: it was one thing answering straight technical inquiries, quite another delivering snap psychological judgements on one of his colleagues. 'Frankly I wasn't that interested. I think I made some crack about it being a chain of dance-halls – beauty contests – that kinda thing. She thanked me and took the stuff away.'

'But she had already told you that it was in connection with a Tetra-Lipp guidance-system?'

'I think she mentioned it.'

'Did that strike you as at all unusual?'

Don Laraby sat forward. 'Listen Mr . . .'

'Jameson – as in the Raid.'

'Well, Mr Jameson, sir, you must understand that this is a big outfit we got here. We deal in every aspect of computers, from simple office equipment to a lotta stuff that goes into the military complex. We do a job, and part of that job is not to run round asking questions. We haven't got the time.'

'Your Mrs Rawcliff evidently had.'

'Okay, so talk to her about it. She's in another department. As I said, I was just helping her out as a favour. She has her work to do, I have mine.' He looked pointedly at his watch.

His visitor ignored the hint. 'For some reason she was interested in the flight-path for a Tetra-Lipp Retropilot Mark 100/4? And somehow she got hold of a print-out of the path, but couldn't understand it? So you helped her out? That is correct, Mr Laraby?'

The American resumed the ritual of removing his spectacles, wiping each lens, then putting them back on again. 'Listen, Mr Jameson, I appreciate that for you fellahs a Tetra-Lipp might sound pretty awesome. For us it's just another computer system. Darned sophisticated, darned expensive, but nothing out of Pandora's magic-box. And I surely don't have to remind you that it's off the classified list?'

There was a calculated pause.

'What is Mrs Rawcliff's principal job here?' asked Jameson.

'In a single word, evaluator. Analysing or processing pretty well anything that drops on her desk. I think she's on sugar forecasts at the moment. Next week it could be tin or nickel or chrome, or maybe gold or oil.'

'Rather a long way from the latest military guidance-system for low-flying aircraft?'

'Okay, you ask her. Unless it's confidential company business, of course.'

'I am afraid there is no "of course" about it, Mr Laraby. As a British subject, Mrs Rawcliff is duty-bound to answer any inquiries we may put to her. She can also be required to sign the Official Secrets Act. I must be quite frank with you, Mr Laraby. I cannot afford to have any misunderstandings about this. As a United States citizen your position maybe slightly different. But I have been instructed to inform you that this matter has been discussed, at the highest level, with your Embassy here, and that we have been promised full co-operation.'

Laraby flushed. 'You trying to lean on me, Jameson? C'mon, let's have it straight! So I've got some info that your people don't want spread about? Mrs Rawcliff and I keep our mouths shut and everything's tickittyboo? Right?'

'That's about the size of it – as far as you're concerned Mr Laraby.'

The American sat back and grinned. He was feeling a lot more nervous than he looked. 'Okay, what's the rub? If I talk outa turn, you invoke some kinda Aliens' Order, withdraw my work permit and sling me out? Or is this thing so important that you'd arrange some fancy car accident, maybe, like they do before the commercial break?'

'I am sure that you'll wish to be sensible about this, Mr Laraby. And I am also sure that you understand that this conversation – like your meeting with Mrs Rawcliff yesterday – is in the strictest confidence. I am very grateful to you for sparing me your time. Don't worry, I shall let myself out.'

For some time Laraby sat and stared unseeing at the cheap lithograph on the wall opposite. He had always liked Judith Rawcliff – she was a nice, bright, attractive woman and damned good at her job. But just now he wished the hell he'd never set eyes on her.

3

Rawcliff lay bruised and puzzled, his body resting on a cushion of soft sand as he watched the five wide, heavy-bellied grey planes closing into tight formation, flying away pilotless into the empty sky. They were losing height, growing smaller, down to 200 feet, which, by the magic of electronics and five slivers of tape, they would maintain, at a steady cruising speed of 240 knots, relentlessly following every contour of the land, every ridge and peak and valley, until a tiny magnetic impulse directed them to plunge into their intricately prepared holocaust.

The sand felt scorched, painful to the touch, and the heat lay on him like a massive bone-aching weight. He could hear the engines droning dully, receding with a monotonous mechanical rhythm that seemed in tune with the pain in his head. He sat up, and was dimly aware of the great silken white shroud of the parachute draped across the sand behind him, its cords resting on his body.

For a moment he watched two white mushrooms drifting to earth, and saw the pilots scrambling up, pulling off their harnesses. He realized that if he lay here any longer he would begin to bake alive in the heat. He felt himself, carefully, anticipating the sharp agony of a broken bone, a torn ligament; then stood up, unstrapping the harness and stepped free of the cords.

Trying to walk up the shelf of soft sand and reach the firmness of the landing strip was like walking in hot treacle, his muscles limp, uncoordinated, dropping on to his hands and knees, half-blinded by sweat, dragging himself forward, all adrenalin sapped, his body drained to the extremity of exhaustion.

The others were gathered around the Beachcraft. It was a quiet, sober scene. No popping of champagne corks; nobody cheering or dancing. Ryderbeit was crouching on his haunches, lighting one of his long cigars. Ritchie and Serge leant against the wing of the little plane, chatting. Matt Nugent-Ross sat under the shadow of the wing and smiled from behind his dark glasses, as Rawcliff stumbled towards them.

Peters appeared a couple of minutes later, limping stiffly. The jump must have been agony on his damaged ankle; and for a dangerous moment Rawcliff felt sympathy for the man.

Peters had stopped several paces away from the rest of them. 'Where's Thurgood?' His clipped voice had a tinny sound in the empty stillness. The drone of the five Hercules had now died into the far distance. They were all staring out at the naked rock-face, the scarred sand, the wilderness beyond. There was no movement, no speck, no sign of a parachute shroud.

Peters turned, he spoke to Nugent-Ross, 'Did you see him jump?'

'I counted four.' The American hesitated. 'All five aircraft were in formation.'

'What's that supposed to mean?'

'Just that he must have switched on the guidance-system,' said Matt.

'Why?' Peters was angry. 'He could have been flying in formation.'

Matt nodded. 'He could.'

Peters stood very still. His blond hair was in place, but there was a thin oil of sweat on his face. He took a last look at the desert, then turned again to Nugent-Ross, 'Can those things of yours be switched off?'

'Nope. Once the switch is down, the course is set. If he tries to override the auto-pilot, he'll crash.'

'We've no guarantee,' Rawcliff said, 'that he switched the thing on in the first place. He might be flying down to Jeddah, hoping to pick up some reward.'

Ryderbeit spat on the stony ground and watched the gob sizzle and shrink to nothing. 'Thurgood's cracked. Come on – I've fulfilled my contract. So have the rest of us. I'm not being paid to worry about what Flight-Lieutenant Thurgood does. Let's get going.'

Peters was still standing away from the rest of them.

Rawcliff watched him, still dazed. There was a thumping in his head. He saw Peters put his hand into his side-pocket and pull out the gun. Not the .22 this time. It looked like the .45 PPK that they'd taken off one of the dead militiamen. He fired it quickly, waist-high, and the three shots made an almost simultaneous crack that screamed across the empty sand, bouncing back from the cliff wall and numbing Rawcliff's eardrums so that he did not even hear the third shot.

Serge's solid body slid back with a clang of metal, as it collided with the Beachcraft's wing; and the little plane shuddered on its struts. Ritchie was still smiling, glassy-eyed, as he slid down and lay still beside the Frenchman. Serge had been hit messily in the throat, and tried to regain his balance, making a quick pirouette, both arms flung out like a drunken dancer.

Matt Nugent-Ross died without a sound, without expression, except that his dark glasses had slid off his nose. The heavy bullet had hit him in the chest, flattening his shirt against his ribs; as he sat down abruptly, and just stared at Peters, as though nothing had happened.

Peters now turned; he gave Rawcliff a funny, rigid little smile. 'I'm saving you for the last, Rawcliff. And you're not going to die quite so quickly.'

Rawcliff stood and watched the big gun move down so that it was pointing at his groin. It was then that Ryderbeit moved. He moved like a snake. His whole body whipped down, left hand still holding the smoking cigar, while his right grabbed at his ankle and flashed back up, glinting in the sun. At first Rawcliff could not see what had happened. Peters' gun roared and sand spat up a few feet to Rawcliff's left foot; then the gun dropped against Peters' boot.

Peters had put out his arm to try and balance himself. He stood swaying, and something black was sticking out of his open shirt, just below the collar-bone. Blood was beginning to swell up round it, trickling down his shirt.

He looked blankly at Ryderbeit. 'You bastard. You knew the fat man's orders. You weren't on the list. He told me to spare you. Why did you do it?' His voice slurred, broken by a cough which brought blood bubbling out of his mouth. He lost his balance and sat down in the sand, a few feet away from the body of Matt Nugent-Ross.

Ryderbeit drew on his cigar, then strolled over and wrenched the knife out of Peters' chest. The blood followed in a spurt, splashing his boots. 'I did it because I don't like your manners, Peters. Now you just lie there and die quietly. You've had this coming to you for a long, long time. Sooner or later someone was going to catch up with you. You're just lucky it was me, and you got it quick and clean, with a knife. Some people wouldn't have been so kind.' He leant down and picked up the Walther PPK, and stood for a moment weighing it in his hand. 'Lovely toy. But too much of a liability.' He stood back and hurled the heavy gun far out across the sand-strip, where it lay lost among the web of grooved trenches left by the five Hercules' landing-gear.

Then he turned back to the Beachcraft and shifted Serge's heavy body from beneath the wing. He did it effortlessly, without expression, like a farmer or a butcher handling a large carcass. Next he systematically searched each of the sprawled bodies, and removed every item of possible identification, right down to wallets, watches, even proprietory labels on their clothing. He worked with a speed and rhythm that suggested to Rawcliff that he had done this sort of thing before. Finally he found a spare five-gallon can of petrol in the back of the Beachcraft. He had begun to empty it over the pile of documents and papers, when Rawcliff said: 'What about the bodies?'

'Sure! If you give me a hundred gallons and about five hours. Any idea how long it takes to burn a human body?'

'You could disfigure them.'

Ryderbeit leered. 'The sun'll do that in a few hours. Let's spare ourselves the smell. I haven't had breakfast, and I want to enjoy lunch, if possible.' He dropped his lighted cigar and stepped smartly back to avoid the burst of white flame that lapped round the pile of dead pilots' belongings. Then he jabbed his thumb towards the Beachcraft.

'Let's get flying, soldier. It's too hot and I need a drink.

357

And we're not going to get one in this fucking country!'

He had opened the door of the Beachcraft and jumped aboard, pinched out a fresh cigar and lit it with a steady hand, before switching on the ignition; then, as Rawcliff climbed in beside him, he reached for Serge's map-case from under the seat and began to squint down at the flight-plan. Rawcliff noticed that he had wiped clean the knife before replacing it inside his boot.

Just as they began to taxi forward, Rawcliff glimpsed a movement from outside. Peters was still alive, hunched up and coughing thick lumps of blood into the sand.

'We can't just leave him, Sammy!'

'So what do you want us to do – fly him down to Jeddah and book him into one of those big modern hospitals they've got there for treating their syph and piles? Come on, soldier, you're too sentimental for this game!'

Five minutes later they were climbing to 4,000 feet, heading west towards Sinai.

It was mid-morning and the heat haze was rising like fog, shrouding the Bitter Lake and the straight dark line of the Canal, which is the best landmark a low-flying pilot could wish for. From now on they would have to rely on the gyro-compass. Ryderbeit was reluctant to use the radio, unless absolutely necessary: and in any case, he didn't trust the air-traffic controllers at Cairo West.

Neither of them liked the idea of Egypt – they would both have preferred a safe haven on mainland Europe, well outside the Arab orbit – but Cairo was the only obvious place within the Beachcraft's range. As though to emphasize this, the fuel warning-light began to flicker and Ryderbeit switched on to the reserve tank.

Rawcliff had never flown into Cairo West, but he knew its reputation as one of the most chaotic and badly run airports on the main routes to the East. Ryderbeit cackled, chewing the stub of his fourth cigar. 'Well, I can tell you, soldier, the bloody place hasn't improved. The Gyppoes are enlarging it, and the last I heard, they hadn't even got a proper control-tower operating. Instead, they had a couple o' bastards using binoculars and walkie-talkies! But I guess we can do with a little chaos at this point. Easier to get lost, with not too many questions asked.' He tapped the map-case under his seat. 'Just remember, we're clean. Aerial reconnaissance for a French geological institute. That's what the man said, and that's what his papers say. We got our passports, licences, vaccination certificates. We're clean as a nun's knickers!'

As he spoke he was bringing the little plane down to below 2,000 feet, working hard to steady her against blasts of upward turbulence. He spat out his dead cigar. 'Our real problems start when we get to Geneva and try and draw the loot. Charlie Pol may not look too quick on his feet, but you've got to move fucking fast to keep one step ahead of him!'

'It was his idea to have the rest of us killed?'

'Sure. He's the one who gives the orders.'

'Why?'

Ryderbeit turned and peered at him with his bright yellow eye. 'Pol holds the purse strings, and this way he's saving himself approximately a quarter of a million smackers – not counting Granty. Anyway, he doesn't want a lousy gang of witnesses sprawled over every bar in Europe, shouting their mouths off about how they helped spike the Soviet nuclear threat to the Arab Continent.'

'But he was prepared to spare you? And Peters?'

Ryderbeit sat forward, squinting ahead. The geometrical shapes of the Pyramids were beginning to form out of the haze; and beyond them the vast dirty sprawl of the city.

'He spared me because I'm useful to him. He's got good judgement, has Charlie Pol.'

'And Peters?'

'Another fall-guy. Third World mercenary, South African background, and nobody to love or miss him. Above all, nobody too keen to claim him.'

They were down to nearly 1,500 feet, holding a steady course towards the dim criss-cross of runways.

'That leaves me feeling rather like a wild card,' Rawcliff said.

Ryderbeit had eased down the flap-lever with one hand

and smacked Rawcliff hard on the knee with the other. 'I'll give you a good reference, soldier. People don't kill friends o' mine and get away with it.' He switched on the radio. 'This is where I start having to be polite to those gibbering monkeys down there.'

Rawcliff looked at his watch. Those five Hercules would be well over their target by now.

4

'I am not here to offer either apologies or explanations. Nor is the Department. If you're so unhappy about what's happened, then I suggest that you bypass the usual channels and submit your resignation directly to the Minister. You'll at least have the satisfaction of having it turned down flat.'

Suchard was tired and ill-tempered; he had drunk too much the night before, which was not his habit, and had slept badly. He was in no mood to smooth down the ruffled sensibilities of the SB or to parry the pusillanimous complaints of the Met in general.

Addison, in his capacity as torch-bearer for the Special Branch, sat across the room in St James' Square, stiff and silently furious – a taunt to Suchard's own secret sense of guilt, even horror. For despite his vain cynicism, his worldly indifference induced by a career spent in the black arts of deceit and distortion, even the occasional small iniquity, all in the supposed defence of the Realm, the reports that had begun to seep through on the wires that Friday morning had caused him a profound shock. Whatever the state of the world, and the precarious balance of forces, for both good and evil, the events of this morning had taken things too far, even for Simon de Vere Suchard. The fact that he had been only a minor unwitting accomplice to what had happened offered no comfort: indeed, it seemed to render his own role all the more contemptible.

The news was still scrappy and confused, coming in special flashes over the radio, and playing havoc with the early editions of the evening papers. On-the-spot communications would be chaotic, even non-existent; and it was likely that the local authorities were deliberately trying to suppress the news in order to avert international panic.

As usual, the wires of the FO were vague and often contradictory; but if only part of the reports proved to be true, it would still add up to a stupendous, horrific outrage, so wanton, so truly infernal, that its implications and consequences were both terrible and impossible to calculate.

Yet here, at one of the nerve-ends of power, and as the truth began to dawn, was come this wretched policeman to nag Suchard about what amounted to no more than a small matter of professional etiquette.

Suchard had stood up and was making himself another cup of black sugarless Nescafé. 'All right, you've got two corpses – Mason, and that miserable Newby, who doesn't belong to us, anyway – and the Yard are whining because they've been deliberately prevented from arresting the culprits. Just bung both on the "unsolved" file! Two more won't make that much difference. And the press have got other things to worry about, after what's happened this morning.

'Damn it all,' he added, sitting down again, and crossing his legs: 'I am not responsible for policy. You can call me all the rude names you like – errand boy, the Minister's chief lickspittle and fag, Government shit-shoveller by Royal Appointment. Just sticks and stones. Complain if you like, but not to me. Christ, man, I'm the last person you should be coming to! *I* know nothing – except that I'm meant to know nothing. I can't even read between the lines any more, because the official cables have stopped reaching this desk – all my sources have dried up. It's the same with the FO. And it's my guess that even the Minister and Number Ten haven't been too fully informed. Which means – again if my guess is right – that they preferred *not* to be informed.' He stopped abruptly: 'That's absolutely off the record, of course.'

Addison gave a short nod, this time barely concealing his rage. 'You misunderstand me,' he said gravely. 'My concern is purely with the police angle. I am anxious about the Rawcliff woman. To be quite blunt, I don't want another corpse, this time smack in my "manor". Nor am I going to spare a full detail to keep round-the-clock surveillance on her for the next ten or twenty years.'

Suchard closed his eyes, stiffening his jaw muscles against a yawn. 'All right, so we scared her off. She's moved out of

Battersea and gone to stay with a friend in Richmond. And taken the kid with her. Sensible girl. They'd be as likely to go for the kid as for her. Providing, of course, somebody twigs – which is only likely to happen if that bloody husband of hers decides to come prancing back, laughing all the way to the local bank, now they've lifted control restrictions.' He leant back, sipping his coffee.

'Otherwise, she's holed up in a nice comfortable house in a cul-de-sac of Richmond Park. Easy enough for surveillance – which, need I say, cuts both ways. The house owner's in merchant banking, and with Lloyds, so he might not like it if he found you boys trampling all over his lawn. That's about the full score, isn't it, Addison?'

'One of my men spoke to her this afternoon – report came in less than an hour ago. He had followed her to a local supermarket in Queen's Road. She had the kid with her and he gave her a hand with some of her things. Nothing obvious – no cheek, and no threats. Until they were outside, that is –then he put it to her, gently but straight. If she wanted to stay alive, and keep her son, she must forget everything that's happened to her in the last few days and get out. Resign her job, sell up everything she had, and go a long, long way away. Above all, keep clear of her husband. That included letters, telephone calls, telegrams, even messages through third parties.

'Pretty harsh words, I think you'd agree? My man was all set for a minor bout of hysterics, at the very least. But not at all. Know what the girl did? Half spat, half laughed in his face. Told him that she'd heard the news, and if he thought she had the least intention of standing by her husband, who was a mass-murderer, he had another think coming. All she seemed worried about was protection for the kid.'

'I suppose we ought to do something,' Suchard said wearily. 'Her house is probably in Rawcliff's name, and there's no doubt a mortgage. And even if Rawcliff's dead – and it can be proved – we can't piss around with solicitors and insurance companies. It would take months. Some sort of *ex gratia* payment can no doubt be arranged. On strictly compassionate grounds, of course. I'll have a word with our

Personnel Department. Needn't go through the Treasury books. In fact, under the circumstances, it's essential that it doesn't.' Suchard turned, gave Addison a very slight wink. 'Enough to set her up somewhere, start again. Canada or Australia. She's an attractive girl, from what I hear. And it would get her off your back, wouldn't it?'

'It would,' Addison said sourly. 'Any news at all about Rawcliff and the other pilots?'

'Not a murmur. We're still expecting the Yids to come through with something. Or the Americans, maybe. We haven't been running this show, remember – all we're trying to do is to keep our feet out of the shit.'

The Special Branch man stood up. 'Very well. I'll put a "red" on the Rawcliff woman for one week – provisionally. And I'd appreciate it, if only as a courtesy, if you would let me know the moment you get anything on the husband.'

'Will do.' Suchard said, without getting up. 'I'll be interested to know what you'll charge him with, if he's fool enough to try and come home!'

But Addison had already left the room without replying.

5

Ryderbeit could pick up only a confused jabber and shouting from the ground, most of it in Arabic. It was so loud that he had to turn down the volume. One voice cut in, in English, and asked them to identify themselves. Ryderbeit did so, then the channel went dead. He tried several other frequencies, but it was like tuning into a very noisy party, sometimes even a yelling match.

'Sounds pretty wild down there,' he said, and shut off the radio. 'Seems we all do our own thing today in Cairo.'

He put the Beachcraft down on a corner of the enormous field that was evidently reserved for private aircraft, which included a number of sleek twin-engine jets; the playthings of the big absentee landlords, corrupt politicos, and probably a few of the rich brethren from Saudi and the Emirates who didn't want to risk advertising themselves on the civil airlines, now that Egypt was in the doghouse following the Camp David Agreement with Israel.

No one came out to meet them. It was a long walk through the shuddering heat, towards the ramshackle confusion of the terminal buildings, some of which were derelict or half-pulled down, others only half-built.

Rawcliff immediately sensed that something odd was happening. A big international airport, at mid-day, should be one of the busiest, noisiest places anywhere on earth. But here there was a strange inactivity. Or rather, the wrong sort of activity. High above, through the dull yellow haze, came the roar and whine of 'stacking' aircraft; while on the ground, across the bleak wastes of concrete, there was no movement – no giant fuel-trucks, baggage trolleys, passenger buses crawling out from the terminal buildings; no mobile generators or brightly coloured runway controllers; no police or mechanics, no trace of an aircraft taxi-ing up to the holding position, nor of anything coming into land.

It was like the approaches to a dead city – until they reached the terminal building.

They heard the noise first, like the muted roar from a football stadium. Rawcliff sensed the vibrations of mass hysteria even before he reached the buildings. All the loudspeakers were bellowing simultaneously, in a cacophony of Arabic; while the floors were packed with people, many of them wailing and weeping, and some of them – including policemen and porters and cleaners, even the girls at the check-in desks – had flung themselves down on their knees and were praying towards the East. A few pockets of bewildered Western travellers could be seen huddled round the edges.

Nobody stopped the two of them as they walked through the barriers, past the Customs and Immigration officers, who were all gathered round transistor radios, one of them howling like a wounded dog. Ryderbeit had grabbed Rawcliff by the arm and soon they were lost in the crowd. It was too noisy even to exchange words. Ryderbeit was heading for the bar, like a horse to water. He paused only to yell at a well-dressed Egyptian in a dark business suit, a transistor pressed to his ear. The man yelled back something in English, and Ryderbeit seized him furiously, forcing the man to repeat himself. This time Rawcliff heard enough to make the sweat all over his body turn cold.

Ryderbeit had released the man and struggled on towards the bar. He leant his face down next to Rawcliff's ear, and said with a long grin, 'You hear that, soldier? Holy Moses, that wasn't in the script! And that script's just rewritten history.'

Rawcliff shouted back, in a voice flat with shock: 'Let's try and get out of here! We're Europeans, remember. Bloody infidels. And I've heard about the Cairo bomb.'

'Take it easy, soldier.' The bar was unattended, and for some reason it was quieter here. A group of small black-suited Japanese, each fondling a camera, blinked at them both through their spectacles. Between the two of them they were able to gather that a JAL flight from the Far East had been due to take off thirty minutes ago for Paris.

Ryderbeit cursed and spat ungraciously in full view of the Japanese. 'Well, by the looks of things I guess we're in no hurry. Before I do anything else, I'm going to have myself a drink. I'm going to have a couple of bloody drinks!' And before Rawcliff could stop him, he had vaulted the bar, selected a quart sized bottle of Johnny Walker Black Label, and began drinking from the neck.

Sammy Ryderbeit was now drunk. Rawcliff had left him sprawled on his belly under a bench, sleeping like a cat.

It was mid-afternoon, and there were tenuous signs that the airport was returning to some degree of order, if not normality. Squads of fierce-looking riot police with batons, shields and machine pistols at the ready, had been drafted in, with some effect. Those incoming aircraft which had not already been diverted were beginning to land. A skeleton staff of Customs and Immigration was back on duty. But most important, some of the check-in counters were now open.

Rawcliff concentrated his mind, forcing out the one memory he most feared – the final contemptuous words of his wife. She'd known all along, and she'd been right. But this, of all moments in history, was no time for maudlin reappraisals, for self-indulgent regrets. He had to act, do something, anything: if he stopped now he would be like a man lost in a blizzard, sinking down, never to get up again.

He discovered that several of the airport shops, run by the more greedy, or perhaps less religious local entrepreneurs, had reopened. He bought two airline bags, some cheap shirts, including one to replace Ryderbeit's grubby olive-drab combat tunic – from which he had not even bothered to remove the Red Cross insignia on the shoulder – and a couple of rudimentary toilet-kits. He remembered, from his own experience, that the one sort of passenger who immediately arouses suspicion is one who travels with no luggage at all. He wasn't worried about heavy luggage – not at this end, at any rate. Those few officials on duty looked as though they had something else on their minds.

Then he went back to rouse Ryderbeit. The Rhodesian might pride himself on being the proverbial Wandering Jew who travelled strictly light, except for the odd throwing knife or elephant-gun. But he was also a born survivor – and a ruthlessly practical one – unlike that impulsive, gullible old plodder, Charles Rawcliff, who threw up everything, abandoning his wife and child, in the simpleton's quest for a crock of Swiss gold.

Ryderbeit stretched himself and yawned. Apart from his leery red eyes, he appeared none the worse for having consumed about half a pint of neat whisky. And as Rawcliff expected, the Rhodesian was not short of money. But nothing fancy or traceable, like credit cards or travellers' cheques; nor anything so soft as sterling or dollars. Ryderbeit had two sewn-up pockets inside the front of his trousers, next to his zip-fly, each containing a wad of big thick one-hundred-franc Swiss notes.

Ten minutes later they had purchased two single tickets on the scheduled JAL flight to Paris, which was now due to depart in forty minutes. But despite several false alarms, boarding did not begin for another three hours.

Passport Control consisted of no more than a wave of the hand from a fat uniformed man whose eyes were still stark with shock. Rawcliff and Ryderbeit were careful to pass through the gate and to board the plane separately, choosing seats well apart from each other. The DC8 was well filled, mostly with passengers from the transit area. Besides the ubiquitous Japanese, there were also about a dozen Europeans – businessmen and a couple of families returning from the Far East, all with the unhealthy yellow tan of the tropics.

Rawcliff was uncomfortably aware that he and Ryderbeit were the only Europeans among the few passengers to join the flight here in Cairo. No crazed-eyed hippies or international pop-idols or smirking, eye-catching little starlets. Just himself, and Sammy Ryderbeit, who stuck up from among the serried rows of seats like the bad fairy at the princess's christening.

Outside, the light was beginning to fade. There was still little activity on the runways. Inside the cabin the air-conditioning had been turned on, provided by a generator truck outside the plane; and the crowded stillness was filled with the soft placebo of Western musak. Little stewardesses moved in their kimonos, smiling down the aisle and handing out warm scented towels, sweets and chewing gum. The intercom crackled in Japanese, then in careful English, regretting that there would be a further delay due to air-clearance formalities.

Rawcliff felt himself drained with lack of food and sleep, yet tense, with a febrile exhaustion that refused to relent, to allow him to relax for one moment. The wheels were still resting firmly on Arab territory and the engines remained silent. It needed no great powers of deduction to realize that anyone interested enough in the first flight out of Cairo that day, after the news of the morning's holocaust had broken, would need to make only a few routine telephone calls to establish who had boarded that flight and where they were booked to disembark. It was just a question of who was interested? Jo's friend with the Mossad in Rome? Or Ritchie's contact, Klein, with his double-dealing between Washington and Moscow? Not to mention the Arabs. Ryderbeit had put it with poignant simplicity back at the airport bar, as he wiped the last of the Johnny Walker from his lips: 'If we're ever rumbled on this one, soldier, you can sleep at night with the thought that we've just become Public Enemies Numbers One and Two of approximately 750 million worshippers of the one-and-only Allah. And I'd say that on this one Allah's going to have a mighty long arm and it's going to wield a mighty swift sword!'

God, what a fuck-up. Rawcliff closed his eyes. He was sitting between two Japanese who at least spared him the ordeal of conversation. Half an hour passed. The Captain's voice chimed in again, exasperatingly apologetic – a pre-recorded litany of Oriental politeness. The girls in their kimonos dispensed more towels, and coffee and tea in paper cups.

An hour passed. Lights came on along the runways and several planes landed, but none took off. Rawcliff's head began to throb from the dry, stale air, and his mouth tasted as parched as leather. Then the rear door opened, with a blast of muggy air. Two men entered the cabin, both Egyptians, sallow-faced with black moustaches, dressed identically in bulky dark suits of artificial fibre. Rawcliff could smell police, even above the scented towels.

They came down the aisle with that familiar, weary, laconic air of self-confidence, checking each passenger's passport. They showed little interest in the Japanese, but spent their time scrutinizing the documents of the few other Egyptian nationals aboard.

They had worked their way along to within three rows of Rawcliff, when a loud argument started in Arabic. Both plain clothes men had closed round a stout bald Egyptian who was half-standing out of his seat, rolling his eyes and waving his arms as though in a macabre burlesque. One of the policemen was holding his passport, the other seized him by the wrists. Rawcliff could not tell whether he were shouting with fury or terror, as the two policemen hauled him out into the aisle and began to march him clumsily down towards the rear door. There they paused, while one of them went back and fetched the man's fat expensive-looking briefcase.

The last Rawcliff saw of him was standing at the rear of the plane, suddenly silent, and adjusting his tie with comic dignity; then he was led outside and the cabin door swung shut.

Almost immediately the Captain's voice announced that they were cleared for take-off. To compensate for the delay, free alcoholic beverages would be served during the flight.

Rawcliff leant forward to tighten his seat-belt, and reached down to rub his trousers under which the sweat was itching out of his groin and down the backs of his legs. He supposed that the incident with the bald Egyptian would have to remain a minor mystery. Even petty, when compared to the enormity of trying to guess who had instigated the terrible events of the morning.

At that moment he heard Number One engine wind up, then Number Four. He caught himself grinning stupidly, dangerously close to hysteria, as he contemplated the absurdity of actually flying as a passenger once more.

Five minutes later they left the ground, heading north-east towards the Mediterranean and mainland Europe.

Eleven-fifteen pm, Paris time. Slack cold rain over the vast expanse of Charles de Gaulle Airport. Japan Air Lines Flight JA 268 from Cairo was one of the last to land before the night lull in traffic.

The passengers filed out into a cool quiet tube of stainless steel, to a series of soundless escalators that carried them up into the molecular complex of the most modern airport in the world. After the stifling mayhem of Cairo, Rawcliff had a disembodied, narcotic sensation: timeless, spaceless, of total unreality. Moving numbly through automatic doors, along rolling floors under stark white lights, into a silent dehumanized world populated only by the squinting, black-suited Japanese and the occasional motionless figure of a uniformed official.

An unreality charged with fear. All round him, like static electricity. This was hardly the place for the solitary 'hit-man', the squad of heavies from any number of foreign agencies, or the long arm and swift sword of Allah.

Part of his brain still registered the presence of Ryderbeit, somewhere behind him: a memory of Ryderbeit being drunk again, on the plane, causing the disturbance, upsetting the fragile kimonoed girls when he refused to put out his cigar as the landing-lights came on. As if his appearance were not conspicuous enough, his behaviour seemed to be signalling to every watching eye.

Again, hopelessly, Rawcliff tried to compute their chances. Of survival, escape, or certain death. He had forgotten about the money, deposited in some respectable institution that only required his signature and a few polite formalities.

He remembered only that they would be waiting for Ryderbeit *and Peters*. That was the way the cards had been stacked; but however efficient Pol might be, there was surely no way by which he could have discovered that the hand had been misdealt? The bodies of Peters and the others might lie forever, rotting quickly down to bleached bones, in that empty corner of the Nafud Desert. There remained nothing to identify them – Ryderbeit had made sure of that.

Ryderbeit was careful. A professional, and slightly crazy with it. Rawcliff caught a glimpse of him now, lank-haired, hooked face and blood-red eyes roaming round the bleak circular hall in which the passengers were filing in two columns through Passport Control. A couple of CRS officers sat behind their shields of bullet-proof glass, snapping through the passports. Two more officers – dark-blue suits, smart white sashes, machine-pistols clipped to their hips –stood immobile in the background.

But Rawcliff knew that there would be other eyes watching them: closed circuit TV, two-way mirrors, hand-picked experts scrutinizing every face, every suspicious expression and mannerism; checking for anyone from a petty smuggler to a known international criminal or someone on the long official list of 'unwelcome visitors'; eyes trained to spot a familiar profile under a wig or moustache, even by the tell-tale scars of a face-lift.

Rawcliff had only one fixed thought, as he moved up to the check-point. Pol would have told them to expect Peters. Tall, grey blond, cold-killer face. Probably carrying a British passport, details supplied, together with both White and Black African records. Sexual assault, gun-running, mutilation and murder.

Mistaken identity was surely out of the question? Not with all the influence and ingenuity of a man like Pol, plus the very latest apparatus and drill for airport security. It was true that Pol had met Rawcliff – but would he have bothered to circulate his description and details, along with the rest of the pilots, on the off-chance that one of them might make it back alive that morning? In any case, Pol could have had no idea that it would be a Japanese airliner bound for Charles de Gaulle Airport which would be the first plane to leave Cairo after the time it took for the Beachcraft Duke to fly in from the Nafud Desert.

Unless, of course. . .

Rawcliff found himself opposite the bullet-proof glass. He rocked back on his heels, giddy with exhaustion. The CRS man had flicked open his passport, glanced at him, shut it and slid it back under the glass, with a murmured '*Merci Monsieur*'. Rawcliff put it back in his pocket and walked through.

. . . Unless Pol had had agents waiting at Cairo, who had monitored the Beachcraft's landing, then been acute enough, despite the confusion, to pick up their trail – identities, flight number, destination – and had somehow managed, probably by short-wave radio, to relay the information in time for Pol to act.

Rawcliff stopped dead. He was in the middle of a bare, domed hall, full of the gentle hum of baggage conveyor-belts. Behind him came a mild stir. The CRS officer was not happy about Ryderbeit's Luxembourg passport. The Rhodesian was swearing, in foul, accurate French, with an atrocious accent, while one of the men with machine-pistols came forward and began to lead him briskly away, without resistance.

Perhaps it was this sudden uncharacteristic meekness in the face of authority that first alerted Rawcliff. The Rhodesian had turned once, his good eye glaring back across the hall, and for just a moment Rawcliff thought he detected a slight nod of that hooked face, before it disappeared through an unmarked door.

Then Rawcliff understood. For the last twenty-four hours – drunk or sober – Ryderbeit had simply been obeying orders, following a meticulously worked-out plan and reacting to a number of pre-arranged contingencies.

His only deviation had been to kill Peters – probably for no better reason than that he didn't like him. The only mystery was why he had spared Rawcliff, unless it were merely out of a frivolous desire for companionship: though Ryderbeit hardly struck Rawcliff as a man in constant need of friends. Ryderbeit was a loner, a pure adventurer. He had warned Rawcliff as much when they had first met in that hole in the wall in Larnaca.

Ryderbeit was useful to Pol and Pol was useful to the French government. Ryderbeit was the man of action who took the risks, as well as picking up any rewards that came his way. Pol was both master-mind and *deus ex machina* who enjoyed playing a devious, perverse game for the highest stakes. And the French government found Pol a convenient agent through whom to pursue their more clandestine and nefarious interests, while the politicians and diplomats looked the other way.

Everything that day had gone like clockwork – right up to the moment when Ryderbeit was led away under armed escort. Pol had got to him first, through his agents at Cairo who had tipped off Paris, in good time to meet the plane at Charles de Gaulle Airport. Ryderbeit was therefore safe – protected from the attentions of other international intelligence agencies, as well as from the host of Islamic zealots who would soon appear, desperate to avenge the morning's awful work.

That left Rawcliff, alone in the baggage-hall – only he didn't have any baggage. He didn't have any money either. Little more than the clothes he stood up in. A bum contract-pilot who had that day participated in an act of genocide for which he could expect to be tracked down by enemies from every corner of the earth. And he hadn't even been paid. For he knew that the moment he stepped into that nice Swiss bank, they would get him.

How to make a run for it? And where to? Buy a ticket to London on credit card? – back to Judith and little Tom, and drag them down with him?

At first he didn't feel the hand on his sleeve. A young man in a well-cut suit said, '*Monsieur Rawcliff? Venez, s'il vous plaît.*' Rawcliff followed him, across the hall, to the unmarked door through which Ryderbeit had disappeared only a few moments earlier. The young man opened it for him and he stepped forward, dazed, to be greeted by a peal of laughter.

The bed at the Lotti was as comfortable as he would have expected. He blinked up at the crystal chandelier, at the heavy draped curtains drawn against the winter sky.

He sat up slowly, once again feeling himself all over for injuries. He was naked under the sheet and his elbow felt bruised from where he must have fallen. He groped out and pressed a bell by the side of the bed.

Nothing was very clear any more. I've cracked up, he thought. All he could remember was Pol standing there in the middle of the room, wrapped in a massive vicuna coat that was lightly sprinkled with rain, giggling at him through his cherry-lips, while Ryderbeit stood solemnly urinating against the far wall.

A valet answered his call, and some time later Pol came in, squeezing himself into a little gilt chair beside the bed. He patted Rawcliff's arm under the sheet. 'You must sleep, *mon cher*. You are very tired.'

'What happened? I don't know any more. I don't know a damn thing. Tell me.'

Pol talked for a long time, gently, reasoning and reassuring, treating Rawcliff like a patient. 'You will be paid,' he said. 'There will be no problem there. Even the dirtiest jobs must be rewarded – when they are necessary.'

'Necessary?' Rawcliff rested his head back against the pillow. 'God forgive me.' He closed his eyes. 'Why didn't you have me killed, like the others?'

'A whim. A sentimental streak, perhaps. When we met so fortuitously in Nicosia, I was rather amused by your cheek – and by the resourcefulness of your wife. You were so obviously superior to the others, that I decided that it would be a waste to squander you. You are an excellent pilot and a brave man. It is not your fault that you are not as physically fit as Sammy – few men are. You have been overcome by sheer fatigue, both mental and physical.' He patted his arm again. 'Have no worries – I don't blame you. I have seen it happen many times, even to the strongest men.'

'My wife,' said Rawcliff. 'My child.'

Pol was shaking his head. 'I am afraid, my friend, that they are the price you must pay. You must never see them again – never attempt to contact them, even through a third party. You would lead straight to her, and she to you. You would both be eliminated – after you had both been thoroughly interrogated, of course. And if they were not satisfied that you had told them all, they might use your child as an incentive. The Arabs, in particular. It would not be pleasant.

'Besides, my friend, I have it on the best authority that your wife does not take a very generous view of our successful operation yesterday morning.' He sat stroking his little goatee beard. 'Women are so rarely rational creatures. Practical, yes. But they lack imagination, they lack the grand perspective. There *is* such a thing as a necessary evil – if only to prevent greater evil. What I helped to plan and what you helped to execute, I see as a drastic operation to remove a cancer from the earth's midst. Unhappily your wife is one of those who interprets it merely as murder – on a very large scale.

'But I have it on the same good authority,' he continued, 'that she and your child will be cared for and protected. Like you – money, a new identity, a fresh start, fresh pastures. You must not grieve for her, my friend. She will survive. So will you. And there are many other women in the world.'

Rawcliff lay for some time with his eyes closed. 'By the way, what happened to Jo?' But he only asked to break the silence: he wasn't really interested. He was thinking of Judith and little Tom, trying to remember what they looked like. He hadn't even got any photographs of them. And he wondered if time could erase such memories, and how long it would take?

Pol was telling him about Jo – making a little joke, about how she was probably at that moment sunning herself by the pool of the Tel Aviv Hilton. He went on to explain that the Israelis had almost certainly found out about the operation in advance – the Mossad always found out about everything – and that they had used Jo as a contact, to keep them informed in case anything went wrong. In one obvious sense, Pol said, the Israelis stood as much to gain as anyone: but in another, they were most likely to take the blame when it was all over. For this reason they had no doubt reserved the option right up to the last minute, of stymying the operation – if necessary, by shooting down the planes before they reached their target.

But Rawcliff wasn't listening. Pol's words rang

meaninglessly round the steel walls of his skull. *Judith, Tom. Oh God, what have I done to them?*

Some time later he managed to concentrate enough to ask Pol, 'So who was behind the whole thing? It wasn't just you? Or the French Government? They'd never have dared act on their own, even through a freelance gangster like you.'

Pol smiled at the insult. 'There are always some secrets, my friend, which are best kept until the grave. Is it not sufficient that the vast majority of the world's Muslim population appear to have been beautifully deceived by the operation? Confused, demoralized, their political will broken, their unity destroyed. Above all, their material greed and extortionate pricing of oil have now, so they pathetically believe, been condemned by the ultimate judge – the one and only God, Allah. We can therefore say, *mon cher*, that for the moment at least, the Islamic Revival had been stopped in its tracks.'

Rawcliff nodded, his eyes still closed. No mean achievement, as far as he was concerned – for the mere price of his wife and child. Poor little Tom. Poor little boy. While his father was now able to enjoy, in contemplative solitude, the luxurious sanctuary of one of the best hotels in the world: looking forward to a hard-earned £50,000 tax free, and the sure knowledge that working for Pol would be more rewarding than selling booze at the wrong end of London's Fulham Road.

He had begun to weep quietly. He did not hear Pol leave.

6

On that Friday morning, at precisely 7.22 am, Middle East time, a crowd estimated at over three million was gathered in Mecca, the holiest city of Islam. It was the height of the *Hadj*, the annual pilgrimage which all devout Muslims are required to make at least once in their life-time.

They had come from all the corners of the Islamic world – from the crescent of the Middle East, reaching down from the Soviet border to the Nubian desert and the jungles of Black Africa; from Morocco and Mauritania and Nigeria, across the sand-seas of the Sahara, to the crowded Nile Delta and the oil-rich lands of the Arabian Peninsula; from the rice-paddies of Indonesia and the Philippines, to the mountains of Pakistan and the coffee-shops of Istanbul. They had come in families, in package-tours, singly, in luxury; crippled and aging and dying, in filth and penury; by bus and jumbo jet, by private plane and leaking boats to Jeddah, finishing the journey in air-conditioned limousines, on camels and bicycles, on feet festering with sores.

They had pitched their tents over miles of sand, on the Plain of Ararat, beneath the ring of naked mountains, eating little, sleeping almost not at all, praying perpetually. Towards the centre of the city the crowd on this early Friday morning was packed so densely that in the centre, in the forecourt of the Grand Mosque, under the seven white minarets, the pilgrims were almost unable to move, unable to reach the Holy of Holies – the Ka'aba, a windowless oblong stone building, draped in black and gold, which is said to have been built by Abraham, and which contains in one corner the 'Black Stone' – a meteorite which Islamic lore decrees was given to Ismail by the Archangel Gabriel.

At 7.22 am a Dru tribesman, who had travelled from the West Bank of the Jordan, and who was an accredited agent of the Israeli Mossad, witnessed the following:

The chanting and wailing was overcome by a distant roar, which soon became a crescendo. Two minutes later, five enormous planes, without markings, appeared over the desert, so low that their shadows passed like great clouds covering the sun. They had appeared over the mountains with a speed and suddenness that seemed to freeze the millions of pilgrims, who halted their chanting and stood gazing upwards.

The planes flew in a low circle round the city, their noise echoing like thunder, so that, now that the first tremor had passed, many of the pilgrims again began wailing and calling to God, certain that these great machines were some visitation from Heaven.

Then the first plane became silent. Its engines had cut, and above the roar of its companions came the words, ringing out over the desert and the Mosque, so that all could hear:

'ALLAH! ALLAH! ALLAH IS GREAT! ALLAH THE ONE AND ONLY GOD! I, ALI, AM NOW RETURNED AS THE MIRROR-IMAGE OF THE PROPHET. I AM THE LONG-WAITED MAHDI! AND I SAY UNTO YE, OH WICKED MEN OF THE EARTH, THAT ALLAH IS MIGHTILY DISPLEASED WITH MAN'S DISTORTION OF ISLAM. ISLAM HAS BECOME A MOCKERY OF ALLAH, A SATANIC TEMPLE BUILT UPON MAN'S GREED AND INTOLERANCE AND UNGODLINESS TO MAN! AND MAN MUST BE PUNISHED!'

As the words rang out, and the millions stood watching and listening as though turned to stone, the great plane began to fall to earth, into the middle of the Grand Mosque. It had passed between the two minarets to the north-west of the building, when there was a flash, and it was as though the whole earth had exploded.

People a mile away felt the ground shudder, and some were thrown on to their faces, while others began to scream and tear at their clothes.

Above the Grand Mosque a cloud was rising as black as night, several thousand feet into the sky, and below this cloud was a boiling mass of flame. The two minarets were gone, and the five others, at the corners of the Mosque, were toppling and crumbling in pillars of dust.

And now, above the screaming, which came from more than a million throats, all calling on Allah for mercy, the second plane was silent and the words were repeated; then it too fell out of the sky and exploded above the centre of the Grand Mosque.

The report went on to describe how each of the five aircraft had flown round the Mosque, at a height of less than two hundred feet, and that each had cut its engines and broadcast its message, before plunging down into the inferno. Several witnesses were to report that at the moment when the fifth plane stalled, and the Mahdi's voice boomed out across Mecca, a figure trailing a white plume – later identified as a half-opened parachute – was seen to leap out of the rear of the aircraft, and be consumed by 'the fire which spread like water', devouring the tall white modern buildings, and the great Islamic Conference Hall, which buckled and caved in under the heat like the collapsing skeleton of a mighty dinosaur; and 'all was bathed in a fiery smoke which was like the smoke of Hell. And when the last plane had fallen, the sky became like night'.

Later, as the smoke settled, a Maronite Lebanese, who had travelled to Mecca with false papers, was able to establish that the city of Mecca – over an area extending from the suburb of Al Tibiyah to the north, to Al Misfalah in the south, and from the desert to the east, to the ancient bazaars along Hayfayir Street in the west – had been totally destroyed.

At the epicentre of the inferno – the Grand Mosque of Mecca – the ground had been blasted into crystals of glass and everywhere underfoot was a thick slime of roasted, congealed bodies. The planes had cut five deep swaths of destruction through the city, and almost no building within an eight-kilometre radius remained untouched. The galleries and minarets of the Mosque had vanished. So too had the Ka'aba, reduced to scorched rubble amid the piles of dead. For those who had survived, the stench was hard to endure.

By noon, when the relief-convoys began to arrive from

Jeddah, there came the sound of gunfire as looters were shot, trying to wrench the gold from the teeth and charred remains of the pilgrims. An estimated half-a-million had perished, with hundreds and thousands maimed or injured in the panic. Many others, having heard the message from the planes of death, chose to take their own lives accordingly.

7

During the final hours of that Friday, while the UN Security Council was in special emergency session, and the major governments of the world called crisis meetings, the international stock-markets – in New York, London, Paris and Hong Kong – closed early. So did many of the central banks.

In the confusion, no undue interest was aroused in the little Swiss town of Aarlau, north of Berne, when various sums amounting to a total of thirteen million US dollars were credited that afternoon to the personal account, in a small private bank, of a French citizen, Charles Auguste Pol.

The money had been laundered through several ghost-companies registered in Liechtenstein, Grand Cayman, and the tiny Pyreneean republic of Andorra. It would have been impossible, afterwards, to track down its origin – debited, on that same Friday, at noon, from a special account recently opened by the Soviet Trade Mission to France, at the Moscow Narodny Bank, in the Boulevard Haussmann, Paris.

THE WORLD'S GREATEST THRILLER WRITERS
NOW AVAILABLE IN GRANADA PAPERBACKS

Gerald A Brown

11 Harrowhouse	£1.25	☐
Green Ice	£1.50	☐

Trevanian

The Loo Sanction	£1.50	☐
The Eiger Sanction	£1.50	☐
The Main	95p	☐
Shibumi	£1.95	☐

Alan Williams

The Widows War	95p	☐
Shah-Mak	95p	☐
Gentleman Traitor	£1.25	☐
The Beria Papers	75p	☐
Barbouze	£1.25	☐
Long Run South	85p	☐

All these books are available at your local bookshop or newsagent, or can be ordered direct from the publisher. Just tick the titles you want and fill in the form below.

Name _____

Address _____

_____

Write to Granada Cash Sales
PO Box 11, Falmouth, Cornwall TR10 9EN.

Please enclose remittance to the value of the cover price plus:

UK 40p for the first book, 18p for the second book plus 13p per copy for each additional book ordered to a maximum charge of £1.49.

BFPO and Eire 40p for the first book, 18p for the second book plus 13p per copy for the next 7 books, thereafter 7p per book.

Overseas 60p for the first book and 18p for each additional book.

Granada Publishing reserve the right to show new retail prices on covers, which may differ from those previously advertised in the text or elsewhere.

GF1781